HÉCTOR ABAD

THE FARM

Translated from the Spanish by Anne McLean

archipelago books

Archipelago Books
232 3rd Street #A111
Brooklyn, NY 11215

www.archipelagobooks.org

Library of Congress Cataloguing-in-Publication
Title: The farm / Hâector Abad ; translated from the Spanish by Anne McLean.
Description: First Archipelago Books edition. | New York, NY : Archipelago Books, 2018
Identifiers: LCCN 2017057968 (print) | LCCN 2018000087 (ebook)
ISBN 9780914671930 (ebook) | ISBN 9780914671923 (pbk.)
Subjects: LCSH: Brothers and sisters--Colombia--Fiction.
Family life--Colombia--Fiction.
Classification: LCC PQ8180.1.B33 (ebook) | LCC PQ8180.1.B33 O2813 2018
(print) | DDC 863/.64--dc23

LC record available at https://lccn.loc.gov/2017057968

Cover photograph by Simón Abad

Distributed by Penguin Random House
www.penguinrandomhouse.com

This book was made possible by the New York State
Council on the Arts with the support of
Governor Andrew M. Cuomo and the New York State Legislature.
Archipelago Books also gratefully acknowledges the generous support from
Lannan Foundation, the National Endowment for the Arts,
and the New York City Department of Cultural Affairs.

PRINTED IN THE UNITED STATES OF AMERICA

THE FARM

But the field of the suburbs of their cities may not be sold; for it is their perpetual possession.

Leviticus, 25:34

I could live here forever, he thought, or till I die. Nothing would happen, every day would be the same as the day before, there would be nothing to say. [...] He could understand that people should have retreated here and fenced themselves in with miles and miles of silence; he could understand that they should have wanted to bequeath the privilege of so much silence to their children and grandchildren in perpetuity (though by what right he was not sure).

J. M. Coetzee

And I was sold in the end,
because I came to be so valued in their ledgers,
I no longer had any value in their hearts...

Dulce María Loynaz

ANTONIO

The telephone rang in the dark, early hours of a New York winter's night. The only people who call at that time are drunks who have the wrong number or relatives with bad news. I hoped it was the former, but it was Eva, my sister:

"Toño I'm so sorry to have to tell you this, but Mamá died in her sleep this morning. Pilar called from the farm to say that last night, after dinner, she'd said she wasn't feeling well. Of course lately, you know, she never feels well when she eats. Nothing agrees with her. So she went to bed. But this morning Pilar got up very early, to see how she was doing, and found her dead."

"I'll go straight to the airport and be on the first flight I can get," I told her.

I felt a deep sorrow, like a thick, gray cloud throughout my body. A pain in my chest and throat, and the wave of sadness rose up to my eyes, uncontainable. How old was my mother? She said 88, but she was actually 89. When she was 25, and her family was pestering her to hurry up and get married, it made a bit of sense to pretend to be a year younger than she actually was. Then not so much, and later, even less, and by the time she was 89, even she thought it was funny to still be subtracting a year from her age. I felt guilty for not having phoned her that week. I usually spoke to her on Thursdays, almost every week. Every Thursday morning she connected to Skype to wait for my call. Jon came out of the bathroom and saw my face, asked what had happened. He didn't ask with words, his eyes and hands formed the question.

"Anita died."

"I'll come with you to Medellín if you want," he said. He sat down beside me and put his big, soft hand on my back. We sat there together for a while, in silence. Finally I answered:

"No, don't worry, I'll go on my own this time." Something caught in my throat. I swallowed. "You should concentrate on your exhibition. My sisters will understand."

We sat together for a while on the bed, in silence, holding hands, knowing that words would only get in the way. Finally I stood up and went to look at my mother's last few messages. The most recent was affectionate and specific, as always: *Settling accounts*, read the subject heading.

My love: I tried to call you, but the little green light was off. I just wanted to tell you that I used one of your checks yesterday to pay your share of the council tax for La Oculta. I also transferred 816,000 pesos into Pilar's account for your share of Próspero's salary and the upkeep installment. I still have three of the checks you signed, in safekeeping. In our joint account, there's a credit balance in my favor of 2,413,818 pesos, which I have no need to withdraw until my next credit card bill, in April. I went to see Dr. Correa today and he found me quite well. For the moment I have not the slightest interest in dying, though I'm a bit down-hearted sometimes with Eva's situation. Last week she told me she's finally going to stop seeing Santiago, the widower Caicedo, you know, who she's been going out with for almost four years. On the one hand I was pleased, because the age difference is too big, almost twenty years, and she'd have no company in old age with him. But on the other hand I'm sorry because she's seemed content since she's been with him. You told me when they went to New York last year, in spite of the age difference and wheel-chair, Eva looked happy. And at Christmas they were fine, you saw for yourself, so it came as a surprise. Whenever she breaks up with someone it's always a leap into the void. She gets depressed, and we never know what's going to come of it. Santiago, in spite of his age, seemed sweet, although sometimes people said he looked more like my husband than Eva's boyfriend. Oh, that's what Pilar said on Christmas Eve, and Eva heard her tell me. It really hurt her feelings. Pilar is not the most discreet person in the world. Anyway, what worries me most is that sometimes it seems nobody's good enough for Eva, but at the same time she doesn't like to be alone. No more on that subject. It makes me very sad. What most cheers me up is knowing that I'm going to see you for Easter. I think your visit will cure all that ails me. Say hello to Jon for me. I send you a kiss and all my love as ever,

Ana

All my mother's letters were like that, practical and warm at the same time: the accounts all clear, and things going on in her life or the lives of her daughters or grandchildren. She looked after my Colombian bank accounts, almost all related to the farm. She was almost ninety years old, but she was more lucid than my sisters or me. Looking after my accounts in Colombia even kept her more alert. In other messages she'd written about the possible sale of a section of La Oculta to pay for the damages a gale had caused when a tree fell on top of the water tanks. She didn't think the sale of more land was a good idea because at the rate we were going we'd end up with just the house left and surrounded by strangers, but at the same time she wasn't prepared to have to take on those expenses, since she couldn't leave herself with no savings for the final years of her life. The problem was that Eva, since she only went to the farm at Christmas, because she was still aggrieved about what had happened there some time ago, didn't want to contribute a single centavo more toward the repairs and it was hard enough to get her to pay her share of the regular installment for taxes, bills, and salaries. She'd rather sell it. But selling it, for Pilar, would be like death.

I didn't want to sell the farm either, even if I do live in the United States for most of the year. Colombia for me was my mother, my sisters, and La Oculta, our hidden-away farm. Now Anita had died, and with her an enormous piece of my life. The strange thing is that she'd died at the farm and not in Medellín, where she lived. Though if I thought about it, her dying at La Oculta on a Sunday just before dawn made a lot of sense. Thinking about my mother, about her death, I realized that we'd never have been able to hang on to the farm – which we'd inherited from my father's side of the family – if not for her. Despite the fact that my mother had no family connection to this land, she'd been the one who sold her own apartment to enable us to keep it when we'd been on the verge of selling, shortly after the death of Cobo, my father Jacobo; she was the one who'd spent part of the bakery's profits on improvements and repairs to the house; she was the one who gathered us all together at La Oculta, in December, in her sweet and firm way of doing things. She invited us all, shopped for everyone, cooked for everyone, and in those weeks together her children and grandchildren revolved around her like planets round a warm, benign, irresistible sun. So even though she wasn't the owner of La Oculta, because Cobo had left it to his children, not his wife, the farm was indivisible from her, and now almost inconceivable without her presence. With Mamá no longer alive, without her cheerfulness, her recipes, her trips to the market, going to the farm would never be the same again. Someone would have to take over her position, Eva or Pilar, but I wasn't sure either of them wanted to. I would never have enough joy, energy, or love to take on the role of gathering the whole family together.

Jon went to the airport with me and helped me find the quickest route. The only direct flight to Medellín had already gone, so I had to change planes in Panama. Since my hands were shaking and my English was failing me, he kindly did everything. He also paid for it all on his credit card and stayed with me until I had to pass through security. We had a long, tender, necessary hug and I left his shirt damp on the shoulder. In the departure lounge I looked through the files on my laptop for old photos of Mamá. Photos from her youth, where she was smiling and pretty, full of life, with her whole future ahead. I found one of her holding me, a year old, in her arms, and we're both smiling and looking at each other happy and in love. I posted it on Facebook, which is where we now announce bereavements, visits, and commiserations, and as I wrote a couple of sentences about her, the teardrops rolling down my cheeks fell onto the keyboard. I don't know if people were staring at me, but I didn't care. A short time later my friends began to leave messages of condolence, some very beautiful, and to write fond memories of Anita.

I managed to get to Medellín that night. While waiting for my luggage I noticed that my shoes didn't go with my trousers and when my suitcase arrived I changed shoes in the restroom. My mother dead and me thinking about silly things like that, my conscience scolded me, but I couldn't help it, that's just the way I am. Benjamín, Eva's son, was waiting for me at the exit. My youngest nephew looked handsome and sad, and we hugged. From there we still had an almost four-hour drive to La Oculta. Pilar had already arranged for a Mass to be held the next day in Jericó. They were keeping vigil over Anita at the farm. Benjamín told me his mother had gone there first thing that morning, after calling me. That his Aunt Pilar had been getting his grandmother ready, that a doctor had signed the death certificate and the priest from Palermo had been down to bless her.

Two or three years ago Auntie Ester, my father's sister, had also died at La Oculta and it was as if the farm was turning into a place to go to die. Auntie Ester had acute kidney failure, but she was very old and at that age they don't do transplants, so she underwent dialysis for something like four years, but her health kept deteriorating until she finally said she didn't want any more dialysis or any other treatments and just wanted to go and die at La Oculta. Pilar took her in, pleased to have her at the farm because Ester was her favorite aunt and glad to be able to look after her. They set up a hospital bed in the same old room that had been hers when she was single, and they hired a night nurse. Auntie Ester's children came from Medellín to visit their mother every once in a while and to thank Pilar for taking care of her. Auntie Ester gradually faded away – she grew increasingly weak, paler and thinner, as fragile as a little bird – and eventually they began to give her morphine. When she lost consciousness and they could tell she was suffering because she was moaning and groaning, Pilar sent the nurse out of the room, asked her to heat up some broth in the kitchen, took a syringe and injected our aunt with a high dose of morphine, something like five ampoules in a row, she told me in secret, and Auntie Ester slipped away serenely, so relaxed that her body just forgot to keep breathing. Then Pilar called Auntie Ester's children and told them that their mother had died peacefully, and began to get her ready so they'd find her presentable when they came for her. Pilar had always been the one to dress the family's dead.

She has been dressing corpses since she was twenty-one years old. My father, who was a doctor, taught her how to prepare someone when they die, so there wouldn't be unpleasant surprises before the funeral. In the midst of the pain, and overcoming it, someone has to get over the disgust and the shock, so that life, or to put it better, death, might be a little less insufferable or a little more bearable. Pilar is the firstborn and being the eldest daughter has advantages and disadvantages. There are responsibilities no one else is able to take on because the other siblings are too young. Pilar doesn't get intimidated by any difficulty; she overcomes just about anything, without ever giving up. Nothing disgusts her, nothing embarrasses her, nothing frightens her. When there's something almost impossible to figure out, in my family we think: if Pilar can't solve it, nobody can.

The dead don't speak, the dead don't feel, the dead don't care if you see them naked, pale, drawn, in the worst moment of their life, in a manner of speaking. Or perhaps there is an even worse moment, underground, or in the crematorium, but this, luckily, we almost never have to see. Pilar has an intimate and affectionate relationship with the dead; she treats them as if what she does really matters to them, as if it would hurt them to be seen in a bad light. She doesn't dress anyone outside the family. She does up the dead so well (leaves them so presentable, almost as if they were alive) that one of Auntie Ester's sons, Arturo, a successful businessman, seeing his dead mother, so well presented, almost a pleasure to see for the last time, proposed going into business with my sister (he offered to put up the capital, my sister would do the handiwork) to set up a corpse-dressing service. My sister didn't want to. She told him that for her it was almost like arranging a newborn baby, because babies are also born looking horrible, and though they don't realize it either, they have to be washed, spruced up, their hair brushed, dressed, so their parents and grandparents, when they see them, will be filled with tenderness. The first and last look are very important, says Pilar, and just as a mother wants to see her child looking good the first time, the child also wants to see her mother looking good the last time and that's why she does it.

In every family, sooner or later, someone succumbs. When that happens in mine, Pilar is always there and she does what needs to be done, but not for money. She dressed our grandparents, some aunts and uncles, her mother-in-law, our father when his heart burst from so much suffering over Lucas, his eldest grandson, and some children of her closest friends. Now she will be dressing, or will already have dressed Anita. We don't really know what it is that she does. I know she uses cotton, gauze, and candlewax to seal up orifices. According to her, death is compassionate to the face because people swell up a bit when they die, and that erases a lot of wrinkles, which is good, and the only shocking thing is the pallor, and so the first thing she does is put on a bit a color. She has to choose the foundation depending on the skin tone, blushers, lipstick, powder, mascara, and injections to give the skin back some vitality. She is an expert makeup artist and from a very young age she's been doing Mamá's hair and makeup for parties, so she's had some experience. Whenever she dresses a corpse, she looks at photos of the person, and makes their face look like it did, preferably a bit younger. When I go from New York to Medellín I always take her cosmetics, little scissors and tweezers as gifts; it's what she most likes me to bring her, although this time there hasn't been a second to buy anything, just a couple of lipsticks I got on sale last week, a vermillion red and an irresistible fuchsia, according to the packages. I was also bringing her the news that now that our mother was gone, our turn to die had arrived. A piece of news that Pilar already knew because when we got there she told us that she had felt, since dawn, that old age had truly befallen her the very moment she'd seen that Mamá was no longer breathing.

When we arrived at La Oculta, the first thing I did was go to Anita's room. Her face was the same sweet, firm face she'd always had; that rare blend of beauty and character. One can make out echoes of beauty even in old age – and character in certain wrinkles, which are like the memory of lifelong gestures. Pilar had put her in a very pretty, embroidered, red dress that

I'd brought her from Mexico once and that made her look very cheerful, in spite of everything. Red was the color that suited her best. Pilar told us that in the early hours a downpour had woken her up so she looked in on Anita. The stillness and silence of the room gave her a prickly, uneasy feeling, until she turned on the light and realized she was dead. My wave of sadness grew, imagining that instant, but hugging my sisters I felt better. We were able to sit and talk all night beside her body, drinking coffee, saying Hail Marys and Our Fathers, which bring a sort of calm when repeated over and over again with the same rhythm. All my nephews and nieces, her grandchildren, started arriving with their children and husbands and wives, and La Oculta gradually filled up as if it were December, though a sad December, in March. When I die, I hope Jon will be able to lean down over the coffin lid, and see me, and talk to me, without disgust or fear, through the glass. In the United States all those things are done in funeral parlors. If I die at La Oculta, which is what everybody in our family wishes for, I'd like Pilar to dress me.

Mamá was lying in her own bed, the one she'd shared with Papá, the one that had been Grandfather Josué's and Grandma Miriam's before it was theirs. The room was just as Mamá liked it. Since Cobo died, Anita hadn't let anyone touch it. His clothes still hung in the closet, hers on the right side and his on the left:

the white shirts, the hat from Aguadas, riding boots, running shoes for going to the little waterfall, shorts, pajamas, and socks. Old clothes, things you wear out in the country that are so worn out you wouldn't even pass them on to the *campesinos*. An old painting of my paternal grandparents, in their forties. Family photos: all our first communions, their wedding portrait, old snapshots from when they lived in Bogotá and, framed above the bed, the imperfect sonnet Papá had written to La Oculta:

> *Beds like rocks, lumpy mattresses*
> *Beneath the night's embrace*
> *Guests sleep without haste*
> *On waking feel the aches*
> *Stiff joints soothed, pain deferred*
> *Doña Berta's eggs, sore hips reward*
> *Yellow on little blue plates*
> *A priest could not eat better*
> *Then reading in a hammock's pouch*
> *Anticipating smells of lunch*
> *Cassava, roast chicken and rice*
> *At three a shower under the waterfall*
> *Later a bean stew savored by all*
> *And hearing you snoring by my side.*

Both Cobo and Anita snored, Papá and Mamá, like an out-of-tune counterpoint, but now they would never snore again. Snoring is a strident, disagreeable music, and everyone makes fun of those of us who snore because it's a sign of aging, but at least it proves we're still breathing, and I felt sad at that moment to think my father hadn't snored for years, and that, even though my mother didn't look so dead, thanks to Pilar's care, her sleep was now an airless one with no more snoring. I missed her snoring as I missed her breathing. Eva told Pilar that she wanted to take over our parents' room, and please don't change anything, don't move anything. Don't throw away the clothes, don't change the photos, don't take the books out, don't put any other blankets on the bed or a different mattress, please don't replace the lamp on the nightstand, don't change the tiles in the bathroom, don't empty the closets or take Papá's poem down off the wall. She ran through this complete list almost in a rage, so our sister would understand. Pilar stared at her wide-eyed, because she hated that romantic clinging to old junk. It was one of the few things she fought with Mamá over. Every time my mother arrived Pilar would say: "Mami, when will you make up your mind to give Papá's shirts to Próspero?" And Anita would simply reply with her confident and tender voice: "Leave me my little things, Pilar, that's how I like it. You can do what you like with them when I'm gone." Pilar could make all the decisions about the farm and almost always be in charge, but in Cobo and Anita's room, she couldn't. That's why Eva wanted that to be her room from now on, her private realm, the only place in all of La Oculta where someone other than Pilar could be in charge.

EVA

I went back to La Oculta only to please Mamá and after several years of not going at all, and only because she decided to revive an old family tradition: spending Christmas all together at the farm. In fact, we all had to stop going for quite a few years; first because of the guerrillas, who robbed, kidnapped, and killed people, and then because of the paramilitaries, who were extortionists, thieves, and murderers. When things more or less normalized, because the state reclaimed the right to be the only organization allowed to kill, Pilar began to go back, and she got in a frenzy about rebuilding the house, repairing the bits that had been burnt down, to make it like it used to be, or even better than before. Until after a while she resolved to go and live there, with Alberto, who'd just retired, and then Mamá got it into her head that we all had to spend the Christmas holidays together at La Oculta. Easter too, she hoped, but if not, at least Christmas. My mother had a theory, and had always lived accordingly, and it was that the elderly have to buy company. Once I overheard Mamá telling her sister, my Aunt Mona, on the phone:

"Listen, Mona, I know that when we get old, we have to pay not to be left on our own, but it's the best-spent money in the world. That's why we can't give our children their inheritance while we're still alive, so we won't end up all alone and hidden away in an old age home."

Mamá invited all of us and paid for everything and that's why Toño came from New York every December, with or without Jon, and almost every Easter too, or as a surprise, at any time of year, when he got tired of life in Harlem. If we didn't get together two or three times a year, Mamá said, then we'd stop being united, stop loving each other and no longer be a family. Mamá shopped for everyone, paid for everything for her children and grandchildren, so there wouldn't be any excuses: food, wine, extra staff. She began planning in June for what she called "the season," and she'd go to all the sales to start buying up provisions for Christmas: canned goods, soap, toilet paper, tins of peas, jars of artichokes and palm hearts, things that last. Not booze, though; she'd say, if you're going to drink rum, beer, whiskey, or aguardiente, you can buy it yourselves. The only alcohol she brought was wine, which she bought up whenever she found bottles at a discount. At the beginning of December she started buying perishables, and around the 15th she'd send a truck full of all the things needed for the holidays, as well as boxes full of wrapped presents, Christmas gifts to put under the tree on the

24th for her children and grandchildren, for the laborers and the domestic staff.

After she died I felt that the single most solid part of my life had crumbled away. And that the less solid parts, starting with La Oculta, now meant nothing to me. I always thought I would rather spend the December vacations traveling somewhere far away, to Patagonia, for example, or to Mexico and Guatemala, after all that Santiago had taught me about Mayan culture, but I never did, so Mamá would be happy at having her whole family around her. Now that she's gone, I don't plan to ever go back to the farm, or at least not at Christmas. Without her it would never be the same.

I always worked with Mamá at the bakery, so it would have been almost impossible for us to have been any closer or to see each other more: we spent all our workdays together. But resisting my mother's will, as well as Pilar's, that we always spend the holidays together as a family, was also impossible. And well, anyway it was an agreeable obligation, because I loved La Oculta too. If I stopped loving the place, if I came to hate it for years, it's because one time I was almost murdered there. The first time I went back after almost getting killed, that first December that we spent the Christmas holidays there all together again, I was still trembling with fright at just setting foot in the house, just hearing the floorboards creak under my feet. But I was with

Benjamín, who hugged me to calm me down, and with Pilar and Alberto, who were living there by then, and with my brother who'd come down from New York, and with Mamá who was alive and as lucid as ever, as well as a whole bunch of kids (Pilar's grandchildren) who jumped into the dark waters of the lake as if it were nothing, so gradually I began to compose myself. When I saw Próspero, our lifelong foreman, after so long, older but almost the same as ever, with just one or two fewer teeth, with that open and discreet kindness that is his way of treating people, I couldn't hold back the tears and I clung to him for a long time, since it was like seeing a ghost, someone who'd been dead for years and then came back to life.

I was able to swim in the lake again, after looking at it with mistrust for several days from morning till evening, after much hesitation about whether or not to swim in those dark, ominous waters. Diving into the lake was maybe the most difficult thing: like overcoming a phobia, like taking a black butterfly, alive, out of a room with your fingers, like catching a venomous snake with your bare hands. I was also able to go horseback riding again. But my whole body palpitated in the lake, remembering and trying to forget at the same time, and in the saddle I still trembled with fear, and felt a twinge of pain, the pain of memory, even though before I'd always loved riding horses. I almost haven't recovered, really, from all that happened to me, and I still have to take pills for the pain and drops to sleep. I think forever; now it'll be forever. Life hasn't been easy, though it's also been magnificent. It was great when I'd cross the lake five or six times, racing against my friend Caicedo, who'd been an Olympic swimmer (in the Melbourne Games, in '56), or when I went for walks with Toño or riding with my son, or when I'd sit and sew and talk with Mamá and Pilar and remember all we'd lived through, and how much we'd laughed and enjoyed ourselves; then it felt like it was worth having suffered so much. Telling it is one thing, but living through it... living it is something else.

Even though it was more than fifteen years ago, I still remember what happened as if it were yesterday. At that time Pilar wasn't living at the farm yet, but she had told me to relax, that I could go to La Oculta without worrying, that things were good there because since the *paracos* had expelled the guerrillas there were no more robberies and the kidnappings had stopped. And I went on my own for a week, to rest, to not think about anything. It was the end of May and the weather was really nice. I was forty and a few years old and still good-looking, or at least that's what everybody told me. I had just broken up with a guy, one of those silly boyfriends I sometimes had, to pass the time and keep from getting lonely. Then I'd regret it, not breaking up with them but having been with them, and I'd get angry, weighing up the time wasted on another pointless dream.

After I'd been at La Oculta for two or three days I received a very strange letter. Próspero handed it to me and said a boy had given it to him in town. On a folded piece of paper, without an envelope, it said simply, *Eva Ángel* (without a "Señora," without a "Doña," without the name of the farm, without any address) and when I unfolded the paper – roughly torn out of a school notebook – the following was handwritten, or rather, printed:

AS WE ALREDY WARNED DOÑA PILAR YOU
PEOPLE HAVE TO SELL OR SELL THE FARM.
THIS ZONE IS NOT FOR LONELY OLD BITCHES.
EETHER SELL NOW OR YOUR ORFANS CAN
SELL. WE WILL BE EGSPECTING YOU THIS
AFTERNOON IN PALERMO AT 3 OCLOCK SHARP
IN THE PARK WITH THE PAPERWERK TO LOOK
OVER AND START THE TRANSFER. THIRD AND
FINAL WARNING.

                                    EL MÚSICO
IF YOU DONT SHOW UP ABYD BY THE
CONSECUENCES

Próspero told me that he'd once been stopped in the atrium of the church in Palermo and they'd told him to tell Pilar that, if we sold, they'd pay us in dollars and in twelve monthly payments.

The price was set by them and even though it was much higher than the commercial value of La Oculta, we knew that when those people bought a place, they only paid the first installment, on signature of the transfer of ownership, they occupied the farm, took over everything, dug up all the land and dredged the streams in search of gold, planted coca or poppies, and then didn't pay any more of the installments. More than that: if someone demanded the rest of the payments, they'd die, or disappear. I had never met any of Los Músicos, but they were famous in the region. Just the disgusting handwriting and bad spelling told me a lot about them.

There were already cell phones back then, big, clunky things, but they only worked in the city. We didn't get a signal at La Oculta, and there was no landline at the farm. So I went to the radiotelephone to speak to Pilar, but I couldn't tell her exactly what was happening because radiotelephone calls could be heard in every house in the region, and in Palermo, the closest village, as well. There was a private channel that not everybody could hear, but we couldn't be sure. I told Pilar, or half told her, what was going on, and she more or less understood, although not entirely. Pilar told me not to take any notice of it, that those guys were crazy but cowardly, that she was going to fix everything by calling the town butcher, who was the contact with them, and that anyway she'd already told them we had no intention of selling La Oculta for any reason, and if they're listening in let them hear. Much better. Pilar's like that, feisty, head-on, less fearful than me. I was alarmed, but I didn't leave the farm, as I should have, that very instant. I was very happy there, reading a lot, doing yoga, eating salads and vegetables, purifying my body, checking out each of the flowers in the garden, which Pilar had looking lovelier than ever, swimming in the lake, going horse-back riding along the trails, up to La Mama in the highlands, and down to the Cartama River in the tropical lowlands. Also, I still felt at that time that if I was on our land nothing could happen to me; outside everything was unprotected, dangerous, and risky, but on the farm I felt safe and sure, as if I were inside an impregnable fortress, in a castle with a drawbridge and the lake like a crocodile-filled moat, like in children's stories, even if the crocodiles were only iguanas, turtles, and carp.

Even though afterward I never went back to loving La Oculta the way I used to, I admit that the landscape of this region is the one that most moves me of all the landscapes I've seen anywhere in the world, and wherever I go I carry it with me. It might not be the most beautiful, there might be better ones, more pleasant and less dramatic, but it's the landscape that is fixed in my head. The landscape that brightened up my father's face whenever we arrived at the farm. I was there with him once, sitting together in the same hammock, looking at the lake and the mountains, and realized that this place, that afternoon, in that light, at that moment, and in that company, was indeed the most beautiful place on earth. And it's something I've felt since then, on other occasions, in those luminous moments that can only be compared to the ecstasy you sometimes feel on seeing certain paintings or hearing certain music, when Antonio plays some concert pieces for us on his violin, for example, along with a recording of his orchestra, or when I used to listen to arias with my friend Santiago, the widower, as my family called him, my companion who I split up with shortly before Mamá died.

Even when I stopped going to the farm for several years I could summon up the landscape from memory if I closed my eyes. And I still dream of it several times a year. It's the landscape of my childhood, when we'd go and spend the season with our grandparents, the place of my youth, the site of the happiest and most wretched moments of my life, where my body has enjoyed the most pleasure and suffered the most pain, the landscape of my true home, our lost and recovered home. My most frequently recurring dream is of something happening, some fright, I'm being chased, and I run outside and I can walk on La Oculta Lake. I run over the surface of the water and start to laugh, happy as the gods, or those little lizards, running on top of the water, away from danger.

Just arriving at La Oculta was enough to make me feel a euphoria mixed with serenity, a tranquil joy, a rapport with the mountains, with the sounds, with the infinite colors of the flowers and fruits, with the breezes that rose up from the river, with the dark water of the lake, with the dawn chorus, with the flashing light of fireflies and the calls of the *currucutú* – tropical screech owls – at night, with the buzzing of the cicadas at midday, with the flight of the cranes, the parrots and butterflies, with the distant humming of bees visiting the coffee flowers, with the mooing and smells of animals in the stable, with the incredible colors of the macaws, with the iridescent feathers of the *soledad* birds, with the noise of the teak leaves when they fall on the dirt path, with the sweltering heat of the afternoon and the dew-drenched cool of the morning.

I'd taken my dog, a golden lab called Gaspar. Gaspar was gentle, but a good watchdog, though he'd never bitten anyone in his life. The most he'd do, if he heard intruders, was growl and bark, displaying a rage that was no more than an inconsequential warning. That's what a good dog does, or at least the dogs I like, the ones who bark but don't bite.

Gaspar and I looked after each other and kept each other company. He was always at my feet, or by my side, he never left me alone. If I stood up, he stood up; if I went to swim in the lake, he jumped into the water and swam with me; if I went for a walk or a ride around the farm, he came with me, chasing me, running in zigzags through the fields, following scents imperceptible to us, sniffing everything, marking out with his urine an imaginary territory that he felt was as much his as I felt the farm was mine, that land that had been our great-grandparents', that our father had left to us, that would one day be my son Benjamín's.

I always go to bed early, before ten, because I get up very early, but that day I'd stayed up late reading in the hammock, enveloped in a novel I'd found in some room in the house, an old novel, its pages yellowing, which had definitely belonged to Cobo, because his name was written in it (*Jacobo Ángel, April 17, 1967*, it said on the title page, and *April 20, 1967*, on the last page: he liked to write the dates he started and finished each book) and it had underlinings and notes in his hand. Cobo had died a few years earlier, and his memory still stung my throat. I'd started to read it the day I arrived and was using the serene hours of the night to get pulled into it again. The book had notes in the margins and a longer commentary, handwritten by him, on the last page. I was enjoying following the trail of my father's reading, knowing that probably during the same passages we were thinking about the same things, that he'd laughed where I laughed, that he'd been frightened where I'd been. In my family everyone always said that he and I were the ones who were most alike. At the dinner table we were always coming out with the exact same phrases, at the same time, ever since I was very small, and I remember we'd laugh and shout: "Jinx: we killed a devil!" Saying the same thing at the same time was to kill a devil, or to put it a better way, to get something bad out of the world. People believe these things, even if they're not true, though more than superstitions they're comforts. A magical thought, as impossible as it might be, can help to console sometimes. At our house we also repeated one of our Grandpa Josué's beliefs, and even though it's a lie we repeated it as if it were true. Whenever an animal died on the farm, if a cow got sick or a calf fell over a cliff and broke its spine, or if a colt got colicky and died, then my grandfather would say: "I've just had a sentence reversed in heaven." He meant that someone in the family was going to die, but God, in His compassion, had liberated us from that horrible death by receiving a lesser sacrifice, the death of an animal. Thinking of that right now while I'm remembering Gaspar gives me a chill.

Reading a novel already read and underlined by my father was like having another conversation with him through the book; it was as if we were reading and commenting on it together at the farm, as we'd done many times in our lives, from one hammock to another, in the afternoons, or in their bedroom, which used to be my grandparents', or in the dining room, during so many long lunches. Sometimes I'd stop reading to think about the story or imagine myself in the situation I was reading about. Meanwhile, I'd reach over the edge of the hammock, stroking Gaspar's coat, staring into the darkness, seeing nothing, distanced from the world, those things that happen to us when we read a good book, and our own thoughts float, dragged along by the ideas hidden in the writing, like two different clouds that meet and mingle in the sky. Sometimes, they even turn black and let loose a lightning bolt, a thunderclap trembles on our brow, and it rains, we cry, a deep chord gets played that we didn't know was so tense in our chest, in the center of our body.

All the lights in the house were off, except for one floor lamp I liked to put beside the hammock to shine on the pages. It was a white hammock, I remember perfectly, from San Jacinto, a coarse canvas that the years had smoothed into something resembling skin. It was soft, cozy, warm and cool at the same time; the fabric gave me the embrace I wasn't getting from anyone during those days. The hammock is the perfect furniture for reading in, a friend of mine says. There were insects flying around the lamp, but they weren't biters; at La Oculta we didn't have plagues of mosquitoes, never any pest insects, or at least we never got bitten. Some frogs were still croaking in the lake. An iguana or a turtle dropped into the water and made that plunking sound, like a fruit falling off a tree and sinking into the lake. The hammock, the dog, and even the insects and frogs, kept me company, made me feel good, safe, with that imaginary confidence that habitual sounds give to living beings, even if they're on their own.

Back then I still thought of La Oculta as my real home. We, our family, have always felt something very deep, something very special when we're there. I don't like the word *energy*, but if I liked it I would have used it at this moment: the *finca* transmitted to us something you couldn't touch, but which was real. A foretaste of heaven, said Alberto, my brother-in-law. Like the dog's serenity, which at that moment was so great as he dozed that it rubbed off on me. If I hadn't had a dog, or a hammock, or a lamp, or a book, maybe I might have been afraid to be alone at La Oculta, at night, after having received that threatening letter.

A few minutes earlier I'd been startled by the rumble of engines that sounded as if they were coming up to the farm from the road, a kilometer and a half down below, near the roadhouse. It was strange, that noise, for I had put the chain and lock on the iron gate myself that afternoon when I came up on my horse, and no one else had the keys. Well, Próspero had a set too, but he went to bed early, as usual, with the chickens, and he'd be snoring away with his wife Berta in his house beside the stable. Gaspar had pricked up his ears too when he heard that noise, he'd hinted at a growl, but he hadn't stood up. Then the noise stopped completely. I thought I'd imagined it, an aural hallucination.

PILAR

The things that have happened, the things that still happen on this farm. First those who've drowned in the lake (five, as far as I know), and who make me feel a special respect for those dark, mysterious waters. Lucas getting kidnapped, which was the worst thing that ever happened to me because not only did they take my son away for almost a year but also took my father away forever, because he couldn't bear it. The arrival of the saviors, which was a salvation worse than the damnation, a remedy worse than the illness, because never before had so much blood been spilt here. The time when they came here to kill Eva. Deaths of previous generations of Ángels, which we didn't live through, but our grandparents told us about. And all the stories that Toño knows about our ancestors back I don't know how many centuries ago. But those old things don't interest me at all, not the genealogies, not the founding of the town, or all those who killed or died defending the land a hundred years ago. That's nothing to do with me. The deaths and difficult things that have happened to me here hurt, but not the past. For example, personally, and just in the last couple of years, two people have died on me at La Oculta. First Auntie Ester; then, Mamá. Auntie Ester's death was not as sad but harder, not just because she was dying for months and I was taking care of her, but because in a way I was the one who had to decide when it was no longer worthwhile for her to go on living. Not Mamá, my mother was perfectly fine to her last day, with her mind intact, independent and bossy as ever, doing deals with Próspero over the calves, asking how many sacks of beans the coffee harvest had brought in, how many centimeters a year the teak trunks were increasing. Mamá slipped away calmly in her sleep, without our noticing. She didn't even ring her bell, didn't even call me. I found her on her side, the way she always slept, on her right side, as if hugging herself. I could barely unlock that embrace to dress her, to do her up. She'd drunk her whole glass of water, she must have been thirsty. There was no anguish on her face, just distance, serenity, rest. I'd like to die like that too; the sleep of the righteous, as people say.

The night of the wake we argued for a while about whether we should bury or cremate Mamá. I said we should cremate her and bring her ashes back to the farm. Antonio, with that silliness of his, believing that our family's dead shouldn't be burned, because we aren't Hindus but converted Jews, he says, he'd rather we put her in the Ángel mausoleum in Jericó, and after a while move her remains, along with those of Cobo, to bury them together where Papá wanted to be, in the resting place, *el descansadero*. Eva said she didn't care, that after death it was all the same to her. Benji, Lucas, and all my other children were for cremation, so Toño was the only one in favor of burying her and had to accept the majority's wishes.

Now what's left of Mamá is under the oak tree you can see from the back of the house, facing the Cartama River, on the small patch of level ground where there is a bench, and everything is a more intense green because it's been sown with groundnut fodder. Próspero doesn't like us to call that place a "tomb" and so he calls it, more subtly, "the resting place," and ever since he said it we've adopted the name. This is the part of the farm with the view I love most, the one that doesn't look toward the west and the lake of the drowned, but toward the sunrise and the open countryside, down below, toward the flood plains of the Cauca, which now belong to other people, to old ranchers or old-guard mafiosos, although they used to be ours too, or belonged to our Ángel ancestors, many years ago.

ANTONIO

After Mamá's death I wanted to stay there for a few days, hidden in the mountains, going over my old notes about the founding of Jericó, about my family, La Oculta, and that region of Southwest Antioquia. Her death gave me the definitive push to finally get down to telling the history of the town and our farm. Remembering is like embracing the phantoms who made our lives possible here. So many things have happened on this land, in this big, red and white house, surrounded by water and greenery. Green, green in all its tones, immense green mountains, and the darkness of the lake water that doesn't reflect the blue and white sky above it, but the black and green crags that appear higher than the sky and rise up to Jericó, the town where my father and my grandfather and great-grandparents were born, the owners of this farm, the ones who cleared the land, chopping down the forest, moving rocks and burning brush, which was all there had been here since the beginning of time.

In the mornings, as soon as I wake up, I walk barefoot on the grass around the house and feel the dew between my toes. I breathe deeply and feel like praying again, like I did as a boy, but now I wouldn't know who to pray to. I say something in silence and it's almost a prayer to my ancestors, although I no longer believe, as I used to, that the spirit survives death. A prayer to nature and to the destiny this farm gave us. At that hour the clouds begin to rise from the river and I hope they pass this way. I see them coming. The clouds rise, slowly, and they pass through and over the house, they dampen it, kiss it. This cloud that rises up along the ground Próspero calls "*la pelona.*" I don't know why, maybe because it brushes over the pasture, as if it were peeling it with a machete. The clouds surround me, caress me, for a moment the world disappears, the lake and the mountains disappear, I feel as if I were submerged in a glass of water with anise aguardiente, as white as milk, until the clouds pass and carry on up higher, tickling the mountainsides. Suddenly everything is tinted pink or orange toward the east, and then the river comes back into view, big and yellow in winter, dark and narrower, with crystal clear waters, in summer, making its way through the deep valley heading for the Cauca. And the two *farallones* reappear beneath the clouds, towering crags, two distinctively shaped hills Grandpa Josué used to call "Doña Quiteria's chest." With the sunlight the colors of the birds and plants also appear: the white and purple orchids that hang from the trees, the orange of the birds of paradise, the purple and pink of the impatiens, the red and black of the anthurium flowers, the marvels that Pilar has planted. Sometimes a blade of grass sticks to the sole of my foot, while I weed a plant, or a clod of earth clings to my heel, and I know that I am this dew, this blade of grass, and this black earth. I have smelled this soil, I have held it to my nose to try to figure out why we love it so. But no, it doesn't smell of anything special, it smells of soil like any other soil. I know every butterfly, every birdsong, the ninety-seven teak trees that form the grove at the entrance, all the sounds (the water of the stream, the cicadas, the chachalaca birds (which we call guacharacas), the black-billed thrushes, mockingbirds, sparrowhawks, roosters, the woodpeckers that hammer away at the dry trunks of the cecropia trees, the macaws that make their nests in the dead trunks of the royal palms), sounds that for me are the same as silence.

I feel that I'm part of this land, this old farm of ancestors I knew and didn't know. I'm the only one in the family who can recite a litany of their names, because I'm the only one interested in the moth-eaten books, the birth certificates and death registries. Not like my sisters, who are more like Mamá, more direct and practical than me, more realistic, and who live in the present. I have a chest of drawers here, and one of the drawers is full of papers I've been collecting or writing for years; every time I come, I take the papers out and correct them or add something new that I read or was told in town. Stories, gossip, truth mixed up with lies, assumptions, and harsh facts. I like to revise and take care of these notes, the way collectors do with their coins, their maps, or their stamps; I cherish them, copy them out neatly, weigh them up and think about them. For years I've been intending to write something about the farm, so my nephews and nieces and their children will know and remember how things were. Then they'll be able to know how it all began, and then they'll also know that to hold on to this farm many people had to sweat and cry and bleed. Blood, tears, and sweat, yes, pure, salty liquids. Many of my notes are no more than digressions and fantasies. Others are historical annotations about Jericó that don't matter to almost anyone, but I like them. This note, for example, refers to the oldest things I know about our family, and I think they're the words with which I'd like to begin the story of the farm:

I don't know if we were Jews, but we couldn't have been very pure-blooded, for we have Jewish names and surnames of conversos, *so in our house we always said, without shame or pride, that maybe we were* marranos, *that's to say, just lip-service Christians, and inside something else, something hidden. The first of us to arrive in Colombia, a country still called New Granada, was a young Spaniard from Toledo, a scribe by the name of Abraham Santángel. What little we know of him is that he arrived in the Indies at Cartagena when he was just twenty-four years old, traveled to Antioquia up the Magdalena River and along the royal roads that led to the Cauca, around 1786, when the Colony was in its death throes, and by the years of the Independence Wars he dictated his last will and testament in Santa Fe de Antioquia.*

Nobody knows the reason Abraham came to live in these rough lands far from the world, in these crags and hills where even a cat rolls, but he surely saw a dark future in Europe and dreamed, like so many others, that perhaps somewhere else fate would smile on him. He probably believed that over here, on the other side of the Atlantic Ocean, breathing fresh air and stepping on unfamiliar ground, fortune could surprise him with some joy, some rain and fertile soil, with the young loins of a generous mulata *where he could sow his seed forever. The longing to expel the sadness from his body, the dream of shunning sorrow and opening a better path under different skies, are illusions that almost all of us have had, but this Abraham Santángel had the courage to convert his thoughts into acts and the bravery to expose himself to a dangerous and uncertain journey, and was able to go off on an adventure when he felt the yearning for distant countries, heeding more the obscure call of his heart than the caution dictated by reason and fear.*

It seems that fate was rather stingy with him, however, for the inheritance he left in his testament was quite poor, almost nothing. In his last will he simply declared that the little he had (the list was brief and precise) – one mare, some clothes, a bit of furniture (a trunk, a candelabra, a harness and trappings, a comino crespo *bedstead, a table with nine stools) – would go to his children who he begged to share as well as they could, without dispute, and listed them, from eldest to youngest: Susana, Eva, Esteban, Jaime, Ismael, Esther, and Benjamín, all born of his legitimate union with Betsabé Correa, from Yolombó, though he doesn't say daughter of whom, which means she might have been black, indigenous, mestizo, or a Creole born and raised here in the Indies, but nor can we discard the possibility – as her name hints – that she might also have been a* conversa, *even if it is most likely she was indigenous or* mulata. *Whatever she was, her children were entrusted to care for and respect Betsabé to the end of her days, under pain of receiving a curse from the other side of life. At the end of the document he added, almost unwillingly, that he was writing his testament because he was suffering serious health problems, and since he had no way of supporting his family nor could he leave them any worldly goods, apart from these trifles, he also instructed his male heirs to work hard and with their own hands, if they didn't want to become useless, without taking advantage of the work of others. He advised his daughters to marry soon and marry well, with gentle and upstanding men, and that all should seek an honorable destiny and none should stain the surname Ángel (in the end he put Ángel and not Santángel), the origin of which, as they well knew, and this is the most mysterious part of the document, "should never be a motive for shame or stain." Finally, he left them a piece of advice that's become a sort of family motto: "Remember that you are no better but no worse than anybody else; work but do not command, nor obey either."*

This very recommendation, which we still follow in my house, is what makes us loved and hated. Rather than command, we explain, we request; and rather than obey, we decide whether what is requested of us is reasonable, can be done, and is well requested. Being disobedient and disinclined to boss others around, in a country of peons and overseers, has always been strange, atypical, and disagreeable. We don't like other people doing things for us, but nor do we like doing other people's things for them. We prefer to do everything with our own hands, and if we need help, we'll still be the first to put our shoulders to the wheel. And we will put our shoulders to other people's wheels too, as long as they're working too and not ordering us around and watching, as if they were from another caste or a better family. That we can't stand.

We, the Ángels of Jericó, are descended from the fifth of Abraham's brood, Ismael, who settled in El Retiro at the beginning of the nineteenth century. We don't know exactly what he did there but he must have prospered somewhat, for he left his eldest son, Esteban, a salt mine in his will. Ismael's second son, Isaías, was the one who emigrated to the Southwest, in 1861, when Jericó was not yet called that, but rather the Aldea de Piedras, in some documents, and in others, Felicina, and all this starts there because with it La Oculta also begins.

La Oculta was a jungle; then it was a coffee farm and a cattle ranch; now it's a country house with a little bit of land around it. The borders were marked out by trees and streams, by ditches and pits, the exact locations of which nobody knows anymore. I, Antonio, maybe the last of the line to bear the surname Ángel, want to reconstruct for my sisters, Pilar and Eva, and for my nephews and nieces, since I have no children, the history of this farm to which we're so attached it's as if it were part of our flesh. Yes, because we are stuck to La Oculta tooth and claw, as if it were the last resort for castaways adrift in the world.

So, that's the first opening I have for my little book, but sometimes it seems too long to me, and so I've written another beginning, a more concise variation on the former, because I don't really know how to start to tell the story from the beginning, which for me begins with the history of the town, which gets mixed up with the history of my family at least since Abraham came to live in the New World:

The first man left Toledo and crossed the sea to arrive in a less tough, less arid land, a land where his name, Abraham Santángel, was not a stigma, and there, some years after he arrived in Antioquia, from the womb of his wife, Betsabé, came forth Ismael, the fifth of his children. Ismael with Sara begat Isaías, who with his wife Raquel begat Elías, who with his wife Isabel had a son called José Antonio, from whom with his wife Mercedes was born Josué, who married Miriam, who gave birth to Jacobo, my father, who with my mother, Ana, had my two sisters, Pilar and Eva, and also had me. This is the whole genealogy of our surname, Ángel, which before being shortened was Santángel, and which with me, Antonio, will surely be extinguished. Those to whom God gives no children the devil gives nephews, they say. Yes, because my nephews are Gils and Bernals, and Ángel is only their second surname. It shouldn't matter, yet it matters to me, and it's almost the only thing I don't like about them. There will be other Ángels, but from other branches of the family, other tribes, so it's not as if with me our name will disappear from the earth. It's sad that I talk so much about my ancestors, that I searched so hard for my origins, knowing that I will be nobody's ancestor or origin. Yes, at least on this flank of the family there will be no one else to bear our surname, first of all because I don't have any children, and second of all because, since I like men and not women, it's harder for me to have them, and in the third place because Jon doesn't trust adoption and I don't think I do either. The names of my ancestors I discovered in the birth, death, and baptismal registers in Jericó, our town in Antioquia, and in other legal documents. I was able to certify that Isaías, our first Jericó ancestor, born in El Retiro and son of Ismael Ángel and Sara Cano, grandson of Abraham Santángel and Betsabé Correa, Christians for not so long, signed and registered the papers for this farm, our farm, La Oculta, on December 2, 1886.

PILAR

T oño is interested in old things, family origins, ancestors, and
surnames. I don't give a fig about all that. I, Pilar Ángel de
Gil, by memory, barely go back as far as our own grandparents,
Grandpa Josué and Grandma Miriam. Josué Ángel and Miriam
Mesa, and that's that. Well, I can remember our great-grandmother, Merceditas Mejía, or Ditas, who we called Mama Ditas,
or Mamaditas (without any of us ever realizing that could mean
something else, something rude). I only remember Mamaditas
because we went to visit her sometimes in the big house in Jericó
and because I have a good memory, unlike Toño, who doesn't
remember anything, so he makes it all up. When I don't know
something or don't remember, what do I do? Well, I keep quiet;
Toño on the other hand does not keep quiet but makes up a story
to complete what he'd forgotten or what he doesn't know. One of
the two: he either invents something, or he believes everything
he reads or everything he's told, like a child, and writes it down.
He hears and believes, believes and writes, writes and thinks,

and then he invents what he doesn't know and with time ends up believing it: that's what he's like. For him, the truth ends up being the lies he believes. He is as credulous and ingenuous as the town idiots or lunatics, and no town has as many idiots or lunatics as Jericó, because at first they were all cousins and married each other, and from there came all possible and impossible defects. All we're missing is the pig's tail, but we've got everything else: asthma, epilepsy, schizophrenia, myopia, arthritis, hemophilia, you name it.

Frankly, as far as I'm concerned, further back than our grandparents, I don't care at all about our ancestors, cousins who married other cousins. If I didn't meet them, if the only thing they are is a pile of faceless names with no memories attached to them, white bones in the Jericó cemetery, what influence are they going to have on my life or the lives of my children? None. Grandpa Josué and Grandma Miriam, however, still matter. My youngest daughter, for example, resembles Grandma Miriam a lot, and not just because she's very short, four foot eleven, like she was, but in her character. Grandpa Josué was more than a whole foot taller than Miriam; in photos they look almost ridiculous, him a giant and her a tiny little thing. But she was a tiny person with a blend of cheerfulness and a wicked temper. When she had an argument with my grandfather, she would raise her voice and always say the same thing to him, a phrase that has become legendary in our house as a threat or a warning. She would waggle her index finger and say to Grandpa Josué looking right into the center of his dark eyes with her hazel ones: "Bismuth, sulphonamide, and quicksilver-iodine!" All she had to do was say that and Grandpa would calm down and admit she was right. At the most, occasionally, he'd answer with a single sentence: "You forgot the arsenic, Doña Miriam, the arsenic." They always spoke formally to each other and whenever we asked about the origin of the phrase, our uncles would say it was a poison to kill army ants, and that our grandfather had once said that if she didn't stop nagging he was going to put a dose of that poison in the soup. Maybe that was it. The fact is that Grandma Miriam just had to say, very quietly, "Bismuth, sulphonamide, and quicksilver-iodine," and our grandfather would lower his gaze and fall silent. He would stop bossing her around and complaining and would be left dumbfounded, as if stunned. Grandma, behind his back, would make faces, stick her tongue out at him, put her thumb to her nose, and waggle her fingers like a naughty girl at school. Grandpa didn't know about that. And Florencia, my youngest daughter, is just like Grandma Miriam; those old genes are still noticeable in her. They're like birthmarks, like tics or obsessions, which we inherit from someone even if we don't really know where they come from.

But Grandma's mother, or Grandpa's father, who I never met, and don't even know what they looked like, don't mean anything to me now. And farther back than them, even less, for they're long dead and gone and forgotten. Maybe something of them lives on in me, but since I don't know what it might be, it doesn't make any difference to me. It might be inherited, but it's mine now, and that's the end of it.

Antonio says, for example, that supposedly we're Jewish to the core and that's why one of the first farms of the first ancestor to arrive in Jericó (I don't know if it was Elías or Isaías or Matías or Zacarías, something ending in *ías*) was called La Judía, and the house with walls of fine hardwood still exists up there, on the banks of the River Frío, that we have to go see it before it collapses from old age, but I don't believe him. I am Catholic, of the Holy Roman Apostolic Church, like my mother and my grandmothers, and that's that, and if we were Jews it doesn't matter because centuries ago we converted to the true religion, and before God we're all equal: Jews, Indians, whites, Protestants, atheists, Buddhists, and Muslims. God is merciful and we'll all go to heaven, even the worst of us, because the pope himself, who knows these things, already said that hell does exist, but it's empty, and that's why bad people don't go there, they just have to spend a few centuries in purgatory, purging their misdeeds and repenting, until they've become aware of all the evil they did and suffer in their own flesh the pain they doled out. That's what I believe, what I've always believed, and if others don't want to believe it, all the worse for them because they'll have to spend more years in purgatory.

Toño doesn't think religious matters are very serious. He used to, he was very pious once upon a time, and I think he even went to Mass in New York when he first moved there, thirty years ago or so. He told Mamá, so she wouldn't worry, that he went to All Saints Church in Harlem, which was very beautiful, Gothic, he said. Then he moved in with Jon, and I don't think he's been a very good influence in this regard, since Jon isn't even Catholic, but comes from an evangelical family, the ones who sing and shout and cry and wave their hands around. They have services that seem like melodramas. Bit by bit, Toño stopped going to Mass on Sundays and Mamá stopped asking. Although deep down I believe he believes, Toño says he is no longer sure of anything, and that religions come and go, like fashions, that there are more dead religions than living ones, more dead gods than living ones, and that there are new religions and gods yet to be born and to die. That he would go to Mass in a chapel that included all religions, because they change, like styles of ties. How despicable: religion is not a fashion or a riddle, like the horoscope or spiritualism; it's a serious and important thing, it's what keeps us steady. And God, no matter how His name gets changed here and there, is always the same. If there was no religion and there was no afterlife, then what would reward the good people and punish the bad? Since prizes and punishments are not distributed fairly in this life, there has to be another, where things are not so twisted. If there was no other life, God would be crazy, and I don't believe that God is crazy. And even if He is crazy, I'd rather have a crazy God than a God who doesn't exist.

Alberto, who is better than I am, and also has much more faith than I do, always convinces me and explains everything when I have doubts. He reminds me how good we have it; he makes me see the privilege of living here, at La Oculta, which for him is a little piece of paradise. I've lived here with him for almost ten years now, with my husband, my only love, my first and only ever boyfriend, my only man. He also has his way of being silent. I kiss him and bite him and taste him still, but even without knowing what he tastes like I understand why I love him so much. I don't know what other men taste like, because Alberto is the only one I've tried, but they must taste similar, surely, the way all the landscapes in the world resemble each other. But this one's mine, and the one I like best, just like Alberto is my man, mine and only mine, and I am his alone.

Once I had a fight with Rosa, the cook, a long time ago. We were fighting and I asked her: "Rosa, if you're so bored, why don't you leave? You're free to go." And she answered: "Ay, Doña Pilar, why would I leave, when all tombs are the same." That made me laugh, and afterward I thought that marriage is like that too. Good or bad, you have to stay once and for all with the same one, all the more so if he's good, like Alberto. But everyone's different. For example Eva, my little sister, has been married three times and has had so many boyfriends that I've lost count. Her last friend was the widower Caicedo, who even though he was too old for her, because he was eighteen years older and looked like he could be her father, at least was decent and generous. But no, she left him too, like all the others. And what for, to get bored again and separate. I don't know. Sometimes I feel so ridiculous and old-fashioned, so different from Eva. She is almost as old as I am, had three husbands, none of whom were good enough for her, has tried out a dozen good, bad, and average men, young and old, locals and foreigners, Jews and Christians, and still holds out hope of finding a better one. She was hurt for several years, resentful of the farm, and didn't want to come back, saying she'd never go back. "I'll never go back to La Oculta," she said. Never, what silliness, never say never. Later she came back, when we all came back and Mamá resolved to organize Christmases again like before the sorrows, before anybody had died, before Lucas was kidnapped and Papá died of sadness, before Eva was almost murdered. When Los Músicos were finally killed or disappeared we were able to come back, to forget, and everything went back to being tranquil, calm, and sweet. Life's like that, after the storm comes the calm, as the song says, and the calm lasts longer than the storms, that's what I say. We all came back and Mamá made tamales again, and custards, pancakes, fritters, like every other year. And the *frijoladas*, the beans, the paellas, *ajiaco*, potato and chili stews, *aji de gallina*, chili chicken, *chupe camarones*, shrimp stew, *salmorejo*, Antioquia-style gazpacho, *posta cartagenera*, blackened topside beef, *asados*, grilled meats, *arequipe*, our version of *dulce de leche*, apple pie, guava paste with fresh white cheese, *mazamorra con piedritas de panela*, corn porridge with little pebbles of brown sugar loaf. Decembers are always like this: songs, games, and feasts. Arguments, fights, tears, reconciliations, the occasional memorable drinking binge with real musicians, a trio from town or a group from Medellín. Novenas, carols, and gifts. The tree and the nativity scene. Now the region is at peace. Now they almost never kidnap or steal, and only kill out of jealousy and threaten for money. Now we can live here peacefully. Now the deaths are no longer from gunshots or pain, but old age, which is the best death, or the least bad, the most acceptable. Instead of Mamá, now Eva and I will have to take care of Christmases, and invite everyone here, our brother, our children, grandchildren, friends, all together. Let's hope this calm will last until our deaths. If there is another storm, let my children handle it rather than me, no, it's not fair, I don't deserve any more storms.

Eva was much prettier than me, and a better student, and a better dancer. In fact, she used to say she was going to be a dancer and a psychologist when she grew up. From dancing so much she had a beautiful body, and not to mention her face, a perfect face, and the kind of smile that a beauty queen would envy. She had long black hair, refined features, the whitest teeth I've ever seen. And she was always cheerful, always laughing. Maybe because she was so pretty, she always thought nothing was ever enough: she wanted more and more and more. More and better. We went to the same convent school, La Presentación, and she won all the medals. I, however, was not even an average student and we were in the same grade because I'd failed a year. Eva always arrived home with her dark blue uniform covered in merit medals: the red medal for arithmetic, the yellow medal for religion, the blue medal for good behavior, the white medal for Spanish, the green medal for geography, the orange medal for discipline, all the medals. She looked like a general. And me without one single little medal. I remember one day, as we got off the bus, I forced her to give me a medal. A friend helped me to hold her arms behind her back, don't be so vain, we told her, and I took the prettiest medal off her uniform, the tricolor medal with the flag. I pinned it on my chest, all smug, and when we got home Papá was so happy, and asked me what medal I'd won, and since I didn't know I told him it was the medal for Love of the School. Eva looked at me with rage from one corner of the study, but she wouldn't tell on me, she kept quiet, resentful, while Papá gave me a bigger kiss for my one stolen medal than Eva for her seven medals won with effort. Ay, how shameful, how sorry I am. Of course our father was also happy about Eva's medals, but he was used to her winning all the prizes, and me winning something was more pleasing because it was so unusual.

Eva went to university and I left before the end of my last year of high school, without even graduating, to marry Alberto. I know that Eva was watching me with all her medals, with all her diplomas, and wondering: will my life be better with all this studying, with so much discipline and responsibility, or will Pilar's life be better, Pilar who was born old and already looks like a grandma? More than half a century has passed since we went to school together, so we should be able to say which life was better. In reality we don't know, they're very different lives but I don't think either is so bad. Maybe the most that differentiates us are two or three things: she doesn't have a husband and I do; I go to Mass and she doesn't; she wouldn't mind deep down if we sold La Oculta and I want to live and die here, on this farm, which (after my children, my sister, my brother, and my husband) is what I love most in this world. The land, the sensation of having a place to die, my own place to be buried, as my brother would prefer, or to have my ashes scattered, as I would, but anyway a place where I can become earth of my earth. I don't know if people in other parts of the world are like us, here in Antioquia, who live with the obsession of owning a piece of land. Here even the poorest people have or want to have a little farm, even if it's just fifty square meters, a little patch to plant three rows of vegetables and one of flowers. Not having land is like not having clothes, like not having food. Just as in order to live one needs water, air, and shelter, here we feel we also need to have land, if not to live off, at least to die on.

Maybe what most differentiates Eva and me is our attitude toward marriage and love. I think it's better the way it used to be: once and forever; Eva seems to think it's best to believe, perhaps because her love life began that way, that love's never forever, but something precarious, uncertain, and almost with an expiration date, like yogurt or jam. There are people who opt for an intermediate route. Near La Oculta, on a ranch called La Ley, the owner of that farm, Iván Restrepo, has two wives. Próspero's brother works there and he tells us that Don Iván always calls when he's coming and lets him know: "Aquileo, tomorrow I'm coming with Consuelo." And then Aquileo knows he has to put out Doña Consuelo's furniture, paintings, photos, and knick-knacks. Or Don Iván calls and says: "Aquileo, I'm coming with Amparo." And Aquileo runs to put away Doña Consuelo's things and put out Doña Amparo's: everything is different, down to the cutlery, dishes, and pots and pans. He has to be very careful not to make any mistakes, for in the photos there are different children with each wife. He has a storeroom where he keeps the things, whether of one wife or the other, depending on who's going to be there, a storeroom locked with a padlock that only the foreman has the key to. Not that Amparo doesn't know of Consuelo's existence, or that Consuelo doesn't know of Amparo's existence, not that they're idiots, just that neither wants to know anything about the other. Once Aquileo got mixed up and left one photo of Doña Consuelo with Don Iván and their children. And it was Doña Amparo, who'd just arrived, who pretended not to have seen the photo. Don Iván widened his eyes at his foreman, and Aquileo ran to the storeroom to switch that photo with the correct one. We love hearing about our neighbor's balancing act at La Ley, Don Iván, a very nice guy, and whenever Aquileo comes by we ask him for details. He tells us, for example, that Doña Amparo loves to go to Miami, and Don Iván takes her shopping there, but what Doña Consuelo likes is Europe, and apparently they go to concerts and museums.

Aquileo says he gives both of them a very good life, and they're very different, because one likes classical music and the other *rancheras*, one likes to read and the other to drink. And they even have different groups of friends. "Don Iván is a wise man," Próspero always says, "but for wisdom like that you have to be very rich. Don't you think?" They're both true, the two lives Iván leads with two different wives, with much skill, in neighboring La Ley. Two very different and complete lives. But I wouldn't live like that because I only like Alberto, and Eva isn't like that either, because even though she's often changed husbands and boyfriends, she's always just been with one at a time, even though each one is always different. She's faithful to each of them, but just for a time, until something shocks her or she gets bored: for me it's a mystery. In reality nobody knows how you should live and everyone lives however they can. Toño lives with a man, Eva searches, Iván Restrepo is a bigamist, Muslims can have four wives. That would be fine as long as the women could have four husbands as well. Me, for my part, I found Alberto, and since I found him I no longer know how to live any other way.

EVA

I can't deny that I was a bit nervous after receiving the note with the order to sell the farm. Let's say my senses were on alert; that even though I was reading I wasn't entirely distracted, but was reading with one eye and keeping the other on reality. I couldn't get that disgusting note completely out of my head, with its bad spelling, clumsily printed letters, scrawled by a person who hadn't even finished primary school. It all bothered me, even the false and annoying name: El Músico. What kind of musicians might those be? They were the very opposite of music; they were the music of bullets, the rattle of weapons, and of threats, nothing more. As far as I knew, the ones who sent the note were some paramilitary guys involved in drugs, theft, and illegal mining, who took people's land by force, operating around Támesis, Salgar, and Jericó, and who'd been invading farms to plant coca and poppies, to set up cocaine labs and kitchens, to extract gold illegally and fill the streams with mercury. They didn't want any neighbors or witnesses. They wanted to be the bosses of everything, by hook or by crook. In the letter they said exactly what they wanted: that Pilar and I had to "sell or sell" La Oculta. They didn't even mention Toño because he's lived abroad for so long they didn't even know he existed.

In any case, I didn't want to think about the threat and was trying to concentrate on the novel. I remember that in the book I was reading there was a commentary by my father on the last page. It was something about how literature should be. I should go find it; I want to reread it. Yes, I still have the book here; it has a charred edge because of what happened later. Here is his note, it must be someone else's thoughts, because it's in quotes: *"That's how literature should be: full of action, with no space for clichés or sentimental meditations. He'd heard much praise for Joyce, Kafka, Proust, but he'd resolved not to follow the path of the so-called psychological school or stream of consciousness. Literature should go back to the style of the Bible or Homer: action, suspense, images, and just a pinch of mind games."*

Having the book in my hands again revives me, helps me remember exactly what happened later: Suddenly Gaspar perked up his ears and, scratching the wooden floorboards of the porch, barking furiously, ran toward the back deck. I jumped out of the hammock like a spring, startled. I turned off the lamp and peered into the darkness in the direction of the dog's growls and barking. I saw streams of light from two or three flashlights. Then the semi-darkness was broken by a flash and at the same time I heard a shot and Gaspar's pained howl. Another flash, another shot. Now there was silence and the flashlights were switched off.

My first impulse was to run and help my dog. I thought better of it and changed direction. I realized my only escape route was the lake. I ran down the porch and climbed blindly down the wooden ladder that led to the dock, kicked off my sandals, without breaking my run, and took a deep, very deep breath when I got to the end of the dock. I managed to think it was good I was wearing shorts instead of long pants. I took a run-up with all my strength and dove into the cold water, as far out as I could from the dock and the house. Even with my eyes open everything turned black, black, black as pitch, darker than the night. I couldn't see anything at all. I held my breath in my chest and swam underwater as fast as I could, away from the house diagonally out into the lake. I remember thinking if I didn't have these damned big tits, which were weighing me down like ballast, I'd be able to swim much faster. I came up for air and took three big puffs, as much as I could fit in my lungs and ducked back underwater.

I began to count *one two three…* I knew I was capable of swimming for almost a whole minute underwater, because it was a drill I liked to do in the pool where I exercised almost every day in Medellín. I wouldn't lift my head until I'd counted to sixty. I have to count slowly, I told myself, so each number will take up a whole second, *eight nine ten eleven*, I seemed to hear Papá's voice in my head, *twelve thirteen fourteen fifteen sixteen seventeen*, never swim in the lake at night unless absolutely necessary, *eighteen nineteen twenty twenty-one*, only if someone falls in and is drowning, *twenty-two twenty-three twenty-four twenty-five*, or to save your own life, *twenty-six twenty-seven twenty-eight twenty-nine*, I'm not going to make it, I thought, *thirty thirty-one thirty-two thirty-three*, my heart is going to explode, *thirty-four thirty-five thirty-six*, they came here to kill me, they'll kill me if they see me, *thirty-seven thirty-eight thirty-nine forty*, I'm going to let out a bit of air, *forty-one forty-two*, I felt a little better after exhaling, I felt my long hair brush against my face, *forty-three forty-four forty-five forty-six forty-seven*, I'm going to burst, my mind is clouding over I feel faint, *forty-eight forty-nine*, I have to get out of the water very slowly so they don't hear anything, *fifty fifty-one fifty-two*, a little bit more, *fifty-three fifty-four*, my head aches, a tingling electricity is running through my whole body, slower, *fifty-five fifty-six*, take a breath and duck straight back down, *fifty-seven fifty-eight fifty-nine sixty*, a bit more, two more strokes *sixty-one sixty-two sixty three*, I'm going up, I'm out.

PILAR

During the holidays, when we were still in school, Eva always went to work in Mamá's bakery; she helped her do the accounts on a calculator with a crank handle, and she drew with a pencil some very neat graphs of expenses on sheets of green paper as big as pillow cases. Mamá had opened a small business in Laureles, our neighborhood, Anita's Bakery, but she didn't have her income and expenditures very well organized: the sugar, different types of flour, oil, butter, the electricity the ovens used, yeast, the salary for the single baker she had at first. The pencil sharpener also had a crank handle back then and Eva used it frequently so her figures would be clear and neat, with very fine, firm, and rounded strokes. When she finished doing the accounts, she went inside as well, with Mamá, where the ovens were, to help her make pastries and prepare the fillings for the pies, which she was starting to sell alongside the bread.

Toño was still very young and lived in another world. He'd arrived late, when we didn't think we'd get another sibling. And as a baby he'd been like another one of our dolls for Eva and me. He was always a beautiful little boy, with lots of very black, curly hair, and refined features like a girl's. In the street people often asked, what's the little girl's name? And he used to answer, with angry laughter: Antonia. He always had a very feminine face, and since he was beardless, and still is, there was something ambiguous in his appearance, male and female at the same time. His voice is very soft and reedy, though I wouldn't say it's affected, but rather a delicate voice, like an Italian's. He's skinny and tall, with long, thin, refined hands, and has always moved with elegant gestures, like a ballet dancer. When Mamá opened the bakery he was still very small; he would have been seven or eight, if that, and was studying violin all day, with a small violin, but a very fine one, said Papá, who'd ordered it from the United States. The house was like a permanent rehearsal, sometimes very pretty, but other times an unbearable squeaking, when he had to repeat the same piece all afternoon, to memorize it, or when he was trying to hone a note that wasn't coming out right, straining his long fingers. Some people, especially other boys, and our cousins, began to say he was strange. Faggy, they used to say back then. Papá would always say: "Be a man, my son, *bien machito!*" when he'd get startled by a bug or spend hours combing his beautiful black locks in front of the mirror. His eyes were very black too, and if he stared at you for a while – hard, deeply – people felt pierced, analyzed. That was his only severity, because in other things he wasn't able to be *machito* and was gentle and soft. He was scared of riding horses at La Oculta; he couldn't milk a cow or catch a cricket. Even though we had taught him to swim, he said he couldn't swim in the lake because when he got into the water he heard the voices of the people who'd drowned there calling him from the depths, saying: "Come, come, come and keep me company, I'm so cold," or worse, in December, they'd sing him carols: "Come, what's taking you so long…" He didn't like boy's games, he didn't go out to play soccer in the street, or throw stones at birds. He was scared of getting hit by a ball on the hands, he took care of his fingers as if they were made of glass: he said his violin teacher had told him that a violinist's hands were his treasure. If Martica the manicurist came to paint Mamá's nails, he liked to get a manicure too. If Papá saw that, he'd shout that he'd taken care of his own nails for his entire life, with a pair of nail clippers and nothing else. Grandpa Josué said that so many women and so much pampering were turning Toño effeminate, and Papá and Mamá suffered, but there wasn't much they could do: Toño was the way he was. He was delicate and sweet, very innocent. Why did he have to be changed into a rude little urchin? Eva and I liked him the way he was, delicate and tender.

I was bad at accounting and worse at kneading dough, so I never helped Mamá and Eva at the bakery. I preferred to go out with my friends, or with Alberto, who took me to movies, to parties, family gatherings. Eva, on the other hand, had this destiny, that no one had assigned her, but that's how it was: to be by my mother's side at work, apply modern methods to the administration of Anita's Bakery, which is still called that, even though it had to be sold during the crisis, after Cobo's death, when it seemed like this country was going to hell and when Eva got sick of trying to keep such a difficult business afloat. Mamá invested the money from the sale and lived off the interest for the rest of her days. With that same income, plus Papá's pension, she always helped us to resolve problems at La Oculta. And more so when she still had the bakery and Eva helped her with the management. Mamá, who hadn't gone to university, managed the bakery's accounts perfectly well while we were growing up, but the business was also growing and when the time came for Eva to start university, the bakery was already a bit big for Mamá to manage alone, thanks to her own success.

Come to think of it, someone had assigned her that destiny of helping Mamá as an unavoidable sentence. When Eva was getting ready to go to university, she wanted to study humanities (her dream had always been to be a psychologist or a dancer), but Papá said she should do a degree in business administration, to be able to help Mamá in the family business. "While Anita devotes herself to this pure and lovely trade of making bread for everyone, you can help her with the numbers and management of the bakery," Cobo declared, like an oracle. And Mamá thought that was a good decision, first of all because Eva was her favorite, and secondly because she thought if she went into humanities she could lose her way. She thought Eva needed to stop dreaming and be a bit more realistic. Since Eva wasn't rebellious back then and was very good-tempered, she didn't take it badly, just changed her plans. She was even cheerful about it, as if it didn't make much difference to her. She obeyed because Cobo said so, because Mamá wanted it, and because it seemed reasonable to help out the family. Eva always put one thing first: responsibility. Although she felt she didn't have the raw material to be an administrator, she obeyed and learned how to do it, and did it well. I remember she applied to study psychology at the University of Antioquia at the same time, and did really well on the entrance exam, in which she analyzed a film called *The Turning Point*, about two ballerinas who had to decide between an artistic career or changing to something more practical. Although she was accepted at both the universities she applied to, she didn't enroll in the University of Antioquia, in humanities, but at Eafit, a new, private, and rather expensive university in Medellín specializing in finances, for the city's future entrepreneurs. But she never seemed to have regretted that decision, or at least she never told Papá she did. She did say so to Mamá sometimes, when she had those cyclical crises that have affected her all her life, maybe due to not having followed her true vocation.

Eva was very happy at university, I'm sure of that, always surrounded by flirting friends. Her classmates, professors, students in other courses, bus drivers, street sweepers that saw her walk by, all fell in love with her. There was a very important French professor who had never accepted that Antioqueña aberration of starting classes very early in the morning, but one year he agreed to teach a course at six a.m., "just for the pleasure of seeing Evita Ángel fresh out of the shower," he said. Every weekend two or three suitors courted her with serenades and recited verses to "Evita, who evades and never invites us." No one ever serenaded me except Alberto. Beauty is like a prison sentence: it opens all doors to you and then closes them. Not that I was ugly, or that I couldn't have had more boyfriends if I'd wanted; I wasn't ugly, just faithful. As faithful as a dog, and for life. I never thought I was going to be able to find anyone better than Alberto and from the moment I saw him I knew I was going to marry him. We were married when I was eighteen and he was twenty-one. And it's not that Eva was unfaithful, just restless; since she was so responsible, she wanted to find the best husband in the world, not the first to cross her path.

ANTONIO

My sisters don't care at all about these things and start yawning and get distracted as soon as I start telling them, but for me it's been important to discover the origins of La Oculta. For years I've researched in books, in old family papers, and I've visited archives of property registries, notaries, parishes, to find out all I can about the farm. I've talked to historians and priests; I've read, I've asked our oldest relatives, Papá's sisters, our cousins, uncles, and my father and grandfather when they were still alive.

It's quite simple. Almost all these lands along the western bank of the River Cauca, from the mouth of the River San Juan (near Bolombolo) and that of the River Cartama (just below La Pintada), up as far as the high plains of the Citará mountain range, belonged to two families: the Echeverris and the Santamarías. These Echeverris and Santamarías were not nobles who would have been entrusted with a parcel of souls and land by the King of Spain, which is the origin of many large estates in this part of the world (the Aranzazu and the Villegas families, for example, were grandees who received land grants and trusts), rather the origin of these properties is more recent and, shall we say, more meritorious. Both families received these lands from the Republicans, who ousted the Royalists, for having been allies of the Liberating Army.

I suspect my sisters couldn't care less, but it matters to me that La Oculta was never a piece of land donated by Spanish monarchs to second sons or third-rate nobles, sent to the New World to get rid of a second litter of cadging and conflictive courtiers. Nor was it ever a mission, or a monastery, or a seminary for training priests, which started up many other towns in the Americas. Jericó didn't begin with conquistadors or monks, but with simple people, and if not equals, at least very similar in their attire and way of talking. La Oculta was an insignificant portion of an immense extension of lands the Republic handed over in repayment of legitimate debts incurred with two merchants, one, Echeverri, of Basque origin, and the other, Santamaría, from Jewish stock, neither of whom had a noble hair on their heads, nor any monastic inclinations either, but much business acumen, much faith in the value of hard work every day, in companies managed with order and moderation. There is some merit in this origin, rather than the sort of unwarranted luck of having inherited a noble title and received lands out of the roulette of birth or the repentance of some Viceroy who paid for his sins by donating land to the Franciscans, Jesuits, or Benedictines.

Echeverri and Santamaría were in-laws and associates. They were merchants and sons of merchants who had come to have a couple of clothing stores in Medellín's Plaza Mayor. They dealt in gold dust, among other things, which they purchased from panners for *tomines*, *adarmes*, *castellanos*, or sterling. They were known to be converted Jews, especially the latter, who was definitely a *marrano*. It can't be ruled out that they might have been smugglers, especially in their early lives, taking melted gold to Curaçao without declaring it to the colonial treasury, and returning with goods to sell here, of which they'd declare half, bringing them in by mule train, and then bring in the second half with the same papers as the first, that is, as contraband, at the same time, but by a different route. In any case, the lands in the Southwest were something else, another kind of deal, perhaps also involving cunning, but not illegality, rather conjecture. What they had done before receiving these lands was to give credit of provisions and supplies to soldiers, officers, and battalions of the Rebel Army during the Wars of Independence, betting that they would be the victors one day and govern.

Since the patriots had no money, they bought the supplies and things with bonds and titles payable when they took power. The colonels and generals signed anything in order to have provisions and equipment. Trusting in an uncertain future (if Spain won they would lose everything), but betting on the insurgents and against the Spaniards, Echeverri and Santamaría had exchanged rice, sugar, corn, tobacco, hats, ammunition, riding gear, horseshoes, nails, bolts of fabric, waterproof material, boots, reins, and ropes for the Liberators' promissory notes. Those promissory notes had accumulated and accumulated until turning into a pile of papers that seemed worthless, but which they kept conscientiously locked in an English strongbox at the back of the store. In Medellín everyone made fun of "Echeverri and Santamaría's bonds," which in the opinion of most had as much value as the faded yellowing paper of old newspapers, only good for ripening avocados and starting fires.

The old men, Don Alejo Santamaría and Don Gabriel Antonio Echeverri, however, kept those papers in their safe and said: "He who laughs last, laughs best." Time seemed to prove them right when the Spaniards finally fled in defeat with their tail between their legs, and the Republic was installed in Bogotá. Every revolution leaves a country broke, and the first few years were times of poverty and uncertainty, with a new government that had no resources to consolidate the newborn nation. Furthermore, with the quantity of dead left by the battles, there was no workforce to undertake any enterprise whatsoever, neither private nor public. Patience was required. They had to wait for the next generation of children to grow up. For a long time those papers seemed impossible to redeem, for the State's coffers were empty after the war and when anything was collected in taxes or exports there were much more urgent matters to resolve. But after many visits, much waiting and insistence with the provincial governors of Antioquia and with successive Treasury ministers, the central government decided to get those Antioqueño merchants off their backs by offering them some distant, forested, inhospitable, and apparently useless lands on the left bank of the River Cauca in exchange for the bonds. Those papers, they resolved, could be redeemed as title deeds to uncultivated lands, state property, in the southwest of the department, in the jungles on the western banks of the River Cauca, down toward the Chocó Valley and the Pacific Ocean. Depopulated lands, densely wooded, with abrupt and entangled mountains, where there were barely a couple of refuges for the much diminished Chamí or Katio Indians – decimated long before by the plagues of illnesses or massacred violently by the white conquistadores – and where not even hermit monks, runaway slaves, thieves, lunatics, or fugitive murderers had gone to hide.

After many comings and goings, those two related merchant families (daughters of one married to sons of the other), the Echeverris and the Santamarías, had come to receive useless land in exchange for the debts. Let's make the best of a bad situation, they said: something's better than nothing, since the government couldn't pay cash for the bonds. In those dense woods on the other side of the Cauca, there was nothing but trees, wild beasts, birds, rushing torrents, bushes, snakes, butterflies, streams, and mosquitos. The climates were so variable that in the highest parts of the sierra the surprising *frailejón* or *espeletia* of the high plains grew, with its soft fur for the cold, and in the lowest parts grew cacao, source of the most delicious drink in the world, which used to be sipped only by gods before some local Prometheus stole the blessing for mankind.

EVA

I raised my head very slowly above the surface of the water, trying not to make any noise. My open mouth began to take deep gulps of air, over and over again, as fast as I could. Two, three, five, seven breaths. My heart pounded in my chest, like the biggest drum in a village band. I heard voices and insults coming from the house. Several beams of light swept over the lake. I ducked down again. I didn't count anymore. I thought I should get as far away from the house as soon as possible and head for the other side of the lake. I couldn't see anything under the water, even if I opened my eyes: a slimy, black, cold barrier that due to my rush to flee felt like a soup of oil through which my arms and legs made me advance very slowly, even though I was moving them with all my might. I pushed the water frenetically with my hands and feet. Again I was running out of air, in a few seconds, but I forced myself to stay under a little longer. I've exercised all my life, it's been one of my passions, and I learned to swim in this very lake, and in the Cartama River, when I was five years old and Cobo taught me how. I thought it best to conserve some sort of order, and began to swim with broad arm sweeps and wide kicks, like a frog, rhythmically, with my best stroke.

If they had arrived through the backyard, then they must have come up the rails from the road. They'd left their cars below so they wouldn't make any noise. They wanted to surprise me, but they hadn't counted on Gaspar's sensitive ears. Oh, if not for my dog, for the life of my dog, I wouldn't have had time to get away. How many of them were there? Who? They had to be those Músicos who said we had to "sell or sell" La Oculta. I couldn't manage another stroke, I'd faint if I didn't take a breath. I broke the surface again. The air entered my body almost with a snort, like a death rattle. A beam of light flashed on my shoulder, and I ducked under as fast as I could, I heard a shot, but I didn't feel any bullet nearby. I veered to the left, to mislead them, my heart throbbing in my temples, in my whole body, from the tips of my toes to the crown of my head. Another three dives and it would be more difficult for them to catch sight of me, but I had to fly, fly under the water. At least the beams from the flashlights let me know which direction I should escape toward; I had to flee from the light toward the darkness. Flee from all brightness, toward the blackest darkness.

I surfaced again for air, out of breath. I looked behind me. They'd turned on the lights in the house. Two men were standing on the dock and sweeping their flashlight beams over the surface of the lake, a bit haphazardly. "Old bitch, I hope you drown!" said one, loudly. I ducked underwater again. Now I was swimming with a more orderly rhythm, with the same technique as breaststroke, but underwater, letting the inertia of the kick propel me. I was going at a good rhythm and now I felt confident that I would reach the far shore without being seen. Even though the water was freezing, every once in a while I found the consolation of big patches of warm water, residues of the sun from the previous day. I could feel my blood pumping all through me, as if my whole body was a giant heart. I was tense from the fear and the effort. But that same beating heart was a message telling me: you're alive, alive.

I thought of Gaspar, my dead dog. I'd had him for four years and loved him almost as much as one loves a child. He seemed intelligent, seemed to read my thoughts, and always adapted to my mood: cheerful if I was happy and melancholic if I was sad. Fierce and frightened if I was scared. That had been his last gesture of solidarity, the one that had saved me. They'd made a mistake by killing him. He was a dog who barked, but had never bitten anybody. Also, Gaspar always swam with me, chasing me when I dove into the lake. If they hadn't killed him, he would have followed me into the water and would have trailed me with his golden head always above the surface. I came up for air again. I was far enough away from the house. They were arguing and shouting at each other. Three more shots went off, a little further off, by the foreman's house. I thought of Próspero and pressed my eyelids in horror. I began to swim, strongly, but silently, without letting my arms or feet break the surface, without stirring up any bubbles, trying not to leave a wake, the way turtles swim, almost imperceptibly, with their heads level with the water, lifting their mouths for an instant to breathe. The disorderly flashlight beams were now very weak by the time they reached where I was swimming, increasingly far from the house and closer to the weeds and guadua bamboo on the other side. The darkness was almost total, but I could see a couple of white posts in front of me at the edge of the water. I heard a fluttering of birds above me. I realized the cormorants and egrets that nested in the ceiba tree had been startled by my presence. I was nearing the edge. I let my feet hang down but I couldn't touch bottom yet, the muddy, slimy bottom of the lake that had always seemed like a dark and disgusting, repugnant gelatin to me, but which tonight I wanted desperately to feel. I wanted to reach the edge, get out, run.

I couldn't take any risks and I swam underwater again. I was very tired and wouldn't have lasted half a minute. I tried to count to thirty. I had to come up for air at sixteen, exhausted. I saw they were walking around the edge of the lake looking for me with flashlights, but they'd gone the other way, the longer way around. The lake was elongated and it would take them a long time to get all the way around it. Besides, they'd run into dense vegetation by the shore of the lake. It was impossible to get through without a machete, you had to cut down thickets, thorny stems, lianas, and branches.

Finally my bare feet felt the muddy bottom; the shore was near. I had to feel my way, from the water, until I found the big rock where I sometimes went to sunbathe. From there a path rose through the guadua grove that would lead me to the dirt road that went up to Casablanca, our cousins' farm. The cousins weren't there, they hadn't been back for months, out of precaution, but Rubiel, the foreman, would be there. Maybe I could ask him to hide me. I found the big, tall, round rock. I swam around it, climbed up one side and got out on the other, on dry land. I was shivering with cold, trembling with fear, breathing anxiously. The shouts and voices were very far away now. The beams of light were now illuminating the men more than the lake. There were people moving nervously on the porch of the house. The ones searching along the lakeshore had reached the edge of the thicket and kept shining their flashlights across the surface of the water. They didn't see me. Thank goodness no one knows this lake better than I do. Thank goodness they tell so many stories about the people who'd drowned in it, and everyone's frightened of its deep and dark waters, even in daylight, never mind at night. I felt the same spirit of the drowning victims of the lake protecting me. Those men couldn't see me and hadn't been able to bring themselves to dive into the water. I stepped on the prickly roots of the guadua bamboo and the pain in the soles of my feet rose to the nape of my neck, like an electric current. I wanted to yelp with pain, but I held it back. The branches and thorns tore my wet shirt, the thorns cut my arms and the leaves scraped my bare legs. I got as far as the wire fence and scooted beneath it. A barb ripped my shirt, in the middle of my back, but I didn't notice that until much later. I reached the road and began to run uphill.

ANTONIO

The new owners of the mountains of Southwest Antioquia had no idea what to do with them. They were burdened with these enormous, empty lands that they couldn't take any advantage of. First they looked for mines and salt deposits, without any success, for in that rough wilderness there didn't seem to be an abundance of gold or silver or salt or coal. Nor did they find Indian tombs of much value, since all they contained were clay pots and bowls, with no metallic treasures, except occasionally a little idol so rusty it couldn't be gold. The odd tomb raider, it seems, had found pieces worth plundering, but they'd just melted them down themselves, without telling anybody, to extract whatever gold might have been in the alloy. As for the ceramic bowls or clay idols, they lacked the beauty and mystery of those of other indigenous cultures, and besides, in those years almost nobody thought them of any worth, and indigenous graves were desecrated without the slightest consideration. The tomb raiders would just smash them, as if they were the devil's work and might bring disgrace or bad luck, which is what they said about those idols, which were there to guard the eternal rest of the bones of the dead beside their few buried treasures. Sometimes, in the rocky ravines they would find mysterious inscriptions, the last signs of an intelligence razed by the whites, and finally erased by the sun, rain, and the elements.

They couldn't get the wood off to market either, because there were no roads to transport it, and tracks were so difficult to create, since the land was all so rough, with its abrupt mountains, almost impenetrable, torrential rains for much of the year, and turbulent rivers full of stones, impossible to navigate. A single downpour was enough to turn any attempt at a trail into a bog. The government had no budget to invest in building roads that didn't lead to a town, so they couldn't count on any help there. At the same time, the proprietors, more merchants than landowners, had neither the means nor the knowledge of how to establish farms in those mountainous jungles. Furthermore, there was nowhere to contract farmhands or day laborers since nobody lived out in those solitudes.

If the inhabitants of Medellín used to mock Echeverri and Santamaría's worthless papers and war bonds, now they laughed at their useless, good-for-nothing lands, which brought them no return whatsoever, producing only cicadas, heat, snakes, jaguars, and mosquitos. They were vast and fertile areas, but completely wild. All that land combined with a shortage of muscle power was the same as not having anything, and it wasn't easy in Medellín to get anybody to leave the Villa de la Candelaria (which was starting to fancy itself a city, while still a miserable little town) for the inhospitable jungle. The city dwellers, rather than wielding a pickax or swinging a machete or digging with a shovel, preferred to watch the sunsets.

But the next generation of Echeverris and Santamarías was not ignorant. They knew they'd inherited the titles to great expanses of land, and a plan was ripening in their heads that would impose on the jungle terrain the much discussed notion in those days known as civilization. By the time their fathers died, without having received any real benefits from the lands they'd been granted, the next generation of Echeverris and San- tamarías had come up with a plan that more resembled a dream. Often, on horseback and by mule, they had traveled over parts of their property. They had opened up some pastures and half marked out some trails up into the hills. They knew of the lim- itless beauty and saw in those empty, inhospitable mountains a potential future. Antioqueños tend to be prolific and it wasn't unusual to find families of twelve, fifteen, or eighteen children, all fed on beans, rice, *arepas*, *aguapanela*, eggs, and a bit of bacon. The first thing they had to do was to attract young settlers to populate the uncultivated land; but those young people had been born in the republic and didn't want to be subordinates or servants; they already had the consciences of free citizens and confidence in the dream of being able to progress thanks to their own efforts, without giving the strength of their arms to others. They had self-respect: they might be humble and poor, but they weren't stupid, submissive, or obedient. If they were going to leave the little cities it was to have their own land, not to go and work as farmhands, sharecroppers, or tenant farmers for others. The slaves had not yet been freed, but their wombs were liberated, and black children born free could not now be enslaved; they were already talking of manumitting all of them.

PILAR

I never doubted that Alberto was and would forever be the love
of my life. The first and only. He lived in the same neighborhood as us, Laureles, three blocks from our house, and we met
one Easter Week, in the afternoon, when we were in the middle
of the Holy Thursday procession and we got caught in a downpour. I don't know why, but whenever something important
is going to happen in my life there's always a downpour. I was
twelve and he was fifteen years old. We went to the processions
not to pray but to flirt; some boys did too. I was with a big group
of girlfriends, and some of them, as we walked along behind the
statues of the saints, poked the boys with a long file they had in a
lace kerchief. Not me, I never poked anybody, I just watched and
laughed. At that age and in those years masses and processions
were places to meet friends and find a boyfriend; religion was
also a pretext for all of us to get together.

Toño says that Alberto and I were engaged ever since our first
communion. Such an exaggeration! It's not true, but almost.
When it started raining hard all of a sudden, some friends and

I ran to take shelter under the eaves of a house, so we wouldn't get wet. Some boys came running up to the same place and he squeezed in beside me. I didn't know his name, but I looked him over from head to toe. Even though we were neighbors, we'd never seen each other before that day. He was handsome, tall and well built, the kind of boy who plays soccer and rides a bike and runs around. He was wearing a suit and tie, which was the style then, I can still see him. The suit was gray, and you could tell he was very strong because of the lines of his muscles in his shoulders and arms. He had lovely hair, a sort of sun-bleached blond, combed up in a high, striking hairstyle, a bit like Elvis Presley's. The usual thing was to wear new clothes during Easter Week, but I didn't have a new dress that time, plus I'd gotten rained on in the downpour. Since Mamá hadn't been home I'd put on a little white dress with red edging, which wasn't suitable for processions, since it wasn't what you'd call discreet, much less when it was wet. But he, that boy, wasn't looking at me. He was looking straight ahead, distractedly, as if thinking about the rain. He didn't even notice me. I on the other hand couldn't take my eyes off him, like someone looking at a statue in a museum. I whispered in the ear of the girl beside me, Libia Henao:

"Who is this guy? Who is he? I'm going to die."

She said: "No, honey. His name is Alberto Gil, but don't even dream of him, not even Mona Díaz could win him over."

Mona Díaz was the tallest, most attractive, prettiest girl in our neighborhood. Libia insisted:

"He's impossible."

"Impossible?" I said, arching my eyebrows. "Well, I'm going to marry him!"

When the procession ended, after the downpour, I looked awful. I'd put on makeup without permission from Mamá or Papá, who were away, and I had mascara running down my whole face, black rivers, like those virgins who cry at the foot of the cross. The boy had gone and I didn't know where. I thought he'd probably gone to El Múltiple, which was the only ice cream parlor in the neighborhood, and where all the kids always went. I convinced my friends that we should go to El Múltiple. Since we didn't have any money, we put all our coins together to buy one single cone to share among all of us. I walked into El Múltiple and saw him sitting there, with his hair a little damp, but not much, and his clothes dry. I looked at him defiantly and spoke to him. This wasn't something that was done back then, talking to someone you didn't know, but I dared to speak to him.

"Hey, aren't you ashamed, look at me, all wet, and you didn't even lend me your jacket to cover me up."

He didn't answer. Of course. He looked at me shyly, smiling. The next day I saw him at church visiting the monuments. That's what we did on Good Friday in the morning, visited monuments. He'd already gone to lots of other churches but I saw him in two: Santa Teresa and in the chapel of the Bethlemitas School. I followed him, trying to guess where he'd go. At least now he looked at me and I looked at him, from afar. We couldn't speak to each other because we hadn't been introduced.

When Easter Week ended, the fourth day after Easter, Pompi, a friend of his, introduced me to him. Every time I see Pompi, to this day, I thank him: "Pompi, what a dear friend you are, to have introduced me to this angel." And Alberto declared himself to me a little while later, on May 7. I was dying inside and happy, but I feigned indifference. That's what you did back then, and I didn't say yes to him right away, as I would have liked to, rather I told him I'd have to think about it, that he should let me think about it until the next day. That night I barely slept, terrified he'd forget about his proposal and never ask me again. But he came back the next morning to take me to Mass. And we went to the seven o'clock Mass. On the way out he asked me: "What did you think?" And I told him yes.

Alberto had a Lambretta, and when he went past our house he'd beep the horn. I would fly to the window and watch him drive past, my heart racing, what happiness to see him drive by beeping and waving. A tiny bit later, on Mother's Day, which is the second Sunday in May, he brought me a serenade. The music woke us all up and Papá asked me very quietly: "Princess, aren't you a little young to be serenaded?" and I answered: "Oh, I don't know, Papi, but I'm happy." Then he said: "That's what matters." At the third song I turned on the light for a second, which was the signal girls gave to let the boy know she was awake and listening to the music. I turned it straight off and opened the blinds a bit to see him for a second. I still remember the little card he put under the door for me. He hadn't written it, but had asked his older brother, Rodrigo, who had better handwriting and knew how to rhyme, to write it for him. *You are the heart of my existence / this passion allows no resistance / any pain that strikes you offends me / far from you my soul feels empty / God made my heart just for you.* And he'd signed it without even putting his whole name. He signed: Albto.

ANTONIO

The one who convinced my grandfather's great-grandfather to go and live on the other side of the Cauca, a land of heat and mosquitos, snakes and cicadas, was an engineer called Pedro Pablo Echeverri, El Cojo, son of Don Gabriel, one of those who were founding villages in Southwest Antioquia. This ancestor of ours, who was called Isaías Ángel, had been born in El Retiro in 1840, was suspected of being fickle, sometimes Jewish and sometimes Christian, depending on the circumstances, or at least that's what I've been told.

When El Cojo Echeverri came through town looking for settlers for his family's uncultivated lands, Isaías was just a twenty-one-year-old kid, recently married to a girl called Raquel Abadi, daughter of El Retiro's cobbler, which either through a scribe's error, or a priest's cover up, ended up being Abad, without the *i*, when she was registered as the mother of Elías Ángel Abad, in Jericó's oldest book of births and baptisms. She had Elías at the age of seventeen, in the same bed where she slept, with the help of a midwife and after seventeen hours of labor.

El Cojo had spent months convincing people in the towns of Antioquia to join up with a venture that had no precedents in the region, and seemed too good to be true. If it worked out, it could be advantageous to the two founding families, his and the Santamarías', but it could also be a good idea for the colonizing families who decided to join the adventure. The most difficult thing was to get them to believe that there was such a venture that all could benefit from. So El Cojo had to go to a lot of effort to persuade them he was not a windbag, a conman who was trying to trick the stupidest and neediest people of every village. The proposal was basically very simple: the founding families, owners of those immense uncultivated lands, would give out property rights of portions of their grandfathers' lands to new settlers as long as they would reside there and help to clear the land and build roads for certain days of the month. There were no other conditions.

From the first day each settler would be assigned a lot in some part of the recently founded town, already drawn up on the map (but not yet in existence), which was then called Aldea de Piedras. And after a few months of serious work, at most a year, each head of a family would also be granted a plot of land outside the town, where they could grow their basic crops. In addition, those who had enough savings to contribute an initial share, could purchase on very good terms and without interest, since the lands were rough, cheap, and difficult to work, larger plots, up to two hundred hectares, or more, for which deeds of ownership could be signed, duly certified in front of the notary public of Fredonia (the only town in the zone that had functionaries at that time), with well-established boundaries and precise markings: the stream, the boulder, the ceiba, the headland, the river, the ditch.

He would reserve the lion's share for his family, and he hid this from no one, since they were, after all, the original and legitimate owners – the flattest lands, on the shores of the rivers (along the River Silencio, the Cartama, the Frío, the Piedras, and most of all the Cauca), where they could establish dairy farms and graze steers. Echeverri himself, in fact, in association with the Santamarías, had a ranch near Tarso, which they'd called Canaan, like the promised land, and another they'd given the name of Damascus, all names they'd found in the Book of Joshua. It would also be the two founding families' exclusive right to charge tolls for use of the future roads. The mule drivers, merchants, and everyone who wanted to make use of these new routes to the west and the south would have to pay these tolls. They would conserve these privileges, yes, but in order to populate the deserted forests they were prepared to surrender a good part of their property. It was rugged terrain, but with lots of good water, and fertile, volcanic soil, so it would be good for growing food crops and raising animals, after the trees had been chopped down, the weeds pulled up, and the rocks dug out.

Struggling to achieve a dream, and following the instructions of his father, Don Gabriel, el Cojo was searching the villages of Antioquia for vigorous young families without a lot of resources, but keen to progress, who wanted to participate in this enterprise, which for the most incredulous was nothing but a collective madness, or a trick. They didn't want bachelors, but fertile couples, with or without children, so that among them they'd populate these lonely hills and farm the land. "If it's so good they wouldn't be giving so much of it away," said the mistrustful. El Cojo was a tall, thin, ungainly man, just over thirty, not exactly handsome, slightly cross-eyed, with one leg longer than the other due to an old fracture from falling off a horse, but with a silver tongue. He had a genuine frankness and a contagious enthusiasm. He had some quality that inspired confidence, and he and his father were sure he could convince one or two hundred Antioqueño families to go and work and live there, in those distant wilds where the devil had yet to arrive.

"Not you, Isaías, but who knows, perhaps your children's children, or the children of your children's children might be able to go to university one day, thanks to these efforts," El Cojo said to the young Ángel, a man of fair features, wide forehead, and a friendly smile. Not very educated, just primary school, and perhaps for that very reason, no nonsense.

"If every family has an average of ten children," said El Cojo, "and that's not preposterous if they're well fed on the beans, eggs, milk, and corn these lots will produce, in twenty years the region will have the population it needs to come from nowhere and build a little paradise. This is our destiny, this is on the horizon, if we have perseverance and a little luck. Within twenty years, when ten- or twenty-thousand souls are living there, no one will believe that just a couple of decades earlier all there was in these wilds were vermin and impenetrable forest. I'm already imagining a geographer writing at the end of this century that the colonizers of the Southwest offered the spectacle of a free, property-owning, comfortably-off, and happy society."

While listening to El Cojo, Isaías Ángel was thinking of the words he'd use to convince his wife, Raquel. Staying in El Retiro would mean resigning themselves to being peons and servants to others for their whole lives; going to the new land meant the possibility of a different kind of life, where they could be owners and rulers not just of a piece of land, but of their destiny. He knew that Raquel – who had received a sum of money from an uncle when she married – aspired to more than scrubbing plates, sweeping up dead leaves, and washing clothes. That's why, as he listened to Echeverri explain the deal, his eyes shone and he couldn't wait to tell Raquel to go and say farewell to her parents, receive their blessing, and help him pack up as much as would fit on three burros.

EVA

My eyes had adjusted to the darkness and could make out some shapes among the shadows. I was on the track that went up to Casablanca, a very steep hill; my sweat was mixing with the lake water. On either side there were lines of striated concrete, and in the center a strip of grass and weeds. Sometimes I walked on the concrete, rough on the soles of my feet, but without thistles, and sometimes on the grass in the middle. When I had the energy I ran or jogged uphill for a stretch, then walked to catch my breath and look behind me.

I was panting and crying, but I didn't even notice I was crying; the tears mixed with the drops of water running down my face from my wet hair, and with the sweat, which was more copious by the minute. The stars were colder and more distant than ever and their wan glow did nothing to help light my way.

The Casablanca dogs sensed my presence when I crossed the cattle guard at the entrance to my Vélez cousins' farm and took the dirt road that led up to the house. The stones hurt my feet and I moved over to the edge, on the other side of a wire fence, to walk on the grass. The dogs ran toward me, barking. When they got close they recognized me and stopped barking; they came over wagging their tails, sniffing my hands, licking my wet legs. I've always gotten along well with dogs. I got to the house of Rubiel, the Casablanca foreman, and rapped on the door with my knuckles.

"Open up, Rubiel, quick, open up! It's Eva, from La Oculta. Open up, Rubiel, open up! They want to kill me, Rubiel, open the door!"

Sor, Rubiel's wife, came to open the door, looking alarmed and sleepless. They'd heard the shots a while earlier. I went in fearfully and closed the door behind me, as if locking out a monster, a phantom. I sat on the floor; I couldn't speak. Sor gave me a towel to dry off; she got me some of my cousin Martis's clothes, so I could change. Putting on clean, dry clothes made me feel better. I would have liked to put on a bit of perfume to mask the smell of sweat, lake water, dirt, leaves, and the thorns that tore my skin. She heated me up a mug of *aguapanela*, lent me a pair of socks to warm up my aching, bloody feet. When I was at last able to babble out what had happened, Rubiel said very quietly that I'd better go. They could come looking for me at any moment and kill them as well if they saw they were hiding me.

I nodded, as I finished getting dressed. Sor brought me a pair of my cousin's running shoes as well. I asked Rubiel to lend me a horse. I told him I'd leave the horse in town, in Jericó, Támesis, or Palermo, or somewhere. Or maybe at the roadhouse, if I could. Wherever I could get to.

Rubiel got out a flashlight and, upset and hurrying, we went together to the stables; between the two of us we saddled a black mare. Her name was Noche. I'd picked her out for her color, as she'd be less visible in the darkness. Rubiel said, in a whisper, that if the men came he wouldn't tell them I'd been there, but that I had to leave immediately, he begged. We were very alert, speaking very quietly as we finished hitching up the saddle, almost in the dark, and sometimes we thought we heard the buzzing of a distant engine.

"I'll leave the mare with someone trustworthy, Rubiel. Turn off all the lights. Goodbye and thank you," I said as I hoisted myself up onto the horse.

"Take the flashlight, Doña Eva," he said, "but don't use it much."

I took the flashlight, turned it off, and trotted up the road.

ANTONIO

Whenever I come back home to New York from Colombia, the first days, when I wake up, I have the strange impression of still being at La Oculta. It's the absence of birdsong and the noise of sirens that reminds me I'm somewhere else. Fire engines, ambulances, police cars. Then, at breakfast time, so silent here, I miss the hubbub of children, Pilar's grandkids, who always wake us up with their games and shouting, a joyful annoyance. Here I eat cereal with yogurt, pancakes, bagels with cream cheese, cinnamon buns, smoked salmon, things like that. Not *arepas* with *quesito*, sausages, blood pudding, frothy hot chocolate, scrambled eggs with tomatoes and onions, or *pandeyuca* like down there. If I bring back frozen *arepas* they never taste the same, and in New York there are so many fine, aged cheeses from all over the world, but no *quesito*. At siesta time – I don't take a siesta in New York, only at the farm – I miss the feel of the hammocks, the midday heat, the sound of cicadas, the strange light one wakes up to, at four or five, which looks nothing like the light at one or two o'clock, when it was so intense it hurt even when our eyes were shut. The light at the farm, so special, the intense light of the tropics, doesn't leave my head, in spite of the darkness of winter, in spite of the cold, or perhaps precisely because of the cold and darkness. I know I've changed spaces, places, I know I've gone back to sleeping with Jon – the best thing about coming home – but inside I remain there for a few days, elevated, spellbound by the memory. He notices, he looks me in the eye and says:

"You're still there, I can see it in your eyes. You're home, remember."

"Give me three days and I'll turn back into the perfect New Yorker, have patience with me, the tropics stick to the skin like toad's milk, which doesn't come off even when you scrub with soap and a scouring sponge."

When I wake up, before taking the violin out of its case to start practicing, I turn on the computer for a moment to check my email. I feel a stab of pain knowing I'll never have any more messages from Anita, but as I think that, on the screen appears my farm, the mountains, La Oculta. I have it in front of me: the lake, the white walls with red baseboards, the wooden floorboards of the bedrooms, which sag and creak a bit, always in the same places I know by heart; the even railings made from the trunks of black palms, along the open corridors that run round the outside of the house on all four sides; the tiles tanned by the elements and covered in moss; the hammocks strung from the pillars that overlook the lake or the view down to the river; the gigantic trees – *pisquines*, samans, oaks, walnuts, cinchonas, ceibas, *mamoncillos*, madrones, cominos, *barcinos*, willows – invaded by parasitic plants, creepers, mosses, lichen, bromeliads, orchids; the crags that rise almost vertically up to Jericó and which I've climbed so many times with friends and cousins, when I was a boy, and now with my nephews and nieces.

Outside it's snowing; a sad, silent snow is falling and melting on the sidewalks; through the window I see people walk past dressed in black and shivering with cold. Here, in New York, in Harlem. Not at home; at home it hasn't snowed at least since the time of the last ice age. At my house it never snows; it's never cold and never hot, like in Paradise. If I want cold I climb the mountain; if I want heat I walk down toward the River Cartama. But in the middle, halfway between the tropical lowlands and the cold mountain air, the climate is always mild, and what surrounds us always looks like that: green and flourishing, perpetually warm. And the landscape opens up before us, immense, mountains and deep valleys that never end but melt into the horizon where the green turns blue like in a seascape. From La Oculta the mountains look big and powerful like the sea. That's what it's like, just as it looks in the photo that opens in front of me. La Oculta is always there, so I never forget it, to maintain the illusion that I'm still there, or at least that I'll return there one day. To go on believing that Cobo and Anita are still alive there, in some way, even if turned into earth, into ashes, into blades of grass, or leaves on the trees. I look at the photograph and it's as though I were praying: this is my home, my real home, my coffee farm in the tropics, in the mountains of Antioquia.

People think I moved to New York, almost thirty years ago now, because I was awarded a grant to continue my violin studies. No, I came to New York to get out of Medellín, to get out of Antioquia, which is an area with a rough but real charm, and at the same time an asphyxiating, religious, intolerant, racist, homophobic, conservative place, or at least it was through and through when I left. It still is, but perhaps a bit less; the news that the world is changing has even reached Antioquia. Distant, isolated mountains produce aloof, reserved, mistrustful people, and that was not the atmosphere in which to exist with the liberty I was determined to allow myself. I wanted to live the way I chose, kiss and go to bed with whoever I desired, out of the vigilant sight of my relatives, friends, Mamá and Papá, and my sisters. They, after the initial fright and scandal, understood, or said they understood me, but couldn't help being Antioqueños in the worst sense of the word. They knew my grandfather would have a heart attack if he found out, and Mamá preferred not to discuss the matter. Papá, though theoretically he understood my orientation, it bothered him a lot, or it made him sad. He experienced it like an illness or a misfortune, as if his son had been born with a deformity, or blind, or deaf, or missing an arm. Once, when he'd had too much to drink, he'd said (unaware I was listening) that the problem wasn't that I was a fag, that wasn't such a big deal, the problem was that I was going to suffer a lot in this world for being a fag, and for that reason I should make an effort not to be, undergo treatment, and if that didn't work, try to control it with discipline, or at least hide it with abstinence. That's what was always recommended in Antioquia, what the priests hinted at as well, and in a certain sense, I've never been able to stop being Antioqueño.

Perhaps that's why sometimes I don't forgive myself, or didn't forgive myself, for being the way I am. Sometimes I'd like to change, for a few days, and be a brave, macho man, with a booming voice and rough, calloused hands, the kind of guy who rides a spirited horse without fear, or tames a half-wild colt with shouts and whippings, which is the ideal man in my part of the world, a guy with a moustache and hat, with spurs and a whip, a man of few words and categorical remarks, cutting, definite, who when he talks does not come out with proposals or thoughts, but judgements. That way of being is the one I most hate, and at the same time what I'd like to be – for a short time – a furious dictator, a tyrant who gives all Antioqueños the order to change, to stop being like that, so macho, so mountainous, so rough and tough, so backward. This is what makes me furious: why is goodness and strength never combined in the same person? Maybe because good people can never force, only convince. But for one instant I'd like to be strong and force them, and after forcing them, go back to being myself, what I am, a gentle person, who doesn't like to impose or force anybody to be any way other than how they are, just to simply be, and to be as I am, because I have no other choice, and not how others might want me to be. I arrived at this tranquil acceptance thanks to a Jewish psychologist in New York, Dr. Umansky, half psychoanalyst, half constructivist. She basically taught me how to find out and accept who I was, what I am in my deepest being. I also owe this to Jon, who paid for my treatment, three extremely expensive sessions a week, for more than four years. Dr. Umansky is wise, but as implacable as a banker regarding payment for her forty-minute sessions. Her bill has to be paid every month, or she won't see you even if you're about to throw yourself onto the subway tracks on a desolate day.

Gradually I started living in New York, almost without realizing. First because I found work in an orchestra, as the last violinist, but in a great orchestra, and later because I fell in love with Jon body and soul. Later came therapy, and then directed meditation, which I also do, with a sage from India who spends a month a year in New York. And many years later, I ended up marrying my dear Jon, marrying a gringo, because they finally approved gay marriage here and in Colombia it's still illegal for two men or two women to marry each other. Actually, I didn't even want to get married, but Jon did. We've been living together for many years, and everything in our relationship was ever more serene; we understood each other better and we'd stopped fooling around on each other. Maturity brings with it a certain tranquility. Because at first we both cheated on each other, we lived the crazy life of the eighties, making love with lots of other men, like bonobos, and terrible things happened, atrocious sorrows like in soap operas.

Jon had always been an activist for gay rights, a leader in the fight against AIDS, a campaigner for the legalization of gay marriage. For him it was important that there should be a ceremony, signatures, certificates, and even though none of that mattered to me, I went along with it to please him, to make him happy. "And this way, if I die first," said Jon, "you'll inherit everything, and not my brothers, who are a bunch of bastards, who've always hated me for being queer." Despite what we Colombians might think, there is still a lot of homophobia in New York as well, and more so among Afro-Americans, or among blacks, as we would say, without meaning to insult anyone with that word or that truth.

One of the reasons I could marry Jon is that he likes my farm in Colombia. Not sharing that would be like a zealous Christian marrying an atheist, or a carnivore marrying a vegan: the perpetual arguments of unsuccessful marriages. He learned to love La Oculta as the years went by, I think, because at first everything about the tropics seemed excessive to him. Or at least in recent years, when he's there he pretends very well to like things he doesn't like (too much heat, too much family, too much rain). He's had to accept my environment, my house, my mountains.

Of course, strange things happen to him at La Oculta. He's the only one who ever gets bitten by mosquitos, for example, and he complains. Pilar consoles him with a theory of her own devising: if someone never gets mosquito bites it's because they have cancer, that mosquitos detect cancer in the scent of the skin. Jon has to put insect repellent on all day and all night, and sometimes, if it rains a lot, he also complains about the humidity, saying it affects his breathing, that his asthma comes back, like when he was a little boy. And his sleep is restless, anxious. If the dogs bark at a horse or an opossum, he thinks bandits have arrived to rob or kidnap us. But if the weather's dry, he sings the praises of the landscape and stops complaining. It's the least he can do. After all, it's taken a while but I've learned to love New York, almost as much as he does. That's why we live here, and I don't complain about the cold or the prices or the tourists, but enjoy myself in the parks, on the beaches, at concerts, art shows, and museums.

Sometimes Jon takes out a canvas and easel and paints La Oculta: the farmhouse, the lake, or the landscape, in an old-fashioned realist, figurative style, in oils, in that style that seems so ridiculous in today's art world. Those are the kinds of paintings Pilar likes, and he does them the way she likes them, so she can put them in her room, or along the outer corridors that surround the house. Then the sun shines on them and they fade, and Jon retouches them every time he comes back, to recover the real colors, though the thousands of tonalities of the tropics are inimitable in any painting. Sometimes, as he touches them up, he takes advantage of the opportunity to add something, almost always some unrealistic detail, something horrible, a monster or a skeleton, a rifle or a chainsaw, some scary effect that Pilar criticizes: "Why did you put that there, Jon? You ruined it with that chainsaw." And Jon just laughs, or he says that at La Oculta some horrific thing is always about to happen and it's good to remind everybody of that when they look at the painting.

When the guerrillas kidnapped my nephew Lucas, and later, when others wanted to force us to sell the farm and sent my sisters death threats, there was a moment of doubt, almost of hatred toward the farm, and we were on the verge of giving in, of letting them defeat us. Jon was furious with Colombia and said it was a failed state with no future, with a distant, uncaring, indolent, and corrupt government. He advised me to sell my share of La Oculta and said together we should buy a cabin in Vermont, on a lake, where we could go once in a while. "If you want we could call it La Oculta," he told me with a smile. "It's hard to believe, but land is cheaper here than in Antioquia, so you sell there and we can buy something similar here, or even more beautiful."

More beautiful? That phrase offended me, but I had to understand him. He is not Antioqueño and doesn't feel what we feel. "It might be more beautiful in the summer and the beginning of fall, but after that it's invisible," I told him, almost scornfully. Jon smiled again, but at least he didn't tell me about the white beauty of winter, tobogganing in January, the iridescent gleam of morning frost. I was thinking it over, or rather I told him I'd think it over, until I explained to him that the coffee-growing region of the tropics was something very different, as beautiful as Vermont might be, my memories and my blood were attached to those lands. That's what I told him, all exaggerated and melo-dramatic: my blood, *mi sangre*. That I was not a great-grandson of Irishmen, or Dutchmen, or slaves, like New Yorkers, but of Spaniards and converted Jews, and indigenous Andean women. I talked to him of the absence of seasons, of lush, green Januaries, warm Decembers, the heat of August, and tropical orchids. Jon just smiled, discreet, tolerant, and understanding, and said that he, on the other hand, felt no nostalgia for Africa and it had never occurred to him to go and clear a plot of land in Liberia. So we kept quiet and weathered the storm.

For several years I lived only on memories, not being able to return. My sisters and Mamá even came to New York to visit us in December, but spending Christmas here, in this cold, accus-tomed as we were to spending it at La Oculta, swimming, sun-bathing, making rice dishes, barbecues, and chicken stews in the open air, going horseback riding, was so strange. I watched Pilar and Alberto here, saw Mamá looking a bit withered in this city, and they didn't even seem real to me, they were like holo-grams, and we didn't enjoy ourselves. We pretended we weren't uncomfortable and drank a lot of whiskey to feign a cheerfulness we didn't feel. The topic of conversation turned again and again to La Oculta. Only Eva was happy, and she said if she sold her share of the farm she'd spend three months a year in New York, going to concerts and winter exhibitions, checking out the new restaurants, the galleries, the science museums, the inventions. Eva had always had an incredible thirst for knowledge, for culture, and in a way her work at the bakery – that destiny Papá and Mamá thrust on her – had diminished her.

To help him to understand me, when he insisted on the idea of a cottage in Vermont, at night I would tell Jon something about the farm that in my opinion was irreplaceable: the aromas from the kitchen, at breakfast or midday. The smell of the stables when there were cows that had just calved and we milked them in the early hours, to the sound of the lowing of the young calves in the corral, with our grandfather and cousins. There was never a cappuccino as frothy as a cup of Colombian coffee with fresh, warm milk squeezed straight from the udder: *de la vaca a la boca*, straight from the cow into the mouth, as Grandpa Josué used to say, inhaling through his nostrils to catch the scent of grass in the fresh milk. The bats that came out at dusk every evening and ate insects on the wing, praised by my father, in spite of how ugly we thought they were, because they kept things balanced so there wouldn't be too many insects and demonstrated that our region was free of insecticides. The toads that hopped inside the house at night, and which we had to frighten away with a broom, because Mamá was petrified of them and if she saw one she'd have a fit. If a toad or a frog got inside the house in the daytime, so much the worse. Cobo would catch it and crucify it with pins on a board. Then he'd get a razor blade and slice it open. He taught us anatomy with the poor little creature that couldn't free itself and we saw how its heart beat, how its pink lungs inflated, where the liver and the intestines were. If it was a venomous toad, its skin filled up with a disgusting milk and Papá said the chemical composition of that poison should be studied, since from the poisons of nature come anesthetics, analgesics, glues, and medicines.

And I kept talking to Jon, unceasingly, of everything that occurred to me about La Oculta. The terrestrial firmament the fireflies created with their appeals of light. The perpetual music of Alberto, who can't live a minute of his life without music, because he hates silence, and when the rest of us tire of his constant *bambucos*, *porros*, and *pasillos*, of so many boleros and so many corny ballads, and we tell him, he smiles and puts on his headphones, to give us a rest from his music but to go on hearing it in his head, always, even at night, even when he's sleeping. The smell of molasses, when the horses go into their stalls and paddocks and Próspero gives them water mixed with molasses and bran, so they drink till they're round-bellied, and the bees and wasps come to taste the horses' sweet, sweet molasses water.

The midday sun, beating down on your body stretched out on a towel on the dock, or on one of the rocks around the edge of the lake, those huge, black rocks, like little tablelands, which came from I don't know where, and the color of your skin that turns darker each day, more alluring, more like the color of the rocks (and more like yours, Jon, like yours). Conversations about science with my nephews who are educated and intelligent, especially Simón. They've done doctorates in physics, in biology, in geography, and tell us about the antiquity of these mountains, their fossils, their formation, the shape the glaciers had given to some parts of the mountain, or a narrow valley. Rum and coke at dusk; ice-cold beer at midday, the various colors: *mulata*, blond, or mestizo, like the skin tones of different members of the family; aguardiente or gin and tonic on some Friday afternoons, for a lively euphoria; Anita's delicious pisco sours, with pisco imported from Peru, which she used to serve as an aperitif before lunch, with the rim of the glass dipped in sugar; the white wines that Eva preferred, Riesling, Gewürztraminer, because of the time she'd spent living in Germany. The sweet delights of alcohol, its gentle euphoria, when it's not excessive and just serves to get us all chatting easily and happily, because everyone talks about the harm booze does, the havoc it wreaks, which is not untrue, but its benefits need to be mentioned as well.

I would tell him again about charades, one of our favorite games, which we played in two groups of all ages. Each team had three minutes to act out a word, and the ones who guessed it fastest won. Pilar's kids liked to make the older ladies act out spicy words, like orgasm, or masturbation, and they wrote them down, anticipating the laughter, so they'd be acted out wordlessly in front of Anita, who with so many years behind her was the one who laughed hardest and most enjoyed seeing her grandchildren embarrassed and excited by their attempts to scandalize her.

I also told him about the neighbors who came from the other farms to share a drink and chat about any subject, at sunset, to talk about everything, land and cattle, music, dreams, as little as possible about politics or religion, to avoid arguments, because they tended to be more conservative and we were more liberal and unbelieving than average: Don Marcelino from La Querencia, Mario and Amalia from El Soñatorio, Camila from La Botero, Mariluz and Fernando from La Inés, Jaime and Ástrid from El Balcón, José from Casablanca, the Sierras from La Arcadia, el Bocha and Martis from Punta de Anca, Ismael from Las Nubes, Miriam and Doña Elvira from La Palma, Álvaro, Diego, and Darío from Potrerito... and others.

All this I told to Jon, to explain why I didn't want us to buy a cottage in Vermont and why I missed La Oculta so much.

When he got tired of listening to me, or sick of my eternal lists of neighbors he didn't know and had no desire to get to know, he would start to stroke my back, the way you stroke a horse's back to calm him down, until he started to kiss me on the nape of my neck, saying he understood, we'll keep waiting, we won't buy any cottages in Vermont or Upstate New York, and he'd gently, slowly bite me on the back, and then lick the bites, he'd reach out for me and me for him, in this simple love men make with men, that people imagine to be so flamboyant and filthy, when it's almost always simple, and lovely, and easy. So, when we finish, happy and smiling, we both fall serenely asleep in one another's arms, like two people who simply love each other, even if their genitals are similar, and that's the only difference.

When it snows and feels like winter is going to last forever I look at the photos I have here of the farm and dream that one day I'm going to be there again, one day, with or without Jon. I don't have nostalgia for Colombia, much less for Medellín, which is a pressure cooker of fetid odors and a slaughterhouse, a swarm of displaced, destitute people, and beggars. You drive down the highway that runs alongside the river, admiring the incredible orange flowers on the *cámbulo* trees, and suddenly you start to see, on the left, an inferno of beings who look like they've walked straight out of Dante, women bathing in the putrid river water, squabbling men smoking *bazuco*, children sniffing glue, couples who shit and mate in the street, like animals, and it's all a shock, a shame for a city so vigorous, so clean, innovative, the little silver cup turned into a hotpot of venality. I don't dream of the *patria*, as patriots say, because my homeland is terrible: what fills me with lethal *saudade* is my longing for that farm. Everybody says, "but you live in New York, what more could a person want than to live in New York," and nevertheless I dream of La Oculta every week, two or three times a month at least, because I carry it with me inside even if I don't live there. I dream I'm swimming in the lake or in the river, against the current. I dream I'm riding a horse without a shirt on, that I'm climbing the mango trees and eating as many as I like, which is like biting a yellow heart, and the sweet, yellow blood runs down my chin, my throat, my chest. I dream I'm milking cows, or climbing fast up the crags, almost weightless. I even dream I'm flying through the air and see La Oculta from a hawk's-eye view. My sisters tell me they dream very similar dreams. La Oculta makes people dream. La Oculta is like a dream we live. And also, if I fantasize about how my future life will be, I always see myself walking or riding around the farm down there, far from the world, in the coffee-growing zone, as if I had no choice but to go back there to die among the stones where my parents are buried. I'm definitely going to be the last of the Ángels, at least of this branch of the family, and the last of the Ángels has to have his tomb there, at La Oculta, the land that gave us everything, that allowed my father to be a doctor and my uncles to be engineers and lawyers, to which I owe the possibility of having had a violin at an early age and later of having been able to come and live here, in New York, where sometimes I perish from the cold and from nostalgia at not being there, at La Oculta. Jon taught me what nostalgia means. *Nostos* in Greek, he told me, is "return," and *algia*, "ache," so just as myalgia is muscle ache, nostalgia is an ache to return. All my voyages, all my voyages, are voyages of return, León de Greiff, a poet of my land, once wrote.

PILAR

I can say that since that day when Alberto declared his love for me we've always been together. We've never spent even a month apart in more than half a century. And everything has brought us closer together, starting with our sorrows. The same year we started being a couple, Alberto's father died. He was a heavy smoker, unfiltered Pielrojas, and he got lung cancer, which killed him at the age of fifty-seven. Alberto was barely sixteen, and his oldest brother, Rodrigo, twenty-six. They were very rich: they inherited several factories and many properties, but at first everything was administered by a relative, Don Salomón Pérez. I remember Mamá saying, when Alberto's father died: "Poor Doña Helena, widowed with all those crazy sons. Let's pray for her, she's going to go through a lot of suffering raising so many boys on her own. Men are troublesome, out of every hundred, eighty are good for nothing."

Since we were already engaged I went to his father's funeral. I felt so sorry for Doña Helena, my future mother-in-law, dressed in black; from then on she always dressed in full mourning, until she died, when she was over eighty. Curt, distant, very pious, a daily Mass Catholic, daily rosary reciter, very charitable with the poor, but cold as ice with everyone, even with her sons and her grandchildren. I never saw her give a kiss or a hug to any of her children, or any of mine, her grandchildren. She was so cold that my children didn't call her Grandma but Doña Helena. She suffered from something she called *colerín calambroso*, which was a stomach sickness that gave her horrible cramps and sudden diarrhea that struck so quickly she could not even make it to the toilet. That's why she practically never left the house, except to go to Mass, or visit friends or relatives, and she always had a sad wince on her face, a gesture of nostalgia and desolation that seemed to make her look forever melancholy and distant. She had her good points though; every year, for example, on Alberto's and my wedding anniversary, she always sent me a card thanking me for making her son so happy. I was very fond of her.

Doña Helena had given up driving, at the insistence of her older sons, and so she went everywhere by taxi. Her sons bought her two taxis: a white one and a black one, so she'd never be without someone to take her wherever she wanted to go and bring her home again. The drivers were also black and white: a black driver drove the white taxi and a white driver drove the black taxi. The driver of the white taxi was called Cucuma, well, we called him Cucuma and he was so nice, happy all the time;

the driver of the black taxi was called Gustavo. They worked as normal taxi drivers in the off hours, but they always had to be available when Doña Helena needed them. Since she hardly ever went out, it was a good deal for the taxi drivers.

The sons, however, did not take taxis. They drove their own cars. When their father died, with a tiny portion of the inheritance, they each bought a car. Flashy, expensive cars, the likes of which weren't seen again in Medellín until the mafioso era. Rodrigo bought a Ford Mustang, the latest model, when he received his share of the inheritance; Santiago, the second son, ordered a red Porsche from Germany; Lucía, within a few years, had a Camaro convertible and was the first woman in Medellín to win a motor race. Juvenal, the youngest brother, had an enormous British Range Rover, because he liked to drive on dirt roads. Alberto, on the other hand, who had as much money as the rest of them, made do with a small, simple, modest, secondhand car: a black Volkswagen Beetle, which we called the *cucarachita*. Alberto has always been like that, humble and simple; he doesn't like drawing attention to himself. I don't know what he did with the rest of the money; either he put it in a savings account or he gave it to the priests. I think if it had been up to him, he would rather have taken the bus. His siblings went around causing a commotion in Laureles, screeching around bends, spinning, sliding, and skidding in the grit on the corners. And every year or two they'd replace their cars with newer, bigger, brighter, flashier models. They were the neighborhood rich kids. Except for Alberto, he always went along calmly, slowly, first on his pale blue Lambretta and then on the bus, or in his Volkswagen Beetle. I saw him like that, with his shy smile, so humble and so handsome, and was more in love each day.

He came to visit me every night, at the low wall out front, before he was allowed in the house. We talked about any old thing, never touching even a hair. Sometimes he'd give me quizzes or ask me riddles. When he posed tricky questions, for example: "Pilar, what's better: almost winning or almost losing?" I'd run upstairs and ask Eva, Eva what's better, what's better, and run back down, and tell him: "Silly goose, of course, almost losing, it's better to almost lose." I owe Eva a lot. Alberto once gave me a biography of Madame Curie to read, but I fell asleep every time I opened the book, so I asked Eva to read it quickly and sum it up for me. She loved it, and Madame Curie is still one of her lifelong idols, she still says she would have liked to be like her. I barely know if she was French, or Polish, I don't even remember anymore. At school Eva always had to whisper answers to me during exams. Sometimes I'd grab her exam paper when she was almost finished and hand her my empty one, so she could fill that in too. I'd rub out Eva at the top and put Pilar, leaving our surname. One time she didn't want to tell me the answers, I don't know why, and I threw a little bottle of Indian ink all over her and stained everything.

Eva never forgot the beret of her school uniform and I often did. She suffered whenever she saw me on the bus with my uniform wrinkled or without my beret. She always put her uniform under her mattress so it would get pressed overnight, without getting shiny, because the material started to shine if you ironed it too much, Mamá had warned us. After her shower she'd put on her impeccable uniform, with all the pleats perfectly marked. On the bus, she sat like a perfect little señorita, so her skirt wouldn't get wrinkled. And she'd brush her hair slowly, with setting lotion, back then, and lastly, her beret. One time when I didn't have my beret on, because I was always forgetting it, I took hers off very slowly, from behind, as we were walking into Mass, without her noticing. I put it on and went to sit in the front pew of the chapel. Eva saw me pass her, in my beret, and she was pleased to see me wearing it. Thank God, she said to herself, where did she find it? When the nun arrived at the church, she inspected us all with her eagle eye from a platform, and saw Eva without her beret and was furious. She called her to the front, with a shout: "Eva Ángel, come up here!" When she got there she asked her where her beret was and Eva touched her head. She couldn't believe she didn't have her beret on, didn't understand where it might have gone. And

I was frowning, in the front pew, with my head lowered, but killing myself laughing inside. Oh, I was so naughty, how embarrassing. Eva was the exemplary, best-dressed girl in school. The nuns even used to take her around to all the classrooms so all the girls could see how the pleats of their skirts should be, how to knot their ties, with two ribbons exactly the same length, how to wear the *piruli*, which was the cap that went with our gym uniforms, a sort of skullcap like bishops wore, but blue. She got in trouble that time, but she never told on me. She would be enraged inside, but since she's as noble as only she is, she never told anybody about the bad things I did. Sometimes, at night, she'd even laugh, a nervous laughter, a mixture of anger and compassion for the way I was, that could never bring me any good, if there was any justice in this world. Since we slept in the same bed, from the darkness, sometimes, she'd say to me, before we fell asleep:

"Pili, sometimes I think you're never going to be able to stop telling lies. It seems like you've learned to lie to get your way. That's nasty, Pilar."

I'd pretend to be asleep. I think in this world it's almost impossible to survive without lying, or without at least a little craftiness. So many truths have not brought Eva anything but problems that she could have avoided just by keeping her trap shut or by telling, for pity's sake, a tiny lie.

When Alberto held my hand for the first time I gave him a furious look (although overjoyed inside), told him to respect me, not to be so forward, did he think I was easy, or what. But I fell asleep holding that hand to my nose, what delight, smelling Pino Silvestre, and kept my hand out of the shower the next morning, to be able to smell him on my hand on the bus and tell my girlfriends that he'd held my hand, that they could sniff it if they didn't believe me. Pino Silvestre, what a lovely scent, though I think that cologne has been discontinued, Alberto's cologne of our youth.

We had a few little problems during our teenage relationship, of course. One day, Alberto went to visit Mona Díaz and I dumped him. Infidelities? I was not going to stand for that, much less with the prettiest girl in the neighborhood. Another time he fell for Olguita Pérez, a pretty girl from the coast, who was tall, tanned, and a divine dancer, she swayed like a palm tree, she always wore red and at a dance the other boys dared him, got him drunk, and pushed him over to dance with her. He was thrilled. But God punished him for me. Two or three days after dancing with Olguita Pérez he came down with hepatitis, and when I went to visit him he told me he wasn't so much in love with me anymore and maybe we should stop seeing each other. That time I almost died. When the situation eased, and his younger brother, Juvenal, started courting me, I pretended to pay attention to Jota, as I called him, though I didn't like him one bit, to see if Alberto would react. It worked, because he opened his eyes and came to the house to beg me to take him back.

One day, about a year after that fight, he went on a spiritual retreat, and I was waiting for him in a new dress when he came back. I'd been saving for a month to be able to buy it. I remember the seamstress who made it for me, where she lived, what the pattern was like, imperial style, the color. I had ordered it in red, like the one the girl from the coast who almost stole him from me had been wearing, a scandalous red. And when the midday Mass finished he said we should stop seeing each other because the priest at the retreat said he seemed very much in love and it wasn't good to be so engulfed from such a young age. That accursed priest, with his black cassock, achieved more than I could with my red dress. What he wanted was to steal him away from me and take him to the seminary. In Alberto's family, since he was so good and polite and humble, since he always went to Mass, and since he was so pious and innocent, they all thought he was going to be a priest when he grew up. I spent about two weeks on tenterhooks, thinking he was going to go into the seminary, that he was going to choose between the red and the black, but finally he came to visit me and I found the way to keep him from going to the seminary.

There, after three years of being my boyfriend, he gave me my first kiss on the lips. I almost forced him.

"I bet you wouldn't kiss me," I said, when I was about to leave for a holiday in Cartagena.

Then he said, oh yes he would, and he kissed me on the lips. I ran to the church to confess that very day because if the plane crashed I'd go straight to hell. But I was the one who proposed everything: holding hands in the cinema, kissing, and finally marriage. I forced him to propose to me. One night I said to him:

"Alberto, don't you think we should get married?"

And he said:

"Um, well, alright. When?"

"When are you free?"

He took out a calendar, a little card he had in his billfold and said:

"It could be December 21st because on the 20th I finish my exams."

I was seventeen years old and as quick as a flash, I said:

"Perfect! Wait a tiny moment."

I ran upstairs to where my parents were and said: "Papi, Papi, Alberto proposed. I have to drop out of school to prepare my trousseau." Papá and Mamá stared at me, half terrified, wide-eyed, but they said okay. And I ran back downstairs as fast as I could, so he wouldn't change his mind on me, and I said:

"Okay, Papá and Mamá say I can get married. December 21st it is, then. But first we have to have our engagement party."

The next day I went to see Sister Fernanda, the mother superior of the school, who was very sweet, and I told her:

"Sister Fernanda, I'm going to leave school, I'm not going to finish my diploma."

"But why? You only need seven more months to get your qualifications."

"Oh, Sister, I'm going to be married."

Her eyes welled up with tears of happiness. I think she'd always wanted to get married. And she said:

"That will be your life's happiness. Don't worry, off you go, in these last few months you're not going to learn anything, especially if you're thinking about getting married all the time. Have children, many children."

I remember that Sister Fernanda, who was such a dear, had Parkinson's, her hands shook when she read pious books to us in religion class. The ideal thing for a woman, according to what they taught us at school, was to marry a good man, and Alberto was the best husband I could get. He was pious, he was handsome, he was good-looking, and he was the best catch in

Laureles. I dropped out to prepare my trousseau, our engagement, wedding, honeymoon, and all that.

In June of that year they fired Papá from the hospital, saying he was a radical and a supporter of unions and Communists. He wasn't exactly a Communist, but he didn't disagree so much with Fidel Castro or union leaders, and he said that some of the things the guerrillas were asking for, such as agrarian reform and redistribution of the land to the campesinos, were not so unreasonable. Don't ask me, I don't know anything, but that made people angry at the university, where they were very conservative, ultra-right, and it enraged them even more because they knew my grandfather Josué, Cobo's father, was a cattle rancher, and the owner of La Oculta, which back then was still a big hacienda, with land enough to fatten up three-hundred calves and produce I don't know how many shipments of coffee a year. They said Papá grew up in a glass house and shouldn't be throwing stones. One day I came home and found all the books from his office in the garage, lying there, piled up in boxes. Papá's face looked dreadful. I thought it was going to spoil my wedding. I didn't worry about Papá getting fired, I just thought: *Now how is he going to pay for my party?* But Mamá told me not to worry, that we'd have the party no matter what, that she'd been putting away some savings at the bakery to pay for the wedding. Besides, she was planning to travel to Cartagena, and up to Maicao, in La Guajira, to buy contraband whiskey and champagne from the so-called Turkish stores, where everything was much cheaper. Maybe the only thing we wouldn't be able to afford was the orchestra for the reception, which was supposed to be Los Melódicos, who were going to play for us so we could dance into the wee hours. In the church, during the ceremony, Toño was going to play violin pieces at the most important parts, when we received the blessing, after the elevation, while the guests took communion, and so forth. He was adorable, Toñito, in a black tuxedo and white bow tie, for the first time in his life, in his first concert as a soloist, so enchanting. His angelic music brought us good luck.

Since we married we've never been apart, and we've been rich and poor, happy and miserable, almost always normal, but we've always been together. I don't forget what I said in the church, when we got married, because even though everyone says it, I did say it from the bottom of my heart, not just to say it but to fulfill it, and I'd repeat it today: "I, Pilar, take you, Alberto, as my lawfully wedded husband, to have and to hold from this day forward. I promise to be true to you in good times and in bad, in sickness and in health. I will love and honor you all the days of my life." I said these words through tears, I cried for the whole time in the church, from sadness at leaving Mamá and Papá, and my little sister and brother. In sickness and in health I have always loved him just as much.

We were both virgins when we got married, of course, with no idea about anything. Nobody talked about things like that at home, or only Papá, and only very indirectly. Eva wasn't a virgin when she got married, and neither was Toño, when he did, because he used to go to bed with women too, at the beginning, when he wasn't sure or he wanted to conceal the fact that he was on the other side. He had two girlfriends, I remember perfectly well, Rosa and Patricia, but later he only went out with boys who you could tell from a mile away what they were. Mamá suffered a great deal over that, at first, though she ended up accepting it. Papá suffered even more, even if he tried never to speak of it, but you could tell, it would slip out, because sometimes at lunch he'd be praising Fidel Castro, because in Cuba homosexuality was forbidden and fags got sent to re-education camps, to cure them, and if it didn't he'd have them shot. And once he even said, speaking harshly, rapping his knuckles on the table, that they should do that everywhere because men were becoming effeminate, and how would there be people in this world, when it was impossible to have children that way, and surnames would disappear, like the surname Ángel, the surname of those who had arrived in Jericó from El Retiro and founded La Oculta, a surname that in our branch of the family depended entirely on Antonio, and he said his full name, Antonio Ángel, and looked him in the eye. Sometimes I think Toño spends so much time finding out about our ancestors as compensation: since he won't leave any Ángels for the future, he'll know everything about all the Ángels of the past.

Finally Toño ended up getting married, to the man he says he likes best of all, Jon, a gringo, and not so long ago, he married almost in old age, in New York, after Papá had died, even though he didn't invite us to the wedding, not even Mamá, or either of us, and Jon's family wasn't at the ceremony either, because he comes from a very religious, very traditional, black family, members of an evangelical church, even more horrified about those things than Antioqueños, and that's saying something. I think Alberto and I are like a hinge between two worlds. Sometimes I think I'm the last one in my family to live the way Grandma Miriam lived, Eva the first to live the way my daughters live, and Toño the first to live as my grandchildren will, because don't try telling me it's not true, there are more gay men every day all over, all the girls complain, when they like a boy, for his kindness, his gentlemanly behavior, because he makes them laugh, and he's sweet, no way, it'll turn out he's gay and that's the end of that.

Which life is better: the old-fashioned way I live or the modern ways of my sister and brother? I don't say my way, or like my parents or grandparents; I don't say my siblings' way; it's better not to judge. Who knows. I'm old now and that's how I lived; they're a bit younger, but not that much, and they lived the way they did too. Who lived better? That nobody knows, everybody does what they can and what feels right. We never know anything. One chooses a route, thinking it's the best, calculating the steps that are going to lead you to a happy life, but no calculation works. We pursue an aim, and we might even achieve it, but once we get there, no one can be sure it was the best possible one. Mamá, who was more modern than I am, and at almost ninety was just as lively and vivacious as ever, said everything's good, that whatever happens is fine. I should have learned from her, and tried to be as open and liberal as she was, always adapting. Sometimes I try and sometimes I forget. That's the way I am, "fancying myself bourgeois," as Toño puts it, and even though I don't know what he means by that, I say, yes, I like the good life, elegant things in their places, and little things make me happy, the garden, flowers, Alberto's company, Colombian music, a well-laid table. I might be very normal, but that's how I am, straightforward and authentic like this farm where I live. But, is this the best I could have done with my life? Eva, I'm sure, thinks no, she thinks she can still get something much better out of her life than this. Sometimes I think it's unfair not to let her search further, not to let her go entirely, cut the string of the kite, give her the money she has buried in this farm so she can fly off to wherever she wants.

EVA

I continued up the road at a trot. I know this region really well: the trails, the trees, the water courses, the woods. I have it memorized like a local campesino, better even than Pilar. It's true that she has spent much more time than any of us at La Oculta, but she hasn't got as much wanderlust as I do. Pilar is a homebody, sedentary, in the image I have of her in my head she's always sewing, sitting in a room or on the porch, just like Mamá, our aunts, and our grandmothers. Sewing and talking, talking and sewing. Telling over and over again the story of her courtship and marriage with Alberto, which we all know by heart. When she gets up, she walks around the house and plans improvements in the garden, which she's always expanding. Then she goes inside and moves from one room to the next in a frenzy of work. She sees spiderwebs, dirt, damp spots where no one else notices them; whenever she sees a termite hole she has an attack, and shouts and gets agitated like a hen. Her life has been spent in a war to the death against termites. She climbs up extremely high ladders, balancing with a syringe in one hand,

and squirts formaldehyde into the holes. I think it's the same formaldehyde and the same syringe she uses to do up corpses. She also battles against blemishes, damp stains, and fungus on the walls. She's always calling poor Próspero to mix up some whitewash, and get out the swab to patch the lime. Every week some part of the house had to be whitewashed, no matter what. And if she doesn't notice anything wrong with the house, then she gets the notion to cut down some trees or plant some palms, buy or order some custom-made furniture, collect the fallen teak leaves and burn them, change the color of the flowers because she's sick of orange, move fences and improve the garden, or make stone pathways. And then she hires day laborers from town and we have to pay their wages between the three of us. But she's always right there, in the house or right around the house. I, on the other hand, have traveled around the area in every way possible: walking, jogging, in a jeep, on a bicycle, and on horseback. As if I were a man, yes, sometimes I feel like it has fallen to me to take on the role of the man of this house, the one who makes money and organizes the bills, who controls and covers the territory.

I dug my heels into the mare's side and began to gallop along the track. The animal's warm body warmed me up too. I'd learned to ride as a very young girl, at the same time as I learned to walk, and felt myself and the horse to be a single body. "We have to form a centaur when we ride!" Cobo used to say, just as Grandpa Josué used to tell him, and anyone who hasn't felt like a centaur, doesn't know how to ride a horse. When one feels that, the body experiences a kind of serenity that's very difficult to describe. Noche felt a sure hand guiding her, and I knew that the mare saw much better than I did in the darkness. I could trust her eyes much more than mine. I'd ridden endless times, day and night, and I always felt sure of the animal. "To ride well," Cobo also used to say, "the intelligent one needs to trust the brute." Sometimes the horseshoes struck sparks on the stones, and those sparks spoke to me about the animal's strength, her potency, which I could feel between my legs.

I began to speak to the mare, in a soft voice, I don't know whether to calm her down or to calm me. To feel less alone:

"Noche, Noche, don't worry, we're going up and quickly, you see, there are men chasing me and we have to escape, you have to help me, Noche, if not they'll kill you too. Let's go up fast. I have to hide in the woods, be careful, don't let me fall off, if you see a wire fence you'll have to stop, but slowly, without throwing me, Noche, Noche."

I don't know why, but I always speak familiarly with horses, as with friends. And my first horse was called Amigo.

I was carrying the flashlight in my left hand, but I didn't want to turn it on and risk giving any clues in case anyone was watching. I had all my senses sharpened. It might have occurred to them to drive up and look for me there, but I didn't hear anything. Every once in a while the hooting of an owl or a *currucutú*. The buzzing of the occasional lost insect, one or two fireflies, the light cool breeze that came down off the Jericó crags. All of a sudden, from the direction of La Oculta, a strange noise started up: they'd turned on a motor, like a chainsaw. Yes, they'd started up a chainsaw and they were cutting something. A moment later, as quickly as it had begun, it stopped. I didn't understand what it could have been and didn't even want to imagine the worst.

I kept going up the road, toward the crags. I had to look for the little gateway that led to the water tank; I'd go in there and up across the pasture, looking for the edge of the woods. At the base of the crags I could wait until the sun came up. As far as I knew, groups like Los Músicos of Jericó didn't do much work in daylight. They preferred to do their misdeeds in the shadows so nobody would see. Night is day for the wicked, Papá used to say.

When I figured we must be getting close to the gate, I turned on the flashlight for a second and saw, between the lines of barbed wire and the *matarratón* trees of the hedge, the gate to the tank. I dismounted to open it. I pulled the mare through by her halter, closed the latch, and swung back up into the saddle, with the flashlight turned off. I went around the side of the

Casablanca water tank and carried on uphill along the little dirt track through the pasture. We went at a gallop. I knew there were two more gates to pass through before the native forest would begin to close in, first undergrowth and ferns, shrubs, the odd coffee plant, and then the first tree trunks. Nobody knew this terrain better than me, nobody. Los Músicos definitely didn't. Maybe Próspero or Egidio, the foreman of La Inés, both born and raised in Palermo, but not Los Músicos.

I could hear frogs croaking, the beating wings of nocturnal birds, and sometimes the lowing of a distant cow. I was breathing easier, squeezing my thighs against the warm mare. I was scared to run into a wire fence without seeing it and I slowed the mare to a walk. The moon wasn't up, there weren't many stars, just a few offerings of light from faraway houses. Once again I thought that maybe, tonight at least, I might not be murdered. It would be difficult for them to find me there. I opened another two gates when the mare stopped; the animal saw obstacles I couldn't see in the darkness. I got down, turned on the flashlight for a moment, shielding most of the beam with my hands, opened the latch, guided the mare through, and closed it again. I got back up on the horse and set off uphill at a trot. When I reached the edge of the woods I looked in the saddlebags. There was a canteen, but it was empty. There was a small poncho. I put it on, to shield myself from a bit of the dampness of the forest. I thought that even though the poncho was white, in the dense woods, no one would see me. I figured it must be about one in the morning, more or less, and I thought to keep warm I'd spend the night on horseback, quiet and still. The warmth of the gentle and noble animal made me feel better.

I was thirsty, but I didn't want to think about that. I discarded the idea of tying up the mare to go in search of water from some stream coming down from the mountain. It was the animal's company that made me feel safe. On horseback, besides, I could gallop away and escape, if anyone did come near. There were still at least four hours until it would begin to grow light. I closed my eyes and tried to absorb through my ears and nose all the sounds and smells of the night. My mouth was dry. I started remembering Pilar's stories, I don't know why, probably to calm myself down and not sleep, the stories she always tells when we're at La Oculta, and that make us all laugh and cry. The evil tricks she played on me at school, when I was so levelheaded and she was such a lazybones. The story of the little turtle on the airplane, one time when she was going to Cartagena, or the one about the United States visas that she managed to get for all the players on the basketball team despite hell and high water, or the story of Don Marcelino, when he died and she had to transport him, disguised and seated in the car, in make-up and a hat, so the army and police wouldn't realize she was transporting a dead body.

I was trying to remember what happened with the turtle in the airplane aisle when I heard something, opened my eyes, and saw a huge brightness down below. Flames rising up to the sky, from La Oculta. There was a wind and it was carrying ashes and sparks. In my nostrils the smell of smoke became more precise, for me it was the smell of death, of defeat. They were burning down the house. Then came the sound of an explosion and an even brighter flash, like a mushroom of fire; I didn't know what it was. Later I was told that it was the gas tank of my jeep, when it exploded, for they'd begun by setting fire to my jeep. I started to cry hard, sobbing convulsively. I pleaded for them at least not to have burnt Próspero and Berta inside the house.

At that moment I began to hear the sound of engines coming up the Casablanca track. There were two pairs of intense, slow lights exploring the night, coming uphill. They were heading for my cousins' house. They didn't turn off the lights or the engines. A light came on in Sor and Rubiel's house, in the distance. I thought I heard a voice, a shout of rage, but very far off, incomprehensible. I was pleading inside, to no one, to fate, not to hear any shots. A short while later the lights began to move up the same path I'd come up a while before on the mare.

I was watching the fire further below and the beams of light alternately. My heart began to pump as fast as it could again. I had to convince myself that nobody knew where I was, not even Rubiel, that nobody could see me, among all the trees. I stroked Noche, so she wouldn't decide to neigh. But even if she did, why would it occur to anybody to think an unseen horse has a rider, or that I was riding her? Horses neigh, that's all there is to it. I took off the poncho and stuffed it back into the saddlebag, to feel safer without anything very bright on. Two big pickup trucks drove very slowly behind the water tank, but they kept going up the road. They were looking for me along the track. After ten minutes the lights disappeared over the hill, heading down toward La Mariela. I began to breathe more calmly; my heart settled down. At least tonight they weren't going to find and kill me.

ANTONIO

Sometimes, at night, I delve into my papers. In New York I also keep copies of the documents I have in the drawers in La Oculta and I try to reconstruct its history, what I know and what I imagine happened there, in the southwest of Antioquia, what I would call my fatherland if the word fatherland hadn't been so sullied by the malodorous mouths of all the nationalist politicians in the world. No, I'm not a regionalist or anything like that, but if I think about it, I say unabashedly that of all the towns in Southwest Antioquia, Jericó is the prettiest. I'm reconstructing the origins of La Oculta, and writing, not as a serious and trustworthy historian, which I'm not, but as an aficionado of various kinds of reading and an enthusiast of what wiser and more educated people have told me.

I know that Pedro Pablo Echeverri was sitting in El Silencio Café in El Retiro, slowly savoring a black coffee sweetened with grated panela. It would be about nine or ten in the morning and a warm sun was brightening up the fresh mountain air. The place honored its name; only the deliberate voices of the engineer and a few neighbors could be heard. Four or five young men (I can see them in my mind: barefoot, badly dressed), between twenty and thirty years of age, would be listening to him carefully, with an almost reverent attention.

El Cojo will have told them that Don Gabriel, his father, and a friend of his, Santiago Santamaría, son of Don Juan Santamaría, had founded a town on the left bank of the River Cauca, facing west, and that the town had already had two names, first the Aldea de Piedras and now Felicina, since it had been authorized to have its own priest. Piedras, he said, not because the land was so stony (it was black and fertile, actually, enriched with ashes from the Nevado del Ruiz volcano, carried by the winds from age-old eruptions), although there were large black rocks scattered among the mountains, but rather for a fast-flowing river, the Piedras, which descended there, between huge rocks, fed by many torrential streams, from the high plains down to the rich lowlands of the Cauca.

Now the proprietors wanted these lands to produce food for the settlers, and eventually, if there was more than enough and good roads were built, they could begin to sell the surplus products. The mining villages, farther south, toward the Cauca Valley, were extracting a lot of gold, but didn't produce any food, no meat or milk or cassava or beans or plantains or potatoes or agave, and all those things could be produced on their lands and that of their relatives, if they chopped down the woods and worked it well. But a good route had to be cleared, or improved where it existed, as far as Marmato, so the mule drivers could go and take swine and steers and provisions to the British and German entrepreneurs, who didn't have enough food to feed their Indian, Negro, and mixed-race, half-enslaved miners, who were starving to death on them, dying of hunger and the horrendous conditions in the pits.

The condition for populating and developing those expanses in the Southwest was to found a town and fill it up with young families who wanted to have lots of children. They'd been gathering people in Marinilla, in Rionegro, in Fredonia, Titiribí, Medellín, and La Ceja. In Sonsón and Abejorral it was futile, for the people there were heading farther south, to Aguadas, Salamina, and Manizales, to invade the former estates of the Villegas and the Aranzazus. El Retiro was going to be the last stop before returning to Felicina, with those who dared to follow him. Anyone who knew a trade would be useful, blacksmith, baker, leatherworker, lumberman, but even those who had no trade would be welcome; all they needed were a couple of strong arms and a desire not to sit vegetating in a corner. They were looking for second sons with neither land nor position, they were looking for fertile couples, at best with children already, bold, but not wicked, adventurers.

"First thing tomorrow morning I'm taking the Minas road as far as Fredonia," said Echeverri in a deliberate, sure voice. "There we'll spend less than a week getting everything ready and interviewing new *settlers. In two or three days we'll reach the Cauca, which we'll cross at the Paso de los Pobres, on a raft, poled across by two expert ferrymen, and once across we'll already be on the lands that for now belong to my father and Don Santiago Santamaría. There is more than enough for all. I assure you that within the year we'll be parceling out the plots, not as gifts, but cheap and on credit. We are going to be fair and generous, especially with the first to sign up and those who work hardest clearing the land and building roads. Settlers who arrive later, attracted by the good news, will not find the land so cheap, as it will be sold to them at a higher price, after other veteran settlers, like yourselves, have received their plots."*

"Can we bring laborers?" asked one of the young men, a well-dressed, fine-looking boy called Peláez with such bushy eyebrows they looked like locks of hair on his head.

"You can invite anyone you want, black, white, mulatto, or mestizo. What will be most useful is to bring women and children, because they get frightened off out there; there's not a soul for miles. The few Indians there were, Chamíes, Katíos, and Caramantas, fled down toward Chocó when they saw us arrive fifteen years ago, thinking we were going to kill them, as whites always had, since the time of the conquistadors. Only a few women stayed behind, who are all now married to the single settlers we took with us. A few blacks liberated by

Governor Faciolince are now working there, and we gave them their little square of land too, just as we did the poor whites. There's nothing but dense woods, but with good lumber, clean and abundant water. We will also entrust laborers with their own pieces of land, if they work hard. It's not going to be a place of masters and peons, but of proprietors. You can bring laborers, but not for them to work while you, as young masters, watch them work and yell orders, none of that. Even the peons are going to be proprietors."

"Ah," Peláez kept on. "So you're one of those modern fellows who believes we are all equal, whites and blacks, rich and poor, intelligent and ignorant?"

"No, I don't believe that," Echeverri responded so calmly that he spoke and smiled at the same time. "What I do believe is that when you begin something you have to give everyone the same things, as when you begin to play *tute* or dominoes. At the start everyone gets the same counters, or the same number of cards, don't you think?"

"That's true," Paláez admitted.

"Well, we're going to do the same thing in Felicina, which is why it's called that, like felicity: everyone will start with the same amount. Later luck, talent, or effort will be the deciding factors. As well as abuses by villains, and the stupidity of fools. These things aren't as static as rocks, but flow like rivers."

"So in the future there will be bosses and workhands, masters and servants…"

"It's possible, some years down the line. Furthermore, I don't deny that my father has laborers, and he pays them by the day. But he knows that with day laborers and wage earners he'd need a century to develop his lands. That's why for now he prefers free men, married settlers, who will begin with the same, or almost the same. Inequalities will arise from the efforts or cunning of some, even from wickedness; from the vices or laziness or simple bad luck of others. Or from inheritance, which is my case, but anyone who has children wishes to leave them what they received or earned – whether through malice or merit or luck – don't they? There are those who are poor because they fell off a horse and were left disabled, and there are those who are rich because a mule knocked them down and on the ground they discovered a seam of gold. Because actually there are not only injustices committed by men; there are also injustices of destiny, as a poet once said. Who knows? Maybe the inequalities will grow and then perhaps, if they get very large, in a century or more, we'll have to shuffle the deck and redeal. But for now everyone is going to start, if not with exactly the same, then with something that is very similar: land."

"And how can we be sure that you're going to entrust us with land, that you're not going to deceive us?" asked someone else.

"For that there is no more security than my word. I do not tell lies. You'll have to believe me, and come along. Or not believe me, and stay here, idle and fateless, warming yourselves lazily in the sun," said El Cojo Echeverri categorically.

Isaías Ángel and Raquel Abadi were the last to sign up on Cojo's list. According to custom, one of his brothers, the eldest, Esteban, had inherited their father's salt mines, and had also received the big house and all the land. Isaías, in El Retiro, would have had no future except that of being a farmhand on someone else's land, a salt miner, or an artisan. Their father Ismael had died before being able to send him to study in Medellín, as he'd promised, because he was the brightest of his sons. He had learned to read, to write, and to keep accounts, but no more. Of their Jewish past, he remembered very little; words whispered on some sincere Sabbath, said in secret by their father, who spoke of the arrival of Abraham in Santa Fe de Antioquia, from Spain. Now he preferred not to be anything, in public and in private, although if asked he would say he was Catholic, and even went to Mass every Sunday, crossed himself, prayed to God – to a god who might or might not exist, he didn't know – so as not to have problems with anyone, and not to have to answer too many questions, from himself or others.

The other young men who were in the café – less needy and yet to start families – asked for time to think about it and left. Isaías remained in the Silencio Café on his own with El Cojo Echeverri, who, after a sip of his coffee, said sadly:

"That's how it is everywhere. Many come to look, and feel curious, ask skeptical questions, but very few sign on. Maybe they don't believe me, or think that all gifts contain deception. In any case, we now have more than ninety families who have agreed to go and we've arranged to meet in Fredonia two days hence. That's why we have to hurry and leave tomorrow. You're going to have to organize everything in the blink of an eye. You'll barely have time to say farewell to your family."

"Then I better go and talk it over with Raquel. She's pregnant, four months along, but it doesn't matter, it's better that she come with me straight away. She's always telling me about her thirst for adventure, her desire for a new life, and I don't think she'll object, quite the contrary, I think she'll be happy that we're going. The only sad thing is leaving behind the family, but she has a sister who might want to come with us; I'll invite her as well. Almost everything I own will fit on three mules. And I'll have Esteban, my older brother, sell the rest, which is hardly anything: a potato crop I have planted in one of his fields, that's half grown. Raquel has a few gold coins, and I know she'll want to use them to buy land, if it's good and cheap. What time are we leaving?"

"We'll meet right here, tomorrow morning at six," said El Cojo. "You have what's left of the day to get everything ready. There are seven other families staying in various houses in town. We're going to leave in a caravan very early. In Fredonia we'll have a few days to wait, maybe weeks, for more people to join, but the sooner we leave the better."

He paused, looked at Isaías with his lazy eye and abruptly changed the subject:

"Don't worry, my associates the Santamarías are or were like you, the Ángels and the Abadi, and nobody's going to say anything if you light a candle on Friday evenings. As long as you eat pork, though it's not allowed, nobody will say a word. What you can't do is get fussy and not eat ham or chicharrón. You know what my father and Don Santiago say? I don't know if it's true, but they say it's easier for you people to be settlers, because you're the ones who most like to move and live somewhere else, because you've been wandering for millennia, as they were condemned to do in the Book of Psalms. There's no one who has a more fervent desire to have his own land, from which you cannot be expelled, and for that very reason you'll work harder than anybody."

Isaías, without a word, remembered a curious recommendation from his father: "Son, remember that we don't like pork, but we have to eat swine so they won't criticize us. Besides, in these crags there's no way that sheep will thrive and it's been a long, long time since we've forgotten the taste of God's lamb, who takes away the world's sins. In the Biblical lands and those of the Koran, pork was harmful, but here in these mountains things are very different, and this is our land now." He looked at Pedro Pablo's lazy eye; an optical illusion made it look like it itched, that from here on in he'd be winking at him eternally; Isaías sketched an understanding smile. They shook hands and that was that.

EVA

O ne morning, while I was swimming in La Oculta, one of
the lake's drowned victims told me this story. He had a
deep, dark voice, but clear and sharp as if he were speaking a
hand's span away from my ear:

"In Jericó, people's houses were always open, as if someone
might just revive and return to the world, or as if a guest from
far away might be able to enter without knocking and without
anyone hearing his footsteps, exactly at lunchtime. They always
set an extra place at the table, with a clean plate and cutlery and
a serviette, with a glass ready to be filled, in case the prodigal
son suddenly showed up, because in every Jericó family there
was always a prodigal son, from whom they'd had no word since
the last war, or since the absurd argument with his father, or
grandfather, which had ended in thoughtless words, curses no
one would take back, and the women, especially the women,
held on to the secret hope of seeing him appear one day, tall
and strapping like a broncobuster, with his smile intact and his

resonant singing voice, with his loud bursts of laughter and the simple confidence that nothing bad could happen to them.

If someone made the mistake of mentioning the absent one while they were having their soup, nobody raised their eyes from the bowl, to make sure not to meet the gaze of the man at the head of the table, because they didn't want to make him feel ashamed of his flaring nostrils, his trembling lip, and flooded eyes. Furtively, in the end, the man wipes not his lips but his eyelids with his serviette, and at that moment one of the women stands up, collects the soup bowls and goes to the kitchen for the first trays of the main course. Sometimes, by mistake, they'd pour a little *guanábana* juice in the absent one's empty glass, and at the end of the meal nobody drank it.

This had occurred so many times, with the sons of the Ángels, the Londoños, the Santamarías, the Abads. It was a constant in the town that some son would get offended and take off, or there would be no trace of one after a battle, or one would emigrate north, or east, in search of fortune, never to return and change his parents' lives into one of perpetual waiting, and that strange sensation of never having a full table."

ANTONIO

Perhaps I also love and miss that farm so much because there, at La Oculta, was the first time. I'll never forget. A friend from our neighborhood, Sergio Ialadaki, had come with me to the farm, and we asked my parents if we could pitch a tent and camp out on the other side of the house, by the lake, near everything but at the same time out of the adults' sight, like an adventure for adolescents who are starting to grow up. They said we could. We were fifteen and didn't want to sleep inside the house, it's true, and I don't think we really even knew why. What I mean is that it wasn't something planned, but something felt, intuited rather than thought out, like a vague premonition of new, as yet unknown emotions. We said we wanted to make a campfire in the open air, with kindling we collected in the woods, like people used to do, to be out in the elements for a while, like explorers, and when we got tired we wanted to lie down in the tent, on top of air mattresses. What we didn't say, but what we did, was to put the air mattresses very close together and cover them both with the same blanket. That day we'd swum in the lake with my papá following us in the canoe, because he didn't like us swimming alone without lifejackets. Not long before, a young seminary student had drowned in the lake, and in the air and water lingered a memory of death, the remains of a tragedy, as if something of the spirit of the boy who would never now be a priest had stayed in the place forever. After swimming we'd gone to climb the waterfall in our bathing suits and stretched out in the sun, very close to each other, on a big, flat rock. I was feeling the pleasure of the hallucinogenic drug that is the midday sun on your bare skin, in that full, warm, tropical light at La Oculta. Just brushing against his skin was enough for me to get as hard as a rock; he looked at my shorts and I looked at his, and we saw the material raised, tense: his and mine. When we stretched out on the rock, on a couple of towels, in the full sun, I took some suntan lotion out of my backpack and started to rub some over my chest and shoulders; I was rubbing it in myself, but I pretended that my hand was actually Sergio's hand and that he was caressing me. I rubbed it in slowly, very slowly, and as I did so I looked at him, to see if he understood that the movements of my hand over my body were actually his covert caresses. Then he put some lotion on as well and stared at me as he rubbed it in, slowly as I had done, slowly caressing his nipples, his arms, his firm, flat stomach. I would have given anything to be his hand at that moment, but I was afraid he didn't want that. He didn't really know what he wanted; only I knew what I did.

The night is a better adviser for such things, which are harder to do, at least for the first time, in broad daylight. We were going to cook on the campfire. Mamá had given us rice, eggs, sausages, and a little chicken broth left over from lunch; we heated it all up in an old, blackened pot, hanging from a branch propped up on two forked sticks right over the flames. Sergio had brought a guitar and sang some Beatles, Elton John, Joan Serrat, and James Taylor songs. He also sang a song by Georges Moustaki, who was part Greek, like him. His soft voice thrilled me and I sang along occasionally on the choruses. I hadn't brought my violin, because, sadly for me, violins aren't suited for those kinds of outings, and you have to take special care of them, because they're expensive and easily damaged by humidity. We'd snuck the remains of a bottle of rum, and we had two or three shots, mixed with orange juice. They tasted strong. We were shivering, not from the cold, I don't think, but from the desire built up over the course of the day. Finally we climbed into the tent and shone the flashlight around. We pushed the two air mattresses together, but we got undressed with our backs to each other, without looking, and then turned off the flashlight. We were breathing for a while in the silence. I heard his breathing;

I suppose he heard mine too. We were less than a millimeter apart, but not daring to touch. All of a sudden Sergio said his skin was stinging a bit because he'd had too much sun and I asked him if he wanted me to put some moisturizer on. He thought that was a good idea. I began to caress his chest, his abdomen, there I skipped over to his thighs, very slowly, face up first, and then face down. I passed him the tube of lotion and he began to massage me as well. We were in total darkness, and could only hear a few crickets, the frogs croaking, the sound of the channel of water that fed the lake, and his hand rubbing my skin. I was straining straight up in the middle of my body, but I didn't know if he was feeling the same thing. I offered to put some more lotion on him and my hand went down to his belly button and then further down, to the edge of his underwear. As if by mistake, two of my fingers passed under the elastic border, beyond it until touching his pubic hair, and then four fingers, all except the thumb, with the pretext of rubbing in lotion so he wouldn't feel the sting of the afternoon's sunburn. I went a little lower down, and there it was, rising up, as hard as a rock, stiff and ready; I barely touched it, one finger just lightly brushed against it. It lifted a little more at my touch and a tiny moan escaped his throat. I felt the happiness of knowing he felt the same as I did. I passed him the lotion again and this time it was he who went below my belly button, he who slipped past the barrier of the elastic waistband of my shorts, he who reached the place where the proof of my feeling the same as him stood. Our faces leaned in toward each other, without kissing, just breathing each other's breath. And then he began to caress me up and down, and I stretched out my hand and reached inside his shorts and began to do the same. We moved our pelvises in unison and hurled our breath in each other's faces. The tension was so high that in less than two minutes we'd both come, in perfect silence, but with a tremendous whole-body shudder, and brief final moan of happiness. I'd felt an electric current surge through all the bones of my skeleton. I think Sergio did too. I held his semen to my nose and it smelled delicious, like mild soap. I didn't taste it, but I smeared it on my chest. It was the first time I made love with anyone, the first time I came in someone else's hand, the first time I touched the viscosity of semen not my own. Afterward we slept, deeply, side by side, without touching each other again.

The next day the ritual was the same. Walk in his footsteps, stretch my shadow over his shadow, breathe in his breath, look at him without missing a single detail of his body: that was my only occupation all day. We went swimming in the lake (under my father's watchful eye, who paddled behind us in the canoe), with the memory of the drowned seminarian, who shouted to us: live, live before you die, youngsters, don't waste the most beautiful years of your lives, and then we went to climb up the waterfall and lie in the sun on top of another big rock, and lying face down we held hands. We took deep breaths. We looked at the bulge in the front of each other's shorts when we turned around. We had to wait until nighttime. And that night, I think, was one of the best nights of my life, at least the night I had the most orgasms. I came five times, touching him, feeling him touch me, breathing his breath again without kissing. He couldn't do it anymore after the third time, but for me it was like nothing was enough, it was a crazy thing, an insatiable desire. A desire like none I've ever felt since, something deep, uncontainable, which I don't imagine would ever have stopped resurging had dawn not eventually arrived. The last time I came no semen came out, not a drop, because there was none left.

When we got back to Medellín, Sergio didn't speak to me again or look me in the face, for months. He avoided me around the neighborhood. He'd turned even more melancholic than before and the dark circles under his eyes, his most attractive feature, grew purple. I think he took refuge in religion and in self-flagellation, trying to bend his inclinations to the traditional side, even if it meant betraying himself. I also felt somewhat ashamed of what had happened, and also went to see the priests, but if he'd given a sign I would have slept with him again in a second, even if it meant I had to confess afterward. I'd secretly kept a pair of his underpants, I remember, they were blue and white checked, and I sniffed them and touched myself. I couldn't get to sleep if I didn't come thinking about those two nights at La Oculta, in the same tent and under the same blanket. It's the only time in my life I've had a fetish. The second night I had turned on the flashlight and shone it on his body while he came: those white spurts shooting up to his chest, toward my face, were the memory that most excited me.

Several months later, one Sunday afternoon, Sergio called me, out of the blue, and invited me to go see a movie. I couldn't contain my excitement. We met at the entrance to the cinema downtown, but he was with two girls, one of whom he introduced as his girlfriend and the other he wanted me to meet to see if I liked her. I felt an unspeakable disappointment. During the movie I felt dizzy. Sergio held hands with his girlfriend and her friend tried to hold my hand, but I didn't want to. When the movie ended, which I didn't pay any attention to or remember a thing about, I left almost without saying goodbye and caught the bus to go back to Laureles alone, while they went for ice cream. I was so sad, so humiliated and disappointed by Sergio's wordless message that I felt faint. Two ladies who were near me on the bus said: "Look how young that boy is and already drunk. What is the world coming to?"

A couple of years went by before I slept with a man again; later I even did it with women, making a determined effort, almost with repugnance, trying to prove to myself that I wasn't a fag, that I was going to be normal like everyone else, or like the majority, at least, or like Sergio, who was disciplined and controlled his impulses, it was during this period that I started going to the Saint Gemma retreats for young people, and since I'd confessed my sin with Sergio, and my thousand solitary sins, the priest insisted that I at least try to approach girls instead of men. But it wasn't the same as that night with Sergio, never that complete, though insatiable, pleasure. In reality, I don't think it's ever been the same as that night at fifteen or sixteen years old, at La Oculta, not even with Jon. That was the first time and the definitive, revealing the path my desire would always take, marking out my sexual destiny. My compass.

Many years later I ran into Sergio Ialadaki in the Chicago airport. We shook hands; he was fat and ugly, with spongy bags under his eyes instead of dark circles, and a potbelly that made him look six months pregnant. He told me he had three daughters, that he'd married a Greek woman. He asked me if I had kids too. I told him no, I was gay, but I hadn't ruled out the idea of adopting a child. He looked me in the eye very seriously, in perfect silence, and I couldn't tell if there was a memory in that look, or rather a signal that he didn't want to remember anything, or even that he really didn't remember anything. One can never read other people's minds. What I do know is that if I concentrate my mind and remember that night in the tent, if I think of my flashlight beam shining on the young Sergio as he was coming in gushes, still today, more than thirty years later, I get hard again.

EVA

I saw again, from the direction of La Oculta, the blaze of the fire, the bursts of flames swaying in the air, orange and red, and thought I saw sparks and ashes carried by the wind. I could still smell distant smoke. I closed my eyes and waited. I imagined the house burned down, Próspero locked inside, the charred posts, the heat, the scorched hammock, the books reduced to ash, Gaspar burnt to a cinder. I thought of the years of effort vanished in half an hour of hatred. Years, more than a century spent building that house. The bed under the mosquito net where I'd made love when I got married for the first time. The dining table, made from a single trunk of a *parasiempre*, a tree from the Chocó Valley we believed to be indestructible, immune to the passing of centuries. The teak stools Pilar had ordered from the Palermo carpentry workshop, according to a design Toño had brought back from New York, clipped from a magazine. Our grandparents' wardrobes and dressers, dark and heavy. The old beds made of *comino crespo* wood, the ancient family photos on the walls, the bad but pretty paintings of flowers and landscapes and horses. In short, all that we, Papá and Mamá, our grandparents, great-grandparents, Pilar, especially Pilar, had done, had acquired, had bought, changed, inherited, received as gifts. The architects who had planned the H shape of the house's structure, the master builders and bricklayers who had erected the walls and laid the foundations according to the instructions, the laborers who had tiled the roofs. The hampers and baskets, all the appliances, the wires carrying electric light to the rooms, the taps, the bathrooms, the pipes, the plumbing, the drains. It was one of the curses of life that everything was so difficult and slow to construct, compared to the ease and speed with which it could all be destroyed: all they needed was a little gasoline and a match struck against its box.

I tried to think of what I should do at dawn so at least they wouldn't burn me like the house. I had to decide which trail to take down to the road, maybe to Juan's roadhouse. I hoped no one would see me; someone could tell Los Músicos, by radio-telephone or by messenger, that they'd seen me go by. I had to try to get down to the roadhouse without being seen. There were three options: through the meadows, opening the latches and wooden gates; through La Mariela, which was the same way Los Músicos' trucks had gone; or down the same road I'd come up, passing in front of Casablanca and behind La Oculta Lake.

I had another moment of crying and an instant later another one of laughter and happiness, because tears were coming out of my body and that meant I was alive, and because my heart was beating hard and that meant the same thing; I felt like a survivor. I put the poncho back on because I was cold. I thought of Benji with tenderness and intensity. At that time he was doing a semester in Berlin, because he went to the Colegio Alemán, Medellín's German school, and he would be in class, not thinking about his mother hidden in the mountains, resuscitated, who was conjuring him up by squeezing her eyelids shut. I thought of my brother in New York, who would be sleeping beside his gringo; I thought of my sister, of my nephews and nieces. I thought of my mamá and of the bakery we were in the process of selling, because I didn't want to keep working there, and I saw Mamá already looking very old and very tired. I thought of my employee, Patri, who came every second day, to water the plants and change Gaspar's water, feed him and take him out for a walk. Now she'd never again greet him as she always did: "Hello, Don Gaspar, come." I half-slept thinking of them, especially my son, and of a theory my niece Flor told me once, that all women who live with cats suffer from sadness. Now her theory was true, for I was not going to live with a dog like before, but alone, and with the thought that I was going to turn into a sad woman, if instead of a dog I got a cat (I even named him: Prrr), I fell asleep, I'm not sure for how long, maybe just a few seconds, maybe half an hour, maybe an hour and a half. In my light sleep I saw Noche, the mare, who turned into Gaspar, who turned into a cat, who turned into smoke. I wasn't really asleep, it was a half doze, anxious and light the way dogs sleep, with one eye open and the other closed. Every once in a while the horse startled me, changing her position or exhaling noisily through her nostrils, brrrr, a huff halfway between bored and resigned, a wordless phrase that said we'll-just-be-patient-because-what-else-can-you-do-when-you've-got-a-bit-in-your-mouth.

Near dawn, a gust of chill wind made me shudder as a shiver ran up my spine. The hairs on my arms were damp with either sweat or dew. Finally the birds and roosters began to wake up and a slight radiance lit up the edges of the mountains on the far side of the River Cauca, just visible between the leaves of the trees. I rubbed my eyes. My mouth was dry and my tongue felt like sandpaper. Beside La Oculta Lake rose a thin column of white smoke. I gave Noche a little kick with my heel and prepared to leave the woods in the first light of daybreak. I'd decided to take the *Camino de la Virgen*, the same way Los Músicos had gone, although not all the way on the road, but taking shortcuts and detours through the meadows. I remembered something my papá used to say: "What's the safest place for a fly? On the flyswatter." That's why I decided to go where they'd gone. When we reached the gate by the water tank the mare wanted to turn left, to go back to Casablanca, but I obliged her to turn right, toward the danger. I soon left the road again and crossed a grove of coffee shrubs; from there I could get back out to the road, a little lower, without fear of being seen. I also wanted to be sure there was nobody posted on the road, waiting for me. It wasn't very likely, since they didn't operate that way, they preferred the cover of darkness, but it could happen, if their only aim was to finish me off. I hoped to reach the roadhouse before seven and catch the bus there for Medellín. There was no way I was going to go back to the farm to get my jeep, I didn't dare. I didn't want to see if Próspero was alive or dead either, or collect Gaspar's body, to bury him. No better idea than the bus occurred to me, for now.

The trail was deserted and I arrived at the roadhouse before six, much earlier than I'd thought. It was still closed, and completely silent. I urged the mare into a trot and went as far as the gate to La Oculta. My heart started its accelerated palpitating again; my palms were sweating. The gate was open. They'd broken the chain with wire cutters or something like that. I realized those men had left their four-by-fours halfway up the hill, so I wouldn't hear them coming. Had they all left by now or would they have gone back to La Oculta? Although I was dying to know how poor Próspero and his wife were, to see what state the burned-down house was in, to say goodbye to my dog, I was afraid to go back up to the place where it had all started, six or seven hours ago. In the air I could only catch a burnt smell, and I could see the column of white smoke, up above, on the lakeside.

I couldn't stay there, a feeling of panic returned, I urged the mare into a gallop and passed the second roadhouse, La Reina, which belonged to the Restrepos, and kept on till La Pava, the Trujillos' farm. Pedro, the foreman there, had known me for my whole life. As I approached the house I saw him in the corral, milking the cows. I almost burst into tears when I dismounted and walked over to him, but I held them back. I asked him if I could take a shower and leave the mare here, if he could unsaddle her and give her some food and water. I was speaking very nervously, agitated, but Pedro prudently asked me no questions. He offered me a glass of milk, and I drank it down in one gulp. Then I saw a hose and drank water without stopping, as if I'd just crossed a desert. It was as if I couldn't sate my thirst. Finally we spoke. Pedro offered me a coffee and squirted a little fresh milk directly into the cup. It tasted glorious.

I didn't want to tell him anything, but he probably guessed many things from my terrified, exhausted face. Pedro told me he'd heard a chainsaw in the middle of the night, up above, and nobody chops down trees at night, before dawn, and then an explosion and the smell of smoke, like from a house fire. I did nothing but nod my head and I think he understood, without my having to say a word. I asked him what time the bus came down from Palermo and he said around quarter or ten past seven. Did I want to send something to Medellín? I remained silent; my hands were shaking. I asked Pedro if he could lend me some money, and he went straight inside and came out with a twenty-thousand peso bill in his hand. He gave it to me without any questions.

"My pleasure, Doña Eva."

Then I asked if the farm had a radiotelephone. He said no, that it was broken; that Don Horacio hadn't wanted to have it repaired because the only thing it did was let people in town know when someone was at the farm. The Trujillos had also been subjected to pressure to sell. I realized that having phoned Pilar the day before had been a mistake. Even if there had been a radiotelephone, I realized I couldn't have used it, because then they'd know where I was. Besides, who was I going to call? Who was going to take the risk of coming to get me? Pilar would, I knew Pilar would dare to come for me, she wasn't afraid of anything, but I didn't want her to take that risk. I had to get out of there on my own. The police? No, that would be worse. I couldn't trust them. I looked at Pedro with fear, desperate, on the verge of tears, and I don't know if he understood what I was thinking or not, if he could see the terror I felt written all over my face; I imagine he could. I was very confused, I hadn't slept, I still felt like I was being chased, cornered, with no idea how to get to a safe place quickly, to Pilar's place, or my mamá's, or to my own home in Medellín, to the telephone to call Benjamín and cry and cry.

"Pedro, you know what they look like, don't you?"

"Who?"

"Those ones."

Pedro moved his head and eyes to say yes. The mere question bothered him, made him nervous. A few months earlier those same men had killed his brother; or they hadn't killed him, but almost, or even worse: they'd shot him several times and left him for dead, lying in a ditch. A bullet had severed his spinal cord and now he was there, in a room in the back of the house, paralyzed.

"Those people are very evil, Doña Eva, be careful," he said in a low voice.

"I know. Could you look inside the bus, when it arrives, and tell me before I get on? You never know if one of them might be on board. I'll hide over there," and I pointed to a bench behind a wall, on one side of the corral.

"Okay," said Pedro.

The bus arrived at almost twenty past seven and was half empty. It was a red ladder bus that covered the Jericó-Palermo-Puente Iglesias-Fredonia-Medellín route. The bus driver said good morning to Pedro when he stopped. Pedro told him there was a passenger. He came back to the corral and told me none of them were on the bus. We shook hands; he had understood that something very serious was happening. I asked him to go up to La Oculta later, very carefully, to see if Próspero was all right, and to tell Rubiel that I'd left the mare with him. Pedro closed his eyes and lowered his head in agreement.

I got on and handed the only bill I had to the driver's assistant, but he didn't have any change. He said he'd give me my change later, when other passengers got on. I sat at the back, beside one of the ladder exits. An hour and a half to Fredonia; two hours to Medellín. I had time to think; I had time to cry; I had time for everything. Sitting in the bus, I sighed with relief, I was moving away from danger and in three and a half hours I would be home.

ANTONIO

There's nothing strange about people falling in love. The strange thing is that there are some people who never fall out of love. That's what Pilar's like. If everyone was like her and Alberto, that would be the end of sin, of adultery, and all priests as well as most novelists would be out of a job. Pilar wouldn't allow herself to fall out of love because then her life would fall over a cliff, lose all its meaning. She and Alberto are the way they are through and through, to their very core. In a certain way our love for and attachment to La Oculta is similar to Pilar's love for Alberto. People love their farms the way they love their husbands or wives, an old love into which we've invested a lot of time and almost all our energy. We learned to love the place as children and teenagers with genuine, spontaneous happiness, love at first sight, in the childhood sunshine and the blue days (as Machado might have put it). But in spite of sometimes having reasons to stop loving it, we could not abandon it without feeling that at the same time we were betraying ourselves, renouncing our own selves, our most beloved attachments and hopes. Giving up a farm like La Oculta is like giving up someone we once believed was the love of our lives. What was the farm? A small fulfilled promise of what America was said to be and mostly was not: a place where you can get a piece of land if you work hard. What was love? Something you were going to receive forever, if you always gave it; somewhere you went to sow, to reap, and to die. Pilar still trusted those dreams that for her never shattered, the dream of a country and a place in that country, and the dream of love with Alberto, and her five children, what she most wanted. Selling the land was a betrayal as grave as if her own children had sold her into slavery.

I was living another American dream, farther north, without being completely convinced by its marvels; I had Jon and I had my hope of retiring to La Oculta one day, or at least to Jericó, even though my love was barren and childless. Eva, on the other hand, as ever in her life, was fickle. Not disloyal, and not unfaithful either. She simply did not get attached to things the way we did, not to people, or houses, or land, or anything. Just in the last ten years she'd changed apartments at least four times, because from one day to the next she'd get bored and decide to move to another neighborhood. She always got excited about starting a new life, in another place, with another love, with another landscape, without ever getting permanently attached to anything. She was the freest of all of us, the one who let herself get swept up by her impulses, which were like wind currents she was carried away by and couldn't or didn't want to resist. She hadn't put down roots in any man or any land. Maybe she was more wary or weary from her experiences. In that sense, perhaps, she was the most deeply Ángel of all the Ángels.

Her last boyfriend, Santiago Caicedo, had lasted for quite a while, almost four years, and it was strange that they'd broken up, because I thought she'd seemed very happy with him. They'd met swimming at the Pablo Restrepo pool in Medellín, and water was the best element in which to meet Eva. Although they swam at the same pool for years they'd never coincided before, because Eva swam at midday, to get tanned and so that thanks to the sun and vitamin D, she'd never get osteoporosis, though she might get skin cancer. The widower Caicedo, however, swam there in the evenings. One day my sister hadn't been able to go at noon and at seven they'd ended up swimming in the same lane. He was in his seventies, but kept pace with Eva doing breast stroke and was even faster than her at front crawl; no matter how hard she pushed herself she couldn't keep up with him. That was the first thing she liked about the old man, his vigor. She asked him why he didn't swim at twelve, so they could see each other again and she could have the challenge of beating him one day, but he said he'd soaked up so much sun in his youth that his skin couldn't take one more ultraviolet ray, his dermatologist had categorically forbidden it. His skin had that blotchy wilted pallor of white people who've sunbathed too much in the tropics. When they finished swimming, he invited her out for dinner and in spite of his age, there was an undercurrent of empathy, something very strong between the two of them. Caicedo, for a start, reminded her very much of our father, Eva told me, because they had similar interests: classical music, films, history, and literature. Furthermore, he treated her with respect, without making fun of her questions or interests, and in that sense was better than my papá, who had always insisted that she should devote herself to the bakery instead of dreaming.

They began to see each other more often. Eva even decided to swim in the evenings several times a week. He had lost his wife a year earlier and was still depressed, eating badly, and very skinny. He told Eva she was the greatest comfort he'd ever had when he was at a moment in his life when everything seemed lost and on the verge of collapsing. The widow Caicedo, who was very devout, told her that one day, not long before meeting her, he was talking to a priest and friend, his confessor, and that the priest had asked him what he thought he'd do with his life now, without Cristina, his wife. And that he'd answered: "I'm going to open the windows so the Holy Spirit can come in." And he told Eva that that's just what had happened: "I opened the windows and in you came, the gift the Holy Spirit sent me." Eva felt useful with him, and appreciated and loved, for the widower was incapable of living without a woman nearby, maybe because that's the way Antioqueño men of his generation were: he had no idea how to boil an egg, how to make something pretty, how to arrange a house. Eva cooked for him, arranged flowers, helped him to choose new furniture, to hang nice paintings, to ease the fading, sad memory of his late wife. He invited her to a cabin he had in La Ceja, which Eva also helped him to decorate, and they read side by side, listened to concerts, watched movies. The cabin had something very special: Caicedo had put up hummingbird feeders all over the property, so the house was surrounded by hundreds of hummingbirds of all colors and all types. They were marvelous, like tiny holy spirits with their invisible wings, Eva said. According to her, the widower enjoyed music more than she'd ever seen anybody enjoy it, not even me or Papá. I witnessed it myself when they came to New York and went to hear a concert I played in and several operas. They prepared beforehand, and he patiently taught Eva what they were going to hear, so she'd enjoy it more. He was very sensitive and although Eva sometimes had to push him in a wheelchair, because he had a bad knee and couldn't walk far (could only swim), she didn't mind, because with him she grew, learned, filled a void that had been growing for a while from devoting the best years of her life to the concrete work of Anita's business, to the family. And

I thought that Eva, at last, was going to stay with him since she told me she loved him as she hadn't loved anyone in the world. I saw him as old, worn out, ailing, that was my only doubt, but I don't think I ever mentioned the widower's age to her. After Mamá's funeral, to change the subject, I asked Eva what had happened with him and she broke down and cried her eyes out, because she was actually living through two bereavements at once, one for Anita and another for Caicedo.

She told me that from the start they'd had problems about his political positions. Caicedo, deep down, in spite of being so cultured and sensitive, was also deeply conservative. He'd never been with a woman who thought for herself, who contradicted him and had clear and definite political opinions. He was right-wing, Eva told me, and he got enraged when Eva talked to him about the paramilitaries, told him what they'd done, about the chainsaw murders near La Oculta, things that he, like so many other people in Colombia of his class, didn't want to hear. The widower's friends were almost all ranchers or industrialists, and one time, at a party in Llanogrande, a general of the Fourth Brigade had arrived, with much pomp and ceremony, the same man who'd been at La Oculta with the paramilitaries, when he was a colonel. My sister, as a result of that, had a big fight with the widower. Eva, however, admitted that it hadn't been the worst, but rather a pretext for her to leave him; that maybe what she hadn't been able to stand up to was something stupider and more intimate: the social pressure. Even though she felt good with him, growing and learning, people kept telling her she should find someone younger. Anita herself said the widower was not going to be company for her in old age and that she was worried about dying and leaving her with him. Eva began to think, first, that she was incapable of being on her own, and at the same time that she should think of finding someone "more suitable" to satisfy other people's expectations, basically because of the age difference, and how old he looked beside her. People despaired of seeing her so vital and cheerful and beautiful at the side of such an unattractive man, such a wreck, at least from outward appearances. Eva had been very upset, for on the one hand Caicedo brought her back to the cultural dreams of her youth (she felt as though she were finally getting to study what she wanted), but at the same time she realized, in spite of herself, that she didn't have enough strength of character to stay with him, because of the pressure around her. And having given up for that reason made her even angrier, even sadder. Since there was no solution to the contradictions she felt, shortly before Anita's death, she'd told her that she'd decided to leave him due to their ideological and political differences, and also to look for someone less old, who would last longer, though deep down she knew she was doing it simply and plainly due to pressure from others.

That had been her last relationship with a man, but in her lifelong search she'd had lots of other failures. Eva wanted to find in her lovers and husbands what she was lacking, but in the end the men never fulfilled her expectations. Maybe her bad luck was also owing to her good luck. "One soon gets sick of grazing…" Grandpa Josué used to say. I mean that, because she was so beautiful, she had far more choices than most, and as Anita always said, "the beauty desires the ugly girl's luck." When someone can always choose something else, it's easier to make a mistake, because of the temptation to change and never resign yourself. That's the syndrome of actresses and other celebrities. But Eva wasn't a frivolous and light-hearted beauty, like some flirt; quite the contrary: she was the most serious and conscientious of the three siblings, the most reliable and definite, and she could be the most joyous when struck by happiness, and the most spirited and hardworking when she wanted, which was almost always. She hadn't been lucky with men. And nor had she been lucky at La Oculta, for she had to overcome something that was perhaps more directed at Pilar – who spent more time on the farm – than at her. Since she'd almost been murdered there, she no longer trusted that land which we'd inherited as our own safe haven, our paradise without snakes, private and immune to the maliciousness of life. It was easier to leave a man than to get rid of an inheritance, which more than an inheritance was an idea, an illusion. Eva had decided not to attach herself to any man or to any country or any land or anything.

I met Jon at an exhibition. As I was wandering by the work, smiling at how bad I thought it was, drinking lots of the wine they give away for free at openings, suddenly a tall, handsome, distinguished man approached me. When I saw him an idea occurred to me which I disagreed with: I thought, unwillingly, and without telling anyone, that perhaps his incredible beauty and bearing had been obtained by the same system my grandfather and great-grandfathers had used to create their best horses: bringing together carefully chosen slaves and calculatedly breeding them, until almost creating a new human species, superior to ours. I immediately discarded this odious eugenic idea and meanwhile he was asking me, very kindly, in a very sweet voice, if I'd liked what I'd seen of the exhibition. My answer came straight from the gut and was as frank and imprudent as my secret thought had been: "Absolute shit, señor, but I suppose one shouldn't say such things." He laughed really hard and went to talk to another group without a word. A little while later I found out he was the artist.

I realized because I started talking to a friend about the artist's name, Jon. I was telling her that in Antioquia the name Jon was very common, especially Jhon Jairo, with the H before the O, and I knew lots of Johns in the States, but no Jons without an H. Then she pointed to him with her chin, saying: "That's him, maybe black people spell it without the H." I looked and it was him, the same one I'd told that the show was shit. I wanted to hide from shame, turn invisible, go back in time, also because the man – in his multicolor African tunic – had struck me as handsome and sweet; I liked his mannerisms and his way of speaking, the elegant way he went from one group to another during the vernissage. After a while I approached to take my leave and told him: "I'm very old-fashioned and don't know much about art; I was born in some isolated mountains in South America and the news hasn't yet reached there that art is like this nowadays." He asked for my phone number and I was happy that he did, that I hadn't offended him.

He called me the next day and we got along from the start. He also thought his art was shit, a farce, he said, but he explained that it was more or less what curators and galleries were asking for now: installations full of theories, philosophical or socio-logical elaborations, lots of boring stuff with found objects, but all wrapped up in sophisticated philosophical dressing. Grand words for very stupid ideas and very poor visual experiences. We agreed. That very night he took me back to his apartment – where he had some of his work that I loved, sculptures of penises and trees, all very erotic and phallic – and that very night what had to happen happened and it was bliss. He was as beautiful naked as clothed, and it was my first experience with a black man, which is also something I don't really know how to explain, but it's like returning to the African origins of our species, something darker, deeper, and more complete. I felt like I was back on the grasslands of the first men, or rather (perhaps I shouldn't have thought this either) I felt like a woman on the primordial plains, and not like the sort of man I am. I'll say something more, although it might sound arrogant: what Jon liked most about me, as he told me from the first day, was my skin, which is smooth, and the smell of my body, which according to him is something like basil, which he loves like nothing else. It was as if I liked the animal in him – and I was carnivorous – and he liked the vegetal in me – and he was vegetarian.

We had an open relationship for a long time, because that's the way things were back then, and we went with the flow. When we met we were both very young, full of life, with the elated enthusiasm we were all feeling at being completely free for the first time in history. We didn't think AIDS could touch us, and if it didn't touch us – I think now – it was only by a miracle, because lots of our friends started to get sick, one after another. That scared us, and enraged us, for it was as if we were suffering from the curse all the most reactionary preachers in the United States had announced. Maybe out of fear of contagion, or the luck of having not been infected, or because we felt that a life like that, so extravagant, resembled the lack of seriousness and limitless disorder of contemporary art, that intellectual ostentation that preferred tangled theories to beauty, one day we distanced ourselves from the perpetual orgy, resolved to be faithful and to devote ourselves more to our work and to taking care of each other, and trying to be happy in moderation and not in abandon. He was the one who proposed it and I was in the perfect moment to receive the proposal. I know I have an Eva, but also a Pilar, inside me.

So in the summer of 1993, when Medellín was so violent that I almost never went there, we moved in together and started to live a New York working family lifestyle, a more bourgeois life, maybe, but also more serene and productive. Not complete fidelity, which unfortunately on my part never quite came about, especially when I went to Medellín and got together with my old friends from the scene, but at least an attempt at fidelity and complete loyalty to him. We no longer say yes to everyone, like before, but rather sometimes, not often, it happens that we're unable to say no, even if afterward we feel bad for having said yes. Anyway, this is something I think inside, hidden within me, because, as far as I know, he has always kept his promise, and as far as he knows, so have I, because it's better that way.

Jon's apartment is on 115th near Lenox Avenue, not very far from Central Park. It's on the third floor and was his parents'. He and his three brothers grew up there. When his father died, Jon took over the lease, which can pass from parents to children, for a ridiculous rent that would be absurd to give up in New York. It was a spacious, bright apartment that he'd renovated, knocking down walls, to make it into a loft. Both of us were a bit tired, almost astonished at having lived through those crazy years, those years of unfettered liberty, irresponsible and delicious years, about which it's not worth going into detail because they're very well known; I don't think there've been many other times in the history of the world when there's been so much liberty. And it had been exciting, and worth experiencing, but also horrible. I'm not nostalgic for those years. Jon and I decided to live differently, in a sort of island of calm, without being sanctimonious about it, strictly monogamous as far as possible. We gradually dropped the habit of fooling around on each other, first out of fear and later out of conviction, until the habit of fidelity settled on us, and it didn't taste bad. Not that there weren't lots of temptations, but we tried to avoid them. It wasn't out of laziness or prudence or chastity that I began to be anchored to Jon. A person gets used to a body the way one gets used to a farm or a landscape: there is something comforting about always seeing the same thing every day: there is charm in routine, the way you appreciate a violin piece more that you've played and heard many times. As La Oculta will always be my home, the only place I feel is my own, joined to me like a limb, Jon is my other half, or I am his rib, in the rewritten bible of our times, the husband I want to have for the rest of my life. I don't know the reason, but it's as if my body and my head had decided without even thinking about it. That's simply the way it is.

He has carried on being an artist. He doesn't work at home, but has a studio near here, on 122nd. He makes artworks that sell for thirty thousand dollars, out of trash he finds in the streets of Harlem. *Carefully Recycled Garbage*, his last exhibition was called, the one he was setting up when Anita died, in roughly the same vein as the long-ago one where I met him. "A gigantic lie," he says at night in bed, with the lights out, and although I can't see his face in the darkness, I can see his ironic, sideways smile, his perfect teeth. He lives off that fallacy – which is a sort of nostalgia for the art of the crazy years – and bit by bit he's become rich and cynical. The farce isn't total, for he manages to give an aesthetic touch even to the most absurd, but it's not exactly what he'd do if he felt less tied to what the galleries, the theorists of the academy, and museum curators ask for these days. Years ago we agreed that this is what the contemporary art world is like, a collective hallucination, a gigantic lie, but we resolved to live within these absurd rules, without shouting that the emperor had no clothes, and adapting to going with the flow, with what Venice and DOCUMENTA demanded. Jon was invited to participate in 1997, and in Kassel I helped him set up an installation of carved-up tree stumps and New Year's Eve rag dolls – the kind they sell along the roadside in Antioquia in December, with sombreros, wearing old clothes, and covered in firecrackers – with old and new chainsaws hanging from the walls; it was very successful and articles came out talking about the experience of an Afro-American artist in the violent tropical Andes. On opening day, when the guests arrived, we had fifteen actors in paramilitary uniforms who started up their chainsaws in unison, and severed the figures filled with cotton soaked in red dye. It was like entering hell. It had a huge impact and since then he always gets invited to all the most important contemporary art fairs. A very famous critic praised the work saying that "installations of this kind reveal the materiality of the civilization in which we live, because they install all that otherwise would obtain no perdurability in the critical conscience of contemporaneity." Ay, I can't stand words that end in "ity," but the attention was good for Jon. Since then he earns more; there are people ready to pay thousands of dollars for an old chainsaw with Jon Vacuo's signature; I imagine they hang them in their living rooms, and explain what they mean. Frankly, although I understand the historical significance of objects, the social statement behind them, and I even helped him to plan it, it makes me laugh. I can't imagine Pilar's living room, or Mamá's, or a corridor of La Oculta, with an old chainsaw hanging from a hook, with a piece of paper beside it, in garbled prose, explaining in dense paragraphs the importance of this work as part of the historical memory of conflict in Colombia. Jon says his only aim is to accumulate two million dollars and retire to do what he likes. Jon has become cynical and practical, but he doesn't suffer the way I do, or ask himself so many questions.

I don't know how much of that sum he's saved up because he never shows me his bank statement. I know he spends a lot on his family, because he's very generous and has many more nephews and nieces than I do, several of them unemployed or addicted to drugs. What I do know is that, for years, all I've had to say is: "Jon, I'm a little homesick. I want to go and see my mother, my sisters, and La Oculta." He immediately goes to his computer and buys me a business-class ticket on a direct flight from New York to Medellín. It is, or was, the only luxury I allowed myself, three or four times a year, when nostalgia was killing me.

It wasn't nostalgia for something lost; it was rather longing for something, for a house that exists. Since I don't really have a steady job (I give private violin lessons, in the mornings, and my engagement with the orchestra is sporadic, when there are pieces that require many violinists), I can feel homesick at any time of year, and go. I also teach, but virtually, courses on music appreciation, theory, and harmony. I have them all set up, with well-chosen music as examples, practical exercises, and classes I can teach via Skype. That allows me to leave New York whenever I want and I take a 4-G device that gives me internet access at the farm, so I won't neglect my duties during the trip and classes carry on. Meanwhile, the apprentice violinists get a break from me, and Jon gets a break from me, although when I'm away, he says, he doesn't sleep well and stays up late almost every night.

I read quite a lot, on paper and on screen, especially history and literature. Sometimes I also write poems here and there, but don't publish them. I polish them up and hide them in my notebooks as if they were sins or odious secrets because what I like is traditional poetry: ten-line *décimas*, sonnets, madrigals… I'm so old-fashioned that there are days when I think that today's poetry is also like today's art: a sort of shapeless farce, all facile form and absence of art, skill, or willpower. Although a poet can't actually work with willpower; one simply waits, and sometimes a poem arrives and sometimes it doesn't, or to put it a better way, a poem almost never arrives and very seldom does the miracle of a theme, a tone, an internal music, and a voice all come together. Poems occur to me most of all when

I'm walking on my own, and surrounded by a foreign language. One occurred to me in Japan, where I didn't understand a single word while I walked among blossoming white cherry trees. One occurred to me in Hiddensee, an island in northern Germany, while around me everyone spoke German and I was looking for amber and pebbles on the Baltic beaches. One occurred to me in Norway, enraptured by the view of the fjords. If I'm alone and don't understand anything that's said, verses well up in my head, as if to combat verbal solitude. It can happen at La Oculta, if no one's talking and I only hear the incomprehensible voices of animals, the mooing, singing, whistling, and screeching. I almost always come out with heptameters, octosyllables, or hendecasyllables, occasionally alexandrines. I've gone to all those places simply for Jon's exhibitions, which have become more and more frequent since his invitation to DOCUMENTA. Thanks to Jon I've seen the whole world, and I'm very grateful to him, even if I'm still only attached to one single place in the world, even after seeing China, Europe, Egypt, Australia, and Japan. Sometimes, Jon smiles and asks me: "Do you want to come with me to Malaysia and Singapore or would you rather go to La Oculta by yourself?" Sometimes I go with him, sometimes I don't.

Jon, Jon Vacuo is his artistic name (and almost his real one, which is Pascuo), shows his recycled trash all over the globe. The galleries that sell his work are the top ones in Paris, Los

Angeles, Berlin, Chicago, Milan, and right here in New York. We have a dear old friend, a ruined aristocrat who amid the ruins of his intelligence is still a very good writer, Heinrich von Berenberg, who we commission to write articles in praise of Jon's work, and we pay him under the table, without anyone knowing. We ask him to employ the most tangled-up style possible. He takes great pains over them and gives us incomprehensible postmodern essays, that Jon polishes up, and the two of them laugh their heads off. *The neo-allegory of the post-verisimilitude* ran the title of Heinrich's latest essay on Jon's work, the first paragraph of which began: "The spatial indetermination of Vacuo's objects, like electrons in an immense particle accelerator, allude to the encounter of Schrodinger's cat and Fibonacci's numbers in one of Turing's machines. That which under the aspect of an extraordinary electronic die dispenses with chance to reach the discursive meridian of Being, penetrates the spectator's neurons like a laser, exciting micro-particles of DNA, axons, and dendrites, until making sparks of illuminated coronas dance through the cerebellum, almost like an ancestral invitation in a rainforest fiesta of *yagé*." Pretty, no? And signed by someone with a Von in his surname, much more convincing, we think, than if any old John Smith or Pepe Rodríguez had signed it. And much more so if the name is a German one, because many believe that only in German is it possible to think. Critics rave about what they don't understand, think they've never read anything so sharp and profound about art. And the dealers and curators do too, and they're the ones who make the most money and understand the least. And their clients are the same, millionaires coaxed with long and tangled words. Whenever they call Jon to ask for a price cut of five or ten thousand dollars, he says no, how could he. He pretends to be inaccessible and does very well selling his big display cabinets of trash ordered in compartments, in cells, arranged by color and shape. There are days when I think that what he makes as art isn't so bad, or maybe I'm used to it, who knows. When he showed at the Museo de Arte Moderno in Medellín, Alberto Sierra, Julián Posada, and Ana Vélez wrote very nice essays about his work that were published in *El Colombian*o.

He's distinguished, tall, sinewy, handsome, very dignified, with the attractive contrast of his black skin, white hair, and goatee possibly even whiter than the hair on his head. It's that neat beard that gives him a profound dignity, like a great African patriarch. He wears multicolored tunics that we have made in Liberia. When we met that night of my faux pas (a faux pas can be an impetus for love) his beard was still black, and I like it that while he's been with me, it has gradually lightened to now being this pure white. He hasn't minded that I've gone from having had jet-black curls, which were the least objectionable of my features, to gradually going bald at his side.

Jon speaks very little, in aphorisms, like an oracle. In bed he tells me that he's as much of an artist as Forrest Gump was an intellectual. He doesn't even understand how he's become such a respected artist, as they say, but he could care less about being respectable. One day when we were celebrating our anniversary, and had drunk quite a bit of champagne at a restaurant, he told me that when he'd saved up all the savings he wanted to have, we could buy a little house in Jericó and spend three months a year there. He had met an odd Jewish man that December, Doctor Ojalvo, the grandson of a Levantine merchant, and had loved the museum of contemporary art he'd managed to set up in the middle of town, a generous, respectable, and useful space. That same euphoric night he told me that perhaps we could donate his collection of contemporary American paintings and videos to the Jericó museum. I thought we'd bought the least bad stuff that had been produced over the last twenty years, what still held a distant aroma of true art. That's what Jon told me that night, though he hasn't repeated it since, and I hope he fulfills it one day, though the idea of waiting until old age to finally do what you want to do is one I've never liked. If I had enough money and could, I'd put the dream into practice today, right now, because while a person waits for dreams to come true, along comes illness or an accident and a person dies. Life is hanging by a little thread, and in the air are scissors that fly in the wind. La Oculta itself, though it seems eternal, has always been besieged by a thousand dangers; when it's not civil wars or the crises, it's crime or guerrillas; it's miners, opium traffickers, or developers who offer millions for properties to turn into recreational ranches. They can't see a green, virgin piece of land, because their eyes get injected with greed, and there can't be a single gram of gold under the beauty of a landscape or they'll want to rip up the whole landscape to appropriate those little nuggets of gold, or copper, or coltan.

My biggest problem has always been uncertainty: not knowing what to do or what to think when many paths open up before me, and I've always had all paths open to me. To begin with I grew up in a world of women, and somehow the possibility of being like them in at least one aspect was offered to me: a taste for sex with men. But that's the least of it, and it's genetic. I'm sure I was born this way, I knew from very early on. I don't think, as Grandpa Josué believed, that I turned into a fag from being so coddled by my sisters. He tried everything possible and impossible to make me more of a man, more *machito*. When he took me to the farm he tried to get me to learn how to castrate bull calves, the way he did, pulling them down with a rope, and without anesthetic, and he also tried to get me to eat the testicles scrambled with eggs. "Eat, my boy, this'll give you lots of virility, make you more manly." I pretended to eat that repulsive offal, but I actually snuck it under the table to the dog surreptitiously, so my grandfather would think I'd taken his medicine. In any case, it wouldn't have had any effect, for I felt myself to be what I was even before I started to grow any hairs or fuzz. And what I perceived didn't make me feel good, because I'd always been taught that it was bad. I struggled against what I saw growing in myself, like a threat, like a mortal sin. To battle against it, the first thing that occurred to me was to start going to spiritual encounters and retreats organized by the fathers of Saint Gemma parish. I believed that with meditation and piety I could get rid of my impure thoughts and impure inclinations. We spent two or three days in silence in a house of spiritual practices on the outskirts of Medellín and I would kneel and beg God to please take this away from me, to take away this wretched attraction to men, to not let me feel enraptured by the other boys on the spiritual retreat.

I confessed, I asked for advice, and Father Eusebio, my spiritual adviser, said that those tendencies could be controlled by willpower and by asking our Lord for lots of chastity and strength. He even put a hair shirt on me, to battle my fantasies, but it didn't work. I would masturbate thinking about men and then cry in repentance. I took cold showers at three in the morning to chase away the erotic dreams filled with male members raining manna over me. There was a prayer group at the parish and they did things to us there to get us away from all kinds of unhealthy temptations. They told us that if we grew close to God and lived a secluded and prayerful life we could frighten away any phantom of impure thoughts. That we should control our gaze, our touch, our opportunities to sin. "One never, two not ever, three passable, four better," was the recipe for company: never to be alone or in pairs. Father Eusebio gave me some prayer cards that served to push away any strangeness or aberration that could occur to me day or night. Sometimes I was capable of going for one or two weeks without sinning, but then I'd lapse again, I'd sink into abandon for a week, until I realized that there was nothing to be done, no matter how much I prayed or struggled what was inside was much stronger than me. It was like putting up with hunger, or thirst. A moment arrives when one simply has to eat or drink, because if not one dies. And I had to have sex, alone or in company, or I'd die. And so I stopped going to the retreats and I began resigning myself to being what I really was within myself. Only in the United States did I manage to replace guilt with pleasure, and even went to the opposite extreme, limitless madness. Balance and acceptance only came to me later, with analysis and with some meditation courses Jon made a lot of fun of, but which helped me to find something luminous, something I'm not going to spurn, something that is within me and that I think we all have inside ourselves, and those who don't see it don't because they haven't looked.

I think there are other things, however, that don't come to us through our bloodlines, but which we choose in life. Beliefs, for example, which we choose from the bouquet of influences we receive, from what we hear and what we read, from friends or teachers. Religious and political beliefs. And that's where things get complicated for me: Cobo was very left-wing, but at the same time very much a believer in all religious things. He himself had recommended the Saint Gemma fathers to me, and later a group of Jesuit Liberation Theologists, people who were very politicized and committed, although in matters of sex almost as closed-minded as the Legionaires of Christ or Opus Dei. Mamá was also quite into praying but without a speck of socialism; a believer in daily Mass, but a capitalist to the core, attached to all that one achieved through one's own work, through individual effort. So politically I've never really known what to be, nor what to think, nor what to believe. Or rather: from Papá I received my doubts about the capitalist world and from Anita a belief in the individual, in merit, and in the economic reward and success that derive from individual talent. I think this is the luminous facet of capitalism, oblivious to its abusive or exploitative side. My Liberation Theologist friends said I was unable to break away from the egotistical bourgeois inside me, unable to work for the good of the community, for others, for my fellow man. But the best thing I saw in Cobo was his love for poor people, his compassion, and the best I saw in Anita was effort and tenacity, her solitary and individual struggle, when she was able to create a great bakery, starting from nothing, and kneading the dough with her own hands. She inherited nothing, was given nothing, she did it all herself, getting up very early every day to work. Nevertheless, I understand those who defend socialist ideas, just as, although I still believe in God (official religion disgusts me now), I also understand those who don't believe, those who are agnostics or atheists. I'm a lukewarm believer, who is unable to share much with my fellows (my heart is not big enough to love everyone) and a guilty capitalist. More than that, there are days I wake up feeling socialist and would burn down a bank. A better way to put it would be to say that I live in uncertainty and insecurity.

I'm a lukewarm person, and many despise me for that. Even when it comes to sex I'm lukewarm, I think, because on some nights of insomnia I think I like women a little bit, that I could leave Jon and have a child at last: we might say I have maternal yearnings, more than paternal, to put it in a totally queer way. There are days when I wake up longing to be a mother, and I would fertilize a woman if she'd let me raise my son, give him his bottle, change his diapers and bathe him, dress him up, powder his little bum, put cream on if he gets diaper rash, choose his clothes, sing him lullabies, bundle him up if he gets cold, dandle him in water if he's too hot, smother him with kisses, all the things that men, who are very macho, deprive themselves of. I love all that, just as I would have loved to play with dolls, as my sisters did, for a doll is much prettier and more fun, with hair, eyes that open and close, with squawks, than a wretched little red car that had nothing but wheels; better to play with something that resembled an animate being than with a stupid little machine that did nothing but roll along a plastic strip. But anyway, in this house I'm also the woman: I take care of the shopping, the cooking, cleaning the apartment, while Jon makes most of the money. At least in traditional families in the old days, this was the division of labor. And I make a bit of music, compose easy salon pieces, little tunes for popular singers, also like a nineteenth-century woman. And I take notes for my family history, like an old maiden aunt. My nephews call me uncle in public, but I know they laugh at me among themselves and call me Auntie Toña, because they say I'm affected, though I don't notice it. Damned kids, if they carry on I'll disinherit the bunch of them, I tell them when I see them, and they laugh at me even more.

EVA

The bus, with its smell of gasoline and overheating engine, drove slowly down toward the River Cauca, sometimes stopping to pick up a campesino who raised a hand or waved a hat on the side of the highway, with a sack of coffee or bunches of plantains. Behind us a wake of dust, on both sides a line of trees: ceibas, *pisquines*, hundred-year-old samans, and the view of the Cauca, intermittently, on the right, up ahead. Sometimes from the window, I would manage to see the orange crops on the other side, in the undivided part of the old Túnez estate. The next stop – if no more passengers flagged the bus down from the side of the road – would be Puente Iglesias, before crossing the river and starting the ascent toward Marsella, Fredonia, and Cerro Bravo.

When we got to Puente Iglesias, I looked distrustfully toward the shop where the buses always stop, and my heart bolted again. Two Toyota pickup trucks with tinted glass were parked in front of the refreshment window where they sold beer, fruit drinks, and fish cakes. I had never seen their faces, but it had to be them. Those guys (one hard, sour-faced; the other scabby, with childish features) were sitting at a small table, drinking beer with an army lieutenant and two soldiers. Beside the truck were more young men, in dark sunglasses, armed. The ones around the table were talking animatedly, without paying much attention to the bus or the passengers, but I knew that if they saw me and recognized me they'd be quite capable of shooting me right there, in front of everybody. And if later someone asked how I'd been killed and who by, nobody would have seen anything, not the soldiers, and much less the lieutenant, or the bus driver, the conductor, the passengers, or the owner of the shop; some out of complicity, others out of fear. If they were already drinking at eight in the morning, they were definitely going to stay there, getting drunk, until the afternoon, so trying to cross the bridge, passing in front of them, was impossible. After thinking for a moment I decided that it would be best to retrace my steps and go seek help at the Toros' farm, which wasn't very far away. Maybe they'd lend me a horse there to go up to Jericó along the trails, or the farm manager might even drive me up to town on a motorcycle, if he had a motorcycle.

I got off the bus, as stealthily as a cat, half covering my face with the poncho and pretending to head for the washrooms, which were behind the bar under a purple, flowering bougainvillea. When I got to the washrooms I turned the opposite way, crossed the dirt road behind the bus, and began to climb up the same slope we'd just driven down, almost running. As soon as I saw a break in the fence on the right I ducked under it and kept going up, feeling very upset, across a pasture between tall trees, black rocks, and Brahman steers who watched me pass indifferently, chewing their cud, lying under the trees in the shade. I was sweating again, from head to toe, and didn't dare look behind me. I had to get as far away as possible. I ran. I ran until I could barely breathe and began to walk. I got a fright when the bus honked its horn twice to announce it was leaving. Maybe they were calling me, when they saw I hadn't come back. I imagined them knocking on and opening the washroom door; I could almost smell the rank urine; I imagined the driver shrugging, the joy of the conductor who would get to pocket the change from the bill I'd given him. I heard the engine start up and another honk of the horn, and then the accelerator. I ducked down behind a rock and saw the bus head onto and slowly over the hanging bridge. The pickup trucks remained where they were parked beside the army checkpoint. The table where the men were drinking wasn't visible from there. I was angry with myself; I thought I should have stayed on the bus, holding myself together, slumped down and pretending to sleep, but it's hard to await death with eyes closed. Now I was there, near them, near the danger, while the bus went away toward Fredonia, around the bends, toward Medellín and safety.

Now I would have to continue on foot. I had no choice but to find the Toros' farm, which wasn't far from there, and was owned by some friends of Lucas. I hoped the caretaker – I couldn't remember his name – would recognize me and help. I had to keep escaping, but I didn't even really know where to. The next bus from Palermo wouldn't come until the next morning. If I could ride up to Jericó, I could possibly risk asking for the mayor's protection there, or that of the police, or the procurator, but in those days it was difficult to trust the authorities, for one never knew whose side they were on, whether they were with the gangsters or the citizens. The police who weren't with the armed groups were murdered or transferred, and the same thing happened to many public officials. Often mayors had to leave and carry out their town duties from Medellín, because if not they'd be murdered too. But things in Jericó hadn't been too bad compared to some places, for the town hadn't suffered atrocities as other parts of Antioquia had, there hadn't been any massacres of more than five, and the town had never been taken by the guerrillas or the paramilitaries, or at least not completely.

My legs were trembling again, my teeth chattering, my hands shivering, and tears were rolling down my cheeks. I was following a narrow dirt path along the mountain, the cattle track to the drinking trough and back. I was looking for the Toros' farm, but I didn't know these lowlands well, down near the

Cauca. If I'd gone across to the other side I could have gone to La Botero; I knew Camila, the owner, and it would have been easier to ask for help there. But getting to La Botero meant passing in front of those guys and the army. Impossible.

The path now descended abruptly toward a ravine; below I could hear the sound of a stream that flowed down the mountainside between enormous, polished round rocks. I was very thirsty again; I needed to drink some water. The path ended in front of a guadua bamboo grove that shaded the current; there was a steep bank above the stream and I began to inch my way down, slowly. I was two or three meters away from the crystal-clear little river, which I could see below. I leaned on one of the guadua to keep going down, but the trunk was rotten and gave way beneath my weight and I fell. I landed sitting in the streambed, straight onto a rock, on the edge. My whole body shuddered from the blow. The spasm shot up from my coccyx through my spine and echoed round my cranium, clouding my vision and deafening me. I felt as though my backbone had stabbed me in the nape of the neck, as if my spinal column had penetrated my brain, inside my skull, and as if my tailbone had become lodged in my perineum and had splintered there like an asterisk. I couldn't breathe, couldn't inhale any air, and the only sensation was unbearable pain between my buttocks and my back. My body fell over onto one side, amid the sand, rocks, and water pooling along the bank of the stream; I was unable to stand up and in my ears my agitated heartbeat thundered. It was as if someone had stabbed a dagger between my buttocks and shot a cloud between my temples. I closed my eyes and waited; I remembered the pains of childbirth, when Benjamín was about to be born. I had never felt anything like that since, until now, but this time was worse since it was a senseless pain, a pain that couldn't bring any good with it. I kept waiting in a cold sweat. I felt a tickling in my legs, like an electric current running up my vertebrae. The intensity of the pain gave way a little. I was afraid I might have broken something important, that I might not be able to move some part of my body.

I let a few more minutes go by, keeping still, petrified, in silence, and several times I was on the verge of fainting. Finally I heard the water rushing against the stones again. My fear had vanished; my thirst had vanished; one single, omnipresent sensation had taken over: pain. I managed to drag myself into the flowing creek and instead of drinking I splashed handfuls of cold water on my face. The pain began to subside and turn into a sort of numbness and tingling in the middle of my body; I felt nauseous, but managed to ease myself onto my side and slowly, gradually get onto my feet. I moved in several ways I'd once learned would demonstrate whether or not a person had a serious lesion in their spinal column:

I stood on tiptoe, stood on my heels, brushed my legs with a blade of grass all the way up and down, making sure I felt it tickling my skin. I could walk, and on foot I couldn't even feel the dagger stuck in the middle of my body. I knelt down beside the stream and drank water, a lot of water, until almost choking from drinking so much. Water, since the night before, the only thing that had saved me was water. It didn't even occur to me to think the water might be contaminated from something upstream, me who doesn't even trust the water from the aqueduct and always prefers to boil it.

Everything is within me, I thought. *The pain, but also the thirst. The only thing not within me is fear: the fear comes from outside, from them. I accept my pain, my thirst, my fatigue, but I don't accept the fear; fear is intolerable*, I thought. I went to the other side of the stream, getting wet up to my thighs in the cold water, stepping carefully on some large stones to retain my balance. I climbed up the ravine on the other side and when I emerged from the guadua grove I saw in the distance, and even thought it might be a mirage, the Toros' house, a modern, elegant, comfortable house. I walked toward it slowly, ducking under the barbed wire when I came to a fence. When I crouched down I felt a piercing pain at the base of my back, between my buttocks, but I didn't cry anymore, I bore the pain the way a pack animal, a mule or a mare, bears her burden and keeps walking.

Julio's caretaker was a gruff, sour-faced guy. He treated me very badly, with suspicion. He seemed like an ally of Los Músicos. He said he didn't recognize me, that Don Julio didn't let him lend out horses and there wasn't enough gasoline in the motorcycle to get him to Puente Iglesias, let alone Jericó; he told me it wasn't easy in this area to receive strangers; he told me to go and to thank him for not calling the people who looked after the farm. The only thing I could get out of him was that there was a *camino real* that led to Jericó along the River Piedras, and I headed for it, with a terrible pain in the middle of my body. I walked up and up, without stopping all morning and part of the afternoon, leaning on a stick that I picked up along the way, asking at campesinos' houses when I lost my bearings. It was strange, many little houses were abandoned, falling down, with initials of various armed groups painted on them (faded *ELN* and *FARC*, and fresher *EPL* and *AUC*); those were years of displacements and many campesinos had to flee, some frightened off by the guerrillas and others by the paramilitaries. When one or the other arrived they accused them of being allies of their enemies, because they'd given them a hen or a drink of sugar-sweet *aguapanela*, and they were always between two firing lines, and always guilty of something. It was much worse for them than for me because I, sooner or later – this was my hope – could get to a safe house in Medellín; they would have to go and live with some relatives as poor as they were, to sleep piled up in a single room or ask for charity at traffic lights with a sign saying, *We've been displaced from San Rafael* (or any other town). *Please help.*

A good woman, now very old, halfway up the climb, gave me two cups of *aguapanela*, despite knowing that being charitable could be a crime; we spoke for a moment. Part of her family had escaped from the violence, but she and her husband were still weathering the storm, trying not to have problems with anybody, she told me, without asking who I was, where I was coming from, or where I was going. She saw me simply as a human being. I drank standing up and the *aguapanela* tasted more delicious than ever and gave me the strength for at least another hour of walking. Later, I started to get dizzy from exhaustion and hunger, and had to sit down every once in a while to recover.

As I walked, leaning on my improvised walking stick, I thought that my ancestors must have gone up this very same path, a century and a half earlier, to help found the town, according to Toño's papers. I told myself I needed to have as much strength as them, and had to climb with some expectation of finding something good. I told myself that I was on foot as the poorest of them had been, and not on horseback or mule, as the more fortunate had arrived. I also thought at least I had shoes. It was a painful, very long ascent, during which I always avoided the road out of fear the pickup trucks of Los Músicos might come by. I thought of how the first settlers, the young men with their wives and children, had arrived sweaty and dirty to the first houses, greeted by barking dogs, with their eyes wide open, their clothes in tatters, and feet aching with blisters, but with great hopes, for them land, for me salvation from this wretched land for which I'd almost been killed. The first settlers had been welcomed happily. They'd been greeted by a Mass and a *sancocho* chicken stew. No one was waiting for me and much less would anyone welcome me. I was coming to leave, to get away as soon as I could.

I was dirty, tired, ugly, battered, with a smell of old sweat. I wasn't happy to arrive, just eager to leave on some form of transport that wouldn't have to cross Puente Iglesias but would go down to Medellín on the Tarso road. I didn't trust anyone and everyone looked at me from a distance with a mixture of disgust and suspicion. I really felt like screaming, shouting like a madwoman, bawling out what had happened to me, so the whole town would hear about the injustice, but I held back. I looked like a lunatic, I'm sure. Being dirty, sweaty, disheveled, and careworn is the first stage of being badly treated: it's the beginning of contempt. And if on top of that you don't have a single centavo in your pocket, you're already almost inhuman, disposable.

All faces looked like enemies to me, allies of the assassins; I was afraid of the police, the army, the mayor. Apart from that, I had a lot of pain in my tailbone, and pain disfigures your face, gives you a sickly severity that increases other people's mistrust, except in those who understand pain and are able to feel more compassion than repugnance. Perhaps for that reason I headed for the hospital and not to the office of any of the authorities. When I got to the hospital, I spoke with a nurse; she at least listened to me and let me wash up a little in the bathroom. I told her I'd fallen and showed her my back. When she saw I heard her gasp and she told me I must have broken something because my buttocks and back were as black as an eggplant. She said I needed to have an X-ray and told me the price. I told her I didn't have any money or time, that I was scared, that I had to get to Medellín that very day and didn't have a centavo in my pocket, that I'd given all my money to a bus conductor and then had to leave without my change to escape from some people who were hunting me down; that I didn't want to take another bus, that I had to go down the Tarso route, or maybe she could tell me some way to get to Medellín without going over Puente Iglesias and without anyone noticing me. She advised me to take a collective taxi and gave me a ten-thousand peso bill to pay my fare. She said I'd have enough left over to buy a coffee and sweet roll. Sometimes people are just simply good like that. I don't even know her name, she who saved me expecting nothing in return. I've never seen her again. The only thing I did, when I said goodbye, was kiss her hands, and she gave me a tender, distant smile, I'm not sure whether it was incredulous, but I don't think so.

I went to the plaza and saw the collective taxis. They left as soon as they had four passengers, three in the back and one up front. I got in line. I could tell I smelled bad. I went to a shop and drank an orange soda straight out of the bottle; I bought a coffee with milk and a sweet roll, too, and paid for them with the money the nurse had given me. I went to the bathroom and drank more water; nothing quenched my thirst. I was sweaty, smelly, my face looked like a madwoman's. I smelled myself and saw my face in the bathroom mirror. When I sat in the taxi a piercing pain shot up through my body from my ass to my neck. I could feel I had a huge swelling down below, like a heavy cushion of blood; a new heart beating in my buttocks. I tried to sit half sideways, but the pain made me faint. The taxi pulled out and I think the pain was so intense I lost consciousness a few times. The other passengers thought I was a drunk or a drug addict and a pig as well. They opened the windows so they wouldn't have to smell me, they kept apart from me, didn't touch me even on the curves.

I didn't feel fear anymore, just pain, for over three hours. When we got to the terminal, in Medellín, I didn't have enough money to pay my fare, and I owed them money; they insulted me, called me a bitch, a disgusting whore, and a thief. I caught another taxi and begged the driver to take me to my mother's address. I arrived and asked the doorman to pay the taxi. I went up the elevator. Anita opened the door and I threw myself into her arms, bellowing like a calf; I was crying for half an hour unstoppably before I could start to tell her what had happened to me since the previous night. She gave me a painkiller, called Pilar, and they took me to see the doctor. The black bruise went up my back and down my legs as well now; they took an X-ray and found I had broken and dislocated my tailbone, my coccyx. The orthopedist explained that they should try to put it back in place, operating on me immediately and without anesthesia, just a tranquilizer, sticking his thumb and index finger up my anus, to reach the bone fragment and push it back into place. I agreed and this was the final horrible humiliation of those two days. Two thick male digits entered forcefully, in spite of the lubricant, and grasped the bone. Nothing had ever, ever hurt so much, not Benji's birth, and the only thing that saved me from the pain was fainting, fainting again. The doctor tried several times to push the bone back into place, without success. Face down I sweated and screamed and howled in pain, until I lost consciousness, but the doctor didn't manage to repair the dislocation or set the fracture; he gave up, pulled his fingers out, and they injected analgesics into my vein. In the mists of morphine, at last, I felt a little bit better.

Since then I haven't been able to sit for more than an hour in any chair, and on horseback I have to put almost all my weight on the stirrups. Since then, whenever my coccyx hurts, which happens several times every day, I think I should never go back to that farm, that the farm is literally "a pain in the ass," as my brother's husband would say, that we should sell La Oculta no matter what, and that I have to convince my siblings to do so before that farm ends up killing us all.

PILAR

My God will punish me, but I didn't get sad when they burnt La Oculta. Or yes, I was sad for the first few weeks, I cried like an orphaned child when I got there and saw the black walls and a piece of the roof collapsed on top of the furniture, when I saw my bed and mosquito net scorched and when I smelled that smell that my nose couldn't forget for days, that clings to your skin and your clothes, but then it struck me as even a good thing to get rid of so much old junk, so many family burdens that prevent a person from looking to the future. And I went there two or three days later, without fear, because if we'd already lost everything, the best thing to do was go see, and if they wanted to kill me too, well let them get it over with. I told Alberto, let's go, let's go or we'll lose everything, and Alberto came with me in spite of the fear.

Of course what had happened to Eva was horrible, and even more frightening to think that maybe they would have burnt her alive, like a witch, that that was what they'd wanted to do, which was why they'd syphoned a bucket of gasoline out of her jeep, sucking on a length of hose: "We burned that slutty witch's house down, and if she comes back we'll burn her too," they said in the village, in Palermo, when they got back. And I have people who tell me. If I had been there, with Alberto, they would have killed us, first of all because I barely know how to swim, three strokes and I get tired, and because Alberto and I would have stayed there, paralyzed, and we would have confronted Los Músicos just with words and by playing innocent. But who can convince those barbarians; Eva did the right thing, fleeing through the water, over the rocks, on horseback and by bus, barefoot and however possible.

We went to La Oculta to see the arson with our heads held high, so they could kill us if they wanted to kill us, but to retake possession of the farm. Próspero and Berta were okay, terrorized, but okay. They'd been insulted, pushed around, and knocked down. Próspero had been pistol-whipped and had a gash in his head, they told him they were going to kill him, but in the end they left them alive, tied to the bars of a window. Juan, from the roadhouse, had arrived in the morning and untied them. They all still tremble with fear when they talk about that night. Próspero had buried Gaspar, the dog, by the side of the house and when we arrived he was still cleaning up the wreckage of the disaster, with an incredulous, stunned look on his face.

Alberto and I were scared too but we pretended to feel self-assured, although we felt like Los Músicos might return at any moment. We were barely there for two or three hours, in the daytime, fearing the night, and we saw the disaster, and tears sprang to our eyes, and we took photos for the insurance company, who didn't want to go, out of fear, because in those days everyone was afraid of the people who wanted to take over the country, and were succeeding. All of Colombia was ending up in the hands of the paramilitaries: the best land, the best farms, the city centers, the most beautiful buildings, everything.

But the fire, I thought later, and may God forgive me, also freed us of old junk: our great-grandparents' cowhide chairs (which Toño wouldn't let me give away), hard as rocks, the termite-eaten stools, the uneven tables, wooden beams so old they threatened to split and fall in on us from one moment to the next, a roof full of leaks and holes. And thanks to the insurance money, which I held on to for months, more than a year, before embarking on the repairs, we remade the house almost exactly the same but different and better. I planned everything very carefully, slowly, with experts, and so we were able to build up the house again, newer and safer, with the ceilings higher, with more air and more light and more views in all directions, though in the same H-shape as before, with more bathrooms and more rooms, respecting the old structure, but modernizing it all. New on top of old, which is the only way to keep these things from falling down entirely. And it was me who took that responsibility on my shoulders, though Mamá also helped with ideas, and even with a bit of money that she gave us from the bakery. Toño was in the United States, and he contributed some of his savings. Eva only said that she'd rather sell it and wasn't going to put a single centavo toward it. She was in bad shape; she was very badly affected, crazed. She never got entirely better, not even when Benji came back from Europe from his semester at school in Berlin.

She locked herself up in her apartment, stopped going to the bakery for a month. She spent the time shivering at home, paranoid, thinking every motorcycle, every sound, every time the elevator went up, was a group of killers coming back for her. She lived through what had happened to her over and over again in her head, and was furious at the whole world, at Colombia, country of shit, she said, with Antioquia, the heart of the shit country, she said.

Because of her mental state, at that same time we had to sell the bakery, because everything was in crisis and because Eva didn't want to go on working there. Either we sell the bakery or we sell the farm, said Eva. And we were left with no choice but to listen to her. Mamá had to give in, because she couldn't run the bakery on her own anymore, as it had become a big important business, with various branches in different neighborhoods of Medellín. Because Eva was depressed, and fed up with bread and accounts, it had to be sold. Eva spent a few years going back and forth to Europe, spending all the money from the sale of the bakery.

From the very moment I saw the burnt-out shell of La Oculta, I got a fever, a rage, an impulse, irresistible urges to reconstruct the house, and two years later I had it looking like before, better than before. Later Toño and Eva and Benjamín, and even some of my own kids, especially Manuela, and Mamá accused me of spending a lot of money, of bankrupting everyone for this damned farm, of having spent not just the insurance money but all three of our savings, and part of the bakery money, on improving the house, on making it much prettier and more comfortable than before the fire.

But what's so sad about the portrait of our great-grand-parents being burnt? It's not like it had been painted by Cano or Roda. Even Jon said it was terrible and made our great-grandparents look ugly. So what if the old stone mortar shattered in the heat? Nobody used it anymore anyway, as no one's silly enough to grind corn by hand in this day and age. So what if the wood stove from the kitchen was lost? Thank goodness, when even trying to light it was a torment, and with all the smoke it leaked it's more to blame for my bronchitis and lung ailments than cigarettes are. So what if the saddles and old riding gear got burnt, the leather reins, the sombreros, the rough, old sheets, the hard beds, the terrible mattresses, the horsehair cushions? Thank goodness, thank goodness, thank goodness: it was long past time to replace all that uncomfortable old junk. Stupid nostalgia for a more difficult past, idealized because people don't know how tough it really was.

They tell me I'm the most antiquated of the siblings, but let's just see, deep down I'm the most modern, the one who doesn't look to the past, like Toño, or to the nonexistent future, which is over for us or ending, like Eva. I'm the one who lives in the present, here and now, in these few moments of life left to us, and it's best to live them without crying, in a beautiful, bright, new house, in a house rebuilt with goodwill, with new toilets and showers, finally with hot water, because we never had anything but cold water here, to build character, as Grandpa Josué used to say, with comfortable beds and decent mattresses, with white towels that dry properly, like in good hotels, without so much useless junk, and having done it all with the same stubbornness that Toño says the original settlers of these lands must have had, without shrieking at cold embers or at the debris of that accursed fire. Not letting ourselves be intimidated, or scared, we'd send Los Músicos packing, or bribe them without anyone knowing, paying their wretched protection money without telling my brother or sister, who get scandalized by everything and make a big fuss of their indignation, to see if they'll leave us alive and not burn down the house again. Those who stay quiet and defeated are soft, and in this life only those who dare get anywhere. It's not that I'm brave, far from it, I'm more cowardly than my siblings, but this is my function in life, maybe because I'm the eldest, as any actor gets assigned a role in a comedy, a tragedy, or a soap opera, and well, I've played my part, as if I were what I'm not: a courageous woman.

ANTONIO

The few dogs in the remote village began to bark a long time before the first settlers of the convoy arrived along the one and only cobbled street. They came from very far away, from different towns in Antioquia (from the old towns to the new ones), and they were happy to arrive.

The first thing they heard in the village, from afar, was something that sounded like the buzzing of a swarm of bumblebees, and then a clearer tumult of voices, shouts, and howling of dogs that were also arriving and would growl and snap at the local dogs, neighing, mooing, and the sound of iron horseshoes and unshod hoofs. Later they began to hear the softer sounds of bare feet and rope-soled sandals, which were like a beat, a pulse of footsteps of women and children, the sound of walking, which is what humankind has been doing since the beginning of the world, since the fantastic footprints of Laetoli from thirty-five-thousand centuries ago: walking from one place to another, far, very far, escaping a volcano or an enemy, with a dream of finding a better land, even if no one has promised us that, just our own imagination, the beautiful illusion of a new land, of good land where food springs forth and where we won't die of hunger, or lava, or fire, or beasts, and that's so far away that not even our enemy tribe's evil intentions can reach us there.

In the village there was great excitement and all the inhabitants – very few so far, two or three hundred souls who nobody had ever counted – thronged the plaza awaiting the new arrivals. A trio (tiple, guitar, and a singer with maracas) sang songs to make the time pass more quickly, to feign sadness and feign happiness. The girls were hoping for suitors; the single men, for potential wives; the lonely were hoping for friends. Even the priest, Father Naranjito, was anxiously hoping for a cook or a substitute niece to make his celibate work of shepherding souls easier and less lonely.

A postal rider, on his way to Carmanta, had announced early that morning that the group would arrive around midday, if they made good time up the last rise from the tropical lowlands without any mishaps, along the path that snaked up the slope to Palocabildo. It was a tortuous and steep ascent from 600 meters above sea level at the river's edge, to more than 2,000 in the village. The postman, before carrying on south, on a fresh horse, said that he'd left them at dawn where they'd camped the previous night on the west bank of the Cauca. As he stopped for a moment to drink a coffee, he'd learned that they were getting up very early to commit to the final climb. He said he'd seen them sleeping on the heap of bundles that shielded them from the night winds; that some sleepless ones were mending horse blankets, halters, and girths. They'd said the worst problem was the plague of mosquitos that had attacked them from sundown until almost midnight, but when he reached them, under clear moonlight, the plague had already passed. There was a group of children with lots of bites on their faces and arms, with a bit of fever, but sleeping together serenely, like little angels. That's what he'd said, with the set phrases learned by heart that humble people always use, and that, more often than not, are the most apt.

In any event, the arrival of almost two hundred people, a long and tired procession of mules, oxen, dogs, horses, saddlebags full of piglets and hens, cows, calves, and many children, men, and women, some on horseback, some on foot, the poorest barefoot and others in espadrilles, the richest in riding boots, was the most important thing to happen in the town since it was founded. It might be said that this was its second foundation, and maybe the real one. Over the following months other settlers would keep arriving, but more gradually, in fives or sixes, sometimes just a married couple hiding out, escaping from their family's disapproval, from the patriarchal curse depriving them of their inheritance, sometimes a dozen adventurers hungry for new experiences, some lively fellow from the capital wanting to buy cheap already cleared land from the naïve ones, other times lone men with wicked faces, who offered to work as lumber-jacks, hated questions, and preferred not to talk to anybody, but sawed up a cedar tree in two days, from sunup to sundown, into perfect boards, unleashing all their contained fury against the innocent wood.

Those who arrived that day might have been as many as the original settlers, who, according to a quick headcount by the priest the previous week, were no more than two hundred and fifty, for a hundred and thirty had shown up for Mass on Sunday and that was not including the children, the sleepyheads, the sick, and those who'd stayed out in the countryside. The town was still barely a town, more like a disorderly camp. There were no more than seventy houses – though calling them houses was flattery dictated by optimism – most of them modest, just huts with wooden walls, dirt floors, and thatch roofs, and around what was planned to be the main square, for the moment, barely four constructions, two of them solid and complete and two yet to be finished.

Paradoxically, the two most important were the ones not yet completed: a wattle-and-daub chapel, with a half-finished roof, also palm thatch, that sooner or later would become the church, and whose primary function – apart from daily masses – was to bring everyone together at the same time; and the second, on the corner of the adjoining block, a small café, which also served as a bar, a place for conversation and, in the back room, a brothel (with just one loose woman, old and outlandish, foul-mouthed Margot, whose official task was waiting tables). It was odd that the priest and prostitute had arrived on the same day in the village and from the same town; but at least in that day and age, both were complementary trades, for, as a writer said, they pursued the same aim: "The church liberated man from his desolation for a few moments, and the same thing happened in the brothel." Or, as a campesino would have put it more plainly, in one house we sin and in the other we are forgiven, or in one we relieve our bodies and in the other they cure our souls. The two completed constructions on the future plaza were two impressive houses, with garden walls and clay-tiled roofs, facing the chapel: those of the two founding fathers of the town, Echeverri and Santamaría, who'd had the outrageous idea of populating their forests with a strange and newfangled system for Antioquia: not the dominion of single men, conquest, extermination, and servitude, but egalitarian discourse, settling families and donating pieces of land.

In reality, to understand the square it still had to be imagined. The future plaza was a field donated by Santiago Santamaría, just a cleared square, outlined as well as it could be by a shallow irrigation ditch, two hundred and fifty yards a side. The plaza wasn't level, for there were no flat surfaces in these mountains, but the plot was the gentlest slope that Don Santiago had found in the zone. It also had the advantage of being well supplied with clean water by a couple of streams and little rivers that came down from springs up in the unspoiled mountain. Everything was so steep in those places, they said if you tied a rooster up by the leg he'd end up hanging. Santamaría himself had traced out the plaza, some ten years earlier, alongside his friend, Don Gabriel Echeverri. After dismounting and finishing the quadrangular outline, which they'd staked out with a length of rope and then marked with a furrow dug with a large hoe, they'd walked around the whole perimeter ringing a little bell, accompanied by ten or twenty peons, who'd helped them with the chore, and a few women who accompanied them praying and singing. "We're founding a town," they said quietly and without any solemnity.

In the center of the dreamed-up plaza they'd left standing a few fine trees that had been there in the middle of the woods: two ceibas, a *romerón* pine tree, a comino, and two white guayacans. The town was so precarious that at the arrival of the new settlers there were still one or two black-eared white milk cows grazing there, as if the plaza were still a farm. It was an invisible town, which had nevertheless already been baptized twice, first as the Village of Piedras and later as Felicina, but actually, as a future settlement, it only existed in some of its inhabitants' heads. With the arrival of the new settlers it seemed that it could finally be called a town because it had the most important thing: living people, flesh, muscles, children, tears, blood, bones, words, ingenuity, the principle material of any settlement. Later would come the school, the theater, the bar, the restaurant, the seminary, the convent, the asylum, the barbershop, the boardinghouse, the courthouse, the town hall, the cemetery...

Along with Echeverri's grandson, Gabriel, an eminent person had also arrived, a Swedish nobleman called Carlos Segismundo von Greiff, who was going to be in charge of the precise layout of the streets. He had experience, for just eight years earlier, in 1853, he'd drawn the map of a new town, San Juan de los Andes, for Don Pedro Antonio Restrepo Escovar, the founder, in the township of Soledad, not too far from there. They called this fine foreigner Míster Grey, and he was a somewhat elderly person by then, with his red beard already turned white, but tall and steady, as straight as a broomstick in spite of his years; he was on his way to the mines in the south, to visit his British friends, but at the request of Restrepo, who was a very good friend of Don Santiago Santamaría, he was going to be so kind as to pause in the town long enough to draw up a freehand map, after some measurements he would take with his instruments, and suggest the best plan for the streets and blocks, designing the checkerboard out from the square chosen for the plaza. Míster Grey, who was a geographer and surveyor, very much liked the climate of the place and the location of the town, and he praised the founders' good taste with his marked foreign accent. One of his sons was with him as well, Bogislao, who would become the grandfather of León de Greiff, who would sing of Bolombolo, his "off-the-map locality," more than half a century after these times.

The two grand houses of the future plaza, that of Don Santiago Santamaría (great-grandson of David, *converso* born on the island of Curaçao) and that of Don Gabriel Echeverri (son of Gabriel the elder, of Basque origin), had been built side by side, the first, some twenty years earlier, and the second, twelve. The first, to serve as an inn and post house, for the mail arrived there, on the abrupt and terrible old trail. And the second to serve as a warehouse and granary. Right there they began renting out horses, selling hay and sugarcane for pack animals, and meals and beds (complete with fleas and ticks) for travelers. The two big houses were stationed on the roadside of the infamous stretch from Medellín that carried on south, so bad and impassable that not even Von Humboldt himself had dared to take it. Both houses had been, successively and sometimes at the same time, hostel, post stop, stables, granary, and roadside inn for the mule drivers who came and went with provisions from Medellín and Fredonia to Caramanta, Marmato, and Riosucio. Both, without having planned it, were eventually to be the origin of the village, alongside a few peons who kept the stretch of road half open, and slept in shacks nearby. Don Gabriel's house, the second to be built, was not only the larger, but also the better preserved. It was two stories high and had fired clay roof tiles, brought from the Guayabal brickworks, on the way out of Medellín, in several mule trains. Right there beside the front door, they had lit a large fire and welcomed the new arrivals with the smell of *sancocho*, the local stew (which would be served after the thanksgiving Mass). The pot of broth boiled and bubbled over the crackling flame of the dry wood, giving off an aroma that sharpened their hunger. The *sancocho* was the same thick soup as ever, the traditional meat and vegetable stew that all cultures in the world have invented after discovering fire and making resistant containers: boiling everything the earth offers in salted water.

In the immense pot a huge wooden spoon stirred the chunks of meat and vegetables, boiled over a slow fire: cabbage, cassava, corn on the cob, ripe and green plantain, carrots, potatoes, arracacha, which were added in turn depending on how long each ingredient needed to cook to become tender but not fall apart. A bowl of diced chili peppers and cilantro on the side, because not everyone likes cilantro or spicy food. On top of the embers as they burned down, beside the *sancocho* fire, on a flat earthenware pan, they were grilling *arepas de mote*, that is, corn cakes of ground maize that had been soaked with ash. The recent arrivals – upon emerging from Mass – brought over their plates or little clay pots and received an abundant serving. None could miss out on a piece of pork loin or fillet of beef. Each would also be given a large, round, crispy arepa. Don Santiago had donated a steer and Don Gabriel a hog for the celebration; the rest of the inhabitants had all contributed ingredients to the stew. Each would also receive, to drink, gourds full of *aguapanela* cut with sour orange juice, ideal for giving a boost of energy and quenching thirst. Jericó's *panela*, unrefined sugarcane rock, was the best and had been a gift of the Tejada family for the fête; they had a sugar mill down in the tropical lowlands, an aromatic mill that drove noses crazy from afar, when they began to boil the sugarcane juice and the air filled with the sweetest perfume in existence. If the serving of *sancocho* didn't sate their hunger, or the *aguapanela* their thirst, they could go back for second helpings as often as they wished. And many did go back for more, some twice or even three times. When everyone was as full as they could get, Gregorio Máximo Abad, one of the young men just arrived from El Retiro, spoke for all the new settlers and, looking Don Santiago in the eyes, said simply and profoundly: "The feast was good, Don Santiago; next year we'll invite everyone to a meal in Jericó."

PILAR

Alberto is lying down in our bedroom with a toothache. His teeth are very bad, poor guy, but he never complains. He could be feeling the sharpest pain and his face would never show it; he's like a horse, in that no matter how much something hurts you can never tell by the expression, or at least I can never recognize a look of pain on a horse's face; horses might be still or agitated, might lose their appetite, and Alberto's the same, he might stay in bed and not eat, but he doesn't moan, doesn't say anything, or put on a long face, is always serene, like a saint.

We went to Medellín the other day to see the dentist, Jaime Andrés, who went to school with my brother, a lovely guy. Jaime said he'd have to perform an operation to replace the front teeth and put some little screws in the incisors, directly into the jawbone, so they wouldn't fall out again. And he also had to put a crown on the left side. Although he barely charges us for the work, just for the materials, the titanium screws, the gold for the crown, the anesthetic, the implants, it's going to cost us close to eight million pesos. We don't have it at the moment and I called each of our children, one after the other, to see if they could help us. Every son and every daughter is different. I love them all as much as each other, the same quantity of love, but I'm not going to say how I love each of them, the quality or tenderness of my love. What hurt most was what Manuela said: "The best thing to do would be to have them all out, once and for all, and for him to get dentures; you can't be spending so much money on dental surgery every year. What does it matter at this stage." At this stage! I'm never going to forget that. It cut me to my soul, seemed cruel, as if we were going to die tomorrow, as if anyone might not die tomorrow, with teeth or without them. Lucas said he was going to talk it over with Débora, his wife, to see how much they could give us. I hope he doesn't forget. Lorenzo has no money, he can barely make ends meet at the end of each month. Florencia isn't working, but said she'd take something out of her investments, each week, to help me out as much as she could bit by bit. She's very big-hearted, Flor, and her husband is generous and discreet. Simón is in Barcelona on a grant that he won and I better not even ask him, because from so far away it's very difficult for him to help out. Each child is the way they are, you see. Manuela says horrible things, but one day shows up with five million pesos in her hand and doesn't say a word to us, leaves them in an envelope on the bedside table. Alberto's tooth-ache hurts me. We aren't that old yet: I'm sixty-four and he's sixty-eight. We're still in the youth of old age, as someone I don't know once said, one of those writers that Toño and Eva read. I don't read much and I read slowly because I take drops that make me sleepy. Ten little drops that dull my senses and knock me out, but if not for those blessed drops, I wouldn't sleep, and not sleeping is the worst, because then I really would end up crazy. Alberto and I are sometimes three years apart, sometimes four, depending on the month of the year.

Alberto and I had no experience when we got married. I was the last person to get married the way my grandmother got married, at the beginning of the last century, or like my mamá, like my aunts: without knowing anything about anything. Once my Aunt Ester told me that she, who was married for five years and had two children, had never known a man. That is, never in her life had she seen a naked man. Her husband was murdered very early on, by the Conservative death squads in the Valley, because he was a Liberal. They made love, of course, but only at night, with the curtains closed, in complete darkness. She felt, but didn't see; they never looked at each other without clothes on. Actually, something had changed when I married Alberto. At least it didn't have to be so dark, and we looked at each other happily, we looked. We looked and looked. And Alberto said to me as he looked at me: "Keep still, I want to memorize you all at once and forever."

It seems to me that a honeymoon is much more exciting for a couple of virgins than for couples today, who've already done everything before they get married and have more experience than the bohemian singers, actresses, and poets of a century ago; or those who called themselves singers, actresses, and poets. You know what I mean. To get married the way Alberto and I did – without having ever done it – was more exciting, and also more complicated. To begin with, the normal thing was to spend an hour in the bathroom, getting dolled up, before going out into the bedroom the first night. I did: I bathed, put on all the perfumes I had, one here, another there, and finally came out in a long nightie and wrapped in a silk dressing gown, like a dessert, more decorated than the wedding cake. The only thing that Doña Helena had told Alberto, preparing him for the first night, was a shy phrase:

"My son, take a little Vaseline."

But he didn't bring any or understand what it might be for. I, although full of emotions and expectations, was rigid and scared; no one had told me anything, and I hadn't asked. Since I was so clear about what I wanted, they thought I knew everything when I knew nothing. I lay down face up, with my legs together, as stiff as a board. When I came into the room I'd seen Alberto's pajama bottoms, raised like a tent in the middle, a pole straining against the cloth. He was ready, and that made me feel very happy, very lucky; but I didn't really know how things were, or what was going to happen, or if it was going to hurt or not. Since he was a virgin too, and without any experience, he didn't know where to put it. His friends had invited him to go with them to hookers, but he'd never wanted to. Alberto was going to be a priest, as I said, and although it had never occurred to me to be a nun, when it came to sex I was a novice.

We were at a borrowed farm, in Sabaneta. It belonged to the Saldarriaga family, the owners of Pintuco, the paint factory. It was the most elegant *finca* there was near Medellín in those days; we had thought of going to La Oculta for our honeymoon, but back then getting to La Oculta was a very long trip, first by jeep and then on horseback, a five-hour journey; you couldn't drive up to the house, so we gave up that idea. Alberto had Plittway pajamas, an expensive brand, pale yellow, almost transparent, like silk. We both had a different pair of pajamas for each night of our honeymoon. His were very elegant and expensive, long pants and shirts with long sleeves. My nighties were pretty, but more ordinary, because there was no extra money for luxuries at my house.

The first night we couldn't do anything, he didn't know the geography, and I wasn't about to show him the way, no, and I didn't really know the terrain that well either. We took off our pajamas, and I opened my legs a tiny bit, but not much, trembling like a little bird, I don't know whether from emotion or fright; he moved a bit on top of me, but finally lost heart. We kissed and that was it. And we looked at each other, and looked. It was the first time in my life that I slept in the nude and, of course, in the morning I woke up with a cold and a sore throat. Alberto went to the pharmacy and bought me some lozenges, on his way out of Mass in Sabaneta. In the morning, when he got up to go to the bathroom, I saw his hairy back and bum. My papá didn't have hair on his bum or his back; much less Toño, because he's completely hairless, like an Indian. Alberto looked like a bear to me, I didn't know men were like that, hairy all over, and I was terrified.

After the first night in Sabaneta we were going to San Andrés, so at midday we went to the airport. On the island it was just as difficult; we couldn't get it together even once all week. Alberto did persevere, on top of me, but I wasn't much help, rigid, full of desire but also fear, with my legs barely apart, and since he was very considerate, he didn't dare push my legs open, to really get inside me. We seemed like two idiots, frankly. When we got back from San Andrés I did nothing but cry because we hadn't been able to do it and I didn't know who to tell. The normal thing would have been to tell Eva, or Mamá, but I felt strange with them. I had always felt closer to my papá than to anyone else in the world; I had complete, absolute trust in him. He was a friendly, discreet, precise person. Also, my father was a doctor, so he had to know more about that than my mamá, so I told him. Papá smiled, then he looked serious and took Alberto into his study and the two of them spoke alone for a while; he explained a few things, I don't really know what he said to him. And he sent us to see Dr. César Villegas, a friend of his, downtown, and Alberto went in alone again. Later he told me that the doctor had explained angrily, mockingly, and almost contemptuously how it was done. He said he showed him some plastic models of a penis and vagina that he kept hidden in a drawer. That was how we both finally, at the same time, lost our blasted virginity, and got out of that one.

He began to buy a magazine called *Lux*, which supposedly gave tips on eroticism, and so, gradually, we began to get going. It took a long time before I had an orgasm; well, to tell the truth, my first pregnancy and baby, Lucas, came before I did. For some years sex was a mechanical, quick thing. Later it got a lot better; we had and still have – because we're still husband and wife in the full sense of the words – a rich and complete life, in that aspect as well, in spite of our years.

ANTONIO

One thing I loved about the farm was the horses. Before I devoted myself entirely to music there was a time when I thought I might study veterinary medicine. Actually, what I wanted to study was equine medicine, horses, just horses. But to get there you'd have to see dogs, cats, rabbits, cows, canaries, bees, and all that bored me. When I was four or five years old, I was frightened of horses, and terrified of riding them; if Grandpa Josué or my papá forced me to ride, I'd cry like crazy and have convulsive attacks of terror, trembling and screaming, with tears and slobber. Thanks to Eva I lost my fear and finally learned to ride. She let me ride with her in her saddle, and held on to me, and explained everything to me slowly, you move the reins like this, your heels like this, until I gradually lost my fear of them, and learned. Now, when I go to the farm, what I most enjoy, aside from playing the violin in the corridor facing the lake, is riding the old La Oculta horses, at least the gentle mares, the trotters less than the pacers.

I liked the story of our horses at the farm, which were nothing out of this world, they weren't horses from millionaire breeders or mafiosos, but they were our own horses. They were like another family who we watched reproduce and die two or three times in our lifetimes, because horses live for about twenty-eight years, at most thirty, thirty-five in rare cases, no more. So we'd all seen our own colts or fillies being born, we'd seen our mares give birth, and they were the great-granddaughters of Grandpa Josué's mares. We'd witnessed, as well, the retirement of horses, because a moment always arrived when they got to be put out to pasture. We didn't sell old horses at the farm, or send them to the butcher's to be made into sausages, but retired them when they got to be more or less twenty-five or twenty-eight years old, if they hadn't died before that. Retiring them meant setting them free and not riding them again and letting them die of old age. Furia, a horse who'd been my grandfather's and then my father's, spent the last four years of his life in the pastures grazing placidly, old, fat, and serene, until one dawn we found him lying under a tree, dead. And the same with the rest of them: Toquetoque, Patasblancas, Horizonte, La Silga, Terremoto, Tarde, Día, Misterio... all those we've retired.

We inherited the mares and stallions, just as people inherit riding gear and farm implements, or as land, furniture, and houses are passed down. Grandpa Josué said that the horses of

La Oculta were from a good breed: gentle and lively at once, often gray duns that end up white, every couple of generations a sorrel. Our animals didn't have weak hoofs and weren't skittish: they were reliable for long mountain rides on the edge of steep precipices, strong enough to cross torrential rivers without getting spooked, had good teeth, were obedient to the heel and resistant to tropical diseases. In recent years, the same trainer has broken them all in, Egidio, the foreman of La Inés, who is very good at it. The most important thing is that the mares conserve their fine, quick, almost imperceptible steps, which makes long journeys in the saddle comfortable, for one sits almost still, without any battering of bums, and this is priceless on day- and year-long rides, up and down slopes.

Grandpa Josué used to say that our Creole Ángel horses needed to breed with an Arabian or Spanish or Lusitanian (but never, ever an English thoroughbred or French dray) stallion, once every seven generations, to renew their fine appearance, to regain the size, intelligence, and good disposition that can get lost in these badlands with the passage of time. Also to moderate the lascivious appetite of the males (the best-looking stallion was always left uncastrated, as a stud, enclosed in a stable on the farm) that drove them crazy from the time they were colts, but without losing the gentleness of the old paso fino, which had been achieved with so much effort, with so many pondered

and discussed crossbreedings; so the males born of the renovated cross had to be sold or castrated, and the mares had to be
mounted (for one time only a rougher ride, but more jaunty)
by paso fino stallions from another Creole ranch, from the stables of the Garcés family in Jericó, or from the Peláez family
at El Retiro, who had the best paso fino horse stock in Antioquia, aside from the mafiosos (who had sublime horses on the
strength of their checkbooks and threats), and knew a lot more
about this than the Ángels, of course, and even more than the
Uribes and the Ochoas. Of course, to the Peláezes this thing of
mixing in a Spanish horse every once in a while was not just a
trick, but also heresy. The Peláez family is conservative, in this
and other matters, and very lazy, but at least they were well-
spoken, and not bandits; decent people with whom you could
speak the truth, and straightforward: if they offered you a Vitral
yearling they weren't going to con you, like the mafiosos, who
always cheated.

Grandpa Josué said that everything he knew about horses
he'd learned from his elders, and this equine eugenics also
applied to humans, as he maintained that they themselves,
his ancestors, also had a theory that in the Ángel family once
a century they also had to inject Levantine or Mediterranean
blood, Moorish or Semite, Portuguese, Greek or Italian, so that
in the beneficial melting pot of the local races – Black, Indian,

mestizos – what had crossed the sea with the hopes of a new world would not be entirely lost, with all their utopian ideals. I don't believe in this nonsense about races, maybe not even in horses, much less in human beings, but that's what our grandfather said, and I can't forget it much as I wish I could. Of course with dogs, horses, and cows one can look for certain characteristics and discard others, but human virtues and defects are so varied, and are less of the body than the spirit, so transferring the rearing of animals to the raising of children was an abuse of the theories of the human race. That was what had driven mad a nation as intelligent and ponderous as the German people, who out of their love for purebred dogs and horses had extrapolated the issue to people, and using absurd eugenics had divested themselves of genetic variety and richness, which is what had made marvels in other lands, and the best example of this is in the new world, in the north and the south, where we are no more but no less than anybody else, as the first of our ancestors who came to these, for him, distant lands said, and where we are, or aspire to be, an amber tone, a beautiful color, the color of mixed races and bastards, and what else are Colombians but mestizos, zambos, mulattos, and bastards?

EVA

He had a motorcycle and I came to think there was no better man in Medellín than this boy; I fell madly in love, for at least two years. His name was Jacobo, like my papá, but we called him Jackie. He was Jewish, Jackie Bernstein. He told me Bernstein meant amber in German, burnt stone, and his skin was a perfect amber color, because thanks to his motorcycle, a capricious old wreck, a Ducati racing bike from Italy, he was always tanned. He also wore a pair of killer Ray-Bans. My father had expressly forbidden us from ever getting on a motorbike, he said we could do whatever we wanted except ride on motorcycles, because motorbikes were more dangerous than revolvers, he said. So I had to arrange to meet him far away from the house in order to ride on Jackie's bike. Back then no one wore helmets; they weren't mandatory, and I never thought I could get killed; the only thing I was frightened of was running into someone from my family, who would tell my papá they'd seen me on a motorbike. I tied my hair up in a ponytail so my messy hair wouldn't give me away. When I got home I'd smooth out my hair with my hands and put it back up in a very tight ponytail.

I sometimes got excited when I went horseback riding at La Oculta, by the rubbing of the saddle between my legs, but when I started riding on the back of Jackie's motorbike, the excitement was double. That trembling, the bike's vibrations, that potency when he accelerated, braked, went around curves, and me hugging Jackie at the same time, my breasts pressed against his back, all that produced a profound emotion. I was terrified when I got down off the back of the bike that the moistness that inevitably formed between my legs would filter through and be noticeable. It almost hurt, down there, when I went out with him. I was very young and still a virgin, but I wasn't planning to be a virgin bride, like Pilar. Jackie said he wanted to be my boyfriend, but his family couldn't find out because they would have disinherited him if they discovered he had a shikse girlfriend, that's what he called me, a shikse, a Gentile, a Christian.

I told him I was prepared to convert to Judaism if he wanted me to, because I didn't give a hoot for religion, but for him I'd be able to learn Hebrew and pretend fervor in the synagogue, if he took me, to shave my head and wear a wig, to dress like an eighteenth-century Polish peasant if necessary, but he told me that wasn't possible, that it didn't work like that, that

Judaism wasn't interested in conversions. He even told me he'd consulted the rabbi of Medellín, an Argentine, and the rabbi had told him that conversions for love weren't valid, only for intimate conviction, an illumination, and that they were very cautious about accepting new believers. I told him that my papá, Cobo, not only had the same name as him, but said that we were also Jewish, that the first Ángel who'd arrived in Colombia was called Abraham and was a Sephardic Jew, for sure, and had even married a woman called Betsabé. I went so far as to ask my father for our family's whole genealogy (which would later become Toño's passion) to try to convince him: and I recited the complete string of our Jewish names. Jackie had his doubts, he said that in Antioquia it was very common to be called Isaías or David or Salomón. He said we were Catholics; that my mamá, Ana, could not be more Catholic and the important thing among Hebrews was the maternal line, which was the only trustworthy one.

In fact, my mother didn't like my going out with a Jewish boy at all either, even though her lifelong, best friend, Clarita Rozenthal, was Jewish. She'd been the first female doctor at the University of Antioquia, and she had also been in love her whole life with a goy, Gabriel Bustamente, a Catholic classmate of my father's, but they hadn't let her marry him either. And even though my mamá had always supported Clarita and Gabriel's relationship, she would not allow me to be in a relationship with Jackie.

"Clarita was going to convert to Catholicism, and not the opposite," she said. "That's very different. If Jackie converts to Catholicism we can think about it. Let him get baptized and have his first communion and then we'll talk about it."

What had happened with Clarita Rozenthal is that when she told her parents about Gabriel Bustamente, they said that if she carried on with him it would be the same as burying her and saying Kaddish and she wouldn't inherit anything from them, and they were rich. And furthermore they were going to curse her so everything would go bad for her in life and she'd have idiot children, or worse, children who scorned her and wouldn't even want to look at her face. Clarita had been unable to stand up to her parents, and her older brother, and her aunts and uncles, who were all against her relationship with a goy. But Clarita had stayed in love with Gabriel, and he with her, their whole lives until they died. Mamá facilitated their encounters, sometimes in her own house, which she would discreetly leave, to allow them to be alone together. There are people who never marry and go on living as each others' widows and widowers for the rest of their lives. I didn't want that to happen to me with Jackie and wanted to fight for my love. I fought for almost two years with all the strategies in reach.

On Jackie's motorbike we could get to La Oculta in less than two hours, for he flew along the highways and we could go along the trails, like a horse. Sometimes I'd say to him on a Saturday or Sunday morning: "There's nobody at La Oculta, let's go." And he'd get out the motorcycle, and we'd go, at full speed, along the road to La Pintada. Sometimes we went horseback riding, sometimes we swam, sometimes we went for a walk. One time we went hiking and I brought cold cuts, a nice cold bottle of white wine, and a blanket. And we went off into the woods. It had rained the previous day and a stream ran down from the crags of Jericó; you could hear the rushing water. In a clearing in the woods we spread out the blanket, drank wine, ate ham and cheese sandwiches (Jackie said, "it's not kosher," but he ate it since he was so hungry). After the wine and food we kissed and kissed as we had never kissed before.

It was a warm afternoon and a *soledad* was watching us from a branch, with her long blue tail, without a sound, as if taking care of us, as if approving of what we were doing with her gentle eyes. I remembered, but didn't tell Jackie, that seeing a *soledad* was a sign announcing a pregnancy. Rays of sunshine fell on our skin and Jackie took off his shirt. Then he took off my blouse and my bra. He looked at me; I looked at him. He said my skin shone like no other skin, that my breasts shone even more than the rest of my skin and that my nipples were the most beautiful things he'd ever seen. He kissed them, licked them, gently nibbled them. I was going crazy and I touched him. I slipped my hand into his pants, pushed them down. He had something smooth, straight, eager, and erect. He didn't have the little hood my brother had: he was circumcised. I thought that was better, as I'd read that circumcised ones were less likely to transmit diseases. I told him to be careful, that I'd never done it before, and he did it with a gentleness I don't think anyone has had with me since. So slowly, so sublime, so delicately that only a couple drops of blood were left on the blanket that I didn't even feel. He pulled out before he came to avoid any risks (the *soledad* watching from the branch), and then he lay on his back, very pensively. He said he was very sorry but he'd never be able to defy his parents. That he was dying to marry me, but he couldn't, and now he was guilty of having taken my innocence. That he'd never tell anyone what we'd done, that I didn't have to worry about that. I felt like crying, but I didn't cry, I laughed. I looked at him smiling my best smile, trying to look cheerful, and said, well, that made me sad, but well, I understood. I stood up and went for a walk in the woods, barefoot and naked. He watched me go and when I came back to where he was, Jackie was ready again, he'd forgotten his repentance and we did it again, more slowly, fearlessly. He came inside me and then we were scared to death for several weeks, until my period came. When it came I was very happy, we both were, it was a relief for us, at that point in our lives, not to have to confront bigger things, a huge family fight or a clandestine abortion, which in those days was dangerous and sordid. I never told him about the bird.

We slept together again sometimes, almost always in the same woods at La Oculta. Sometimes we'd hop on the motorbike and go all the way to La Oculta just to do it. Sometimes we couldn't stand such a long journey and we'd go to a pine forest in El Retiro. I had my first orgasm with him, lots of orgasms. I mean my first orgasm in company, and multiples very soon too, because I'd already figured out how to have them with my own fingers long before. I think that women who don't learn how to have them on their own have more trouble having them with someone else later. After a while I realized that he loved me more than I loved him, and that he was suffering desperately for not being able to stay with me, to marry me. After coming on my chest, he'd lie on his back and cry like a baby. I'd caress him and think he was a coward, but I'd say, never mind, he'd find a Jewish girl he could love, that there were the Lerner girls, the Zimermans, the Maneviches, the Dyners, that he should go out with one of them and he'd forget about me. He said he'd been introduced to all the Jewish girls in Medellín and none of them was as pretty as me with clothes on, let alone naked. None of them had skin as radiant as mine, none had hair as long or as black; none got as wet as I did. I was enraged that he was comparing me to others, but I stayed quiet, feeling like crying, but laughing myself silly. Laughter is often – at least for me – the best protection.

One day someone came to my house with the story that I was seen with a boy on the back of a Ducati motorcycle. My papá called me into his study after dinner and shut the door behind us. He didn't chastise me, but his blue eyes welled up and he told me he couldn't take it if I were killed in a motorcycle accident, he'd never forgive himself. He begged me in the name of what I most loved to please stop exposing my life to danger in that way; that in the hospital he saw victims of motorcycle crashes every week, injured and dead. He said he'd lend me the car whenever I wanted it, even if he had to go to work by bus, but he begged me please not to get on a motorcycle ever again. I couldn't disobey him, and I saw Jackie on foot, in other places, but never again on the bike or at La Oculta. I told him that in my house there were taboos too, like at his. Not religious ones, but almost religious; that at my house the sin was to ride a motorbike, much worse than eating pork, or sleeping with a circumcised Jew.

Finally they sent him to Israel to work on a kibbutz for two years, and he met a Russian girl there who he ended up marrying. Before getting married he wanted to say farewell to me with one last trip to the woods at La Oculta. I didn't want to anymore, I was very disappointed in him, in his cowardice, and had started going out with another guy, a classmate at university. But I agreed. And I even rode on the back of the bike again, defying my father's request. I didn't have an orgasm, but he did. He came in my belly button again, like Onan in the Torah, he said to me, and then burst into tears.

"And who in the Bible are you crying like now?" I asked him.

"I don't know," he answered. "I don't know the Bible by heart either."

We got back on the motorcycle, drove back to Medellín, he went back to Israel, and I haven't seen him since. Someone told me he lives in the United States with his wife; that he graduated in medicine, specialized in obstetrics, and makes a lot of money looking after rich women, doing fertility treatments, in vitro inseminations, births, and abortions, in a small town in southern California. Good for him. And to think I would have turned Jewish for him, Buddhist for him, Muslim for him, atheist for him, whatever he wanted. Love drives you crazy and that thing I felt was love, my first love. Maybe I was spared from being bored my whole life in small-town California, how would I know.

ANTONIO

They were sweaty, tired, dusty, but happy at having arrived. They talked loudly, sang *coplas*, challenged each other with *trovas*, told of the adventures of the trail: injuries they'd done themselves with machetes, wandering mules, exhausted donkeys, runaway horses, the calf swept away in the Cauca when she fell off the raft and the swimmer who dove in after her, to save her, and almost drowned too, when he got to the rapids. They showed each other the blisters on their feet and described the throbbing of their legs, the itching of the crab bites in their private parts, the colic and pains in their guts, the pustules, the fevers diagnosed by touch. In the two and a half days of the crossing from Fredonia (six or seven for those who came from Marinilla, Rionegro, and El Retiro), no child had died, and that was a good sign. There were no old people with them. Many, almost all of them, had had to spend two weeks in quarantine below Fredonia, to prove that they weren't diseased, but most of all to prove their patience and civil conduct.

There had already been deaths in the Aldea de Piedras. Measles, scarlet fever, and cholera had visited even these remote lands. But people were buried in the fields, where they'd fallen ill, for it was futile to take them into a town where there was not yet a doctor or a priest, and where the cemetery had not yet been consecrated. In the lot set aside for this purpose, donated by the founders, no one had yet been buried, and Don Santiago's calves were still kept there as they were being weaned, and from his herd came milk, butter, and cheese to sell to the settlers. That was why – people said – there were no ghosts in town, or apparitions, or fear of the dead yet, or of death. No one wanted to think of death; there would be plenty of time to get old and die in peace, here, in this new land, and they hoped to God there would never be a Cain in this town, that no one would ever dare to raise a hand and kill any of his brothers.

The sad thing, however, is that the first two official deaths in Jericó were two brothers, the Trejo brothers, originally from Envigado. They both wanted to marry the same woman, a girl who'd grown up in Aldea de Piedras, and they were the first- and second-born sons of their household. The girl had made eyes at the eldest boy first, but had then resolved to accept the proposal of the younger one, who was more even-tempered and inspired more confidence. The older one could not resign himself to this disdain, and something gripped his heart. A deaf hatred, a limitless resentment grew within him. One Sunday evening he got drunk in the new town's only canteen and went to look for his brother at home; he asked him to come outside, insulted him, and told him to bring his machete. Their parents had gone to bed and were fast asleep when the eldest brother issued his challenge. The younger brother didn't want to fight a duel, much less with his brother, but nor did he want to be intimidated or humiliated. The machetes flashed and they both rolled their *ruanas* around their left forearms, like woolen shields. Since the eldest was drunk, he received the first cut, a deep wound in the left shoulder. He grew furious and managed to slash his younger brother in the thigh. They were both bleeding heavily and kept injuring each other more and more, in the arm, in the neck, in the ribs. None of them were fatal blows, but they both lost a lot of blood. Unfortunately there was no one there to separate them and the trails of blood drenched the ground. They both bled to death little by little, without a word.

In the town they called them "the two Cains," from the moment they picked them up off the ground early that morning. The younger one was already dead and the eldest, conscious but in his death throes, did not ask for forgiveness. He himself told the story of how the duel had gone. From then on, the fiancée, a girl whose last name was Arcila, never looked at another man. When the nuns of the Order of St. Clare came to town, years later, she was the first to request entry, and cloistered herself with them. No one saw her face again in the fifty-four years that followed until her funeral. The two brother suitors were buried near each other in the cemetery, one beside the other, face to face. They buried them both with their machetes in the coffin, as a reminder and a warning. There could not have been a sadder or less promising inauguration for a cemetery.

The new arrivals had traveled for eight or nine hours a day, with one or two stops to eat, on the banks of a clear stream. Sometimes Isaías and Raquel, at dusk, would take themselves away from the rest of the group and bathe or cool off in the woods; Isaías would look with enchantment at his wife's belly which was beginning to become convex, full, and he touched it tenderly. Raquel was frightened to make love, but they lay down on Isaías's white *ruana* and she touched him very softly, with her perfect hands and fingers, until he finished and could rest. Afterward they embraced and laughed, and talked about the future of their firstborn in the new land. They dreamt big dreams for him, and didn't just discuss the name they'd give him, whether it would be a boy or a girl, but also the name of the land they'd leave to him, as El Cojo had promised. If it were a boy, they decided, he'd be called Elías or Israel; and if she were a girl, they'd name her Eva, as the first woman. And the first land they resolved to call La Judía if the child was male, and Palestina if female. They enjoyed these dreams and enchantments and laughed.

Since the new settlers brought convoys of cows and calves, colts and oxen, and since they came with mule trains and donkey convoys, they proceeded very slowly, and the trail was not very wide. Sometimes an animal would take off into the woods and they'd have to wait until it was found. They'd slept at roadhouses where there were any, or out in the open, under roofs of rubberized canvas, in circles made of the harnesses, saddlebags, bundles, and equipment, taking turns to keep an eye on the oxen, cows, and horses. A couple of children had fevers, and two horses had died of exhaustion on the final ascent from the Cauca, on the toughest part of the snail trail (that's what they called the part of the trail that rose like a corkscrew) and were now the vultures' pleasure, but all the rest were good and healthy.

At the front of the long procession came Don Gabriel's son, Pedro Pablo, El Cojo, riding his white mule, and at his left was our ancestor, Isaías Ángel, that young man from El Retiro who from then on would be Echeverri's best friend, which I know from a couple of letters that were preserved at La Oculta until the night of the fire. Pilar, who throws everything out, thought those charred papers weren't worth the trouble of saving, and chucked them into a hole with all the debris. Echeverri and Míster Grey, during the journey, had talked to Isaías about the world and what was going on in it, for him so distant and strange. They told him about the war in North America, Lincoln's great battle to liberate the Negroes from slavery and unify the country; about the settlers in that huge country who received uncultivated lands in the west; sometimes barren lands and sometimes fertile lands, but with little rain to make them flourish; they told him about Europe and the new countries they were cooking up, big and prosperous and free, with Bismarck in Germany, with Garibaldi and Cavour in Italy. Míster Grey spoke nostalgically of his native Sweden and the sea of the Vikings, which he now had few hopes of ever seeing again. Here, in this wild, mountainous country where a hidden voice had called him, similar, if not greater, projects than those of Europe had yet to be realized: constructing a worthy, united, and free nation, where the space was shared out fairly and not arbitrarily as the Spaniards had done, and where everyone would have a house and land of their own, water, air, and home, because only the labor of individuals, combined with public works, created national wealth. It was no longer a time for violent conquests, or domination and extermination, but a time of pacific conquest. Things like that were also what he, El Cojo, wanted for Antioquia and for Felicina, the name he favored for the town: a promise of happiness, a sort of commune of free men, all with land, all proprietors without envy, with a couple of days a month of communal work. That would have to work well. They talked very animatedly, El Cojo pleased with the temperament and manners of the young man from El Retiro, and Isaías thrilled that the wise old man and young dreamer were opening his eyes to a wider world, and also happy to see the new land, the land where all would have land. That year, 1861, was a marvelous one in many parts of the world: people were breathing optimism, unity, liberty, friendship, the dreams that almost a century earlier the French Revolution had not been able to fulfill. El Cojo had read enlightened authors and said that with education and well-being, without abuses or injustice, people would be good. The Swede was less optimistic, he distrusted human nature, but he was pleased that there were young men with utopian dreams even in these rough tropical mountains, so far from what for him was the heart of the civilized world, his old Europe.

Three days before, when they arrived in Fredonia, El Cojo extended another act of goodwill toward Isaías and his family. Once they'd arrived in that town, and after the long conversations they'd had on the way from El Retiro, he had to confess that Don Santiago Santamaría was very rigid in the selection of the settlers and had therefore established a sort of quarantine for all those who aspired to live in the new town. Below Fredonia, in the Marsella hermitage, he left all the new families for a couple of weeks and gave them food and shelter, but put them under the observation of a priest and a barber who lived in the village. Those who drank, the lazy ones, those who didn't go to Mass or showed signs of bad tempers (the ones who hit and shouted at their wives, mistreated children or animals), were sent back to where they came from under the pretext that all the places in the Southwest were taken. Well-mannered, meek, hardworking, and patient Christians were allowed to carry on toward the Cauca. This quarantine was known as "the sieve," but El Cojo wasn't going to submit Isaías and his family to this test, and he let them go on, vouching for them, without making them fulfill Don Santiago's prerequisite. The rest of the families who'd come from various towns he left there for the required two weeks, and continued the journey with those who had already passed through the priest and barber's colander.

Maybe for this reason the Ángels were even more content and enthusiastic. Isaías exclaimed, excited and happy, that he had never seen such crystal-clear waters, such delicious *sabaleta* fish, such colorful birds, and most of all such inspiring air or such a blue sky. He could not believe that the Toledo of his ancestors was as luminous or as green. All his descendants have continued to repeat the same things like parrots, right down to me: that nowhere in the world, not even in Greece, is there a sky as blue as that of Jericó, when it's clear; the same blue that's only seen in a few Italian Renaissance paintings, Fra Angelico blue (as our writer friend Von Berenberg called it), and maybe in Madrid, on a few afternoons.

The climate – the sunny mornings – was perfect; the transparent and very clean air, the kind that dries sweat while one barely notices, refreshing the skin without cooling it down too much. Raquel, his wife, was riding sidesaddle on a little sorrel paso fino mare, a little ways behind. Pedro Pablo, El Cojo Echeverri, had lent them the mare, called Simpatía, which was his spare mount for when his main horse needed a rest, considering Raquel's condition. A couple of years later he sent the mare to their home with saddle and reins and all the gear, as a Christmas present on the 24th, and with that mare the Ángels of my family began to raise horses, that first mare was our Eve, our equine Lucy. With this single gesture of lending Simpatía, El Cojo had earned Isaías's eternal friendship and gratitude. They had so often mentioned their appreciation, the beauty of that first gesture, They had so often mentioned their appreciation, the beauty of that first gesture, that El Cojo ended up sending the whole horse as a gift, to reiterate the pleasure he'd derived from lending her to them. In spite of her pregnancy, Raquel had withstood the long journey from El Retiro well. They didn't know what sex the baby growing within her body was, and would only see five months later: he would have testicles, testifying to his virility, and would be called Elías, like one of his Abadi grandfathers who'd come from the Canary Islands.

Saying goodbye to her parents, hastily and unexpectedly, had been sad. Don Abel, her father, had blessed her four times, and four times had dried his tears with his handkerchief. Her mother, Barbarita, more phlegmatic and curt, had just said, "May things go well for you, my dear, and when you can, send news of that new town." Raquel also liked that new land that welcomed them with a hearty stew, with cheers and songs, with hats in the left hands and right hands outstretched. At the last moment two of Raquel's siblings had joined them as well, her younger brother Gregorio Máximo, and her older sister, Teresa, who were almost going hungry there in El Retiro. Don Abel, the shoemaker, had blessed them too, and Doña Barbarita had said the same thing to these two, "May things go well for you, my children, and Teresa, I hope you'll write when you have time." She hadn't asked Gregorio because, although he spoke well and clearly, he didn't know how to read or write. They came along under the pretext of helping their pregnant sister, and the only parting gift Don Abel could give them was a new pair of shoes each, "so they would go far." Teresa, who was twenty-eight years old, already had a spinster's look about her, and had been very attached to her sister since childhood. The boy was just fifteen, but tall and strong, handsome and a good worker, and El Cojo had welcomed him to the adventure of settling the Southwest. Gregorio Máximo would eventually marry one of the Restrepo girls, and would be the father of another Antonio, Antonio Abad, who would eventually be called Don Abad, the almost legendary patriarch of Jericó, who would found another lineage in these parts, of timid and kindly people, rather quiet, but not at all stupid, with lawyers, doctors, engineers, and brewers among them, and even the odd patchy man of letters.

Many years after this triumphant arrival in the new town, one of our ancestors, our great-grandmother, Merceditas Mejía, wanted to refute the rumors circulating in Jericó, that the Ángels and the Mejías (Mexías or Mesías, odious tongues claimed they were called), or the Abads (who, it was said, had been called Abadi), were descendants of converted Jews, the deicide race. For that reason, she spent the last old Spanish gold coins she had hidden behind a special tile in the kitchen, in an old velvet pouch, and gave them to Father Cadavid so that he would take them to Monsignor Arango Posada, who was thinking of traveling to Spain to undertake genealogical studies of various Antioqueña families. Through Father Cadavid, José Antonio's widow, great benefactress of the Jericó cathedral (her family had donated the Virgin's crown of precious gemstones) at the beginning of the century, began to receive little by little the replies arriving from the Iberian Peninsula. And the news was not very rosy, not for the Ángels or the Mejías or for the Abads or the Santamarías, whose children all bore these surnames and repeated them from memory, like a litany of saints. The Ángels could be traced back to a certain Rabbi Yehuda Abenxuxán, which didn't seem like very pure blood, to tell the truth, for all they'd done was change Abenxuxán to Santángel, which later in the Americas got shortened to Ángel, and the Abads descended from a certain Abadi sent into confinement in the Canary Islands, for religious fickleness, and the ancestors of the Santamarías and the Mejías he dared not even utter, more *conversos* than anybody. In light of this information, Monsignor Arango Posada recommended, from the dry and distant lands of Castille where he found himself, following a very old custom, dictated by modesty and prudence: "If you allow me to say so, esteemed Doña Merceditas, in this matter it would be best to let sleeping dogs lie, as they say over here, and I would rather counsel you and your family to be content in knowing that since the ancestors of your husband's family, and your own, arrived in Jericó, no one has ever doubted that you have all behaved with the utmost decorum, and very Christianly. Don't forget that after all Jesus was also of that wretched race, or at least his mother was, and that didn't prevent him from redeeming us all as brothers nor does it prevent us from venerating his sainted Virgin Mother and her patient husband Saint Joseph, or her mother Saint Anna, who taught him to read. But as far as the certificate that you wanted, it will be very difficult to get an authentic one, and in order to obtain it we would have to invent it, or pay a very high price to get them to give us one here in Spain, homemade, for certificates of cleanliness of blood are still issued, but the less authentic they are the more onerous the price, and I don't know if you want to leave Don Antonio's sons without any property, only in order to reply to murmurs you could simply ignore." Those monies were lost, Mamaditas used to say about those old coins that were not silver or nickel, but pure, solid gold. And meanwhile she kept giving alms to the poor, every Friday afternoon, and prayed to a litany of saints, and said her holy rosary, every day, and begged our sainted Virgin Mary and her sainted mother Anna and her husband the patient Saint Joseph, that no one find out that the surname Ángel used to be Santángel and before Santángel even worse, Abenxuxán.

PILAR

Lucas almost wasn't born; I was in labor for four days. The contractions started on Sunday night, and on Monday morning we called the doctor. Alberto went to the university because he was still studying back then. My obstetrician, Dr. Henao Posada, said that it was just starting and that first-time mothers' labors tended to be very long. I spent Monday at home, with contractions, but still with lots of time between each of them. My papá, who was very excited about his grandchild, stayed with me – more nervous than I was – and occasionally called the doctor to tell him how things were going. On Wednesday we went to the El Rosario Clinic and Dr. Henao examined me and said I was I don't know how many centimeters dilated; he declared that the baby would be born at dawn.

There was a tremendous rainstorm that evening, as there always is when something important is going to happen in my life, and at nine at night they took me into the delivery room because by then I was nine centimeters dilated. After pushing for more than an hour I was in so much pain that they had to give me an anesthetic. What happened after that I don't remember, but I've been told. It seems that after struggling for a long time with their hands, they tried to get the baby out with forceps; afterward with something like a plunger, like they use to unblock drains, a giant suction cup they attach to the baby's head and that deformed poor Lucas's skull. The forceps gave him a black bruise on his brow and damaged his left ear. There was no way: my pelvis was too narrow to have a baby the way you're supposed to. Dr. Henao went downstairs to ask permission of Alberto and my father to perform a caesarean. They pushed the baby back in, by hand, and sliced me open with an enormous incision, not like the caesareans they do these days, so discreet and slick they barely leave a scar, but a dreadful gash, like from the First World War. Alberto started to cry because he'd just read some old novel about a woman who dies in childbirth. Women were always dying in childbirth in the past, and children too. Papá says our species pays a high price for our big brains: with a lot of pain, lots of tearing, and high mortality at birth, because of the exaggerated dimensions of our heads. And that, on top of our being born before we can fend for ourselves, without being fully gestated, making for such a long rearing of such defenseless newborn creatures. Thank God my son was born in the second half of the twentieth century. When the anesthetic wore off and I came to back in the room, I saw a monster lying in the crib, with a horrible, pear-shaped head, covered in bruises all over his body. Giving birth isn't like that easy happiness they show in some movies; giving birth is tough, painful, full of blood, smells, and sweat and danger. A hundred years earlier we both would have died during that labor, my son and I. Not only that, but a hundred years ago I would have died seven times by now. And yet, there are still people who miss the past, the marvels of natural childbirth and the blessings of life in harmony with nature, without technology or science. Idiots.

A pediatrician came and started to examine Lucas. She looked worried and immediately took him to the special care nursery. She said he wasn't breathing properly, that his reflexes weren't perfect. She told me the baby was probably going to have some cerebral problem, with mental disabilities, because he had a lot of lesions on his head, deformed by the forceps. That was the day my mother-in-law began to suffer from *colerín calambroso*, that illness she never managed to get rid of. Papá told me, in dismay, that it didn't matter if the baby died, that I could have another one. That night the obstetrician, Henao Posada, came again, but he didn't agree with the pediatrician's diagnosis ("I was gentle. What happens is that babies are very delicate and noisy: they look like they've been mistreated, but they're strong too; they're tough, and the work of childbirth helps them to become pluckier.") and he went into the special care nursery. He went in without saying anything to anybody, without permission. He saw the infant wide-awake and restless, hooked up to an I.V. to keep him hydrated, and stuck a finger in my baby's mouth, to see if he'd suck. Right there the boy sucked strongly, and the doctor told a nun to bring a couple ounces of milk in a bottle, and gave them to him. When he came out, he asked that we not say anything to the pediatrician about what he'd said, but he reassured us by saying: "The child is perfect, what was wrong with him was hunger." The pediatrician went to examine him in the evening and found him looking much improved, and lively. She brought him to me in my room, saying that thanks to her care the baby was safe and sound, and all his vital signs were much better. When she handed him to me, Dr. Henao Posada winked at me from the corner of the room.

But in any case, Lucas was hideous; he looked like a boxer after losing a fight, with his eyes swollen and his whole face covered in bruises, scrapes, and scabs. He wasn't beautiful 'til he was about three or four months old. Luckily, everything he did was normal. He nursed normally, crawled normally, walked normally, started saying words at twelve months, and spoke perfectly by the age of three. The only strange thing was when he got a very high temperature he had convulsions. Later it happened again, at the worst moment.

At that time, Eva was in her second year of university and in love with Jackie; when her classes finished for the day, she'd come and visit me in the evenings and watch me feed Lucas, so beautiful, so chubby, so cute, and I know that she would have liked to have a baby too. Even though she was at the top of her class at university, just like at school, she looked at me and said, without saying it out loud, but in silence in the darkest part of her skull: me too, I want to have a baby too and breast-feed. But she had to wait 'til she graduated, got married for the first time, separated from her first husband (a selfish womanizer, only interested in power), got married again, and finally, when I already had three children, had her first pregnancy, which I was the only one to know about, and later made the decision not to have the baby. How sad, a baby that would have been an Einstein, a great doctor or a great physicist, I think, because he would have been the son of her husband the banker, who hated being a banker and would have liked to have been a mathematician, and of Eva, who won all the medals at school, but one day she told me, "I lost it," with a long, deep, dark look. "I lost it," and it was as if the baby had drowned at sea, as if that child had sunk to the bottom of the Pacific Ocean.

I don't know why she did it. I've always known that she didn't lose it but had it removed – and may God forgive her – out of fear of having so much responsibility, out of the terror of not being able to decide everything for herself but having to think about a child. I'm going to say just to myself here, without anyone hearing, and may God forgive me as well: out of selfishness. I've never told her, but on the subject of abortion I've never been in agreement with her. I accept abortions in cases of rape or if it's certain that the child is going to be born deformed or with some horrible illnesses that will make him suffer for his whole life, him and his family. But just like that, no. Maybe a fetus isn't the same as a person, but it's the same as a seed of a mango, and not even the most convinced abortion campaigner is going to deny that. Women know, even women who've had abortions. They would do it again, if necessary, yes, but they know it's a very difficult, very serious decision, almost impossible to make, and not because it's murder, but because it's the denial of something very beautiful, a life, a life that's just beginning, and life is better than death, always. Or not always, then, okay, but almost always. Eva came to understand later, much later, and she finally had a gorgeous child, Benjamín, Benji, but she had him without a father. I mean, without a father she was married to, because she had him with one of her husbands, the second one, but a long time after separating from him, and that's why Benji's last name is Bernal. Eva chose his father carefully, of that I am sure, for he's the director of an orchestra, and is cultured and good, though bad-tempered, and Eva asked him only for fertilization and his surname, as a special favor, because he hadn't had any children either, and he wanted them, even more if he didn't have to inconvenience himself by living with them, as he's a person who's always preferred to live alone. There are fathers like that, who prefer a more sporadic and less intense relationship with their children, not like Alberto, who seems like another mother to mine. Sometimes I think Eva, in her life, might have lost other babies, unintentionally or by choice, but without telling us. It's one of those mysteries that nobody really knows, and that some women take to the grave. I, on the other hand, have almost no mysteries, I tell almost everything.

I've never had an abortion, and it would never, ever occur to me to have one. After Lucas I had four more children, all normal, all caesareans. This used to be the usual thing, to have lots of children in a row, but not so much anymore. More and more I notice that I'm the unusual one. "It's just that you live according to the traditional family model," Eva said to me once, Eva, who sometimes talks like a book. *According to the traditional family model*, what a ridiculous phrase. She means I lived like Grandpa Josué and Grandma Miriam, married by the Church for life, without the slightest intention of ever separating, wedded not so much to each other, but to marriage, and giving birth to as many babies as God wanted to send them. She was trying to tell me that I'm a very conservative, old-fashioned stick-in-the-mud. Well so I am, but that's like saying I like to eat by candlelight, I get around by horse-drawn carriage, wear a wig and crinolines… I'm the odd one, yes, the only one who's only married once, as a virgin and in the church, and the only one who never thinks of separating, no matter what happens. The one who had five children by five caesareans and would have had more if Dr. Henao Posada hadn't told me that my uterus wall was as thin as paper and if I got pregnant again he wasn't going to keep me as a patient so he wouldn't have to watch me bleed to death.

That was when I decided to get my tubes tied, after the last caesarean, when Simón was born. I know the Church forbids it, but I went to see Father Gabriel and I asked him, Father Gabriel, do you want me to die? Of course not, he said. Does the Church want me to die? I asked, and he said: No, of course not. Then I have to have my fallopian tubes tied because if I get pregnant one more time, the doctor told me, he wouldn't even take care of me. Lots of women used to bleed to death a century ago, when there was no way to stop having children. And then Father Gabriel said he was going to consult with the bishop and the bishop gave me the authorization to have my tubes tied. Of course I'd already had the operation before Father Gabriel and the bishop gave me permission. I'm not an idiot. I asked them because they like to feel important, and I feel sorry for them thinking they're not anymore and that we don't even take them into consideration. And the thing is no one considers them anymore, not even me. I feel sorry for the Church, when I think about it. It's older and more outdated than me. A pachyderm, an endangered species. I see it when I go to Mass in Palermo: only us old folks go these days and it all seems like a pantomime, an act, at best a custom, but nobody gives a fig what the priest says, nobody really believes that the wine is blood, that the bread is the body of Christ, his real flesh, that confession saves your soul, or that not going to Mass on a Sunday is a mortal sin. I'm the only one who still believes in all that, or tries to believe it, because I lack faith and would like to have more. And who knows, the Church is a very old, very rich, very solid thing. Life takes many turns and maybe its power will come back. Or maybe it'll disappear entirely, nobody knows.

ANTONIO

I've found the birth and death certificates for almost all the Ángels in our family, since the first one who arrived in Antioquia, as well as marriage and baptismal certificates for all or almost all their children, even those who died before the age of two, who were the majority. Often they kept using the same name over and over again, as if they could replace a lost child, as if one could be reincarnated in the next until finally one of that name would grow up, cling to life, and reach old age. I could even tell you what they died of or how they were killed, the ones who reached adulthood, one by one. Isaías, Ismael's son, Abraham's grandson, died of bilious colic on the trail from La Mama and Jericó, on the back of a mule that was taking him to see Dr. Zoilo Mesa Toro, the first sawbones in the village, but he didn't get there in time and died on the way, fell off the mule as if struck by lightning, in the eighties of the nineteenth century, and his son Elías had to tie him to the saddle, half covered with four sacks, bent over the back of the mule, to take him into town, for his wake and funeral and burial. Raquel Abad, his widow, had the strength not to sell the recently cleared farms (La Judía, La Mama, and La Oculta) and to put them in the charge of her son, who had come of age not long before, our fourth known ancestor, Elías.

All Elías's brothers were taken away by the civil wars of the nineteenth century, recruited by force and lassoed in the village like cattle, sometimes in the service of the Conservative army and sometimes in the Liberal one, and they never returned to the village, either because they stayed somewhere else or, more than likely, because they were killed in battle. It was said that the recruits were taken to the sites of the battles tied hand and foot, and there they put a rifle in their hands and let them go, to try to kill more people on the enemy's side than on theirs. They were boys, almost children, scared to death, and if they fired those guns it wasn't for any just or unjust cause, but only to save their own skins. They were not fighting for liberty or for religion or for justice or to have their own country; they weren't fighting for the color of a political party, not caring whether it was blue or red; they were simply fighting for their lives. And thus the country sank deeper into backwardness and the lands became depopulated, unworked. Elías was spared, precisely because he was able to hide at La Oculta, the farm his father had bought shortly before he died. The farm was in such a strange spot on the mountain, a dip in the middle of the cordillera, almost invisible from any angle, and for that very reason it was and is a good hiding place, and its name itself means hidden: nobody arrives there who doesn't know the way perfectly, and from a distance it can't be seen. In those wars so many died and were killed, and so far from home, that sometimes the dead were left lying in the middle of a field, or in a swamp, or in the jungle, and the vultures would eat them. Or maybe they settled in distant lands, on the coast or on the eastern plains, and they never came back due to the shame of returning with blood on their hands from all the people they'd had to kill to be able to survive, or because they forgot the way home, their hearts hardened by war. From these wars there are interminable lists of names of boys who went by force and never returned. Those wars were almost never fought in Antioquia, where everyone was related and didn't want to kill each other for being Liberals or Tories, federalists or centrists, but the new towns of Antioquia had to contribute, against their will, lots of cannon fodder to stoke the bonfire of the old quarrels of the republic.

Elías, then, the second Ángel to take charge of La Oculta (and also to expand it by buying adjoining lots), the one spared from the civil wars because he could hide right there, was killed by falling off a rock, on May 15, 1906, up in La Mama, when he was explaining to José Antonio, his firstborn, what the exact boundaries of the farm were. From a secret cliff edge of

La Mama, leaning out over an abyss from a rocky outcrop, on the edge of the mountain range that faces the Cauca gorge, you can make out a section of La Oculta. It was the only place from which the farm could be seen in the distance, and that's why he was explaining where the boundaries were and how far away the white blotches they could see scattered about were their own cattle, which could be sold when they were fattened up, and how far the green rows of coffee and shade trees were theirs. He gave him this explanation, as if it were an involuntary testament, shortly before falling over the precipice. He spent several weeks hovering between life and death with fractured ribs and legs, and in the end he didn't make it. In those days a broken femur, when they didn't yet know how to surgically repair it, much less in a rural village, was a death sentence. Elías left two sons, José Antonio and Antonio Máximo, and a string of daughters whose names I'm not going to list here, but they all married locally and left descendants, or became nuns and died saintly deaths, like all the nuns of Jericó, from the Arcila girl, who took to the cloisters to atone for the deaths of the Trejo brothers, up to Mother Laura, the saint who prayed each night for the Liberal soldier who had killed her father. José Antonio inherited La Oculta, the lowland farm; his brother Antonio Máximo, La Mama and La Judía, the farms up in the highlands, for dairy cattle and potatoes. José Antonio was the most successful of all the Ángels, and the one who added the most land to La Oculta and cleared fields to sow good vegetable and coffee crops. He died young, of typhoid, in 1920, in his house in Jericó, in a bathtub filled with cold water they'd put him in to try to bring down his 107-degree fever, and when he stopped breathing, Josué, our grandfather, had to suspend his medical studies in Medellín to take charge of La Oculta and all the family businesses, which he ran well until the depression of the 1930s.

Grandpa Josué was a tall man, with an imposing demeanor, but timid and with gentle, almost sweet manners. Very decent and very fair, with a social conscience, he was the first in our family to declare himself a liberal in public and a Mason in secret, for which he was even excommunicated in Jericó. He was so furious when they excommunicated him that he rode right inside the church on horseback, as an act of independence and desecration. You excommunicated me? Swallow this little protest, which will never be forgotten in Jericó. He was also a womanizer, more than by vocation, by a strange magnetism he held over women. He didn't have to ask them, they asked him, and maybe this got him accustomed to intimacy and to an almost unconscious flirtation with them all, young and old, ugly and pretty. He was flirting until the day of his death, in the last week, with the nurses who took care of him in the clinic, and who liked to go into his room and look after him and laugh with him, a dying man.

Josué lived for more than eighty years and died in Medellín, in 1982, of cardiac arrest, after two heart attacks. I was present when he died, and my sister Pilar took charge of bathing and dressing his corpse, with my father's help. Jacobo had taken up the career his father had been forced to interrupt, almost as a duty to the lineage, so besides being the firstborn, he was a doctor. But in spite of being the firstborn, he received only one eighth of La Oculta. It was to be divided evenly between the eight heirs. His portion, however, perhaps in honor of his primogeniture, included the dilapidated shell of the old house beside the lake, with a few coffee fields and pastures to fatten calves, no more than fifty *cuadras* in total.

Jacobo, our father, died of pancreatitis in 1994, while his most beloved grandson, Pilar's eldest son, Lucas, was being held hostage by guerrillas. I am alive today, in my late forties, rapidly approaching my fifties, with a pretty healthy body and habits, but I could die at any moment like any one of us. It could be tomorrow, it could be twenty years hence, most likely I'll reach an age somewhere in between the 69 years my father reached and the 82 my grandfather died at. The only thing I know is that the year of my death will begin with 20 and be followed by two digits, certainly less than 50. All that will remain of me will be my notes on Jericó and an old coffee farm in Southwest Antioquia, if we manage to hold on to it until I die, and my bones get to be buried in the earth of La Oculta, in that place I call the tomb and Próspero prefers to refer to as "the resting place." Próspero always finds a Castilian word for things; what we, with our gringofied vocabulary, call the "deck," he calls the *tablao*; and *el descansadero* for the tomb, and *pudriero* for the septic tank. Yes, in the resting place I'm going to tire of resting forever, so dead, so inert, and as unconscious as a stone. Just like my ancestors, to whom I attempt to give voice, to resuscitate them for an instant in these words. In these words that are also air, that are also smoke, just the shadows of thought, but they last at least a little longer than flesh and our breath.

EVA

Long ago it was only male heirs who received and divided up the farms, because it was men who inherited the land, back then; the women got the houses in town and the old furniture, the dinner services, the beds, the dressers, the cutlery, and the silver trays, if they had such things, but not the land. Then that changed for good or ill. If women had been inheriting all along, like we do now, then there would barely be an acre left for each descendant.

All my father's sisters and brothers, all my uncles and aunts, sold their lots off bit by bit. It was very sad when they wanted to sell and we didn't have the money to buy them out. That's why what's left of La Oculta is not much land and not much else: a herd of dairy cattle, fourteen cows, and a few heifers to replace them. But nowadays milk isn't worth anything and it's very hard to break even on what we spend on concentrates, pasture, vaccinations, inseminations, and everything else. A dozen horses, because Alberto likes to go horseback riding, and everyone knows that horses don't bring in anything but pleasure and expenditure. We also have fifteen acres planted with coffee, which yield two crops a year, but that doesn't even bring in enough to pay Próspero, who's now almost as old as we are and at harvest time contracts day laborers to help him pick the beans. Another eighteen acres of teak plantation, but those trees can't be cut for another twenty years, so I don't think it'll be us who saws them up. And the garden around the house, with fruit trees and flowers, lots of flowers, a small forest of native trees and a path through the woods.

For me, the lake is the most important part of the farm. La Oculta Lake, as everybody calls it, looks natural and is as integrated into the landscape as the mountains, but it's actually artificial. Our grandfather Josué had it built in 1939, when he was 39 years old, since he was born with the century. Where the lake is now there was a natural swamp, where a few springs drained out, a marsh full of toads and mosquitos, especially in the rainy season, according to Grandma Miriam. Until it occurred to our grandfather to build a dam with rocks and earth and dig a channel from the stream called La Virgen, to fill it up with freshwater. La Virgen comes down from Jericó and traverses La Oculta, from one end to the other, until it feeds into La Cartama River. La Virgen, Cobo used to say, was like the spinal column of the farm, the backbone, and on each side was our land. Our grandfather said a piece of land with no water was worthless, and La Oculta had three streams, La Virgen, La Guamo, and La Doctora. Now we just have this little piece left, and La Virgen passes unseen through the lake, feeds it with freshwater, and carries on down the slope, to rejoin its main course. The other two streams now pertain to other people's land.

These days they'd probably not allow the lake to be built, and they'd even be right; you'd have to request permission from the municipality, from the Ministry of the Environment, from the Mining Ministry, from the indigenous peoples, but in 1939 you didn't have to request permission; a person did whatever they wanted on their own property. As a result of our grandfather's idea the unhealthy hollow filled up, the weeds died, the toads hid from so much water, the mosquitos went elsewhere, and there's the freshwater lake, big, black, imposing, as if it were eternal, as if it had been there for centuries and centuries. The only thing that frightens me is that one day the water will come rushing down with such force that it breaks the dam. If all that water suddenly gushed down the mountainside there would be a tragedy below: it would carry away the roadhouse, kill people and animals caught in its wake. When engineers come by I beg them to take a look at the dam, but they look and look and don't say anything. They don't want to commit themselves; they say it might last a century, ten centuries, or break tomorrow. The ground is unstable in these mountains where there are landslides, slippages, floods, and earthquakes. Sometimes I look at the lake for hours and although it feels eternal I know that one day it will be a muddy bed and a disaster: let it not happen to me, or to my sister or brother, let it not happen to my son or my grandchildren, I beg.

Many people have drowned in the lake. Many that we know of and probably others that we don't. In my count: Emilia, the youngest daughter of one of my grandparents' caretakers. A medical student who came up here to camp without permission, supposedly to study for an exam, and who dove into the lake for a swim and never came up again. He left a physiology textbook open, in the shade of a tree. A seminarian who was never found and who Próspero says is the ghost who walks the corridors and makes the floorboards creak even when there's nobody in the house. The Nadaist poet Amílcar Osorio, who didn't know how to swim, one night got drunk and dove into the darkness to die.

Well, that's what they say, that he was drunk, but according to my cousin Mario, who was with him that day, Amílkar U (as he signed his poems) hadn't had a single drink the night of his tragedy. Mario says that on February 12, 1985, around eight at night, the poet, a refined and intelligent man, had the strange idea of taking a boat out and rowing on the lake on a moonless night. He had been talking for the whole evening, without smoking or drinking anything, with two friends, Mario himself and Fabián. Shortly after dinner, and when Mario had already gone to bed, the poet decided to go out rowing on the lake. Nothing could be seen except the luminous splatter of fireflies. After a while of silent rowing, there was a splash, like someone falling or jumping into the water. And then a shout that came from the lake. The poet was shouting: "Fabián! Fabián, tell Mario I'm not going to make it!" Then there was silence. Mario jumped out of bed, startled by the shouts, and managed to see Amílcar's head that was still above the surface of the water. So he dove into the lake, to swim to him and pull him to shore. When he looked up, he saw the poet gazing at him, staring, melancholically, for some moments, and then he sank, very slowly. Forever. The next day they found him on the muddy bottom. Próspero touched him with a bamboo pole, while they probed the lake inch by inch, in the same boat Amílcar had used. In the poet's only published book, *Vana Stanza*, Amílkar U wrote of his drowned body among the water lilies, a sort of masculine Ophelia. In 1985, La Oculta Lake was covered in water lilies around the edges. Mario says that the morning they found him, Aurita López was talking with Amílkar U on the Cámara de Comercio radio station, broadcasting an interview she'd taped with him the previous week, about his only book. And while they pulled his dead body out of the lake, on the radio the poet was talking and talking, and spoke beautifully. That's how these things are. Later some crazy, scandal-loving *nadaístas* went so far as to say that Osorio had been murdered, drowned for fun. A lie as big and deep as the lake: slanderers, no one murdered him. He wanted to jump in the lake at night, and no one knows why.

Another one who drowned there was my cousin Carlos Fernando, my Uncle Javier's son, when they sold their share of the farm; that sale filled him with a cold, contained rage; he, who had been the most cheerful and most promising of all the cousins, couldn't accept that the farm had been sold, and began to do crazy, risky things, like scaling the crags with a cattle rope, up the steepest side of the range. And what he did one day was to fill a pair of saddlebags with big round stones, the kind the Cartama's full of and that are used for stable floors. One night, he drank a whole bottle of aguardiente, took out the canoe, paddled to the middle of the lake, and threw himself in with the saddlebags tied to his back. Divers had to come to bring him up, two days later, because he was so weighed down. Sometimes I take the same wooden canoe that Carlos used to kill himself and paddle around the lake thinking about him, our dear cousin who was going to be an eminent physician, but I realize that I would never commit suicide. It's just that so many things have happened in the lake that your heart beats faster just looking at it, and your memory gets stirred up with old stories, and absent presences of people who, although they're not here anymore, you can still sense.

ANTONIO

The first piece of news they received when they arrived was that the village had changed names, and would no longer be called Piedras or Felicina, but Jericó. There had been many arguments about that biblical name. The Echeverris defended the name Felicina; the Restrepos and the Jarmillos wanted it to be called Palestina; the Santamarías voted for Jericó. Finally there was a clear majority among the settlers who had held the first town meeting a few years before. The scrutineer had been the new parish priest, Joaquín Ignacio Naranjo, a short, fat, red-headed man from Zaragoza, recently sent to the town by the Bishop of Antioquia. They called him Father Naranjito, and he was the main banner-waver for the name Jericó, which was from the bible. Eighty-three voters had a part in the decision (only 82 men could vote, landowners with solid roots, and one widow with money), and Piedras only got eleven votes, those of the oldest residents, attached to the original name; Felicina, twenty-seven; Palestina, twelve; and Jericó, the majority, thirty-three, the widow among them, swept up by the priest's rhetoric and the support of Don Santiago, the founder. El Cojo Echeverri felt somewhat disappointed when he found out, but he wasn't a stubborn person and much less spiteful, so eventually he thought his utopian projects could be realized in a place called Jericó.

More than a year before Don Santiago had written to the bishop – with a not very original image, but still effective back then – telling him that a town without a priest was like a flock without a shepherd, and therefore urging him to send someone to take charge of the chapel, which was like the sheepfold of the village, even if it wasn't finished yet. The chapel was a shed with a few cedar benches and walls of comino planks, but it already had a bronze bell, donated by Don Santiago himself and hanging from a prop at the entrance to the temple, which was rung not just as a call to Mass, but also to summon all the inhabitants for any special occasion. Up until that year of 1861, the village had only received visiting priests, barely once a year, who came to baptize the babies born in the previous twelve months, marry those who were already cohabiting or those who could wait no longer to set up house together, and bless the dead who had been buried far and wide (in a field, up in the hills, in a yard), wherever they'd breathed their last breath. Now that he was the priest in residence, Father Naranjo had officially received the cemetery lot and the keys to the chapel, but the graveyard still had to be enclosed with a high wall and someone needed to be found who wanted to take on the job of gravedigger. A large lot had also been set aside for the construction of the presbytery on one side of the main plaza. To raise the money, he'd been selling special spaces in the cemetery, to build mausoleums, but these sales wouldn't start to come through until one of the town worthies died, someone with the means to import a marble statue and set a good example of funereal ostentation. Not caring that the land had been a donation from the founder, he had already turned death into a business, for the Church needed to make a living, and not just off the uncertain and timid alms of the parishioners. Tithes and offerings were very hard to collect, since Antioqueños have never liked to talk about their earnings. And for atheists, pederasts, suicides, and heretics, he was considering the garbage dump, to one side of the cemetery, squalid and stinking, watched over not by angels but by vultures, to serve as a warning to all.

Father Naranjito welcomed the new settlers with a Mass before lunch, so they could take communion without breaking vigil, and during the sermon gave a long explanation about the name Jericó, with quotes in Latin that no one understood, and perhaps for that very reason admired all the more. With his shrill little voice he told them that when they had crossed the Cauca, by the Paso de los Pobres, they had embarked on the same exploit that the Jewish people had realized by crossing the River Jordan. *Mysterium tremendum.* And that the walls of Jericho had fallen to let them enter, after the people had circled the city seven times (the seven days they'd taken to arrive there), and that all the riches of Jericó now belonged to them. *Intra tua vulnera absconde me.* He did want to advise the new inhabitants, indeed he did, that one part of the riches they found there, especially if these were gold (in mines or Indian tombs, *Ab maligno defende me*), must be handed over for the construction of the barely begun temple, so that it could have sturdy walls, a well-tiled dome and belfry, and a floor not of earth and sand, as now, but of fired-clay tiles or even, if possible, of fine travertine marble. This was very important to remember if they didn't want to suffer a Biblical curse. *No permittas me separari a te.*

Zaragoza, where the priest had been born, was a mining town full of slaves and rough overseers, and he seemed not to understand that this new population wanted to be very different; he carried on speaking with the same covetousness and the same tone with which he'd spoken to the miners of his hometown.

The recently arrived farmhands and artisans looked in astonishment at the old settlers, who were no less surprised to hear this rash sermon. And they were even more surprised when the priest said that, finally, he was going to recite a prayer to counteract the Lord's terrible prophecy. And there he read a passage from the Book of Joshua, in the Latin of the Vulgate, which he then translated into Spanish, more or less saying: "Cursed before the Lord be the man who rises up and rebuilds this city, Jericho. With the loss of his firstborn son he shall lay the foundation thereof and with the loss of his youngest son shall he set up its gates." The chosen reading did not seem like a very good omen, but the priest clarified that the prophecy was no longer valid since Christ had come to redeem the Jewish people and all men, and that it was now possible to build a new Jericó without danger and without fear of the terrible curse being fulfilled, as long as – he repeated, wagging his finger like someone brandishing a whip – the recent arrivals, Jericoians of the New Alliance (that's what he called them), donated a tenth of their earnings in gold and silver, a share of their animals and crops, and finished building the Lord's new temple as soon as possible.

The settlers didn't understand the sermon too well, but they did note the priest's covetousness, and looked at each other raising their eyebrows, scratching their heads, and shrugging their shoulders. But, to be on the safe side, they handed over – from the little they brought with them – alms toward the future church. The priest, finally, after almost an hour of dark words, sent them out with the well-worn formula: *Ite in pace missa est.* The parishioners, who the whole time had been dreaming of lunch (the scent of the *sancocho* reached them from the pots on the street), came out hungry, hot, with their hats in hand, almost in a stampede, to line up in front of the steaming stew.

EVA

The first thing I did when I got out of the clinic was try to get in touch with Próspero. I wanted to see him, talk to him, and I sent him a message to come to Medellín any day he could to have a meal with me, so he could tell me what had happened after my escape across the lake. Pilar had gone to the farm and had already told me what had happened to Próspero that night, but I wanted to know all the details. As for Los Músicos, Pilar hadn't been too clear, but she said some of the neighbors were going to help her convince them to leave us alone. The fact is Pilar and my mamá went back after a year, and hired builders in Jericó and Palermo, and brought in material, without anyone doing anything to stop them, and that was very mysterious to me, and no matter how many times I asked Pilar I never got a satisfactory answer. Suddenly Los Músicos who almost murdered me were no longer our enemies but almost allies. I couldn't bear the idea, but I kept my mouth shut.

Próspero took the bus that stops at the roadhouse, came up to Medellín, and had lunch with me in my apartment in his clean

Sunday clothes. Almost without tasting a bite of food, Próspero told me, to start with, something he hadn't been able to tell me when I'd gone there the last time. That Los Músicos had already been close to La Oculta – a few months before – committing horrible, monstrous deeds, doing what they maybe would have done to me if I hadn't escaped through the lake. Or to him and Berta, if a miracle hadn't happened, a miracle Próspero attributed to the ghost of the drowned seminarian.

It had happened one day at dusk. He had seen the black jeeps go up the track toward Casablanca and they'd stopped on the other side of the lake, on the small, level clearing where there was room to park cars. Próspero told me that he spied on them for two or three hours, from behind the Virgin's rock. The first thing he saw was them dragging out three young guys with their hands tied with wire from the backs of the jeeps. Próspero managed to recognize one of them, the son of the barber in Palermo, but he didn't know the other two, and so he thought they must be from Támesis or La Pintada, or some other little village, but not Palermo or Jericó. Los Músicos were drinking aguardiente and smoking marijuana at the same time as they beat, kicked, and swore at the kids. They'd left the doors of the vehicles open and played music: salsa, merengue, *vallenatos*.

He heard them working the kids over from dusk until night had fallen. When it got dark, they turned on the headlights of the jeeps. The three boys howled with pain, begged for help; the thugs shouted and their nasty words could be heard above the music: disgusting filth, threats, swear words, mocking, and curses. "They were martyring them," Próspero told me, with one of his beautiful old-fashioned words. "The *paracos* were martyring them, Doña Eva," that's what he said, "and I didn't want to tell you when you were there because all I wanted to do was forget about that; it would have been better never to have seen it. And also because I was scared, because in Palermo everyone says that nobody can say anything about what's going on, that we all have to swallow our words. Fear and fury; fury at the cowardice of not being able to do anything." Próspero didn't dare approach the place, and hardly even raised his head, but he could hear everything from behind the rock with his heart in his throat.

He heard them say: "You going to talk or not, you son of a bitch; tell us or I'll rip your nuts off with these pliers, fucking scum." They were smoking, knocking back the aguardiente, asking them questions, turning up or turning down the music, but the boys only screamed and begged them not to kill them. From the back of one of the jeeps they took out a chainsaw and started it up. It made a deafening noise, "like when they're felling a cedar or when a plane flies over very low to take photos," said Próspero. They started it up, revved it, and shoved it near the boys' necks, with its atrocious buzzing. They laughed evilly like madmen; the air smelled of *bazuco*, liquor, and marijuana. Próspero couldn't look: he heard over the music and the chainsaw noise, he smelled, he sensed, he imagined. At some point they turned off the chainsaw. They stubbed out their cigarettes on the boys and burnt them with their lighters. "I'm gonna light your ear on fire, haha haha, look how well this torch burns with all the grease, look at how black it's getting, like a pig's ear!" The boys screamed and cried and begged: "We didn't do anything, I swear on my mother we didn't do anything, the worst we ever did was maybe steal a sack of oranges." The others said they were thieves, guerrillas, snitches. Finally Próspero began to smell the iron scent of blood, and a sound of machete blows or stabbing, because the men said they weren't going to waste bullets on those lowlifes. By then it was very dark and the moans started to grow weaker, the last screams, the gurgling, the death rattles. Then the chainsaws started up again to chop them into pieces, to leave the bodies in bits scattered on the ground, carved up like beef cattle. Próspero didn't know what was worse, the noise or the iron blood smell. The last thing they did was hack off their heads with the chainsaw and kick them into the ditch. They started the engines of their cars. They left them naked, in pieces, tortured, thrown on the side of the road that goes up to Casablanca. The police came the next day to gather up the bodies in plastic bags, after Próspero called it in on the radiotelephone. On top of the body of one of the young guys, they left a sign that said:

We Músicos are cleaning up the zone of guerrillas, drug addicts, and pickpockets. Gentlemen farmers, don't forget to send your contributions on the tenth of each month.

They left another, which Próspero took from the chest of the other boy and that one he put away, with brown coagulated bloodstains on it:

I died for being a snitch and a blabbermouth and because I'm a guerrilla bastard.

We couldn't eat a single thing, Próspero and I, that day, remembering what they'd done to those three boys, and then the visit they'd paid us, the night I'd been reading in the hammock. He'd woken up when they shot Gaspar and had looked out the window. He'd grabbed his machete, just like the night the guerrillas had come to the farm for Lucas, but then he'd put it back in its sheath. What could he do?

"I was very afraid for you, Doña Eva, but I couldn't go outside. When I saw them go in holding their flashlights and pistols, I knew they were going to kill you, and I also knew that if I appeared at that moment, they would have killed me too. I didn't turn on any lights and locked us inside. I hugged Doña Berta, both of us scared to death, crying quietly. After a while I realized something strange was happening because I heard those guys arguing; then we heard more shots and thought they'd killed you, but then they said *that old witch had flown away on them*, forgive me, those were their words, and I prayed to heaven that you'd had time to hide in the woods. I never imagined that you would have dived into the lake; if I dove into the lake without a lifejacket I'd drown, especially at night. After a while they came and broke down our door, dragged us out and made me open the main bedroom, your mamá and the doctor's room. I lied and told them that I didn't have a key to that room, that it was always sealed up. Then they went down the track and came back up carrying a chainsaw; you don't know what I felt when I saw that, I thought they were going to chop us up in pieces. But no, what they wanted was to cut a hole in the door to your mother's room, to get in. They started up the chainsaw and began to slash it, but right there came the first miracle: they ran out of gas, the chainsaw's tank was empty.

"Then they asked me for the keys to your car, the jeep. I went to where you always leave them and handed them over. Then they asked me for a hose and chopped off a piece of it with a machete, stuck it into the gas tank of your car, the Palomo, as I used to call your little white jeep, and started to suck on the other end to fill up a milking bucket. At first they said it was to put gasoline in the chainsaw. They were drunk or high or on crack and weren't thinking straight, every few minutes they changed their plans. Whether they should kill us or not, whether they should steal things from the main bedroom, look for the documents, they said all kinds of things, crazy things, like they were deranged. Luckily they got sick of sucking gasoline and spitting it out, if they'd managed to get any more they would have burned down the whole house. Because the new plan was no longer filling up the chainsaw, but setting the house on fire. They took the little gasoline they'd managed to get out, half a bucket, and sprayed it around on the deck and the edge of the house until they ran out. They tied Berta and me to the window bars of the bathroom beside the stables. I realized what they were planning to do and told them they were going to burn us alive if they left us tied up there. They laughed and slapped and kicked us. 'Before you were thankful we didn't kill you right away,' they said. 'Don't worry, the smoke will get you before the flames do.' They made a trail of gasoline from your jeep and set it alight; there was a smell of gasoline everywhere and then heat, blazes, a noise like a gust of hot wind blowing through. The first to burn was your car, the Palomo, which exploded pretty quickly with a horrendous noise, like a bomb, but the gas started to burn all over the place then. The heat was awful, but neither the smoke nor the flames reached where we were tied up. If the wind had been coming from the other direction the whole house would have burned down and we would have been burned alive or asphyxiated. Luckily the wind was blowing the other way, off the lake, that was the miracle of the sainted drowned seminarian, and the flames went out toward the garden, instead of coming inside the house, they went up into the branches of the trees. That's why everything didn't burn down, just a part, and that's why we weren't burned alive. The gasoline burned up quickly, but later some wooden things kept burning, the straw roof, the floorboards, and the posts of the deck, which burned up completely, and some chairs, tables, benches, part of the wooden floorboards of the corridors.

"We spent the whole night tied up until Juan, from the roadhouse, showed up, having heard noises in the night. He came up at about eight in the morning to see what had happened and untied us and asked in terror what had happened and where you were. Later Pedro, the caretaker of La Pava, rode up. He came on a black mare, Noche, which he had to return to Casablanca. He told us you'd gone on the seven o'clock bus and by the grace of God should be arriving in Medellín by then. That you'd looked terrible, all bruised and scraped, but that you were fine, that you were alive. We were pleased to know they hadn't been able to harm you, and put out whatever was still smoldering with water and dragged the charred things out onto the patio. Berta begged me, and is still begging me, to leave La Oculta. But where are we supposed to go at this stage, already as old as we are. We don't have a house to go to, and our kids aren't going to take it well if we show up to live with them. I still have almost ten years till I can retire, you know. So we're going to carry on enduring, and hope one day things change. Doña Pilar has already been there and she said not to worry, they're going to rebuild the house and Los Músicos aren't going to come back to bother us. I don't know what she did to arrange that, but I hope it's true."

PILAR

We didn't use to live year-round at La Oculta, but in order not to lose it we moved here. We had to rent out our house in Medellín to be able to buy food and cover everyday expenses, and moved everything to La Oculta, which is our real house, where we'd always dreamed of returning, if the region ever became less dangerous. Now we live here, comfortably, on Alberto's retirement pension, which is not great, but helps, and the rent from the Medellín house, where a Jehovah's Witness temple now operates. Oh, if not for them, those blessed Jehovah's Witnesses, so noisy, shouting about all the silly things they believe in… they believe the world is going to end. I believe the world is going to end one day too, of course, but not so soon. The house, which thirty years ago was beautiful, is ruined now, it's like a big shed without walls, a storehouse where they don't stockpile things but believers. We had to allow them to knock down the walls because if not, they wouldn't have rented it from us. And there they get stirred up, pray, sing, and jump around. They shout about the world ending half hysterically, that our

Lord's silver head is already peeking over the mountains of the East to come and judge the living and the dead, most of all the living who don't think like they do, who haven't seen the light of truth, but in the meantime they pay us a good rent, and thanks to that we can live at La Oculta. Sometimes, on long weekends and at Easter, we rent it out to groups of doctors, or pilots, or to big families nostalgic for the family farms that no longer exist, and we have to go and stay at Eva's place in Medellín, or with one of our kids, because renting it out for holidays is what enables us to pay for the repairs the house constantly needs. We return and have to air out the mattresses because they don't smell of us, but of other people's sweat, other people's sex. A handful of glasses and plates always get broken, a few forks and teaspoons always get lost, or a toilet gets plugged up with toilet paper or pads. A lame horse, a broken chair. Half the money from renting it out goes to pay for what they damage, and I work on the repairs until the next time we rent it out, which is like another earthquake. Eva's the one who insists we rent out the house, because it matters less to her, she doesn't even think of her own bed as hers, and her monthly contribution gets considerably lowered. Toño, who's so far away, doesn't say anything, and doesn't even notice, because he's a man and men don't notice these things.

The rental of the Medellín house, however, is a long-term contract, five years, and now we don't worry about what they do to it; it's lost to us as a house, and we no longer think they're damaging or defiling it. That house, now converted into a temple and storehouse, is all we have left of the years of opulence, when Alberto was the director of Gacela Plastics, one of the many businesses his father left them. It was a factory that made cheap toys, very cheap. They were distributed in the poorest towns and villages of Colombia, but then it was bankrupted when people began to smuggle in toys from China; there was no way to compete with the Chinese. Nobody can explain how they can produce things so cheaply; it seems like workers must be forced to work fifteen-hour days over there and they pay them terribly, almost like slaves. Well, that's what people say, I have no idea. Besides, Alberto, being such a good person, and being so influenced by my father, who just for saying people should be paid fairly was called a communist, accepted everything the workers asked for in the petitions they brought every two years with their union. Education subsidies for workers' children: okay. June bonus and Christmas bonus: okay. Housing subsidies so they could get their own houses, of course, why not, that's what Cobo thought correct. A cafeteria in the factory serving lunch and dinner, yes. Shorter work days and the whole weekend free like rich people: fine. My papá said it was possible to build harmony between proprietors and workers if the bosses were fair. Between my dad's altruistic advice, the union, and the

Chinese, the factory went bust. Alberto pampered the union for ten years, and when the business went bankrupt from having given so many bonuses and benefits and a soccer field and a gym and education and housing subsidies, when they had to close the plant because the toys didn't sell anymore, when they had to liquidate the land the factory stood on to pay the social benefits of the laid-off workers, they put up posters with Alberto's photo, saying: "Alberto Gil, enemy and murderer of the working class." Oh, my heaven-sent sweetheart, how awful. That was the first blow, when Gacela went bankrupt. And then we lost almost everything we had left when the guerrillas kidnapped Lucas right here at La Oculta.

Lucas was seventeen when he was taken and turned eighteen in captivity. We marked the day from afar, lighting candles at home, and singing *happy birthday* to him over the radio. I've never suffered as much as during those nine months that he was held in the jungle. Alberto hasn't entirely recovered either; and not because of the money, that was the least of it, since at least we were able to save him, but the anguish, the awful nights and worse days. Since then he's become quieter, more disappointed in the world and people, and takes more refuge in music and his fruit trees, especially the mandarins and the oranges. All day he prunes, fertilizes, brushes the trunks of the citrus trees, removes lichen and mosses, affectionately caresses the fruits as they grow, and maybe that's why there are no sweeter or more delicious oranges than the ones from La Oculta. Not even Spanish, Sicilian, or Egyptian ones can compete with his.

We are born believing that people are good, until life comes along to prove us wrong and show us that yes, there are good people, but there are also many very bad people, with evil intentions, calculating, underhanded, and ungrateful. People with tiny hearts, not like a mango but like a bitter, unripe little guava. Until Lucas was kidnapped I believed with the optimists that the good people are the majority; yeah right, Lucas getting kidnapped was the worst rebuttal I could ever have gotten: every day with the fear that those bandits – idealists, those fighting for a fairer society, good revolutionaries – would kill him. What were we guilty of, tell me? Having a forty- or fifty-acre farm that gave us nothing but expenses and a couple of jobs? Was it our fault that we were less poor than the majority of Colombians?

They phoned us and threatened to kill him if we didn't hand over the ransom money quickly. One day, in about the third month since they'd taken him, they sent us the first photograph of him, holding the previous Sunday's *El Colombiano* newspaper, as proof he was still alive. Not much later they sent more photos where Lucas looks sad, pale, with a chain around his right ankle, as thin as a noodle, beaten like a dog, head down, with a lost look in his eyes. As we sold things we offered them more and more money, a hundred thousand, two hundred thousand, three hundred thousand dollars, but they wouldn't accept, they wanted a million, which we didn't have, not even by selling everything, including the house in Medellín and La Oculta. We had people from a foundation, *País Libre*, by our sides, advising us on how to negotiate, and who told us to gradually increase the amount, but slowly. It was heartbreaking.

The night that the guerrillas came almost everybody was asleep, except for the men and me, as I always stayed up listening to music and talking with them until they went to bed. Suddenly we heard a racket by the stream and the dogs started to bark. We turned off the music to hear better and the lights so we could see what was going on. Everyone knows that night is daytime for thieves, that the worst things almost always happen at night. Several flashlight beams were coming up the gully. The radiotelephone didn't work at that hour, and there was no one to call to ask for help. We went to wake up Próspero, but nobody here has ever had any weapons or anything, and the only thing Próspero could grab was a machete in need of sharpening which he had to hand over to them as soon as they pointed a rifle at him. They came in through the stables, single file, as if they didn't mean us any harm, as if they were just passing through on their way up the hill, to Támesis or Jericó, impressively calm, as if they were anesthetized, with a coldness and faces as hard and inexpressive as I've ever seen in my entire life. You could tell their souls were damaged by hatred and resentment. They were walking hatred; they were people – men and women – who had killed and watched others kill. Who had tortured and been tortured. They had their hearts wrapped in an icy bark. They didn't speak, they grunted with cold rage, gave brief orders as if they were in barracks and we were all recruits. I remember that Eva's boyfriend at the time locked himself in one of the bathrooms, with several women and the youngest children, Benji, Florencia, and Simón, trembling with fear, crying in terror. Eva broke up with him as soon as they got back to Medellín, because she couldn't stand such cowardice. Alberto, Lucas, Eva, Próspero, and I went out to the stable. Toño was in New York. We tried to reason with them, but it was impossible, they just grunted and barked, trained their guns on us. They wouldn't let us speak: "Shut up, you old bitch; shut up, you rich bastard!" That was all they said to us.

They put a sack over Lucas's head. He was the one who suggested they take him because he was in good shape. He played basketball and was seventeen years old. He offered himself so they wouldn't take me, who they'd asked for ("Which one of you is Pilar Ángel?"), for back then everyone thought I was the owner of La Oculta, because I was the one who went most, and contracted day laborers and carpenters and builders in Jericó or

Palermo. Lucas said that Alberto and I were sick, that I smoked and got tired out after walking ten steps, but if they took him it would be the same. I didn't want to let him, but the guerrillas liked the idea. "How old are you?" they asked him, and he lied and said he'd just turned eighteen. Alberto objected to their taking Lucas, said no, that they should take him, that he was strong because he rode horses and bikes, but the guerrillas chose Lucas and when they heard the word horses told Próspero to go and get them. And we barely got a chance to say goodbye, but we looked at each other with streaming eyes, before they tied the sack over his head. I screamed: "Why are you putting that on him?" "So he doesn't learn the way," they said. "But he already knows it," I answered and they shut me up with a shove. They also said that it wasn't a kidnapping, but rather a retention to guarantee the payment of a revolutionary tax. That the faster we got the money together, the sooner they'd return the boy.

They went on uphill with him, toward Casablanca, toward the chilly uplands; they forced us to saddle horses for them to take. The horses came back at dawn, on their own, without riders, saddles sideways, in search of their feeding trough. Later Lucas told us how he and three guerrillas rode up the crags until the horses could go no further because it was too steep, and from there they'd kept walking for the rest of the night, until they reached a camp. As well as the sack over his head, while they walked they'd kept him tied up, like a calf, so he wouldn't escape into the woods. Every day they moved him to a different place, farther and farther away, higher and higher up into the mountain range, and at night they chained him to a tree.

They'd given him a plastic sheet for the rain, and a blanket, but Lucas says that what he felt most all the time he was kidnapped was intense cold, the kind of cold that goes right to your bones and that made him shiver like jelly, cold that didn't abate even in daytime, because he almost never saw any sunlight, under the canopy of the trees. Finally they stayed put in some part of the Citará mountains, and more kidnapped people were brought there. For some weeks, at least, he had someone to talk to, because he was not allowed to speak to the guerrilla fighters, much less the female ones. Those were the least awful weeks, he told us, because one of the kidnapped men, Señor Angulo, knew about orchids and birds, and he taught him how to recognize them, by their calls, by color, and by the leaves. One of the guards even lent them a small telescope to distinguish the bromeliads from the orchids on the tree branches. Later, unfortunately, but fortunately for him, they'd let that knowledgeable and calm Señor Angulo go free. But we didn't know anything about this; we were in Medellín, with no news, receiving the odd phone call to frighten us and repeat the ransom terms.

We got up early every day to try to sell something to be able to pay. That was when my papá despaired of ever having sympathized with the communists, of having been so understanding with Cuba, with real socialism, and began to hate the guerrillas. When they sent us a photo of Lucas without a shirt on (so skinny his ribs stuck out), with a sad look on his face, and with an iron manacle and chain around his ankle, Papá began to drink outrageously. He would have whiskey for breakfast, or rum or aguardiente. His eyes were always red, his face looked congested, his nose was red and deformed, and his hands shook. Day and night Papá cried like a baby because Lucas was his eldest grandchild, and his favorite ever since almost dying at birth. My papá also wanted to sell the apartment where he lived with Mamá, the car, the furniture, whatever would keep them from killing Lucas. At night we thought about how frightened Lucas must be in the jungle, about the wound he must have from the slave manacle fastened on his ankle, and we'd think about what would happen if it got infected, if he got tetanus or leishmaniasis, as many did in the mountains when they went barefoot, about his solitude, the horrible way he must be being treated, and his sadness; we cried when we thought about what he'd be eating. In the early mornings we'd go to a radio station that broadcast a program called *The Voices of Seizure*, and we'd send him messages of encouragement, trying to keep our voices from breaking, but with our hearts broken in two. Lucas told us later that the guerrillas let him listen to a small transistor radio, and hearing our voices in the early hours was his only solace during that time, which made him think we hadn't forgotten him, and the guerrillas were lying, to weaken him, when they said that we didn't care about his life and didn't want to spend a single peso to save him. That he might as well join them since he didn't have a mother or father anymore. Another day, by phone, they told us that Lucas had been having attacks, that he went into convulsions and thrashed around and foamed at the mouth. We didn't know whether to believe them or not, the *País Libre* people said it was most likely a lie, but it turned out to be true; he'd developed epilepsy while he was in the jungle, we don't know whether from his suffering, or as a delayed consequence of his birth trauma, or something else.

It was really hard, living without living, sleeping without sleeping, eating without eating, dreaming horrible dreams every night; nothing was really real, for life went on, but my mind was always on something else, always elsewhere, in the jungle, in the solitude of that open-air prison where they had Lucas without any contact with anyone, or any affection. Alberto and I sold everything we had left, except the house where we still lived, which was spared. We sold a really good warehouse that we rented out in the industrial part of Medellín; a lot in La Estrella; an apartment in Laureles that my mother-in-law, Doña Helena, had left us; my car, which was brand-new, a portion of the bakery, which Mamá had given me and that Eva bought for much more than it was worth. We sold everything to pay. Everything except our house and La Oculta, which anyway didn't belong to us kids yet but was still my father's. La Oculta was not sold; the farm is not for sale. I have this engraved like a tattoo upon my memory: La Oculta is not for sale.

Papá got sick while Lucas was kidnapped. When they told us about the attacks and convulsions over the phone, Papá screamed. He got sick from suffering and drinking because he couldn't bear that the guerrillas had kidnapped his eldest grandson, his *ñaña*, the child he loved most in the world. He'd talked to all the contacts he had in the leftist movements in Medellín, in Bogotá, but with no results, nobody paid him any attention. Lucas had already been held for half a year and had just turned eighteen in the jungle, when Papá developed pancreatitis. I was so anguished, without any news of Lucas, no proof he was alive, and suddenly the person I most loved, my greatest support at that moment, my papá, was in the clinic, with pancreatitis, dying. Sometimes misfortunes come like that, all together, they don't space themselves out over the years, but arrive all at once, as joys also do sometimes, one after the other. Life is made up of gusts of happiness and gusts of sadness and long years of calm, with no surprises, which are the best.

Papá knew that he was dying, he told Eva and me himself: "The pancreas is the seat of the soul, *mijitas*; if the pancreas gets damaged, it's time to get ready for the funeral straight away." I had no life either; every night counting money we'd collected in cash: a hundred thousand, two hundred thousand, three hundred thousand dollars. In the end they settled for four hundred and thirty thousand, which was all we could raise, at the same time as my papá was dying. Those were the months in which I most clearly perceived the tragedy of life, of motherhood, of the love we have for our children, for our parents, which caused me that unbearable heartbreak, and double, side by side: my son in captivity and my father dying. Maybe the worst moment was when I had to go on the radio and tell Lucas out loud that Cobo, his grandpa, had died the night before, but that he'd left him a message advising him to be very strong, and optimistic, and hold on, because now very soon, they would let him go. Those things people say, always the same ones in those circumstances, because only ordinary phrases seem to tell the truth when life is horrendous. That my papá's soul was accompanying him and helping him from heaven, that's what I told him, because I believed it, I still believe it, and I can almost see him up there watching, watching me, protecting me, happy that I've now come to live on his farm, on his land, at La Oculta.

One afternoon like any other afternoon, a day like all the days of those horrible months, I went to visit my father at the clinic. He was confined to bed, down to skin and bones, his profile sharp, insatiably thirsty, and his complexion was that sallow color of death. He couldn't stand up or walk as far as the bathroom and that made him feel offended, humiliated. When I was not dealing with the humiliations of hasty sales and loans from speculators to get together the ransom money for Lucas, I'd go to the hospital. I sat with him for at least a little while each day as long as he was sick. I passed him the bedpan every five minutes because he felt a constant need to urinate, but he barely managed to get out, with much effort, sweating, a few drops of a thick, cloudy, dismal liquid. Like lynx urine, he'd say. We'd dampen his lips, always burning and dry, with a wet cloth. Eva came to visit him too, even more than me, and took turns with my mamá to stay overnight. Toño came late, men are like that, they're almost never any use at all when someone gets ill. He arrived for the final days, when the orchestra finally gave him leave, even though they were in the middle of a series of very important concerts that week; it cost him a promotion to the second violins. He arrived from New York virtually just to say goodbye, because Dr. Correa said there was no longer anything they could do and he always told us the truth, though not coldly like most doctors, but gently, and that's why we're still so fond of him. On that same trip, I'll never forget, Toño brought a briefcase full of dollars that Jon was lending us for the ransom; he smuggled it in, without declaring the money, and if they'd found it he would have ended up in prison as a money launderer, which was all we needed. We received Jon's thousand hundred-dollar bills and we kept them for several weeks in the safe at Mamá's bakery, stuffed inside black X-ray bags and in a briefcase, ready to use them if necessary. Fortunately, in the end we didn't have to, and we returned it all. It was in the same briefcase for years, in the bakery, because Toño was scared to travel with such a large amount of cash. Finally Jon decided to buy some Botero drawings with that money, and they converted the hundred thousand dollars into three sheets of Guarro laid paper, with a series of drawings of interiors (a kitchen, a living room, a bedroom), rolled up in a cardboard tube. They say one day they'll donate those drawings – which they like more than his oils – to the Jericó Museum of Art.

My papá also went to the radio station to record messages to Lucas, or phoned them in, with his tongue thick, half drunk, to beg his forgiveness, always asking his forgiveness, although he never said exactly what for. He begged his left-wing friends to help, to talk to the guerrilla leaders, to tell them that Lucas was the grandson of a leftist, of a revolutionary, but they all turned their backs on him. He devoted himself to heavy drinking, in order to endure it. And he would scream insults at the guerrillas, drunkenly in the street, and insult himself with the same curses that he used against them.

One of those afternoons, the same as any other, in the hospital, I was sitting with him but with my back to him. He was breathing badly, with an oxygen mask, and they were giving him a saline solution to hydrate him, and some morphine to keep him sedated. At that moment I was looking out the window of the hospital room, concentrating on the rain, on the wind, for an immense, furious downpour was falling, with thunder and lightning that echoed through the air and gushing water forming yellow rivers in the streets. I was thinking of Lucas outside, under that icy shower pouring from the sky. Suddenly, Cobo (Lucas was the one who started calling him Cobo when he was first learning to talk) asked me to come over to the bed and came out with something I'd never expected. He told me, with a barely audible voice, almost a murmur: "My love, I have to ask you something very special that might sound strange to you." And I said: "What, Papi? I'll do whatever you want, you know I'd do anything for you, but what is it?" Then he said, very slowly, looking straight at me with his gentle, blue eyes: "What I want to ask you is that you never sell La Oculta, not even if – when

I die – your mother and brother and sister say you can sell it to raise the ransom money for Lucas. This is what I want to ask you: that you take charge of La Oculta never being sold, not now or ever while you're alive. And that you make Lucas promise, when he gets back, and when he inherits it from you, that he won't sell it either." "All right, Papi, but why?" I asked. He said that the farm was all we had, that the farm was the land that had fallen to us in the struggle of life and we couldn't hand it over to anybody, no matter what; that his ancestors had arrived in Antioquia with nothing, with only the hope of a better life. And that La Oculta is what had given them a decent life. La Oculta had given them education, work, liberty, independence, the feeling of having a place in the world to leave and to come back to, a place to live for and a place to die. And that couldn't be lost for anything in the world, not even the most beloved person in the whole family, and that was Lucas. He told me that I, his eldest child, would have to sacrifice my eldest if necessary, to defend our land. He also told me where he wanted to be buried, on the farm, and asked not to be cremated, he didn't like the idea of cremation, just like Toño now. That he didn't want a tomb but just a hole in the ground, without any marker, at most an unpolished, round, black stone, from one of the streams, he said. And that we should wrap him, or his bones, in a simple shroud, in a white sheet. I began to cry, my silent tears fell warm and slowly onto the yellow skin and bones of my papá, but I agreed. And my papá cried just like me, in silence, because we were saying goodbye forever, and he was asking me to be more attached to a wretched piece of ground than to a person. He was asking me to endure, for La Oculta, his death and even the death of my son. I didn't understand him, frankly, though now that I'm old I understand much better.

I asked my papá if we couldn't sell La Oculta if one day we were starving to death, and he said precisely for that reason, no; that if one day we were starving to death, we could alleviate our hunger by farming the land of La Oculta. That I should imagine that one day – due to a solar storm, a meteorite, a computer catastrophe – we were left without electricity for ten years; there wouldn't be any gasoline, or food, or news, or anything. In the cities people would kill out of desperation, rage, and hunger. Only those who had farms would be able to save themselves with land to cultivate, horses to get around on, cows to milk, pigs to fatten, hens for eggs, and firewood for cooking. Or think of a virus like ebola, or an airborne contagion; it would also be necessary to hide from the plague in a remote place, like in the Middle Ages. At any moment the time could come back when men had to rely on nothing but their hands, without technology, facing nature, as in the distant past. And that's why we had to defend it however we could, always, as if we could go back to being like the Indians of the Amazon and like the first men, our ancestors. I didn't really understand him, but he kept talking, it seemed to me, like a biblical prophet announcing a misfortune and at the same time saying, on the day of the Flood, how we had to build Noah's ark. That very evening my papá slipped into a coma and two or three days later he died; he didn't speak again, and Lucas never again saw his grandfather alive.

When we could finally arrange the handover of the ransom money, which was a total odyssey (we had to take the cash hidden inside rubber tires to a zone in the jungle on the border between Antioquia and Chocó), and they set him free, skinny and wan, with a bushy beard and a festering sore on his right ankle, months old, which left him with a dark scar for life, with convulsions that hit him from one moment to the next, the first person he asked for was Cobo. He didn't understand how Cobo could have died while he was held hostage in the mountains, because he had left him healthy and robust. He wasn't listening to the radio the day we gave him the news, and even though other companions in captivity had repeated the news to him, he hadn't wanted to believe that Cobo had died while he was kidnapped. I have never known, as old as I am, a grandchild who loved his grandfather so much, or a grandfather who loved a grandson more. He'd been buried for a month and a half when they freed Lucas, and Lucas didn't know whether to not forgive himself or not forgive his grandfather for having died like that. We told him, he died when they had you in the jungle, he died of his pain for you. And then Lucas sat in a corner, very quietly, with his eyes closed, and finally he said that this was worse than the kidnapping, worse than being chained up day and night like a dog or a slave. Later we went to the cemetery and Lucas sat all morning on top of Cobo's grave. At the cemetery I told him what he'd said about La Oculta, and he listened to me again in silence. Later he promised that one day he'd take Cobo's bones there, to the place he wanted to be, wrapped in a white sheet, and that he'd put a big, round, black, unpolished stone from the stream on top of the place. That was a long time ago, when we couldn't even go to La Oculta to sleep, afraid of being kidnapped or killed. Much less could we think of taking Cobo's remains there. We could go once in a while, by day, to take Próspero some money, but without telling him ahead of time, and returning before nightfall. We wouldn't even drive there, but went by bus, dressed as campesinas, Eva and I, like people going to the village to visit their families. The whole region was plagued with guerrillas and if someone slept overnight they'd be kidnapped. Later the paramilitaries arrived, they said to clean up the zone, and yes, they cleaned out the guerrillas, and we could go back, but then it started to fill up with them and the corpses of their victims, and we could see that they were even worse than the guerrillas, more bloodthirsty. But anyway, we resisted, we hoped, we were able to hang on to the farm, and here I am, here we are, living here. Lucas comes here every once in a while without fear, with his children, my grandchildren, and he takes them for walks and explains why this farm is so important to our whole family, and he teaches them to swim and to ride, and I feel that the thread that began with my grandparents and continued through Cobo and through me, still lives, through Lucas and his children, and will continue through his children's children, like in those biblical litanies that Toño likes.

ANTONIO

The siesta ended with a start because the church bell rang again; after the priest's sermon, after the feast of stew and a siesta, came the lay sermon. Don Santiago Santamaría was going to speak to them. He walked toward the dais that sometimes served as the altar, took off his white, woven straw hat, cleared his throat, and began to speak in the second-person plural, something still used in those days, especially in speeches:

"Jericoians of this new alliance. Forgive a man of few words and few sparks addressing you, but that is what my friend and partner in this enterprise, Don Gabriel Echeverri, as well as the residents who've been here longest, desired. Doña Quiteria and I, and all the inhabitants, extend our warmest welcome, not to this village, which barely exists yet, but to this dream, to this collective endeavor for the future of Southwest Antioquia.

"The first thing I should tell you," he added, smiling and pointing to the clear, blue sky and the idyllic, tropical temperature at two thousand meters, "is that for anyone who doesn't like the climate, there's still time to leave and reach the first inn on the road, in Palo Cabildo, before nightfall, or even go as far as the Trappist monks in Tejada, who'll lend you a niche to sleep in."

Here he paused rhetorically and, seeing that nobody left, carried on: "Well, then, if we are staying, it shall be to work very hard, from sunup till sundown and with no excuses, under rain or hail, with scorching sun or frost and dew. In these solitudes everything is yet to be done, and what needs to be done shall be done solely with the strength of our arms. In this new town we have only one thing: the future. I wish to clarify, as much to the laymen as to the clergy," and here he looked at Father Naranjito directly, "that we are not nor can we be miners or panhandlers or tomb raiders, but only settlers. Those who want to dedicate themselves to the hazardous occupation of mining can carry on south, for there are mines down there. Sleep here in town, if you wish, but first thing tomorrow take your deceptive trail. Go to Marmato, to Riosucio, even to the Chocó, or turn north and go to Segovia or to Buriticá (there indeed are mountains of gold), but go away from here. We have not come here to pan for gold or to desecrate graves. Nor have we come here to conquer, that is, to dominate and kill or humiliate Indians. The conquistadors passed this way already, two hundred years ago, and didn't even leave Indians to humiliate; they either exterminated them or chased them all away. If there were any here, they would be welcome in this endeavor to colonize a land in its raw state. We have not come here to dominate anyone, much less to enslave: the black and mulatto people among us should feel free from now on. I see a pair of black brothers from a distant region, recently liberated from the ignominy of slavery; well, to you I say the same: work the land and be welcome here in this new town of free men. We have not come here to play cards or dice or to drink aguardiente, that is, to enrich ourselves on luck or to traffic in vices that bring men low. And we have not come alone, but with women, or to marry the women already here, for there will not be servile work, but familial work. In Jericó, we don't want bachelors, and any man older than twenty-five who hasn't found a wife will be charged a singleton tax, because single women are aplenty in this world of wars; so, young men, find yourselves a wife, for we haven't come here to waste time or to desire our neighbors' wives, but to care for and pamper our own, and to procreate many children with her. Here we shall not be judged by the color of our skin, but by the sweat of our brow, and may the sun tan all our hides, for there is no better school in life than the elements. We have come here because we wanted to, but we'll only stay if we have strong will and patience…

"Here my godson, El Cojo, Don Gabriel's son, has suggested that the lands be distributed immediately, and in identical-sized plots to each family. He is a very good man, an idealist, but an unrealistic dreamer. His father and I do not believe in anything given away. We believe that those who've been able to amass some savings in their lives deserve more land, and those who are just starting out will have to make a greater effort. The largest pieces of land, suitable for farms, ranches, and even productive estates, will be sold very cheaply, and furthermore, those of you who already have the money for a down payment can pay in installments, and with no interest, over the course of years. When will this good fortune occur? Very soon, after a brief period during which we'll see which of you are truly hardworking people of good conduct. Those who've come to drink, gamble, or idle away your hours, can head back the way you came. If anyone wants to go, let him go now, and may the Virgin accompany him!

"This business of handing over plots of land, or entrusting larger pieces of land at a giveaway price, we are not doing just because we are good or very stupid men, but because it is a business which over time will benefit us. We don't want our lands and our families to face the same fate as the Aranzazu family, in the south of Antioquia, who finally had great extensions of their lands expropriated by the state because they had not been capable of exploiting them. Or worse, what is happening to the Villegas family, who have had people invading their properties for years and now spend their lives in court cases and disputes, paying expensive lawyers in Bogotá to take their cases before the government, fighting against settlers well established on other people's lands, which they consider their own, and who are not going to be removed by fair means or foul.

"We also have faith that commerce will bring some traffic to the region; there are already many muleteers who pass this way, and take to the south news of what is brewing here. Jericó's fame will spread far and wide. And things will go very well for some of you, not so well for others, and for some, may heaven grant it shall be very few, it won't go well at all. Be that as it may, what we hope is that merit will do better than sharpness, hard work better than cunning. Here there are no suspicions or secrets; everything is open. You all, in receiving, in the very moment of receiving, for having had the valor to come all the way here, are giving too, for you are giving your work in exchange for uncertainty, your present in exchange for the future. So you must not be humble, nor humble yourselves, but feel your-selves proprietors and protagonists in a work of progress in these virgin lands.

"We cannot promise felicity or prosperity, and that is why our town will not be called Felicina, as our utopian godson wished, always so virtuous and dreamy, but we do have firm confidence that work is better than idleness and laziness, at least almost always. And I am now at your disposal to resolve whatever doubt or question might occur to any of you. That is all. Oh, one last thing: as you'll have noticed, in Jericó there is no prison and no police, there is no mayor, no judges, no notary. The government in Medellín has named me a justice of the peace so I can settle any dispute or difference that might arise between settlers, whether it's a matter of water rights, boundary lines, drunkenness, or jealousy. I expect all of your good conduct will defer as long as possible the arrival of those institutions, the arrival of which will indicate certain development, undoubtedly, but also the beginning of problems, disagreements, and disputes. One day here there will also be judges, constables, mayors, one day there'll be a jailhouse, guards, and police, we'll even have to have a gravedigger and break the ground of the cemetery one day, but the later the better, for I hope no one has come here in much hurry to die, and that we'll all die of wrinkles, the least horrible of deaths," he concluded with a smile.

One of the recent arrivals, José Bernardo Londoño, who came with seven offspring, asked if there was a school. Don Santiago said there wasn't one yet, but they were in a hurry to build one and already had a lot reserved, donated by his friend Echeverri. A town, he said, is not just houses and people. A true town needs to have a church, a theater, a school, and places to get together and converse. But most of all a school, so the children can learn to add up, subtract, and express themselves well. If among the new arrivals there was someone who was good at reading, writing, and sums, and who also liked to teach, they could immediately be named teacher and be put in charge of the school, which between them they'd all start to build. He, for a start, would also donate a chalkboard and desks, plus a monthly salary, for the first year. Later they'd see if they could all contribute to pay the teacher. At that moment Father Naranjito asked for the floor and said that a school was a very good idea for the boys and that he would offer to teach religion and biblical history. But as far as the girls were concerned, he thought they should open a separate establishment where they'd be taught gardening, embroidery, cooking, and at most basic notions of how to add and subtract to be able to help with the administration of the home. Reading, on the other hand, was not a good idea for girls, as he had seen how they grew careless of their duties when they got caught up in sinful novels and immoral stories that damaged their behavior. Here, El Cojo Echeverri, with his face contorted with rage, interrupted the priest brusquely: "Look, Father, for the moment there is no way to build two schools here, but what we'll do is begin with them all together, little men and little women, and if we eventually see that the latter are little brutes and only fit for sewing and cooking, we'll make them their own separate school, where they can learn the things you suggest: embroidery, gardening, and culinary arts. But for now, let the boys and girls all start together, don't you think, godfather? Remember what Governor Faciolince said, about ten years ago: 'In Turkey where women are debased and degraded, men are likewise, debased slaves. In France where woman is queen, liberty wields everywhere her sovereign rule.'"

"We shall do as my godson suggests, and later we'll see," said Don Santiago. Father Naranjito made the expression of one resigned to the error of others: he raised his eyes toward heaven and lowered his head with feigned humility. Teresa, Raquel's sister who had also come from La Ceja, raised her hand and offered to be the teacher. There was also a man, Jorge Orlando Melo, who, according to those who had been walking with him, knew absolutely everything anyone might ask, on any subject. Don Santiago, after asking both of them a couple of questions, named the woman teacher and Melo professor and principal, and had them step forward to introduce them to everyone. One of the first works undertaken a few days later, communally, everyone putting in a day's work, was the construction of the new school, on a plot behind the future church. Almost all our ancestors who were born in Jericó studied there, starting with Elías (son of Isaías) and José Antonio (son of Elías). The last were Grandpa Josué (son of José Antonio) and my papá, Jacobo Ángel, son of Josué. Not me, though, I was born and raised in Medellín, but with our eyes always turned toward Jericó.

Something that always inspired wonder in travelers who passed through Southwest Antioquia in the second half of the nineteenth century was the healthy look of the people, the great number of children the women gave birth to, and the good size, strength, and posture of the inhabitants. Boussingault admired their strong constitution and Schenck said that nowhere in the republic were there "taller or more athletic figures than the inhabitants of the mountains, or prettier women with healthier colors or such agreeable appearance." There was no great secret in this, I don't think, just something very simple: good food and healthy, hygienic habits.

My grandfather said that they taught them at school to think of the flags of Antioquia and Colombia at mealtimes, in the following manner: "We need to eat something white (rice, arepa, grits, milk, cheese), something green (vegetables and salads), something red (beans, meat, fruit, chocolate), and something yellow (eggs, plantain, corn, cassava, arracacha, potatoes, other fruits)." At this point everyone would always ask about blue, and the answer was very simple: "The blue is nothing more than the pure, fresh water from the mountain springs, uncontaminated by human excrement or animal manure."

The diet of the Antioquia mountains was simple and frugal, but complete and balanced: every night, in every house, whether the women wore fine shawls or rough ponchos, beans were served, an excellent source of protein, which cares for the neurons. *Mazamorra*, or corn porridge, was always there for dessert, sometimes with guava cake or at least with pieces of *panela*, or raw sugar loaf, which supplies energy. Beef and pork, when the new farms were cleared, began to be abundantly available, and not all of it was exported to the mines down south. The hard thing was preserving it, but salt was brought in by mule train from El Retiro, and the meat was dried in the sun in strips which would later be ground between two stones. Ground meat, or powdered meat as we've always called it, sprinkled over beans, sometimes crowned with an egg fried in pork dripping, was the most appetizing dish in the world, especially when complemented by ripe plantain, baked or fried in slices, which gave a sweet touch to the whole meal. At midday they might add that same powdered meat to the rice soup, which would have a bit of chopped potato in it, and on a separate plate some slices of ripe tomato with grated cabbage, cilantro, and a squeeze of lime, and ripe avocados if they were in season. And always a white or yellow arepa on the side, the way they'd have bread in the Old World, because, as a German traveler put it, "where corn doesn't grow, neither do Antioqueños."

The clothing, according to descriptions in documents from the time, was simple: "Men wore pants and a long cotton jacket, a palm-straw hat, like a Panama hat, but locally made (in Aguadas or Sopetrán), plus a poncho and the indispensable *carriel*, the shoulder bag typical of the region. Women wore short skirts and the same hats as the men, their hair in long braids hanging down their backs. Some wore black merino wool shawls with long silk fringes. Everyone went barefoot, rich and poor, and only wore shoes, which they found tight and bothersome, for very special occasions." My grandfather always told us that his grandfather, despite being one of the most important men in town, always went barefoot, and that's how he is in the only full photo of him that we still have, a daguerreotype damaged by damp and mold, in his elegant suit with his calloused, rough feet sticking out.

His great-grandfather, Isaías, with Gregorio – his wife's brother, who was still a minor and planned to save up for a while before getting married and choosing his own plot – began to clear the first piece of land he was awarded. They could saw the best trees between the two of them, but they didn't know what to do with so much oak, comino, and cedar wood. Since they didn't want to burn it, they piled up the logs under a roof, to protect them from the rain, to wait for the day when they could use the wood. After chopping down the trees and hauling away the logs, they burned the stubble that was left, and planted the first seeds in the ash-enriched soil, plantain, corn, beans, arracacha, and potatoes. After two crops they let grass grow and put two or three black-eared, white calves on the patch. Meanwhile they cleared another patch of woodland. What they grew was mainly to eat, but they would also take some of the products to the new town, on mules, to sell on market day, or to exchange with artisans for tools, or for work with recently arrived young settlers.

In the yard of their house in town, which over the years became a walled-in garden, the Ángels constructed a pigpen where they fattened swine on leftovers and products from La Judía and La Mama (the first two farms they cleared) they couldn't sell on market day: worm-eaten carrots, potatoes drilled by *mojojoi*, moth-nibbled beans, extra plantains. Every six months, drivers arrived to take the pigs down south to the gold mines, where people didn't produce food, but money, and it was easier to get a good price for them. That's why it was so important to keep the road to the south clean and paved – at least in the worst sections – for without that road there was no way to get their products out. In the other direction, the road, which came from Medellín and rose up over La Cabaña from the Cauca, began to carry fine timber. The Santamarías and Echeverris charged a tax for the wood or animals taken down the road. All merchandise had a fee to be paid. Many years later, at the edges of town they planted the first coffee shrubs, and those plants arrived with the promise and the dream of a product that, finally, would give them something more than mere subsistence.

Cultivating coffee had been the idea of a visionary priest, Father Cadavid, who arrived in Jericó in 1875, to replace Father Naranjito, and through his tireless initiatives had been like a third founder of the town. He was an energetic man full of ideas who had read about the fever over that drink in Europe and the United States, and so he distributed plants to many campesinos and taught them how to use the seeds and grow the crop. In Jericó, as in other parts of the country, he also ordered the penitence of planting hundreds of coffee seedlings, or thousands, if the sin was a very grave one. The paradox was that after a number of years the very sinful people did a lot better than those who never sinned. A few years later Father Cadavid was the one to import the first coffee thresher, and there they bought the crop from the campesinos. Elías, the firstborn son of Isaías, was one of the first to grow coffee, on the highest part of La Oculta, which was his father's then and he would inherit at his death, soon afterward. He planted so much coffee that in town he was known more as a sinner than as a coffee grower.

The people of Jericó were conservative and puritanical: they did not tolerate billiards, forbade cockpits and bullfights. Adultery was not easy in a town where everyone knew everyone by first and last names. There were only three prostitutes (María Medallas, Malena, and María Esther) who lived together on the outskirts – ruled by the old madam, Margot, who had retired and become an adviser on intimate matters and a successful businesswoman – and who took the virginity, at the end of the nineteenth century, of nine out of every ten teenage boys in Jericó. Since old and young men owed this debt of initiation to them, they were tolerated with certain sympathy, as one tolerates a beauty spot on one's body. Even the wives thought it better that their husbands and sons unburdened themselves with public women than with their neighbors' wives.

Not everything was easy, because there are wise guys and barefaced liars everywhere. There were some very clever men who took advantage of the stupider ones, or the needier ones, and gradually accumulated lands, bought at a pittance, or sometimes through illegal sophistry, in order to get control of greater expanses. The cemetery began to fill up little by little, because old age and diseases arrived. Widows were the ones who most often had to give up their lands at the price they were offered, or old couples who'd lost their sons to the civil wars and didn't have the incentive or the means to hold on to the land. Others hadn't done well due to bad luck (there was a plague that destroyed all the tobacco leaves in the hot lowlands), or even due to laziness. After a while, some sons of those who had been property owners were day laborers (earning very low wages), or renters or sharecroppers on other people's lands. There were even cases of poor cousins working for rich cousins.

Isaías Ángel had arrived young, vigorous, and full of dreams at twenty-four years of age. By forty-two he had seven children (two sons and five daughters), La Judía and La Mama in full production, and the straw house in Jericó had its wooden walls thickly plastered, the poor stools had been replaced by furniture carved out of the fine wood from his own lands. Toward 1880 the small village was becoming a fair-sized town, one of the fastest growing in the whole republic, with almost ten thousand souls. His eldest son, Elías, who had arrived in El Retiro traveling in total comfort in the warm womb of his mother, was now twenty-one years old – he'd just reached the age of majority – and had received a basic education at the school from the now very elderly Melo.

The first Ángel born in Jericó, above all else, was agreeable, honorable, and hardworking. From La Mama, Isaías, his father, had worked his way gradually down toward the Cauca, clearing the trees and underbrush, and had discovered a spot with good air and a good view, full of crystal-clear waters, halfway between the chilly uplands and the tropical lowlands. A hidden spot. Which is why, when he bought it, quite cheaply, from one of Don Santiago Santamaría's many sons, he called the place the hideaway, La Oculta. That happened, as I've said already, on December 2, 1886, and we still have the papers, handwritten by a notary in Fredonia, in the voluptuous calligraphy of the time.

EVA

When a man is a womanizer they say he's successful with women; I would say, rather, that he has had success with none of them, because the good thing – I suppose – would be to fall in love and stay in love. All my life I've felt sorry for Don Juans. In this sense, I could say that my life with men has been entirely successful, or rather a complete failure, a failure of success, a disaster, depending on how you look at it. Although I've fallen in and out of love many times, I've never been a Doña Juana. I always fell in love looking for someone who would bring out the best in me, at the same time as I would bring out the best in him, and I've fallen out of love when I've seen that it wasn't worth it, for they didn't know how to give or receive, or they didn't love me the way I wanted to be loved, or they didn't like the way I loved them. I had all the men I loved, at least for a while, even though they were later frightened by me, by my freedom, and by the way I am, and they ran away in terror. We women can have many men, as many as we want, or almost, but we don't tell anyone, because it does us no good.

Not Pilar. Pilar is made of different stuff, older, tougher, the stuff of my grandmothers or my aunts, the ebony or carob wood of my great-grandmothers. The only man she's ever had is Alberto. And, like my aunts, like my mamá, and all my grandmothers going back as far as you want, all she does is improve her garden, pray, look after her children or grandchildren and arrange the house, cook, and decorate. She was never interested in studying. Less in reading: she reads little and slowly. Talking about politics gets on her nerves and strikes her as bad manners. Religion is a bad subject as well, she doesn't like to argue, and is simply Catholic like her elders. She crosses herself and goes to Mass like she gets dressed or drinks water every day: it's a duty and that's all it is, something she doesn't think about or argue about, she just does it, like brushing her teeth. She thinks divorce is a huge stupidity, according to her, marriages always go from bad to worse: the second husband is worse than the first, the third worse than the second, the fourth worse than the third, and so on and so on until you end up in a solitary old age. Just like the husbands. For her the important thing is to choose well the first time and stick with it. Her recipe for long-lasting marriage is very simple, she says, and according to her our Grandma Miriam gave it to her before she got married: "Mijita, always say yes to your husband, never contradict him, but always do what you want to do." That's how she is with Alberto, she never contradicts him and never pays him any mind.

At the farm, with us, something very similar happens. She always says that she'll do what we decide between the three of us siblings, after arguing for hours and hours, but then she does whatever she wants, and since she's the one who lives there, she always gets her way. She spends her life arranging the house and the surroundings in a continuous frenzy, like an ant constructing or reconstructing her anthill, untiring. She caresses the house the way she caresses her husband. I think she sometimes knocks things down so she can spend her time putting them back up again, injures to cure, because the worst thing that can happen to her is to have to keep still. She drives poor Próspero crazy with requests: move this for me over there, help me clean this wall, let's whitewash this section of that wall, bring a pair of pliers so we can pull these nails out, let's move those staghorn ferns to another tree, let's plant a basil bed, another of cilantro, and one of parsley, plant some peppers, melons, and eggplants, chop down that tree, cover that window, oil the hinges of the stable doors… Anything not to keep still. And she goes racing off to Medellín, flying in the jeep when her children or grandchildren, friends or husband, call her, to help them with something.

Pilar, when she's not arranging things in the old house, is embarking on improvements and changes to the landscape, moving fences, flattening hills, pruning trees or planting trees, planting a new type of coffee with higher yields, combatting the beetles that eat the hearts of the royal palms, moving stones from one place to another, canvassing the neighbors for contributions to repair the road, which always gets damaged by the winter rains. And if she's not busy with those things, she's helping someone who's ill, taking an injured person to the hospital, bringing a midwife to an expectant mother, or preparing a corpse, though only when it's someone in our own family or someone very close to her heart. Doing favors, giving gifts, helping others' lives to be a little easier, turning her own into madness. I see this for a single hour and I get exhausted just from watching her. No, I've never wanted to be like that.

When I was very young they invented safe, latex condoms and the pill, feminism grew in strength, but none of those inventions had any influence on Pilar: she never used any methods of controlling her fertility, not even the rhythm method, and she had all the children God chose to send her and she always thought feminism was an exaggeration that was going to mean the death of marriage. For me it was different: the pill and antibiotics took some fears away, and feminism made me aware of how men had oppressed us (when Pilar was born, women didn't even have the right to vote yet), and I've always been freer with my body, although I've always taken care of myself, and I didn't do with it what my grandmothers would have recommended. I resolved that I was not going to be the way women have always been in my country: slaves to men and slaves to themselves, to their desires to arrange their domestic worlds and nothing further, to their husbands and children, instead of helping to improve the whole world.

I've lived a different way, and not just in relation to men and love, but also in relation to what the majority of people think. I confronted the traditionalists who criticized my way of being, I fought with them and tried to change at least those who were closest to me. I seduced, allowed myself to be seduced, kissed, danced, and sometimes went to bed. I took as my motto that every person is the proprietor of her own body and did what I wanted with it rather than what my husband might have wanted. I have never agreed with men simply to keep them happy in their illusion of power and dominion. No, I am audacious with them, and contradict them, and if they get bossy or demanding I stop them cold, though affectionately: they can make their own coffee and juice, they can pour the water or wine and serve the dessert. They have two hands just like us.

I didn't believe the nuns at school when they told us (I can still hear Sister Fernanda saying it), "Girls, never forget that your body is a temple." A temple, a temple, and what is a temple, a marble glacier, a stone slab, a confessional. They didn't say the same thing to the boys, no, not to them, they were taught to go to brothels, as if their bodies weren't going to become ill, until in my generation, finally, we could have boyfriends and go to bed with them without getting pregnant, and they didn't have to keep exploiting the poverty and desperation of prostitutes, or at least that's what I hope. Maybe the liberation of women will end the business of prostitution, though I doubt it, not even in Sweden has that sorrow ended. Or maybe there are cases when prostitution is a remedy for a necessity. There are lots of men who can't find anyone to sleep with, and perhaps there are always women willing to resolve – as a well-paid job – this problem for crippled, abnormal, or old men. It seems such a complex problem that I've even joined study groups on prostitution, and we haven't been able to agree on whether it should be banned or not.

I lived as only men had lived before: free to move around, to choose, to try out. And it seems right to me, fairer, less unequal. If I feel like going to bed with a man, I find one I like. If they were polygamous, then we can be polyandrous, and if they don't like it, they can go find a temple. I've been left; I left some of them. I've changed lives the way a snake changes skins; I leave behind the withered, dry one and put on another, which I hope is fresh and new, ready to live again. That's how a woman's life can be nowadays, at least, and if someone criticizes me for having left my husbands, for not having adapted submissively to their demands and mistreatment, let them criticize, and let them grin and bear it as well because the time for humility and submission is over. Families – luckily – are no longer what they were; a couple who stays together for their whole lives, no matter what happens, understanding each other or not, sleeping together or not, loving and respecting each other or despising and rejecting each other, some even beaten, together forever, no, not that. What horror. Couples getting bored together, couples in a restaurant saying: "Let's whisper the rosary so people think we're having a conversation," dying of boredom, of tedium, of spite.

I am third-hand; and the men I've had, all of them, have also had previous owners. These days almost everyone is secondhand or third, either widowed or most often separated after failed attempts. It doesn't matter to me, I think it's preferable. In Medellín they say – about cars – that the best brand is new. It might be true about cars, but not for marriage, I don't agree. Virginity, now that we have antibiotics and contraceptives, no longer makes sense, and was never a big deal to me. I never asked a partner if he was a virgin (I wouldn't have liked it if he was) and they didn't ask me either; it was obvious I wasn't, and if they'd complained about that they would have felt a burst of laughter on their noses, disdainful laughter, who do you think you are.

Husbands, what we call husbands, I've only had three: the president (who wasn't president then and in my opinion should never have reached that position where he's done more harm than good), the conductor, and the banker. I haven't gone from bad to worse, as Pilar says; the first was the worst, the second the best, and the third was the middling one. The president was not president or anything close to it when I met him, but everyone knew he was going places, though not that far, because super intelligent he was not; he was just astute, arrogant, sure of himself, sharp, and almost without scruples. He had a dark, frightening side, which he kept hidden, a concealed capacity for violence, undoubtedly pitiless, and without regrets, truly Machiavellian. A madness that escaped from him, and that he had within, lying in wait, like a monster inside him. But this could only be clearly seen when he was drunk, then his most sincere and deepest demon came out, a will to dominate and a deaf rage if he was not obeyed, which frightened me. An alpha male, tough, implacable, full of testosterone. Tall, about six foot three, with a booming voice that intimidated people at the first syllable, surer of himself than a shark that smells blood.

His friends called him "minister" from an early age. Minister of this and minister of that, because he liked to listen to and give speeches from the time he was in primary school. Left-wing or right-wing speeches, it didn't matter, but always speeches full of big words, the kind of words Colombians capitalize: the People and the Fatherland and Justice and Liberty and the Church and Enterprise, and whatever.

When he reached the presidency he called me and said, maybe a year after taking office: "Evita, my dear, let's get together." And we got together. Even though he was president of a pernicious government, I didn't refuse.

We arranged to meet on a Thursday at La Oculta and he arrived by helicopter. He concocted a visit to some town, Jardín or Bolívar or Tarso, I can't remember which, to inaugurate a school or a slaughterhouse, more likely a slaughterhouse than a school, and decided – he told his wife – "to spend the night at the estate of some old classmates." A lawyer, he's one of those who says spend the night instead of sleep, estate instead of farm, deceased instead of dead, classmate instead of friend, steed instead of horse, educational institute instead of school, and other idiocies like that. Whenever I see him I have to tell him: try to speak normally, dear, in Spanish, with your unseeing people and your sex-trade workers and your afro-descendants you're not going to win me over. I've always said blind people, whores, and blacks, which is normal and has nothing bad about it because at least it's clear. As for the friends with whom the president was going to spend the night, that was me, and I'd arrived by jeep a few hours earlier. In reality he didn't have friends, much less female friends: he had allies, subordinates, party members, people who loved or hated him for his acts, many who feared his powerful fist, or thrived in his shadow, but real friends, not a single one, just lots of servants, secretaries, and subordinates. A flick of the president's finger was enough to behead whoever he wanted. If he couldn't do it with the law, he'd do it fiscally, delving into their taxes; if he couldn't do it fiscally, he'd do it with their private life, tapping telephones and hacking into their email accounts; if none of that worked, he'd resolve it with lead, without even giving an order, but simply by allusions. He came, took me to bed, like a rooster as usual, he came too soon, infuriatingly, and fell asleep. He slept nervously, uneasily; he tossed and turned like a cement mixer; when we were married he didn't move so much; after a restless hour or so, he fell into a deeper sleep. *Veni, vidi, vici*, he could have said, like Caesar. As if conquering me was some great feat. He came, he came, but he didn't gain anything, just my scorn. He slept at my side and I thought: *I could put poison in his ear and murder him, like in a Shakespeare play, sink a knife into his jugular, put a viper in his bed*, but I didn't have any poison at hand, nor the guts to kill anybody.

I opened my legs without any real emotion, simply out of curiosity, to find out whether time and power had worked a miracle of metamorphosis on him; whether the youthful bad lover had turned into a warm and calm, even wise mature man. Whether power, as some say, had brought some charisma over his soul. Whether he had finally received a gift and acquired any grace, at least in bed. As if. Brusque, tactless, disagreeable, quick. As if I were a mannequin, an inflatable doll, a hole. He even hurt me. He made love as if some superior power had given him an order to make love: militarily. He moved his pelvis with rhythmic momentum, like a metronome. His instrument very firm, like steel, the sword entering like someone killing an enemy, like the torero going in for the final pass, but it all turned out to be more like the final blow, a failure. And he extracted his dagger bathed in blood to hide it quickly in its sheath. At four in the morning he was up, impatient, shouting hysterically, waking up his ministers with some ancestor of the cell phone, Avantel it was called, an advanced telephone, calling the pilots to prepare quickly, because for him there was no one more despicable than those who sleep a lot. That's why they took off at first light, the blades frightening the poor tricolored macaws and little green parrots and raising a dust storm. I pretended to be asleep.

Twenty or thirty years ago we'd spent our honeymoon at La Oculta and it had been the same. The worst lover I've had in my whole life: hasty, brusque, impatient. A stallion lasts longer mounting a tied-up mare. He'd get an erection, jump my bones, and that was that. Sex of a procreator, not a lover. Or conquistador, a violator of the neighboring tribe. "Who are you sleeping with?" was the only thing he said to me, the last time, as he penetrated me, and I said, "With Gustavo," but he corrected me: "No, ma'am: with the President of the Republic." And I started to laugh. I felt like I was in a Fernando González book, a dictator novel. Our marriage didn't even last a year because he was as conceited as a feline and as unfaithful as a canine. He was teaching political science at a university and ended up getting involved with a student who got pregnant, his little wife now and forever, for he pretends to be monogamous. She declared herself by having a child of his and he had no choice but to leave me and go and live with her. They couldn't even get married because in those days there was no such thing as civil marriage, only Catholic, and they hadn't annulled ours. Later he fought for an annulment for years because appearances are what matter most to him. Paying papal lawyers, he finally managed it, declaring I don't know what immaturity on my part, or his part, when we were married. And he married his student, without ceasing to betray her as well, no matter how strongly his speeches defended matrimony, conjugal fidelity, and the family as the supreme good.

It was never good being with him or talking with him or walking with him and much less sleeping with him; not the first time, at La Oculta, nor the last time, in the same bed. Thank goodness we didn't have any children. I did get pregnant by him, during our marriage, but he never knew. He never knew I had a second-month abortion, either, all alone, without ever telling anyone. I had seen his darkness and would never have wanted to raise a descendant of his, someone who looked at me with those eyes of a monster, which would emerge from his entrails. I had forgotten about that, luckily, or not forgotten, but buried it in one of those zones of the mind we hardly ever return to, and only now do I let it rise to consciousness. I had two abortions; I only want to remember one, the one I've occasionally talked about, but there were two. I never recognized that horrible pregnancy with Gustavo, because I never wanted to have a child of his. In his genes lurked something dark, sick, ancestral, the worst demons of our nature. A kind of irremediable evil, like that of Cain. His ancestors, who were also from the Southwest, from Jericó, had been expelled from there and sent to Salgar, for being wicked. The mad, the lazy, and the bad-natured were sent to Salgar, confined there, not allowed to leave without being sent to rot in a dungeon, and the grandparents of very bad people ended up in that town; I know them and I see them in the mirror of my mind, I have their names on the tip of my tongue but I won't repeat them, in case I might be able to forget them. Poets with the gift of the gab but without souls, who think they're marquises but are just thugs, more resourceful than intelligent, heartless, earsplitting politicians, victims of cruel parents who mistreated them until their bodies and souls were deformed. However, one cannot generalize, it's always unfair, and even in Salgar there are very good people, I don't deny it, and I can see their faces in my memory.

I don't remember my politician husband with displeasure, however. It was one more experience in my life. I felt what many women have felt: the attraction for the abyss, for the malevolent and violent but powerful man, dark in his wickedness, unscrupulous in his customs, implacable, who will protect you with his infinite power as long as you're as submissive as a meek dog. We women are disgraceful in that way.

The last night I spent with him he asked me if I'd like to be consul or cultural attaché in some country. I told him I'd think about it. For a couple of days I thought I'd like to live in Rome for a year, or in Paris, or in Madrid, I became enchanted with the idea of living in Barcelona, by the sea. Then I felt lazy, or more than lazy, the certainty that I'd despise myself if I accepted that charity, and I told him no, thanks anyway. In Colombia the ex-girlfriends and ex-wives of presidents always end up with a little diplomatic post in Europe. A little something to keep them happy as compensation. I decided to stay in Medellín, at the bakery, improving my mother's business, going to La Oculta every once in a while as well. Wretched farm. Three or four years later I had my run-in with Los Músicos. I told him what had happened with them, by phone, and I think he was one of those responsible for keeping Los Músicos away from La Oculta; I think we owe him that favor, but I'm not grateful. Now we're even more tied to that piece of land that we inherited. My life has tied me to it as if it were a bad husband from whom I couldn't manage to free myself. When they almost killed me there, I was finally able to divorce myself from that farm, break free, stop truly loving the place, see its real face, dark like its lake, dark like the heart of my first husband. I hate you, La Oculta. I hate you as I hate the black heart of a powerful man I was once capable of loving for a very short time. For this I also disdain and distrust my own heart, which must have its black cavities as well, because whose doesn't; we're all made up of the same things, though probably in different proportions.

There are days when I wake up lucid, and then I despise the countryside. The cows, the hens, the smell of manure, the mosquitos, the toads that Cobo dissected with frightening ruthlessness. In the countryside people walk around in a stupor, in the best cases, and others turn suspicious, sly, mistrustful. They spend their lives looking after fences and pigs, hating their neighbors, mistreating their animals, gossiping, because, since there's nothing to do, they devote themselves to hearsay, to malicious rumors. The countryside dulls the wits because there's no cinema, or newspapers, or libraries, or concert halls, theaters, exhibitions, lectures, universities, or people of all kinds coming and going and arguing in the cafés. There is no intelligent, informed conversation, which is the best way to stop being ignorant. There are no foreigners to open your eyes to other places, everyone is a villager and a local and all think themselves the center of the universe, their universe, their tiny little world. In the countryside it's possible to die of boredom and for your mind to be extinguished through lack of use. Cobo, who loved La Oculta so much, used to sometimes say: "With just a tiny predisposition toward foolishness, the countryside can turn us into complete idiots." They'll tell me that nowadays with the internet it's possible to have everything you want in the countryside: music, films, theater, lectures, conversations, social networks. Well yes, but it's not the same. Those who stay in the countryside gradually become savages, they start to turn the color of the earth and end up resembling cows or, in the best of cases, birds. It's the direct contact with other people that civilizes us, and civil comes from *civis*, a "citizen, one who lives in a city." Cobo taught us that too, he was fascinated by etymology, and didn't call himself a doctor but a *poliatrist*, according to what a colleague of his had taught him, Dr. Abad, one who cures the *polis*, doctor to the city.

I think almost all campesinos would choose not to be campesinos, if they could. It's easier and more interesting to be a doctor or a botanist than an expert in shovels, pickaxes, plows, manure, and hoes. The thing is, in Cobo an attachment survived and an affection for the place that had enabled his family not to have to work with their hands from sunup till sundown. In Cobo love for the countryside was more like weariness of civilization: a rest in silence. It's strange, he profoundly loved this part of the country, perhaps because La Oculta was the proof of an effort, the palpable proof of something achievable not by cunning, luck, or deceit, but by work. It was these fields, tamed by his forefathers, that had enabled two generations of Ángels to study and live in the city. When he went back there for a few weeks, he felt complete and if his friends asked him what he was doing, he always replied with the same words: tending my garden.

It's the contrast that makes us love La Oculta: time devoted to contemplation and silence, the pause in a life of work whether routine or even intellectual, getting away from it all, even though it's true that it's within the mundane noise of the cities where progress occurs. Although perhaps a tranquil atmosphere apart is the best place for thinking. Darwin lived in the countryside and developed his most brilliant ideas there; Einstein would go to a cabin outside Berlin to think. It's difficult to miss city life if one doesn't spend time in the country, and vice versa. There you can read and study more and concentrate better. And it's difficult for me, now that I almost never go out to the country, to miss the city, which I'm fed up with. It makes me tense, puts my nerves on edge at all hours. The traffic, the smoke, the noise, the thousands of commitments, arrangements, emails. It's always the same: we only want what we don't have. And it's always the same: I never know what to think, I contradict myself, I agree with A and disagree with A, I love and at the same time hate the countryside. But maybe La Oculta might not be exactly the countryside, but rather something else. La Oculta is the deepest and most obscure part of our origin, the black, smelly fertilizer that everyone in our family grew out of.

In any case, I'm going to tell Toño and Pilar that I'm selling them my share of La Oculta very cheaply; they can give me as little as they like, I don't want to ever go back to that blessed, that wretched land, and much less now that my mamá no longer exists, what I loved most about this family, my incredible mamá who always tried to understand me and supported me despite my being so different from her, despite my having lived in such a different way than she did. When I was a little girl, Silvia Roltz, a young classical dance teacher, lived across the street from us. I asked my mamá to let me study ballet with her, told her there was nothing I would like more than to be a ballerina. My mamá, with her gentle firmness, looked me in the eye and said no, that it would serve no purpose. I finally began to take dance classes with her – she, who has managed to live her life as she wanted, without bowing to pressure from anyone – in my fifties, and now I'm enjoying it. But I have no grudge against Mamá, I can say now that she's dead, for she taught me other things. She taught me, for instance, that money cannot be despised, that form is important, and that you don't always have to say the pure, unvarnished truth. From her I learned, I tried to learn at least, that although we disagree with someone we should maintain our composure, the elegance of disagreement. When I was twenty it bugged me that my mother should be so diplomatic, so polite. But over the years I've come to understand that her old-fashioned courtesy was not hypocritical, that it's better to be indirect (to tell Pedro so Juan will understand) than rude. Whether I liked them or not, the manners she taught me were a social necessity, a lubricant of daily life, and a way of being more civilized, less frank, less direct, less craggy, less of a campesina, and less like someone from Jericó, like my papá, who held nothing back and said everything he thought to your face, and that's why he had so many problems, so many futile fights that wore him down.

I don't want to undervalue his realism. Doing accounts and making myself necessary at Anita's Bakery, it's true, I abandoned my passion for dance or psychology, but I learned other things. And when in my personal life I never abandoned the search for a better partner, a man who would respect me for what I was, and whom I could truly, completely respect, my mamá never criticized me or my curiosity for everything and my thirst for knowledge and accepted with tranquility and without ill will my husbands and boyfriends and lovers and friends. I had total intimacy with her, and we were always together. We arrived at an arrangement: I would dream less and help her with her company, but I could live freely, and she wouldn't interfere in that with her religiosity or her old-fashioned views on life. Maybe she saw in my liberty a liberation of her own, once she was old, although she never said so, a life very different from the submissive life of the majority of women from her generation.

I better get back to my loves and losses. I don't want to recount all the men I've had, boyfriends or husbands. They're gone now; I'm not so attractive anymore. If I start making lists, I'll skip names because I've forgotten them, and for the best, or I'll omit them because there are some I want to forget. It's sweet to be able to forget a few of the men I've dated. I don't have as many urges as I used to have either. Sex could be wonderful, exultant, years ago, for example with the cyclist, who was the exact opposite of the president: a sweetheart, a pleasure, a gentle laugh, a great lover. He was simple and patient as if I were a field for sowing. But now taking a man to bed is almost like a task, a duty. Getting old is very sad. I have this body, which now turns on very slowly, like an old grill, like an iron that takes ages to heat up. Now I just go out with girlfriends, and only see Caicedo every once in a while, but without sleeping with him: he was my last companion, the most important of all, and I call him sometimes and we go out for lunch. He says: "Evita, why did we split up? What's wrong with me? What did I do?" He didn't do anything to me, in fact, and he had been the man who gave me the most, taught me most, who recovered music for me, ballet, a taste for opera and for the best books. I left him out of cowardice, because I couldn't stand people criticizing me for being with a man so much older than me, and not very attractive, even though I loved being with him and found it sweet to dissolve in his embrace. I also left him because of his right-wing friends, his military and industrial cohorts with no social sensitivity, and I left him because of a car he bought, it makes me laugh to remember. That was the day we split up. He came to pick me up at home and told me he had a surprise for me; he took me to a dealership of gigantic trucks and showed me an immense car, a sort of disguised Hummer that looked like a tank, a weapon of war. I told him, outraged, that I would never get into a car like that, aggressive and ostentatious, in a city full of poor, hungry, miserable people. That it was a pure Mafioso car, a gutless rich man's car. The salesman told him he shouldn't change his mind, but rather his girlfriend. I told the salesman he was right and told Caicedo to decide. I turned my back on him, hailed a taxi, and left. That same night he arrived at my house in the immense, ostentatious, shiny, new, yellow car. Let's take her for a first spin, he said, and I told him never to come back, that he'd made his choice. It was the straw that broke the camel's back, the drop that overflows the glass of water, Llorente's flower vase. Sometimes we leave people we love over a stupid incident, a shirt we don't like, a scent, a lemonade he didn't pour us, an enormous car we disagreed with.

I have this house, I have a third of that farm where I almost never go, and even less often since Mamá died. With her death we Ángels had our wings broken and we haven't been able to raise up the farm again. Pilar digs her heels in but it's out of stubbornness, more of a denial; she denies the farm is not what it once was and stays there hardheadedly. I could quite easily never return to La Oculta, I might even leave the country forever, if Benji stays in Germany or goes to live in Canada, where he's been offered a position. But Pilar says never say never. I've always been like this: myself and the opposite of myself. I'm going to phone Toño and tell him I'll sell him my third. Yes, that's what I'm going to do. I don't know. I've never really known, because another thing I've thought to do is give my share to my brother and sister. If it weren't for Benjamín, I would give it away. Or take whatever they want to give me for it, even if it's a pittance, and I'd donate it to some foundation that's doing something for people's health or education. The thought of Benjamín is what keeps me from doing that. Perhaps it is our children who make us selfish, who make us think of property as if it were food for our children. If Benji didn't exist, I wouldn't have any property now, none. I'd live in a hotel, I'd make sure to have a minimal income for food and shelter, and no more. Have no things, no furniture, no books, and especially no house or farm. Property is a headache and an injustice: property makes us stingy and mean. Property ties us down. If I had nothing, what freedom and what purity I'd feel. Rid of everything at last. To not pay taxes, not think of the payroll or the leaks in the roof or the fences or the animals. That would be ideal. But I can't, I still can't, damn it. At this stage of life and still not able to do what I want, exactly what I want, it can't be, I need to be able to, in spite of what anyone and everyone thinks.

ANTONIO

Grandpa Josué, even though he was Liberal or called himself one, whenever anyone talked to him about agrarian reform he would turn red, get nervous, confused, and turn back into a Conservative like his parents and grandparents. That began to happen in the seventies, during the Lleras Restrepo government. The complicated thing is that Cobo, my papá, was in favor of agrarian reform, and then they'd have tremendous arguments. "Look here, son," Don Josué would say, "I understand that there are a lot of people without any land, but is that my fault? We have defended this little patch of land tooth and nail for almost a hundred years and we didn't win it in a raffle. I knew my grandfather Elías, who was called Don Ángel in Jericó, and he walked barefoot and had hands more calloused and rough than any farmhand nowadays; he had cleared the jungle with his own hands and ax blows. He was a *patirrajo*, as you city folk say, although by my time we all wore shoes. But, tell me, because we are no longer *patirrajos*, thanks to effort and hard work, does that mean we have to hand over our land to the new *patirrajos*? My own father, your grandfather, who died so young and didn't go barefoot, taught me to break in colts and geld calves, to prune coffee trees and produce good beans. I knew how to do all those things, and when I had to give up my studies to return to the village and the farm I did so willingly, without complaints or feeling sorry for myself. I harvested, washed, peeled, and dried coffee beans in the sun. I've done all this with my own hands, following his example, washing the beans gently, sorting them by hand, discarding the husks, so I feel no guilt of having been lazy, having exploited or taken advantage of anybody. I have farmhands and campesinos working for me? Yes, but they're people who had no work who I pay a decent wage, with bene-fits, as required by law, as a minimum. But I work with them, shoulder to shoulder, not watching over them from a distance and giving orders as if they were slaves. They're the same as me with less land, less luck, that's all. And it was your great-grand-father, my grandfather, who left this land to us, that is the luck we had, and he had inherited from his father, just as I am going to leave it to you. Or do you want me to change my will and leave it to the poor? If that's the case, let me know and I won't kill myself trying to keep it, I'll drink it away."

Cobo listened to him while looking at his hands and then answered: "Look, Papá, agrarian reform is for the huge haci-endas on the coast or the plains, in the foothills of the Andes, thousands and thousands of barely used hectares; they have thousands of skinny cows out there running loose, and a couple of hands who don't even get minimum wage or any social security, and the people in the villages are starving to death, without a square foot of space to plant a bit of cassava, surrounded by fertile, green fields, and they're threatened or killed if they dare to sneak under the wire fence; and those lands, at least out on the coast, are fertile and flat, not mountainous and rough like La Oculta. That's where the large estates need to be shared. In the Southwest the land is not so badly distributed, and that has been the secret of Antioquia's success, even with bad land."

Our grandfather's land, in the middle of the last century, was no more than 400 *cuadras*, 250 hectares, most of which was devoted to cattle ranching, but with thirty thousand coffee trees in the uplands. Don Josué lived in fear that his land would be considered a large estate and parceled up into twenty-five plots to be handed out to the poor people of Jericó and Támesis. La Oculta had already been divided into three pieces, shared between him and his two brothers, and it didn't seem like that much land to him, since his father had three times as much. At my grandfather's death, his eight children, my father among them, each received fifty *cuadras*, slightly more than 30 hectares, which was more or less the size of plots that the agrarian reform bill was going to hand over to each campesino family on the coast (though they never fulfilled that promise), so the threat of agrarian reform didn't affect the next generation. Rather, since those lots weren't big enough to provide any revenue, but only worries, expenses, and headaches, one by one all our uncles and aunts sold off the pieces of land they'd inherited.

We were not campesinos, like our grandfather had been, but we still had our last little piece of land, to honor his memory, maybe, although probably rather to enjoy the privilege of watching daybreak there, to feel what we feel – it's something deep and ancient – to be at a place we know to be our own, and that no one can take away from us. I think this happens in all parts of the world and that's why people are killing people in Israel and in Ukraine and in Syria. Here too. But something has changed, in any case, since Anita's death. Since we cremated her and scattered her ashes in the resting place, Christmases have lost most of their charm, despite Pilar and Alberto's efforts to liven up the season. There were ridiculous arguments about the shopping (about whether Pilar was wasteful, buying absurdly large quantities, squandering food), about paying the servants, even about gifts for the staff. And now the older nephews and nieces have opinions and want certain things done their way because everyone's contributing to the expenses. They forced us, for example, to get an internet connection and television, when for us La Oculta was a place to be free from television and internet, where one could disconnect from reality, from the news of the world. I heard the sound of television and saw children watching it from their bed, and I felt that it was heretical and that the children were committing a grave infraction by watching cartoons instead of frolicking in the waterfall in the stream, watching the birds, lassoing calves, or climbing trees. When it was my mamá who paid the bills and dominated, there was peace, but since her death everything has become more complicated, and any decision, any extra expense, every change in the old daily habits, turns into a neverending argument.

Near La Oculta there were still people looking for gold. Sometimes small planes or helicopters spent entire days flying over the zone, apparently taking aerial photos, studying topographical maps, and tracking geographical signs in the shapes of the ranges, in search of veins of metal. Apart from the miners, there were also ever encroaching groups of people who would buy a hacienda and divide it up into lots. Chainsaws were heard again, not decapitating people, like in the times of the paramilitaries, but felling trees. They stole land from the mountains, and the sources of water, woods, and fields disappeared and lavish weekend houses appeared where once a stream had begun. It had happened in Tínez, the great hacienda that had belonged to the founders of Jericó, near La Pintada. The threats approached, no longer in the form of guerrillas or paramilitaries, but as real estate speculators, with pamphlets in full color that spoke of the development of the area, of its valuation, of how close to Medellín it would be once the freeway was completed. We, at least Pilar and I, kept holding on for the time being, while Eva – again and again – kept giving us reasons why we should sell.

We insist on opposing death and change with a surname and a piece of land. It was for our surname that I, when I was very young, even went so far as to have girlfriends. I slept with them without desire, how absurd, because the idea of being damaged (as they used to say when I was twenty) bothered me, and I struggled against the deepest part of myself, because I suffered at the thought of not having children and being the end of the line of the Ángel name, which was so important to my papá. I tried many strategies, to supposedly cure myself. First religion, which didn't work. Then I thought I could spend the rest of my life sleeping with women, but thinking about men while I was with them, so I could come and inseminate them and then have Angelitos. For a while I wanted to give up sex completely and become celibate, an ascetic, unsullied bachelor, but that was like fasting, something one can manage for a while, but it's not possible to fast for a whole lifetime. Even chastity can turn into an aberration that deforms your character. Celibacy is like fasting; if one is a decrepit old man, without any hormones left and therefore without desires, who can even stop eating and still live for a while as he dries out, then fasting and being celibate are possible. Chastity is a recipe dictated by sanctimonious old men who are chaste due to a lack of testosterone and call the fact of having desire lust, simply because they don't miss sex. And temperance when it comes to eating is also a rule of old dyspeptic men: since they have bad digestion, they don't want anyone else to eat very much, and they call someone with an appetite a glutton, because they get indigestion from one tomato and a couple leaves of lettuce. Young people, on the other hand, are able to digest a fork, if they happen to bite it, to feel hunger and desire seven times a day.

When I began to live with Jon, I suggested we do what my friends Andrés and Lucho had done. They'd adopted an orphan who'd been rescued from a garbage dump in Moravia in Medellín, and they have him here, in New York. They're neighbors of ours, and he's growing up very well, and even makes fun of their gay tastes and gay mannerisms, and he has quite a few girlfriends. He's a handsome teenager (Gregorio, he's called), better looking than his fathers, with very long lashes and curls that almost touch his eyebrows. But the thing is, apart from how complicated it is for a gay couple to adopt a child, even if they're married, I have some disagreeable genetic beliefs: I believe in direct descent, in the biological inheritance of blemishes, virtues, and defects. Children put up for adoption in general come from parents with problems such as drug addiction, alcoholism, prostitution: it's like entering a raffle for a tiger, and may adopted children and their parents forgive me because no one is to blame for being what they are and there are adopted children who are angels, perfect wonders, like Andrés and Lucho's son who as well as being handsome is very intelligent. Enthusiasts of adoption are convinced Rousseauians: they believe that everything depends on nurture, and that's not true, if only it were. I like to see my father's face in mine, I like to recognize my grandmother's toes in mine, the tics of my uncles or some other relative in my tics. It doesn't even bother me to know that my asthma is inherited and if one day my gallbladder or prostate fails, it'll probably be because one of my ancestors suffered from that same Achilles heel. I am not an expert on the laws of inheritance, neither civil nor genetic, but apart from the odd exception, our illusion of immortality, or at least of posterity, has to do with the survival of our genes and our possessions.

Sometimes I think of another solution closer to that of a couple of lesbian friends, Consuelo and Margarita. They asked some handsome and intelligent acquaintances (I don't think anyone requests ugly and stupid when they go to a sperm bank) to donate semen. They had a party and with plastic syringes they'd bought at a pharmacy (without needles), injected the fresh semen themselves, on fertile days that they'd calculated with charts, and now they have a girl and a boy. But that's much easier for women; in Jon's and my case, we'd have to hire a womb, something that's legal in the United States, but not in Colombia. Well, in Colombia everything can be resolved with money. I could even have asked a woman I liked to donate a handful of ova, and fertilize them myself, in vitro, and then implanted the fertilized ovum in a healthy young woman willing to carry the pregnancy to term in exchange for payment. But I never did and now I'm too old for that; I never wanted to enter into the judicial complications of that tangled kind of paternity.

I am left with my nephews, Eva's son with the orchestra conductor and Pilar and Alberto's five children. Though I don't see them often I always have my nephews and nieces in mind; they are the tiny bit of me that will still be alive when I die: they are a distant proof of paternity, an hors d'oeuvre or dessert at the meal I wasn't invited to, a quarter of their blood is like mine. Eva had Benji late, because she almost couldn't decide whether to have children, and the strange thing is that she didn't have him when they were married, but after separating from her third husband, the banker, during a few weeks when she started seeing the second one again, Bernal, and going out with him. She got back together with him, just to get pregnant, I think, because Bernal – with all his defects: as conservative as he became over time, his neurosis, his desire to always be alone – seemed to her the least bad of all the men she'd sampled in her life. I love my nieces and nephews, sometimes I even think they are the motor that makes me exert myself in this life, the impulse that keeps me playing violin, to save some money, to keep La Oculta, to investigate the past of Jericó and the farm. I only wish I had more than these six: Lucas, Manuela, Lorenzo, Florencia, Simón, and Benjamín, because I get so much from each of them. Lucas is strength and enthusiasm, vital energy; Manuela is beauty, and capable of helping without expecting anything in return, like Pilar; Lorenzo has goodness, Alberto's saintliness, and no one could ever expect a betrayal or anything bad from him; Florencia is the spitting image of her grandmother, with her character, her permanent good mood, because she says she suffers from such a cheerful disposition that she laughs her head off in her dreams, and I've seen it; Simón is scientific and sane, intelligence on legs, and best of all he has a joyful spark, intelligence with laughter, like Pilar at the best moments of her life; and Benji, being the youngest, and Eva's only son, with a misanthropist hermit for a father, is the one I feel the most paternal connection to; he has a scientific and rational brain, a sharp mind, and is a moral, practical, serene, and inspiring presence.

Sometimes I wonder if I mythologize my sisters as I mythologize our ancestors in Jericó, if I see them as more special than they are. Perhaps they are two regular women of Antioquia like any other women born there in the middle of the twentieth century. They're so different from each other that it might seem strange that I love them each as much as the other. If I put them on a set of scales, the pointer would be exactly in the center, without leaning to one side or the other. As long as I can remember I've observed them with interest and curiosity, with love and passion, the way you watch the drama of a film unfold, two films showing at the same time. They are a mystery I have to decipher day by day. My heart could be shared between them like an apple cut exactly down the middle into two identical and symmetrical halves. I don't judge them, I don't think that one is better or worse than the other. I believe that they don't judge me either and have accepted me as I am, with light and shadow, virtues and defects, with Jon and without Jon. I think that if Pilar had not had at her side a man like Alberto, who is completely exceptional among men, she might not have been able to form such a traditional family, as she always wanted. If Alberto'd had adventures, lovers, little flings, as almost all men do, and Pilar had found out, it's not impossible that her path would have been more complicated, closer to Eva's, or at least her loyalty wouldn't have been as joyful as it is but more resentful and angry. And if Eva's first experiences hadn't been with such disagreeable, macho, selfish men, maybe she wouldn't have had to assume that attitude of mistrust, liberty, and evening the score. Since they were free, she chose freedom too, out of a private feeling that it was only fair.

I've had a lot of partners too. I lived the first half of my life like Eva: searching, sampling, without guilt, in liberty, to see if I could find one with whom I wanted to put down roots, enjoying the variety, in light of not being able to enjoy the pleasures of permanence. And the second half of my life, since I met Jon, has been more like Pilar's, though with the odd, brief adventure that I don't want to recount here because just thinking about them makes me feel guilty. He tells me he hasn't had any other lovers since we've been together. There are things in life that you only tell yourself, as long as you're not found out, hidden things that are nevertheless not the core of life, but a dark part of our intimacy that we don't share with anybody, and that are like clouds that would cause useless wounds, desolate ruptures in a relationship that runs along well and happily because there is a small field of open air and secrets. I know that Pilar and Alberto have no secrets, and that strikes me as purer, cleaner, nicer. But how many couples can live like that? They're like the ten just men of the Bible, those few who manage to keep God from evaporating the world in a ball of fire. But anyway, the sins of the body are not enough to warrant the Flood, or the fire and brimstone destruction of Sodom and Gomorrah. The Catholic God is a drama queen. Learned morals are much more rigid than the inclinations of our bodies. One does what one can; Eva has done what she could; Pilar and Alberto have done what they could; I've done what I could.

There is a certain private prejudice in defending one's relatives, taking care of an inheritance to leave it to a family member. It's possible, it's almost certain, that our properties will be squandered by a useless son-in-law, a careless nephew or a hedonistic granddaughter: we know that everything is exposed to the mishaps of the future, but at least for the time being we want to protect our paternal and maternal heritages. People will say that all this is no more than a bourgeois preoccupation, further complications for proprietors of movable and immovable goods. I have a Marxist friend who likes to argue with me and he explains it like this. "To begin with," he tells me, "property is theft," quoting Proudhon, the French anarchist. And then he carries on with his stream of thought: "What happens is that if one does not have land or a house or any objects of value – works of art, family silver, china, books, etc. – rather these goods are public, this selfish and stingy manner of thought disappears. And even more so if we don't have children to leave all these things to. I even think it's better not to have children or a traditional family, because it's the family where selfishness is implanted and developed. For that very reason the Church, which is old and wise, forbids its priests from marrying and having children. For the same reason, the Russian Leninists thought the best way forward was to take children away from their families and let the State take charge of them." He was a Leninist about that and about many other things; but the idea of taking children away from their families in Russia failed. It's impossible to dictate rules that contradict human nature: people rebel even in the midst of the toughest and most oppressive regime; there are some things that are unacceptable to our deepest psyches.

But in any case maybe it is children, paternity, maternity, that makes us worse, more selfish, more calculating and stingy. Or more prudent, urging us to rise at dawn, exert ourselves, know the purest love. As I don't have children, my argument is based on hearsay, but those who do have them get furious with me and say I understand nothing: that children are everything, that their children have taught them altruism and goodness, and their grandchildren, even more. The fact is that those of us who never had children – monks, gay men, nuns, hermits, single or sterile people, Catholic priests who faithfully practice celibacy – have a less small outlook on life: we can envision a future without ourselves or our children, but rather with other similar beings who should be better than we are now, and instead of leaving an inheritance for our descendants, we can think of living and working for the benefit of all. I have done nothing more than investigate my ancestors like an ant, as if my family background were my life, since I can't have a family life going forward. What for, what for? I don't know, simply to find out where I come from, or better yet, to be able to control and replace with words what I haven't been able to realize with deeds, to have at least a paper child that will be a testimony of my time here, a useless but beautiful form of paternity and posterity, at least for a while. And I love this kind of child, my papers and notes, like a descendant who will speak for me when I die.

EVA

There is always something that hasn't been said and I am an expert in detecting silences, half-truths, words barely whispered in secret. I watch from a corner, quietly, pretend to be reading or sewing, but my ears are wide open, and I watch, watch out of the corner of my eye, watch with the eye that occultists say we all have in secret places. Someone hides something, always, people hide what they don't want to be known, and we only discover it by indirect indications. They're not big things, not necessarily, it doesn't have to be a skeleton in the closet, it just might be one little bone, the last vertebra, the tiny bit left of our monkey's tail.

I know for example that Pilar, after Los Músicos almost killed me, or maybe even before that, had started to pay them a monthly fee, protection money, which they call a vaccine, without telling Toño or me. Paying those people, paying those who kill kids who smoke dope in the village (smoking *bazuco* while killing them), those who had carved up three kids on the road into the farm with a chainsaw, those who had burned down half our house but had meant to burn it all, those who told us we had to "sell or sell" La Oculta. Pilar never told us, but once I heard her talking to a neighbor. She gave the money to him and he took it to Los Músicos, at first. Later they resolved to make another deal, which would allow Pilar to save face, to keep her from blackening the Ángel name, so she wouldn't have to hand money directly over to the thugs. The arrangement consisted in us renting some fields to him so he could graze some cattle there and he, in compensation, would pay the fee to Los Músicos in town so they wouldn't do anything to us. I understand that went on for years. I had stopped going to La Oculta by then, and Toño wasn't going either, out of rage and repugnance for what was happening. Jon had him almost convinced about a cabin in Vermont, where the autumn was a fabulous explosion of all the shades of ochre, orange, yellow, and red. Toño wasn't even coming down from New York in those years. What for, he said to me, if I can't go to La Oculta I'd rather not even go to Colombia. My country is La Oculta, a few friends, the taste of mangos and *curubas*, but especially the farm. He'd rather invite Pilar, Mamá, and me to go to New York, and we'd all squeeze into Jon's apartment in Harlem. But Pilar and Alberto got bored in New York, since they weren't interested in the museums or art exhibitions, and even though Pilar loved the stores on Fifth Avenue, she said nothing was worse than walking along there without money, like poor children in Medellín going to the ice cream parlor to watch rich children eat ice cream cones. My mamá felt strange not being able to organize Christmas in her way. She'd make buñuelos, but they'd explode in the deep fryer, and the *natilla* custard didn't taste like *natilla*, and the leg of ham in Jon and Toño's oven came out burnt or undercooked, never quite right.

Of the three of us, for years, only Pilar kept going to the farm with Alberto every once in a while, and they even talked to those bandits, I think, though they didn't tell us. Once she had to give them lunch, because they'd camped near the house. She has that levelheadedness; even if she's dying inside, she'll never show anyone her fear. They would have killed me, because I would have insulted them. Pilar gave them chicken stew. She served *sancocho* to the same men who had gone there to kill me, no less, the same ones who'd set our house on fire and carved up those boys. Once – Próspero told me – she even lent a room to an army colonel who'd gone there to have a meeting with them. I happened to meet that colonel once he was a general, in Caicedo's house, and when he heard my name and saw my hardened eyes – I looked at him with rage as I said, without offering my hand, "My name is Eva Ángel, from La Oculta" – I saw something very odd in his demeanor: a mixture he couldn't disguise of anger, mistrust, and fear, most of all fear.

It's something shameful, but if not for Pilar, for those depths she stooped to, La Oculta would by now have been lost to our family. She has defended it even by cheating, with vileness, like paying protection money to the paramilitaries. Toño and I would have let them invade it, would have traded it for a plate of lentils, anything but sully our hands with those men who were smeared in blood.

Later Los Músicos disappeared, or rather, were disappeared and killed one by one. But there were several years in which they worked shoulder to shoulder with the military. The time Pilar gave them *sancocho* that same colonel from the Fourth Brigade was there. He was the one who met with them on our land, and later slept in the house, I don't know which room and I hope at least not in Cobo and Anita's room, which is now mine. He, that colonel who later became a general and then a commander, and when he retired was given homages, told Pilar: "Don't worry, Doña Pilar, we're thick as thieves with these boys, hand in glove." For once the colloquial expressions were literally true. They did their dirty work for them.

For a while, after Lucas was kidnapped, and some others in the region were as well, the people with farms thought it necessary to protect themselves. They called the politicians and military officials they knew and sponsored those "self-defense groups," and hired them, transported them, armed them, paid them, and brought them together at their haciendas. The ones who gave them the least, gave them *sancocho*, like Pilar. "Death to kidnappers, no more extortion, no more guerrillas, death to thieves, clean up the marijuana smokers." The region filled up with slogans like that, painted on every wall, on every stone, and signed by the Autodefensa Unión de Colombia. Until they started to murder and kidnap anyone who didn't pay their "vaccines," and even those who did, and to ask for more and more protection money every month, and to bring in miners and form alliances with drug traffickers who offered to buy farms, and whose very offers were threats and blackmail. That's why Pilar paid, so they wouldn't do anything to us, but then they wanted to buy the land, and started to send those notes.

Then the landowners turned against the *paracos* and made war on them. They forgot that they had summoned them up and began to say it had all been by force, extortion, that they'd had no option but to pay the "vaccines." Allied with the government, they forced them to demobilize and then killed the ones who talked too much, and later they extradited almost all the leaders to the United States, as drug traffickers, but that was only when they started naming the companies, politicians, military officers, and landowners who had summoned and financed them, who had trained them with their officer friends, even with experts brought in from Britain and Israel, revealing that they'd given them provisions, weapons, ammunition, help, silence, and protection. They got them out of the country so they wouldn't reveal the whole truth, so that the oldest and supposedly cleanest names in the country would not appear on the lists of paramilitary funders. So they wouldn't reveal the names of all the colonels, generals, sergeants, and captains who had helped them in their massacres.

By a miracle they didn't give Pilar's name, but no, what nonsense, we're small fry, a tiny drop in a lake of blood. Pilar was able to do something very ugly to conserve the land, but Toño and I, though we never gave a peso personally, always suspected, knew that our older sister had to be doing something like that, and preferred to close our eyes and mouths, we played the fools. And they have also done to us the most disgusting and abject things to try to take our land away, first the guerrillas, supposedly to return the land to the people, to the poor, to the campesinos, to the Afro-Colombian and indigenous comrades. Liars. To keep the ransom money for themselves, and then buy the land cheaply because it wasn't worth anything because they were there, devaluing it with their mere presence, doing their own deadly business. And later the paramilitaries, supposedly to protect us from the guerrillas. Deceivers: to take possession of the land themselves as well, by fair means or foul: either you sell it to us or your orphans can; sell it to us or leave it to your widow to sell, they used to say. To hand over that land to the miners and drug traffickers, their closest allies.

ANTONIO

When I was investigating and reading about the history of Jericó, three or four years ago, I went and stayed there for a few weeks. I didn't want to know everything only through the filter of reading; I wanted to breathe the air of the place and had the illusion of feeling something old in its streets, the urge to perceive something of the nineteenth century while living in the twenty-first and coming from New York. Anita was still alive and I spent a few days with her in Medellín, before carrying on to the town. I took the chance to go to a concert that Bernal, Eva's ex-husband, was conducting, with an orchestra of young people from the barrios of Medellín, the Academia Filarmónica. They played Beethoven's Fifth so well and then Tchaikovsky's Violin Concerto, with a Spanish soloist, that I managed to reconcile with my city for a little while and think there might be a future here, with music and violins, which have always meant so much to me.

When I got to Jericó, the town was papered over, on almost all the red, green, and blue balconies, across the lacy latticework over the windows, on the open, polished, wooden gates, on the stone walls, were white notices or stencils proclaiming a succinct, unvarying slogan: *No to mining!* These signs told me the town had self-respect, that there were people here who still believed in working for a living and not in receiving royalties for handing over mineral rights, and that having to choose between beauty and riches, they'd prefer the former.

That opinion, however, was not unanimous. Some politicians and many lazy citizens preferred to live off rent, scratching their bellies. I was told that there were more legal and illegal miners every day conducting explorations in the vicinity of the town. A pernicious government had sold off the entire subsoil of the region at bargain prices and, ignoring any measures of environmental protection, had no qualms about turning over the earth and invading the land with machines and temporary mines. I was also told that some bureaucrats made agreements under the table with Canadian, South African, Chinese, and Colombian mining companies to allow them to dredge the riverbeds, pry under the crags, and tunnel into the mountains in search of signs of gold, silver, copper, uranium, whatever there might be. There was a quiet struggle going on between the town businessmen, habitual conquerors and predators, who saw easy money in royalties, in spite of the landscape, the water, and nature, and those who wanted to defend the land as it was, the natural wealth, and most of all the beauty, the beauty that is preserved and created by farming the countryside and protecting the woods and the land. I didn't want to get more involved in the current situation than I should and I pretended to be a quiet tourist. I said my name was Joaquín Toro and that I'd been born in Titiribí. Although I was on the side of the environmentalists, what I was interested in at this moment was the past, the town's foundation, and the early years of the twentieth century. I thought if I concentrated more on the dreams and efforts of the past, I could better defend the present, demonstrate that what had been achieved was no accident, but the fruit of the vision and work of thousands of people who had settled the town with healthy and genuine hopes a century and a half earlier.

While I was in the parish archives, at the History Center, or at Dr. Ojalvo's house, I felt really good; when I walked along the trails and by the sides of the crystal-clear rivers, I felt really good; when I talked to the campesinos and young people, it was all very pleasant, and I encouraged them to keep fighting for the water, the trees, and the air. But the town, especially on the weekends, filled with commotion, with rude people, with incessant music at full volume, and arrogant people who thought they were more important because their truck was bigger, their horses more spirited, their farms more ostentatious. If I wanted to live here with Jon, I had to think it over very carefully. A place like La Oculta was one thing, hidden up in the hills, serene and silent, but being subjected to other people's whims, to their noise and high-handedness was quite another.

There were several little internet cafés in town and I'd go into one or the other of them to talk to Jon on Skype and see him for a while. I told him good and bad things about the town, and Jon listened in silence, probably with even more doubts than I had about our plans. And there, in the internet cafés, or on my laptop with my 4G dongle, when it was working, in the hotel, I investigated things about the past. I wanted to know, for example, how long a technological innovation took to arrive in Jericó, a century ago. A good innovation such as safe drinking water or electric lighting, not a bad and dangerous one like mining with mercury, which contaminated the waters. I didn't miss the darkness of the night, although I knew it was better for sleeping and seeing the stars, so I decided to accept electric lighting as something good.

In a few hours of searching I found tons of interesting information: on October 21, 1879, Thomas Alva Edison, in his laboratory in Menlo Park, New Jersey, "mounted one of his carbon-coated filaments in a glass tube and managed to get it to burn continuously for forty hours. On New Year's Eve, he illuminated the main street of Menlo Park electrically as the first public proof of his invention." Among the curious things I learned was that this invention saved the whale from extinction (for a substance in its skull – which was called spermaceti due to its resemblance to another white and viscous substance – was used to make the majority of candles people used to light their houses) and resulted in fewer house fires every year around the world. In 1881, during the display of electricity in Paris, the light-bulbs surprised everyone as the latest marvel. In 1882 the first electricity plant was built in New York; Rome and Venice built their own in 1886.

The new invention arrived in Medellín just twelve years later, on July 7, 1898. One of its most engaging chroniclers, Lisandro Ochoa, described it:

After intense work and huge setbacks, the long-awaited night arrived for the inauguration of the service of 150 arc lamps. Berrío Park and the adjacent streets were crowded with people; everyone came out of their houses overjoyed. From the smallest children to the oldest grand-parents, everyone pressed into the mass of humanity that filled the park.

Outdoor lighting – another chronicler tells us – had previously been supplied by petroleum lamps located on the four sides of the square. The new invention, it seems, provoked Marañas, local rogue, as he was directing his gaze at the wan and waning moon: "Now you're really screwed, moon, go light our villages!"

Jericó, where the Ángel family lived, where I was now sleeping and reading about electric lights, was still illuminated only by the moon – when there was a moon and it wasn't cloudy – or oil lamps mixed with petroleum, for almost another decade.

The moon outside and candles within, as well as the glow from the wood fires. The world, the whole world, was a very dark place by night, until those early years of the twentieth century. But here too, thanks to the untiring work of Father Cadavid, an electric generator was installed, and Jericó saw the light on April 15, 1906, a quarter of a century after its invention in the United States. I also found the tale of that memorable day in the words of a local reporter. First to be lit up in Jericó was the church, not the streets, a very clear sign of who called the shots and who brought the miracles of God and science to town:

The night, although dry and calm, was dark. As the hands of the clock on the church struck seven, great crowds of people made their way to the temple, to the beautiful, artistic, spacious, and luxurious temple. Father Cadavid entered, followed by a mob of children, men, and women (my grandfather was among them, it was one of his first childhood memories). Out through the arches and windows came, like the first arrows of a battle, some notes that the expert hand of Don Daniel Salazar coaxed from the organ. Something grandiose and unexpected was about to happen.

Suddenly, the light of eighty lightbulbs melt the black darkness; the straight columns, the imposing arches, the multicolored windowpanes, the acanthus capitals, the tabernacle surge from the heart of the night, against the azure background, the simple draperies and flamboyant festoons of leaves and flowers. And the notes from the organ spill out of the temple, and the deep voices, and the cheerful shouts, and the moving tones of the *Te Deum*, enrapture all the souls and elevate the hearts. *And there, at the front, eyes on the ground, haloed more by his modesty than by the light, humble and trembling, the author of that new creation: Father Cadavid!*

It was such a great event that several people wrote about it. Here's the speech that one of the notables of the day addressed to Father Cadavid, and, after praising him for bringing nocturnal light, he praised him for having endeavored to illuminate souls as well in his temperance campaign. For some years temperance was Jericó's leaders' favorite subject:

Not long ago, the axes of our laborers had broken through part of the primitive jungle and changed into fertile haciendas what had once been covered in thick underbrush; not many years ago, dens of wild animals were replaced by farmhouses and tilled land and a tiny village or hamlet, which occupied the center where we now have this flourishing city, when the parish was entrusted to your wise direction. Your voice, persuasive and eloquent, has thundered through the sacred cathedral against vice and corruption, achieving the triumph – almost exceptional in Antioquia – of ending cockfighting and all kinds of gambling here, where young men can get lost; your word has been abundant in the Temperance Society to demonstrate that alcoholism is an asp that destroys our capital and our reputation, that poisons our body and our soul, that turns us into useless and damaged members of society.

Among the members of the Temperance Society, according to the documents in the History Center, was José Antonio

Ángel, our ancestor, his signature one of the first, as one of the town notables. The campaign against alcohol lasted years and maybe wasn't a bad idea in a country so prone to drunkenness. These days that banner has been taken up by the evangelical churches and I have no doubt that's one of the keys to their success. They're fanatical and intolerant, in general, but they keep many from falling into one of the most widespread of Colombian vices. I enjoy a drink, I admit it, but I'm a terrible old hypocrite when I think of the general drunkenness of my compatriots. Which is why I read with certain pleasure the old signs that covered the town a century ago. In different locations in the plaza, on huge squares and long strips of white cloth, in big, black letters, legible from a block away, were warnings like these:

FOLLOW THE PATH THAT A TEMPERATE SOCIETY MARKS OUT, AND YOU SHALL FIND TRANQUILITY.

TEMPERANCE IS THE SLOGAN OF VIRTUOUS TOWNS.

INTEMPERANCE WILL BE THE STIGMA OF WICKED TOWNS.

A DRUNK IS SOCIETY'S SCANDAL.

A TEMPERATE CITIZEN IS A GUARANTEE FOR SOCIETY.

At the banquet offered to celebrate the arrival of electric light, only one glass of sweet wine was served, as a blessing. As a token of gratitude, they gave Father Cadavid a painting by Francisco Antonio Cano, the best painter in Antioquia at the time, having studied in Italy, and a good portraitist: it was a picture of his mother, María Luisa González de Cadavid, donated by the señoritas of the Association of the Daughters of Mary. Among them were several of Don José Antonio's daughters, and his wife, Merceditas Mejía, Mamaditas. And when they turned on the lights, the chroniclers related, in spite of the happiness and the celebrations, five days later there was not a single drunk in Jericó.

The governor of Antioquia, Gabriel Mejía, had sent a message brimming with enthusiasm that said: "The doors of the liquor store are not open, and even if they were, the people would not flock there in search of abominable poison, father of madness and crime." And in fact, according to what others recorded, "no liquor was imbibed; there were horse races, prizes, trays of honey, allowable games and theater, and thousands of pretexts for taking a drink, but no one did, because Jericó stuck to its word of honor. Jericó will not be like Sodom and Gomorrah, nor will it be buried by an earthquake like San Francisco."

A few years later an earthquake toppled the temple raised with such effort. Then they designed another church, much uglier than the previous one, if rather more solid, and today the plaza is nothing but a parade of canteens and drunks, but anyway, I better not say anything because I drink too and sometimes I think that life is so hard that only with a certain amount of alcohol can we bear it. If not, it's impossible to explain the success of this drug, which is greater than that of all religions.

In any case, when electricity arrived in Jericó, more than a century ago, the town had more inhabitants than it does today; the theater was open and running; there was a musical ensemble and a literary magazine; despite the sanctimoniousness of those years, the citizens associated with each other in pursuit of common goals. The first years of the new century had been like a fresh start and everyone dreamed of a beautiful future and had sincere intentions to forget about their grievances. There were common ideals and any number of people anxious to fulfill them. Everything seemed like marvelous promises, for the War of a Thousand Days had just ended and there was optimism and desire for forgiveness and reconciliation. There was, as is cyclical in my country, an illusion of perpetual peace, of peace at last, of a new era when brothers would stop killing each other. The economic crisis would not take long to arrive, nor would the mid-century *Violencia*, and later all kinds of plagues all together: drug trafficking, guerrillas, paramilitaries. With the turn of another new century, there are once again yearnings for peace and progress in the air. Could I live here with Jon, in a town with fewer inhabitants than a century ago? Well, I didn't come here hoping Jericó might resemble New York, which would be impossible and absurd. If I came to live in this town I would be looking for something different: the peace of a simple life, the contrast of a country life to our life in the big city, and most of all to be close to my little personal paradise, which I shared with my sisters, La Oculta. I'd give violin classes to children, help to found a new ensemble, perhaps a string quartet. I've said so to Jon, but he's always answered with evasion and delays. "Calm down, Toño, take it easy," those are his slogans.

I rented a jeep with a driver to take me to the farm along the old route by way of La Mama and Palermo. It had rained and it was almost impassable, but we managed to get there after driving for an hour and a half, with a few brief stops to look at the majestic gorge of the River Cauca. I arrived just as Pilar and Alberto were getting ready to sit down to lunch. They had a *sancocho* waiting for me. A *sancocho*, I thought, like the one that had welcomed the first settlers to the area, a century and a half before. They had made it in the traditional way, on a wood fire, even though we'd had electricity at La Oculta since the 1970s, in spite of its remoteness. I remembered the Peltón turbine my grandfather installed on the stream, that he'd only turn on for a few hours, before we went to bed. Its monotonous noise, the pale, dim, flickering light. It was a long path back in time, but I didn't really know what my path was, our path ahead. We've never done anything important in the Ángel family, nothing very glorious. Neither have the people of Jericó. No invention that has improved the world came from the inhabitants of our pretty town. The most we can boast is the local shoulder bag, the *carriel* and a few verses and novels by two writers with the last name Mejía: Manuel and Dolly. I looked at my simplified *carriel*, a leather satchel I can wear diagonally across my chest to carry my things, notepads, wallet, books, notes. My grandfather always carried a pistol in his as well, just in case. At least I don't need to carry a pistol anymore, and that consoled me.

EVA

I keep in touch with some of my Ángel cousins in Medellín.
I always tell them they were right to sell their share of this
blasted farm, that at least they didn't get kidnapped by guerrillas or have to pay off the paramilitaries or live out their lives
fighting with their siblings. Among our cousins there are rich
and poor, successes and failures, decent people and not so
decent ones. That's the way all families are. A few of them are
businessmen; others are cattle farmers, and some have even
bought much bigger properties in far-flung parts of Colombia.
One of our cousins is a big landholder on the coast. Another is
poor, but decent, and doesn't let anyone know. There was a distant cousin who was sent to jail in the United States, for money
laundering; with his dirty money he bought several haciendas
around Jericó, but he couldn't even see them or enjoy them, his
wife is enjoying them, an old, frivolous, vain, uncultured woman
who was a model in her youth and is now a surgical model (six
kilos of silicon and botox in her body), and their children, who
are as untrustworthy as their father. In the same family things

go like that, like in the tango: some are born under a lucky star and others are ill-starred.

Our grandfather Josué, for example, always talked about his father's brother, David Ángel, who had inherited the same amount of land as his brother, and was relatively well-off, comfortable. And he was a good man, generous in town, kindhearted at home, a friend to his friends and lover of his wife and seven children. Early in the century, in 1912 or '13, on a hacienda he had near La Oculta, La Lorena, he had a heart attack at the age of thirty-nine. His wife and his children, who were all still small, were not able to run the hacienda. La Lorena, two years after David's death, was already what was known as a "widow's farm," that is, a piece of land covered in weeds where the woods were beginning to take back what was once an open and well-managed farm. When the coffee plants don't get fertilized or weeded and no one combats infestations, harvests are reduced and pastures disappear. On the abandoned fields calves don't fatten, and the farm can't support as many cattle. Sooner or later the widow has to sell the deteriorated, devalued land. And then raise her children and feed them as best she can, with that money, for five or ten years. Then the money runs out, and she sells the house in town; they move into a smaller one. When the oldest son turns sixteen, he's not going to start working as the boss of his father's farm, but as a laborer. And the same thing happens to the second son. The eldest daughter gets married early and badly, in order to get away from the worries of her mother's home, and has many more children than she can feed. And thus, the whole family goes downhill. That was the poor branch of the Ángel family, as my grandfather put it, who he helped as much as he could, when he could.

And in my generation it's not much different. There are servants, artists, tramps, hardline leftists and extreme right-wingers, Tories and Liberals, everything. People tend to think that everything is the fault of other people's wickedness, or bad blood, or bad upbringing, or lack of education, but sometimes the bad times begin with just a moment of bad luck, a heart attack or a fall from a horse. But I don't want to make excuses for men. If I'd been killed by Los Músicos when they came to kill me, if I hadn't known how to swim well and hadn't had the luck to escape, now Benjamín would probably not receive a peso of my share of the inheritance, and my brother and sister would have had to hand over the farm for whatever was offered, with their sister dead in a hammock, full of holes like a colander, disfigured by bullets or chopped up by a chainsaw. Luck and evil; effort and merit and luck; luck and goodness; drought or floods. Nobody should boast of what they have or feel ashamed of what they don't have: the chain of events, the wheel of fortune, everything is so difficult to define and to know. Ideologies and religions teach us indignation or resignation: point out the guilty: capital, sinners, laziness, alcohol, envy, greed. There is something to that; but there is also a lot of luck, plain and simple good or bad fortune.

ANTONIO

What Cobo used to tell us was that when he was eleven and lived in Jericó, Grandfather Josué had gone broke and lost everything he had in the depression of the 1930s. When I think of our grandfather I always imagine him old, the way I knew him, but he was a young man of thirty then, who had three children, my dad, Aunt Ester, and Uncle Bernardo, who'd all been born in Jericó like him. This young man, Josué Ángel, my grandfather, had had to sell off one by one all the properties he'd inherited from his father, José Antonio, and there were a lot of them, although they also had debts, inheritance tangles, and complications. Casablanca, La Inés, La Mesa... those were legendary names, but there was one, one single property that he'd managed to save from the general debacle, and this was La Oculta, the one his father and his mother loved most of all.

Don Josué, as my grandfather was called in Jericó, was a tough man, but very honorable, and his only determination, at the age of thirty, was to leave his mother, Mamaditas, at the very least secure despite the economic crisis. He struggled for two years to pay off all he owed, liquidate the lands that had been seized, redeem the promissory notes and expired mortgages, and in order to do this he had to sell off the cattle herds, the future harvests, and bit by bit the land of all the rest of the farms, with the sole aim of getting one on a sound footing: La Oculta. His mother and two brothers, who were still at school, would live off the oldest and biggest of the family farms, without danger of seizure or forfeit. Those tensions had given him a gastric ulcer, which he'd suffer from for the rest of his life. "It feels like I've got ground glass in my stomach," he sometimes said, when he spat up blood and the pain wouldn't let him sleep. But as well as giving himself an ulcer he'd managed to save what was most important to the family: La Oculta.

He entrusted Don Chepe Posada, a dependable friend, with the administration of the farm (for his widowed mother was not able to run it, nor did she have the experience with those struggles, and his brothers were far away) and then he informed his wife and children that they were going south, to Sevilla, a town the devil hadn't yet reached. And the devil was the Depression. He took what was left, the furniture from the house in Jericó – which he also had to sell to pay off debts – distributed it over seven mules, and put his wife and each of his children on horses borrowed from La Oculta. Early one morning they left town, before the sun rose, and they set off in stages for the south, traveling at first along the same route that half a century earlier had been one of settlement and hope. They had passed through Palocabildo, they'd stopped on the heights of La Mama, for one last look at La Oculta, and they'd carried on to Jardín, Caramanta, Riosucio, Anserma, La Virginia, Cartago, La Victoria, and finally arrived at Sevilla five days later. As the crow flies there are barely two hundred kilometers between Jericó and Sevilla, but in that steep region they had to cross rivers and mountain ranges time and again, climb and descend slopes by impassable routes and take detours to sleep in villages off the trail one way or the other. This time it was a flight toward another new land. Miriam, his wife, was pregnant, just as Raquel, mother of the first Ángel born in our town, had arrived in Jericó. Sevilla is in the foothills of the central range of the Andes, on the way down into the Cauca Valley, and it was a town that had been founded barely thirty years earlier, in 1903, at the end of the war, by Heraclio Uribe, brother of the famous Liberal general who led that party's army in the War of a Thousand Days.

In Jericó they'd left behind the devil, which was laying waste to the town, as well as their friends and family ties. In those years a branch of the Ángel family split off and they never spoke again. Grandfather Josué had business dealings in partnership with one of his father's brothers, Antonio Máximo (in that generation all of Ismael's sons had the first name Antonio – like the Aurelianos in Gabriel García Márquez's books, since fiction is almost always a copy of reality, or an exaggeration, or a cover-up of what really happened – and that makes all the genealogies complicated, and one never understands quite who was the son of whom), and from there the story is told differently depending on which branch of the family you hear it from. According to the daughters of this Antonio Máximo, who they called Papá Toño, who only had girls and baptized them all with names beginning with E (Emilia, Eunice, Elisa, Eliana, Elena, Esther, Eva, and Emma), our grandfather Josué had been responsible for their father's bankruptcy, since Papá Toño, our grandfather's uncle, had been the guarantor of his loans. According to our grandfather, he and his uncle had businesses in common on various inherited properties, and they had both lost everything, except for two estates, La Oculta for us and La Tribuna for them. In fact, that's where the Elisas (as they were known in town, to simplify things) were raised, and Papá Toño ended up marrying them all off to engineers who in the 1930s were constructing the railway in the Southwest. Since they were all girls, there are no longer Ángels on that side of the family, and all their children are called Ceballos, Orozco, Puerta, Hernández, De la Cuesta, and things like that.

What is certain, because our father, Jacobo, Cobo, lived through it, is that our grandfather Josué arrived in Sevilla with what he was wearing, and the bleeding ulcer in his stomach. Our grandmother, Miriam Mesa, shortly after arriving in the Cauca Valley, gave birth to her fourth child, Javier. And there in the south our grandfather started from scratch. He'd go to a farm on the outskirts and buy a steer on credit, and sell it in town for a little bit more. Then two steers on credit and he'd sell them somewhere else. So, he devoted himself to buying and selling cattle, which is what he knew how to do, since he'd only done a year of medical school, and had to give up his studies at the age of nineteen (and take charge of the inheritances and businesses) when his father, José Antonio Ángel, had died in Jericó of typhoid fever. For ten years business had prospered, the land and cattle had been there to support his mother and his siblings, but in the depression, when nobody paid, nobody bought, and debts piled up, almost everything was lost, except La Oculta, the drowned man's hat.

Almost two decades later, in 1950, when our father, Cobo, lived in Bogotá, the devil finally arrived in Sevilla, in the Cauca Valley, and there he took on his most damaging form. After the Bogotazo in 1948, the *Violencia* began. And since Sevilla was a Liberal town and our grandfather one of the most renowned

Liberals in the region (after twenty years of hard work, he was by then the owner of a farm just outside town, the only notary in Sevilla, and a well-established cattle dealer), the hit men of the Conservative Party were going to kill him. So he had to pack up his things again, sell off his land at a loss for whatever he could get for it, and go to live in Medellín, displaced, as they say these days, for in Medellín they were killing less, or at least the police didn't let the Conservative hit men kill all the Liberals.

It was our father, Cobo, with Pilar just born, who had advised our grandfather to return to Antioquia but not to Jericó, where there were groups of Conservatives disguised as crusaders making the rounds at night to kill or *aplanchar* Liberals (farmers, shoemakers, shopkeepers, good men had fallen victim), but rather to the regional capital, Medellín. And Don Josué was finally persuaded to leave Sevilla when the Conservative hit men killed his son-in-law, husband of our Aunt Ester, and all of Cobo's classmates from the General Santander Secondary School. With the money from selling all his property in the Valley, grandfather was able to buy a house in Medellín, and that's where we got to know him.

Mamaditas, our great-grandmother, died when I was a little boy, in the 1960s, and Chepe Posada, to facilitate the inheritance, divided the estate into three equal parts to divvy up between the brothers. He gave each lot a name: La Coqueta for the lower land, La Abadía for the upper part, and La Oculta (with the old house) in the middle. The part with the house had less land attached. Don Chepe cut three strips of paper and on each of them wrote the name of each of the three parts of the old hacienda. Then he rolled up the three papers in the same way and, to be completely sure they couldn't read them, he went into the kitchen and wrapped each piece of paper up in tin foil, making a little ball. He came back from the kitchen with the three identical little balls in his hat and explained that each brother had to reach in and take one out. Grandfather, being the firstborn, got the privilege of choosing first, and then Eduardo and Elías. When they read the names of their lots (La Oculta for Josué, La Abadía for Eduardo, and La Coqueta for Elías), the first two were satisfied, but Elías, who had hoped to get La Oculta, could not hide his disappointment. He was furious and ever since that day he always insisted that his older brother had tricked them in order to get the old house and the lake. Elías said that Don Chepe, who was closer to Josué than to the other brothers, had put the one for La Oculta in the freezer for a moment and my grandfather had selected the cold one. Grandfather always said that was a crazy invention of Elías, and the proof was that La Coqueta was at least as good as La Oculta. Because of that fight the two brothers never spoke to each other again. Eduardo, who remained friends with both of them, and enjoyed La Abadía till the end of his life, said that the freezer trick was nothing more than an excess of fantasy from the imagination of Elías, who was very distrustful.

PILAR

To think that I lived my whole life laughing my head off and that my stories always made everyone laugh. Now they're rather depressing, stories tinged with bitterness by the ailments of old age, that contaminate the past with sadness, without it having been real, because there were many luminous years, full of happiness, which I tend to forget on the bad days, and it shouldn't be that way. We've been gradually losing our sense of humor and our cheerfulness over the years. Sorrows, illness, pain, and resentment mount up. It's hard to laugh with a toothache, or a pain in the coccyx, or this cough I wake up with from smoking so much. Nevertheless we do laugh sometimes, we really do, at ourselves. When life is no longer interesting, when memorable things don't happen to us every day, when the future shortens, we take refuge in the past, and one's memory turns into a cork in a whirlpool, circling around the same things all the time: our grandparents, the house, the kidnapping, the fire, the death of those we love most, the betrayals by friends that make us mistrustful. Over the course of a long life things get tainted by the ugliest, foulest incidents. The past weighs on us and distresses us. Only a few fortunate people, like my mamá, know how to live to the end full of humor, vivacity, sharing encouragement and joy, immune to grievances and sorrows and eager for life and the future, no matter how short the future might be. It's strange, she who suffered so much in her life – widowhood, kidnappings, losses, robberies, attacks, betrayals, everything – carried on to the end having that high-minded, independent, solid spirit, but most of all full of love, comprehension, and joy. She looked at everything from a distance, with a touch of irony, wisely. And she was the one who knew the most of what went on here. At eighty-nine years of age she had more curiosity than her children, and was more eager to know everything. She'd call us at eleven o'clock at night, speaking quickly, and say: turn on the television, look at the president saying such and such a thing, look how Eva's ex-husband is really going mad now, look at him shouting like a madman and if he gets into power this country will be going to the devil, it'll be another setback of twenty years, like in the time of the *Violencia*. She was the one who told us about the Twin Towers; she told us about wars or attacks, horrible viruses coming from Africa.

I'm not like her, I don't even watch the news anymore, I don't want to feel rage, or fear, I don't want to feel like leaving. Besides, there's nowhere to go in this world, and there are no longer any new worlds to discover. I'm old and tired, like this world. Even global warming seems to me like the hot flashes I'm still getting all these years after my period stopped, as if the Earth was also going through menopause. I'm old and tired, like this house, like this planet. Worse than this house, because I at least paint this house, repair, plaster it when a corner of the wall falls off, I mix up a batch of grout and put several layers of whitewash on top, improve its skin, remove the marks and freckles, cancerous lesions, cure it with injections of formaldehyde when termite holes appear on the posts or the beams, clean away the cobwebs, fumigate the roach nests, stamp on the scorpions, carry out toads by hand, sweep out the snakes, banish the bats with sulfur, catch the drips, stop the damp, disinfect the floors and mop them furiously until they shine and smell clean: I fight against decline. If only I could do the same with my body, my spirits: apply patches and mend, slap a coat of whitewash over the wrinkles. Sometimes I can; there are days and nights when I can, and I am happy again, forgetting myself.

If a friend of mine was elected president I wouldn't ask for anything for La Oculta. Not that he pave the road, or build an aqueduct nearby, or find jobs for Próspero's children in some ministry or anything like that. I'd just ask him to help those in the village, in Palermo, so they could have a decent school, drinking water, a hospital (because Palermo doesn't even have a rural doctor, and that's the worst, people die of the stupidest things), jobs, because people here want to work, to be able to buy a little house, a little piece of land, what we already have, it's not much to ask, here in this country of rain and sunshine, lush and green. There is enough land for every family to have a little house, a patch of earth. La Oculta is a dream that we all have, a dream come true in our case, in our family, but an unrealizable dream for almost everyone else: a place, a roof, a view we enjoy, a way of waking up in the morning, looking outside, and feeling comfortable with the air you inhale, the tree you can see, the flowers that bloom, the water that flows, the sun that warms us, the cloud or person passing by, or the skinny mare grazing in the field. Yes, I believe that all the people in this country, and if not all of Colombia, at least those in Antioquia, have a dream hidden in their heads, the secret dream of having a piece of land, a little bit of land that makes us feel secure, a hidden reserve for the thousand misfortunes that might befall us. That dream was fulfilled for one moment in history, or at least that's what Toño says, and then was lost.

In every family of Antioquia there is a lament for a hacienda lost by their uncles, their grandparents, or great-grandparents. It was a large piece of land, fertile, covered in cattle, crops of corn, and beans, with horses and dogs, but they had to sell it when Uncle Such-and-Such gambled it away, or because

Grandfather was a drunk, because Aunt So-and-So got cancer and they had to pay for her treatment in Los Angeles and she died anyway, because father put it up as collateral for a friend and the friend went broke and then it was taken away. Some smart-aleck cousin who ended up with it all by playing the saint while actually being a thief. The most common is that the grandfather had many children and left the land in the hands of the grandmother and it was kept intact while she was alive and didn't let them fight over it, but when the grandmother died the kids fought tooth and nail because they couldn't agree on how to share the inheritance and had to sell it in the end. Or they divided it up into thirteen lots, each too small to plant a lettuce. That was the story for Próspero, who had seventeen siblings and didn't inherit anything, just the death taxes. There are thousands of stories like that, and all are regretted. In reality it's the local version of the lost paradise, of the promised land that was once given to us and for some sin or some mistake we weren't able to retain.

That's why Alberto and I wanted to retain La Oculta and we were going to retain it no matter what until we died. And it's not out of selfishness, it's so Antonio and Jon can come from the United States and feel happy here. So my children and grandchildren can come and feel the same happiness I felt as a little girl and young woman, when my grandparents and parents were still alive, and youth itself was happiness. Even if they go to the seaside and to faraway places. But even if they'd rather spend their vacations in Spain or Morocco, they know they can always come here, and they have their house here, their old landscape, a plate of hot food, daybreak with the same fantastic view their great-grandparents saw, the perfect climate that makes Alberto feel like he's in heaven. I don't want my grandchildren driving past here some time when they're grown up, saying, "This used to belong to my grandparents but for some reason they left it, they sold it, because they fought with their brother and sister or wanted money to travel to China, what idiots." If this place has always been a paradise for the Ángel family since they discovered it and cleared it, why are we going to say it's a hell that we have to get rid of. It can't be that they were all mistaken. Cobo was not mistaken when he told me not to sell it. The mistaken ones were those who sold the land. When our uncles or cousins who sold their land come to visit, they sit by the wall or lie down in a hammock and weep in silence. They know this landscape was theirs, that this view was theirs as well, and out of indifference or stubbornness, they lost it. But at least, while it still belongs to us, all our relatives can come even if just for a few days, because we want others to come and take it in. This house is like the papers Toño writes, which he doesn't want to keep locked up in a drawer forever, but hopes to publish one day, so many can enjoy or suffer what's happened here, and think about things, think about their own houses and their own fathers and grandfathers, even if they were never here but in other towns, other parts of the country, or the world, because the whole world is full of Ocultas, of Ocultas that, whatever they might be called, resemble our Oculta.

ANTONIO

The only bad thing about La Oculta was how far away it was from the sea. The view from the top of La Mama had oceanic dimensions, it's true, but that immensity is not the sea, in any case, nor could it be, because the sea is very far from there and there is nothing on land as big as the sea. The Pacific, by air, is actually not that far, between La Oculta and the shore of the Pacific Ocean there is a strip of land one or maybe two hundred kilometers wide, at most. But it means crossing mountains, plains, terrible roads, and then the densest jungle in the world, the Darién. The River Chocó, geologically, Simón, my scientist nephew, tells me, is an ancient Amazon, all that's left of the ancient, primordial Amazon, when the Amazon River flowed into the Pacific. Then the Andes rose up near the ocean, and the Amazon had to reverse its course, all across the American continent, toward the other side through interminable plains, to the Atlantic. On the western side of the Andes only one intact piece of the original, primordial Amazon jungle remained, for the mountains here are a little bit more inland: and there it is, impenetrable, with Amazonian plants older than the ones in the other Amazon, a unique forest, wet and tough, impenetrable, as ancient as the most ancient jungle on the planet, as rainy as the rainiest place on earth. And that was the jungle that kept the people of Jericó from reaching the nearest ocean. Not even today, in the twenty-first century, is there a road to take us there. It's not even possible to overcome this block that keeps Central and South America apart. In this corner of the world, everything is detained. And just before you get to the densest and boggiest jungle in the world, you come across our little paradise, La Oculta, in Jericó.

The eyes of the people of Jericó, in the time of my grandparents, great-grandparents, and great-great-grandparents, had never seen the sea. Abraham, the first, had crossed it, it's true, when he left Spain to come to the Indies, but then his children and grandchildren and great-grandchildren would never see the ocean. They withdrew to this remote part of the world, into these impressive but inhospitable mountains, far from the sea. They carried on speaking the resonant, old form of Spanish that their elders spoke, and even today, if you ask the residents of Jericó if they've ever seen the sea, more than half of them have only seen it on television.

When I tell Pilar this, and speak to her of the sea, of what I feel at the seashore, near New York, in the summer, she shrugs, almost with rage, and says: "And who says you have to see the ocean to be happy, or New York, or Europe, or Japan, or Africa, or wherever? You've seen almost the whole world, from Brazil to Australia to Hong Kong, but nowhere have I seen you happier than right here. Alberto and I are happy here, and even if the sea is far away, when we've gone anywhere else we've always wanted to come back to this very place. This is what we like. Is it so hard to understand such a simple thing?"

PILAR

We were alone, Auntie Ester and I, in the old dining room of La Oculta. That's when she was already very ill, in the last weeks of her life. She had spent almost the whole morning talking about her memories of Jericó, of her childhood in town, of leaving for the south, with her parents and my papá, on horseback down into the Cauca Valley during the crisis in the 1930s, in search of a second chance, of a new life. The only thing our grandfather hadn't sold in Jericó was his mother's house and La Oculta, so she could live off what the farm brought in. She told me that her brother, Cobo, was always asking questions, and that he'd talked so much all along the way with Grandfather Josué that when they arrived in Sevilla he hadn't gone into fourth grade, as he should have, but fifth, since according to our grandfather he'd asked about so many things during those days that it was the equivalent of a whole year of schooling. She spoke for a while, as usual, of the *Violencia*, of her husband murdered by the Conservatives and the return to Antioquia, as if the family had always lived like a pendulum that flees from hunger or from blood. They called us for lunch and I helped her walk to the dining table, very slowly. When we were having our soup, with her sweet and worn-out ninety-year-old voice, without lifting her eyes from her bowl, she started telling me something with all the inflexions alerting me to the fact that she was about to say something important:

"*Mijita*, there's something that you and I have never talked about, and we talk about everything. I think all these investigations Antonio's been doing about us and the surname Ángel and Jericó are really wonderful, but there's something I have to tell you before I die, a very nasty sin my father committed, your grandfather, that is, the person who gave us all this name that you girls and Toño are so proud of." Here my aunt stopped, glanced over at me with her eyes as sharp as needles, to make sure I was listening attentively, ate three spoonfuls of vegetable soup, very slowly, looked back down at her plate, and carried on speaking:

"I don't think anyone knows what I'm about to tell you, and you'll see if you tell or not, but don't tell until after I die, because I don't want gossip or questions from anybody. I came here to die and I think the day is fast approaching, so I have to tell you this to see what you think, and you can decide if you want Toño and Eva to know, or if you'd rather keep this secret story all to yourself. I've carried it for half my life, since your grandma Miriam told me, and I wish she hadn't, because since that moment I loved my father much less, I stopped feeling the respect I'd always felt for him. He stopped being the idol who'd pulled us up out of misery over and over again, and became an ordinary man, a being of flesh and blood. Your grandmother Miriam and I talked a lot, much like you and I in these months, because we lived together from the time I was widowed, which means we lived together for more than thirty years, but she never told me about this offense of my papá's in all those years, perhaps to protect his image in the eyes of his children.

"You remember," she said, "that your grandma Miriam wasn't born in Jericó but in El Retiro, don't you? Well, I always knew that she, before meeting Josué, had had a boyfriend there, a real fiancé, who she adored, the son of a family from the coast who'd moved to El Retiro and who was called Fadi Ajami, son of Don Hussein Ajami, a Turk, or to be more precise, a Palestinian, although back then they were all called Turks, all those who arrived with Ottoman passports. Fadi had a printing press, one of the few, or maybe the only one in El Retiro at the time. She and Mono Ajami – as he was called due to his blond hair and blue eyes – were going to be married in 1919 or '20, I'm not sure, and they were engaged, but something happened and Fadi's brother, I can't remember what his name was now, I think maybe Hassán, one of those Arab names, was killed by some bandits at his hacienda over by Sonsón, and left two very young orphaned daughters, I can't remember what their names are, or were – I don't even know if they're still alive. Their mother, Fadi and Hassán's mother, told Fadi that he had to marry his brother's widow, who was Palestinian like them, Farah Abdallah. He didn't love his sister-in-law, he didn't even like her, or get along with her, but that was the custom and the law of the household: if one son died, and left a widow and descendants, if there was a single male in the family, then he had to take care of them and marry her. And there was no discussion possible: that's how it was and that was the end of it.

"So this Fadi Ajami had to tell your grandmother Miriam, with an aching soul, that they couldn't be married because he was obliged to marry his young widowed sister-in-law, Farah. Imagine, we were all about to be Ajamis, and Palestinians, and not Ángels and Jewish, as your brother says we are, although this thing about our Judaism I don't entirely believe. The thing is that your Grandma Miriam was very hurt when her Arab fiancé left her in the lurch and resolved to get married quickly to the first suitor who appeared. And that's when your Grandpa Josué showed up, our papá, who had some investments in salt shipments together with Miriam's father, Don Bernardo Mesa, who was also a cousin of Mamaditas and, you know what they say, 'blood is thicker than water,' or, as your own grandpa used to say, one has to find a spouse among one's own tribe. The thing was, there was no salt in Jericó and so salt was shipped by mule train from El Retiro, and your grandpa sold it in Jericó. You don't know how important salt was back then, salt was like today's refrigerators, the only way to keep many things from rotting, especially meat, beef jerky, that was a way of preserving it. Anyway. He was very young and he'd had to take charge of his family's business dealings because his father… well, you already know, the typhoid and all that.

"The thing was that your grandpa, who was a very young man, very fine-looking, was in El Retiro shortly after Miriam's Turkish boyfriend left her in the lurch. That was when the young man from Jericó caught her eye, and they became engaged, and a few months later they were married. I have the letters they wrote to each other during their engagement, which are very romantic and quite pretty. But here is the secret and the sin, *mijita*, which is not nice to tell, but I'm going to tell you. What happened was not so unusual in those days when there were no antibiotics and men lost their virginity in the brothels: your Grandpa Josué had syphilis when he married your Grandma Miriam, although he didn't know it, and their first child was not your papá as they've always said, but a little girl, who was baptized Ester, like me, but who was born blind, sickly, and syphilitic. That little girl died when she was a few weeks old, and just as well with all the problems she had, but they promised that the next daughter they had would also be called Ester, if they got cured and could have more children, and that's why I was called Ester. If you go to the Ángel mausoleum in the Jericó cemetery, you'll see a little plaque with my name on it, as if I'd already died. It says, 'Ester Ángel, born and died at the beginning of 1920, two short weeks,' in other words, three years before I was born. If you want when I die you can bury me right there, beside the girl I wasn't, or who I replaced.

"You don't know, *mijita*, the meaning of rage and shame. Your Grandma Miriam got married, more resigned than in love, more hurt than sure, to someone who she didn't love as much as the Turk Ajami, but who she at least liked, and right away she got pregnant, but as a result of that pregnancy she also got infected; your poor grandma, in the very act, got the best and the worst, life and sickness. That's hard to forgive. Luckily your Grandpa Josué's younger brother, Elías, was studying medicine by then, and in those days there was a treatment for syphilis, a long and painful process, for to treat a person they poisoned the whole body with arsenic, mercury, various things, and people either died or got better. You remember when Grandma Miriam got angry with your grandpa, she always said the same phrase?"

"Yes, Auntie," I said: "Bismuth, sulfonamide, and quicksilver-iodine!"

"Yes, exactly, 'bismuth, sulfonamide, and quicksilver-iodine.' All she had to do was say those words for your grandpa to fall silent, dumbfounded, as if sunken in his own guilt and disconcertion. That phrase obliged him to go back in time, to a time when he'd had to get down on his knees and beg for your grandma's forgiveness, on his knees. Well anyway, that's what they were given to treat their syphilis in Medellín, *mijita*, so they could try to have more children, but for a year they were forbidden to have relations or even to sleep in the same bed. When they were finally cured by the blasted mixture of bismuth, sulfonamide, and quicksilver-iodine, your grandpa returned to Jericó, to look after the salt business and especially La Oculta, the cattle and the coffee, and your grandma Miriam went to spend a few months with her family in El Retiro."

Auntie Ester had served herself the main course, but she'd barely touched it. The look in her eye was hard, cold, but she felt lightened, alleviated of a weight. Her eyes seemed to be looking backward, even though they were looking off into space or fixed on an unimportant spot on the ceiling. She smiled with a slight sweetness, and began to speak again:

"Well, you know how my uncles used to explain away that phrase with a silliness that my papá had threatened to put rat poison in your grandma Miriam's coffee. What rot. What shut him up was his deepest, oldest guilt at having infected his virgin bride, who he loved so much, with his brothel sin. I think it was that guilt that made him a gentle and timid man for his whole life, as if forever purging an indelible guilt, of which your grandma took care to remind him every once in a while. I know that your grandma, when she was recovering in El Retiro, saw her former fiancé, Mono Ajami. Then she returned to Jericó and your papá was born. I'm not saying anything more, because that's all I can say, *mijita*, with full knowledge. From there on in I can imagine many things, but I've never said what I imagine because that would be like letting madness loose, and it's best to keep that chained up with seven locks, is what I say."

EVA

The glory and tragedy of love are so simple. I can't understand why poets, psychologists, and treatise writers spend
so much time going over it, when it's such a simple thing, which
for me is this: two people fall in love, and while still loving each
other (while still in love with each other, I emphasize), little by
little, almost without noticing, they fall out of love, until eventually they end up hating each other. The reason is so simple,
so animal and human at the same time, so low, so high, so
normal, so sad: boredom with sex, boredom, that is, of having
sex with the same person. It's precisely sex, the essential factor
that carries us away with delirium, to love each other madly,
to the exaltation of happiness, of harmony, of communion,
which is called love, and is its most human and most beautiful
mask. Something so fleshbound it becomes spiritual. And that
same thing that made them unique and happy, inseparable and
faithful, with eyes for no one else, gradually wears away. And one
tragic morning, one night on the town, on an unimportant trip,
sex with someone else, a prostitute, an idiot, an ugly or useless

woman, seems more erotic than sex with the beautiful, kind, glorious loved one. And that furtive sex, if it gets found out, and even if it doesn't (because these things are known unknowingly), is unforgiveable for both. He can't forgive himself, and gets confused, and she can't forgive him and curses him.

I know, I've lived through it so many times, I know men and I know myself as well. When I was married to the banker, I couldn't believe it, but that's how it was: he would go off with women who weren't worth – and I don't say this out of vanity – my little toe. Silly little girls, tacky, brainless, and without any spark. But these women had different tits, different thighs, other scents, different hair, different eyes, other voices. And that made them profoundly attractive to him, much more attractive than me, even though he loved me, and I know he loved me, but his eye was caught by other bodies, the way dogs follow the scent of a female dog in heat, unable to resist. I'm not playing the saint here, I felt it too, perhaps less forcefully than him, but I felt it too: that a clandestine, furtive, occasional love would make me scream with pleasure more intensely even if afterward I felt angry and only wanted to get dressed and for the other man to get dressed and go, quickly. Yes. I felt it too, though a bit less than them, and less than him. But maybe since I've been like that I can intimately understand what they do, what happened to my banker – I couldn't forgive him though, no matter how rationally I thought about it, I could not forgive him. We are like that: free and liberated in mind; if a friend asks if we think it's okay if they're unfaithful out of pure carnal urgency we say of course, go ahead, we only live once, tomorrow the worms will be eating us: we give the same advice to everyone. But to our spouses no, this sin is not permitted to our own partners, because each of us is a god unto ourselves, and betraying fallen angels is all well and good, but you don't do that to the true god. The problem, I believe, is insoluble even if there are solutions proposed by culture and history. Pilar's solution, as dictated by religion and tradition, is not to sin and that's that. Trying to take importance away from sex, and live that way, eating the same traditional meal every day and suppressing the desire to taste exotic dishes. Some, very few, manage to live that way, but it's very unusual in these times of so much freedom. With men, in this culture, we're more permissive. They have adventures and their submissive wives wait for them at home until they come back. They have children out of matrimony, who show up when they die, and there didn't use to be a problem, for natural children didn't have many rights, but these days they have to be given a share of the inheritance, a share of the farm.

I never had an Alberto, so faithful and so calm, nor have I ever wanted to be like Pilar. I've known men more profoundly, having had all sorts of types of men, some much worse, and much more unfaithful and more sexual than Alberto, real dogs, but amusing dogs. They did it behind my back, and I knew, but at least for a while I forgave them, I tolerated their vices, and got even with them without their knowing. Unfaithful to me? Take that, my love, same to you, without your ever knowing. For a woman it's easy to find someone to sleep with; all men always want to go to bed with a good-looking young woman who's new to them. All of them, all, or all except for one in a thousand, to not leave out some rare cases, mysterious and almost unique, the way saintliness, heroism, and disinterested goodness is unique. But sex for revenge doesn't give one a sense of getting even but of failure; it's good for nothing, it doesn't console. Since revenge didn't do any good for my third marriage, I separated from him as well, and now I can barely remember him, he passed through my life without glory or sorrow.

When I split up with my third husband I realized I'd soon be too old to have a baby. I went back over all the men I'd had at that stage, official boyfriends and lovers, the three husbands, friends to spend time with. I made a chart and tried to think which of them was best, or the least bad, in his habits, genes, and appearance, and concluded that the best of all had been my second husband, Bernal, the orchestra conductor. I invited him out for dinner, we went out a few times, until I sprang on him what I wanted: not to sleep with him, since neither of us was interested in each other anymore, but to have a child with him, and so we wouldn't have to go through the embarrassment or trouble of sleeping together again after so long, we could do it through artificial insemination. I asked him to be my donor. He didn't have any children and he hesitated for two or three months, but in the end he agreed. He told me he was curious to see how a child of his would turn out, curious to watch a child grow up, but that he didn't have the time or inclination to raise a child, to be a proper father. He'd give him his surname, he'd see him once in a while, but no more. That was more or less all that I wanted, a boy who looked like the conductor, with his honesty and good nature, as far as possible. And that's how Benji was born, like a calculation, and I raised him on my own, practically on my own, though he knows who his father is and they see each other once in a while, but no more than that. I don't think I played that part of my life badly, at least I've never regretted it.

ANTONIO

The last time I went to La Oculta before the disaster was when Próspero's brother-in-law drowned in the lake. Maybe that was one of the last omens that the disaster was approaching. I don't know. I had gone down from New York for Easter Week and was staying there on my own, since Pilar had gone to Medellín with Alberto for some expensive and complicated dental work. I was studying a Brahms quartet that I was going to be playing as second violin a month later, and when I wasn't practicing in my room, I'd go out for walks, or horseback riding. Próspero's brother-in-law had come down from Medellín for a few days' vacation with his wife and three children, a boy and twin girls. He was a nice guy who I'd been talking with the night before; Próspero had asked me to let them stay a few nights in his house, and I said of course, what could be wrong with that.

His brother-in-law had had a hard but good life. Shortly before his son was born, seeing he had no way of supporting his family, he'd gone clandestinely to the United States, crossing all of Central America in trucks, passing through Mexico, slipping over the border. Once he was on the other side, he'd stayed there for more than twelve years, first illegally, then with false papers, and finally with his papers in order, after one of the amnesties. Little by little he'd managed to save a bit of money. During the first years he couldn't visit and didn't get to watch his son grow up, see him learn to read or ride a bike, because his wife and son stayed behind with her parents in one of the poor neighborhoods of Medellín. He sent them a money order every month, to support them, and she worked cleaning offices. After seven years he was able to bring them up to the United States, because he was granted residency. And they were there for another five years, and had two more children there, twin girls. Finally he decided with all he'd been able to save in twelve years they could come back. He came home, bought a taxi and two buses with the money he'd made. That's what they lived on. He drove the taxi (they'd arrived at La Oculta in it) and rented out the two buses. He'd also built a nice little two-story house, on the same block where his in-laws lived.

That morning I'd gone out riding early. When I came back from my ride, Próspero – who'd never learned to swim – was screaming that his brother-in-law had drowned in the lake, and that they'd been looking for his body for two hours, unable to find it. I galloped to the lake and found the police, the firemen, and people from civil defense. They were looking on from the shore. Finally they launched a boat and probed for the body from there, with a guadua bamboo pole. Próspero's wife, the drowned man's sister, was crying; the drowned man's wife and son were crying; the two girls were crying.

What had happened was that the man had gone out rowing, happily, in the bright sunshine, with the two little girls, in my father's old beat-up canoe, which we hardly ever used anymore. In the house there were lifejackets, but they hadn't put them on, I don't know why. In the middle of the lake the canoe began to leak, and it slowly started to sink, until it sank completely. The girls didn't know how to swim, and their father, who was a very weak swimmer, tried to keep them above water, holding them in his arms. At the same time he shouted for help, going from one twin to the other, pushing them up so they wouldn't sink. The girls swallowed water, they sank and came back up again, scared to death, crying. It's fear that drowns us, more than water. If you stay calm, you can lie on your back with your head back and float, but they don't teach that to anyone. Próspero, his sister-in-law, and the boy were watching, shouting, going crazy, but they couldn't do anything because they didn't know how to swim. They ran back and forth on the shore. They watched him struggling to save the girls. And they threw ropes that couldn't reach the middle of the lake, to try to save them, to pull them in. Finally a farm laborer came by, took off his shirt and pants, and doggie-paddled out to where the girls were. First he brought in the one who was on her own, then went back and took the second one from her father's arms. Próspero's brother-in-law was exhausted by then and unable to make it back to shore, he asked for help, said he was out of breath, that he couldn't make it; the laborer was also very tired and stayed on shore watching. He didn't have the strength to dive back in and help him keep afloat, although he was begging for help and moving his arms. He was scared that Próspero's brother-in-law, who was a big man, would drag him under trying to save himself and that they'd both drown. His wife and son and his rescued daughters, his sister and brother-in-law, all watched from the shore as he sank for the last time.

I dove into the water to look for the corpse. The civil defense people and the police were looking for him with poles, from little boats. When someone drowns the lake becomes smeared with death and everyone grows afraid of swimming in it. Próspero showed me more or less where his brother-in-law had gone down for the last time, and I dove underwater, with my goggles on. I was doing that for a long time, diving down and coming up again. I couldn't see anything underwater. I had to just feel around.

I had never touched the body of a drowned person underwater. The hair on his head, the inert flesh, the complete abandonment. "Here he is!" I shouted, and I stayed in place, brushing against the body with my toes. Others came to help.

When we were finally able to get a rope around him underwater and pull him out, I saw his blackened face, with a grimace of anguish and pain. The drowned man had managed to save his daughters, but he hadn't been able to save himself. The wife and son watched us pull out her dead husband, his dead father, from the shore; the rescued girls, owners of all the air, could scream with all the power of their lungs. The zippered plastic bag hid the body from the curious eyes of neighbors. The mother, as a symbol, gave his wedding ring to their desolate son. The police wrote a cold forensic report: black shirt, green pants, forty-seven years of age, taxi driver by profession.

The water of La Oculta Lake, three meters below the surface, is a very dark green, almost like the night. Diving blindly I had touched the body of a drowned man. And it was as if all the drowned victims, from one moment to the next, were there, in that gloomy lake where I like to swim. I have always swum in La Oculta with the fear of dying. Since that day, much more so. Sometimes still, in the Harlem nights, I dream of that man who I touched, underwater, with my own hands. I still think if I'd been there a few hours earlier, if I hadn't gone out riding, I could have saved him. There wouldn't be another three orphans, another widow, in this strange world where all it takes is a moment of carelessness or bad luck to turn a whole life into an unhappy one.

EVA

There's a strange passion in our family that's appeared in various members since the time of our great-grandparents, and that Pilar has manifested more than anybody. It's difficult to understand its origin, and its nature, but it consists of an attack of irresistible generosity. Neither Antonio nor I have it, but Pilar does, to an exaggerated degree.

With a strange frequency, but always when one least expects it, she gets the irresistible urge to give gifts, to hand over everything in exchange for nothing. Without having the means and even with things that don't belong to her, she sets out to distribute whatever's at hand. A friend of theirs, for example, went to the farm, and was enchanted with the mare that Jon rides, with its gentle pace and easy handling, and so Pilar gave her to him, saying in any case Jon hardly ever came to La Oculta. There was a picture of Grandma Miriam in my room, a picture I loved, for the dark face of my grandmother with her look of bismuth, sulfonamide, and quicksilver-iodine, and someone admired it. In a flash, Pilar took it down off the nail it was hanging from and obliged the admirer to take it away with her. If an acquaintance had a birthday and invited her to the party, she'd buy extravagant gifts, with her credit card, and much more than she could afford. Then she'd spend months paying it off, with interest, but she never learned her lesson.

She's capable of spending millions of pesos in a nursery, buying bedding plants, exotic palms, native trees to plant at the farm. She'd get into a sort of frenzy of repairs and renovations and hire gardeners, painters, plasterers, carpenters, to do useless improvements, which were suddenly urgent and unable to be postponed. When the bills arrived, there was no money to pay them and she'd turn to Toño and to me, to our mamá when she was still alive, to cover what was missing. She would replace practically new mattresses, buy new sheets after giving away perfectly good ones, new pillows, cutlery, glasses, giving away the previous sets without really knowing why she'd given them away.

When she cooked a meal, she'd buy enough meat to feed an army, and her barbecues and beans always produced two days worth of leftovers, but she sent everything to the nearby houses of the farm laborers or to the school in Palermo, so the children could be served it for lunch, or she'd give it to the maids to take home: paella, desserts, fruit, everything on the pretext of helping the poor and not letting things spoil. She'd gone as far as lending people plots on the farm to cultivate, because she'd felt sorry for a young couple of campesinos fleeing the violence of some criminal band from who knows where, from the mountains near the Chocó or the mining towns farther south, and she let them sleep for nothing in an old sharecropper's shack from our grandfather's day, and which she fixed up at her own expense, ordering roof tiles, cement, bricks, and other material from town, so those people wouldn't get wet, and then it turned out they were not good people, lazy and useless drunks, and she'd have to pay them to leave or evict them by force.

She's given away calves, pigs, fighting cocks, teak boards, sacks of coal, sacks of coffee. If there was an abundance of anything, she didn't sell it, but gave it away. Anyone who wanted to go to the farm, at any moment, was invited, and if necessary she would borrow money to be able to feed the crowds that arrived, and she'd hire cooks, servants, launderers, to wait on the guests like kings, and paid them all daily wages that were twice the going rate in the region, because the poor girls had so much work. She would never ask visitors to pay any share of the expenses, for the groceries or the staff. She gave away the clothes she had, her children's clothes and her husband's, even mine and my brother's. If I left a pair of shoes, a hat, or a pair of boots to wear the next time I came (months later), when I returned they'd be gone because Pilar would have given them away to someone.

At Christmas she always bought presents for everyone at the farm, everyone in the family, the employees, the farm workers, day laborers, girls who came to help out when there were a lot of people staying, their children, and even those who showed up at the last minute to visit. No one knew where she got gifts for everyone, but nobody ever went without a little package. Even though Mamá, when she was alive, gave Christmas bonuses to everyone, Pilar thought it was too little, and bought more, without asking us. She'd bring us the bills afterward because – she'd ask – how were we going to leave So-and-So or Such-and-Such with no gift on Christmas Day, that's not right Eva, Toño, you owe me this amount.

The bottles of wine or rum, the hammocks, the corkscrew, the ashtrays, the saddles, Cobo's books, the ponchos, the riding whips, visitors just had to admire something and they'd be taking it with them as a gift. "Doesn't matter to us, does it, Eva? Of course they can take it with them, right?" she'd ask in front of the person she'd just given something to, and I at least was never able to discredit her in public, and I'd just smile. Later, at night, Pilar would ask me why I was always so stubborn about selling this farm when it was so beautiful and what a wonderful time we always had here and how much our friends always loved coming to visit us. I would just say, "Ay, Pilar, you won't understand."

ANTONIO

Why did I do what I thought I'd never do? It was like falling out of the sky and breaking my spine, like a loose tile falling on my head while I was walking calmly down the street. But no. It was more like walking through a rugged, dangerous landscape, on the edge of a precipice, trying not to fall, and, exhausted from trying to keep my balance, letting myself fall into the abyss, as if attracted by the vertigo of death, and almost resigned. Sometimes it seems like the most important things happen for no reason and all of a sudden, as if they fall out of the sky, like an avalanche that comes loose from a mountain and drags you away. Many things are like that, brusque and sudden, but since many others are not, one prefers to think everything is a slow process, with gestation and development. That's how things get built, almost always, arduously and slowly, but what is destroyed, what gets lost, is a matter of a second. Creating a human life takes, at least, five minutes of sex, nine months of gestation, two years of intensive attention, and then twenty more to form a person entirely. Death, however, often arrives as a bolt from the blue, as a bullet, as a hurricane, as a rapidly fatal heart attack. Only if one dies in old age does death seem like the work of days or years, of a constant and gradual wasting away, the drip that wears away the stone or the moth that eats its way right through a dictionary. One can die bit by bit – and that's the most normal – but also suddenly as if struck by lightning, like a thunderbolt out of a cloudless sky, or an unforeseen storm. A tree that has been growing for two centuries can be felled in two minutes with a chainsaw.

It also sometimes happens that what seems sudden and motivated by a single, isolated cause, is actually obeying a cluster of hidden or invisible events that coincide at the same moment until becoming irresistible, and everyone gives in because at just that moment nobody has the force to resist. Fate is like that, or maybe destiny, because all this has very little to do with will-power. A feared but unexpected, even mistaken decision, gets made because many things happen, almost at the same time, that force you to commit that error. So you crash, you kill your-self in an accident, because there was a moment of carelessness and because at that very moment that truck was coming the other way, or the motorcycle, and not at another time, because you leaned on a branch that seemed sound but was rotten inside.

In this case, circumstances left me with no option but to commit the mistake, knowing perfectly well that it was a mistake, or at least an irremediable decision, which could never be undone. And I made that decision; I was unable not to make it. For more than a century La Oculta has so often been saved at the last minute, when it seemed we were going to have to hand it over or lose it. In the last few decades it's been saved, always, by some *in extremis* help from my mamá, who solved problems by some miracle, pulling money out of places there didn't seem to be any. And this time it could have been saved too, even though our mamá was no longer around to save us as she always had, Pilar was still firm and not prepared to give in, but it was me, her ally in all the other crises, the most convinced that we had to preserve the farm, who weakened. Actually there were a whole bunch of things clustering, hiding like a virus, waiting for the perfect moment, and they fell on us right then and there when they saw our defenses were down, and they took over the farm.

There are days when I feel resigned and days when I can't forgive myself, or even worse, when I can't forgive Jon, because in some way I hold him responsible for what happened. Or Lucas, my nephew, or Eva, or all of them together. But poor Jon's not to blame, or not only him; Jon had only been sincere, and I should understand that. Just as my grandfather wasn't responsible for the economic crisis of the '30s, Jon isn't to blame for having been born in the United States and for feeling almost nothing for a piece of someone else's land that meant almost everything to me, to us.

A person is unfair, in any case, and always looks for others to blame for the bad things that happen. I'm angry with him now that I know that our plans to live in Colombia one day will never come true, he has enclosed himself even more inside his world, in his studio, with his friends from there and his family. He has thrown himself into New York life completely, with the fury of a recaptured youth, now that he no longer feels the danger of that fatal attraction, of the call of that world away in the tropics I've felt all these years we've lived together. I've just told him, as coldly as I was able to, that I'm not going to spend Christmas with him, that I'm going to go to La Oculta, to visit Pilar, who is still there, entrenched in the house as if it were the last bastion under siege by barbarians. I want to see how everything is after what we did. I'm afraid to go, but I have to go. Jon shrugged with indifference as if to say, "Do whatever you want." He knows that if I go it won't be to stay, for there's almost nothing left of La Oculta. Lately he just shrugs and says, "that's okay," never contradicting me; it's worse than arguing; it's as if he had a lover and was happy I'd be going away. Before we didn't like to be away from each other even for a few days, but now I see him as if liberated, calm, even happy to regain his solitude, and I don't know whether it's solitude or freedom to be with another and not with me. He manages to make me jealous, but I'm still going to La Oculta, to see it, probably to say goodbye as well, and to be aware of the consequences of my signature, or my actions. I tell him we'll see each other in January and he shrugs again, says relax, to stay until February if I want.

EVA

Pilar asked me to come to the farm before the work began. It was torture; I shouldn't have gone. When I arrived at La Oculta the first thing I heard was an unbearable noise of engines rising and falling in pitch, disturbing the silence all day long. "What's going on?" I asked Pilar. "It's the chainsaws. They're chopping down the coffee bushes, the teaks, and the shade trees," she told me. I'm sure Pilar invited me so that I'd be hurting in my bones and skin, as a tree hurts when it's cut down. I felt like a trunk that was going to be sliced at the ankles and toppled over. The teaks were barely ten years old and they were tall, but they weren't ready to be harvested as they didn't have the width or density yet to make good timber. "They're going to use them for the fences, as stakes and crossbeams for the roofs of some of the new houses," Pilar explained. "They're not good wood yet, but they have to clear the land for the building work." Some of the shade trees, the guayacans or the carobs, would supply wood for furniture, doors, and windows. I didn't want to hear that noise of chainsaws, much less all day long, from sunup to sundown.

Pilar's face looked awful. Alberto tried to pretend things were like they were centuries ago, the chainsaws like "your ancestors' axes." A hundred and fifty years ago La Oculta had started the same way, with the chopping down of trees, and in the end history was repeating itself, symmetrically. I didn't appreciate his black humor.

To change the subject, I tried to give them some good news: Jon had managed to sell the four Botero drawings in New York, and he'd gotten almost the same as he'd paid for them after Lucas was released: eighty-thousand dollars, just twenty-thousand less, at a time when the art market was difficult. And that they might be buying a log cabin in Vermont. That Jon thought Vermont was much prettier than Antioquia, especially in the fall. Pilar just said: "Oh really? How nice for them." Alberto said he was going to the orchard, to prune and fertilize the orange trees. He put on his headphones to drown out the chainsaws and everything else with music. Próspero's eyes were popping out of his head, which he kept shaking, and he just walked aimlessly in the tiny space left around the house, as if he were witnessing a tragedy. I couldn't stand so much tension anymore. I could see in their eyes that I was to blame for everything that was happening, that my selfishness was why La Oculta would never again be what it had been.

I dove into the lake, which is what I always do when I want to be saved. The water washes me, cleans me, calms me. Swimming in the lake is my meditation. I don't speak, no one speaks to me, I move my arms and legs rhythmically, breathe deeply, exhale, tire myself out, stop thinking. An hour swimming back and forth from one shore to the other, without Los Músicos pursuing me, without siblings making comments, without eyes that look at me in silent reproach. I put earplugs in so I can think better. While I swim I think about Benjamín, who is still studying in Europe. When he returns he might not recognize La Oculta, if he comes with his cousins to visit Pilar and Alberto. In any case this time I don't swim peacefully and the water does not calm me. Maybe I now prefer swimming in the pool in Medellín, which has never been mine, and where nobody has drowned. While I move my arms I do nothing but think about the people who have drowned in the lake and feel that they're looking at me with their white eyes from the muddy bottom, with anger, with reproach. I received a lot of money, in euros, for my third, and I sent it to Benji so he could invest it there, in Germany, which is a solid and safer country, a country with public lakes where I've swum without feeling I'm swimming in a cold soup of drowned people. I am achieving what I wanted: I have almost nothing now: a few pesos in cash to survive on here, austerely, in a mini-apartment where I sleep, as if it were a hotel, to feel light, unencumbered by baggage. I don't even cook anymore, and I've filled the kitchen with old books of my father's that were at La Oculta. I don't want things, or maybe the only things I want are books, to leave them in my will to a public library, and that'll be it. Pilar told us to take what we wanted, when we signed the papers, and the only thing I took from the house were books, nothing else: not one object, not one painting, not one piece of furniture, or any souvenir. Books, only books. Now in my apartment if I open the pantry I find books; there are magazines in the oven; books in the kitchen cupboards, in the bathrooms, in the medicine cabinet, in the front hall closet, behind the sofas, and even in the dining room where I never dine: books and more books. I have breakfast at the kitchen counter, without cooking anything. Raw food, cereal with milk, fruit, so I don't have to cook, and then I have lunch and dinner out, on my own or in company.

I had a surprise for Pilar as well, but I'm not going to tell her for a while: I have a new love, a good love, a different love, very different, Posadita. I didn't take her to the farm, as I'd thought I might, because it seemed unfair to expect Pilar and Alberto to deal with another piece of news at this moment. If I had taken her I would have had to sleep with her in Cobo and Anita's bed, and that would have been one last desecration, another one. Too much for a moment like this. I didn't want to tell her. It's a recent thing, something I didn't expect. It was like a discovery around the same time as I was feeling fed up with men. Being with a woman is something different, softer, something I'd never allowed myself to experience. It's easy, actually, very natural, and it doesn't feel to me (as I once thought) like a confusion of instincts. And besides, Posadita is very young, almost as young as Benjamín, with that softness of youth, that delicacy of youth. Smooth and radiant skin, timidity. For once I wasn't going to learn, but to teach. I didn't want to verbalize anything or explain either, and Pilar wants everything explained in words, always with words.

I did tell Toño, because given how he is, I thought he'd understand without a word. But Toño, when I told him on the phone, said one single word, in a very loud voice: "What?!" After a while he said, half apologetically, halfheartedly, that it was fine, not to worry, perfect; then we hung up. I know what Pilar would have said if I showed her or if I told her. She'd open her eyes as wide as a frightened calf, and that look would be enough to say what she'd then say in words: "That's all we need." I don't plan on telling Benjamín anything, or explaining; I want him to realize gradually, and if he wants to know anything more, anything specific, he can ask me and I'll explain. I'd like the answers to arrive in his case before the questions. I feel something sweet and tranquil inside, something consoling like a compensation for this tragedy of selling the farm. I'm surprised myself that I can like a woman so much. I finally hope, and I'm convinced, that a relationship is going to last, because I'm built to last as well, if things work out, and maybe this one, so different, might work out. Everything is so new that I still don't know. It's like a softening throughout my entire body, like swimming under water, but not stifling.

Posadita, who's name is Susana, advised me to make the deal. She's an architect and agreed after looking at the budget, the expenses, and the proposal by Débora's friends' company, which is very important, one of the most respectable construction companies in Medellín. "It's a serious offer, and a very good one, that you shouldn't turn down," she told me. "If you and your brother and sister don't accept it, they'll find another farm in the region, and you'll lose the opportunity. They already have all the permits from Jericó, and those construction licenses are hard to acquire and take a long time; you have to grease a lot of palms and use a lot of leverage. It's now or never." Now or never. Susana has never seen La Oculta and perhaps for that very reason she could speak so surely, without a single doubt.

That's another reason I didn't want to take her, so she wouldn't get doubtful.

I felt that I was going to the farm for the last time. I wanted to dive down into the lake and I did, as if escaping from myself. I dove underwater and counted to twenty-six before coming up for air. The body is stubborn and does not want to die. Well, I don't want to die yet either. In the water, all of a sudden, I burst into tears. But, what are a few salty tears in a sea of fresh water? Even if they'd been drops of blood they'd have gone unnoticed. When I got out of the lake, Pilar had already served the fruit. Then there was a *sancocho*, as there always was on the first day of a visit. On one wall of the dining room were the photos of Mamá and Papá, like an altar to the ancestors on the wall. Each one had their flower, a fresh rose for each. All they needed were lit candles. Their eyes looked at me in reproach as well, and not so much for Susana, but for having sold. I went into Toño's room, to see the paintings and photos of other older relatives; their eyes didn't say anything to me: inexpressive, inert, cold. The *sancocho* tasted good, tasted as good as all the *sancochos* in my memory, the ones Mamá made, but the lunch was tense, silent. When we finished, I put the earplugs back in my ears and had a siesta in a hammock. I tried to think of bees on the coffee flowers, when the buzzing managed to penetrate into my eardrums. It was not a restful siesta and I said goodbye the moment I woke up. I didn't want to hear Pilar's laments or her nagging complaints and I wanted to get straight back to Medellín, to be with Posadita, to hold her. I had no desire to listen to the horrendous concerto of chainsaws. They insisted I stay overnight, said that the night was still and silent as ever. I didn't want to. Somehow I managed to escape from them, from everything, from the past. Especially from the past, from all the burden of family. Let Pilar carry it, if she wants, I don't want to carry that burden anymore.

She, as obstinate as ever, stubborn as ever, will probably carry on living there, in the old house. One day she'll die there and I'll have to come and prepare her body, even though I don't know how. Who would be widowed first: Alberto or Pilar? I tried to imagine it and didn't know which would be worse. She smoked more, she had more of a chance to die first. I said goodbye to the two of them as if to two dying people. When I climbed into the jeep I didn't cry, but tears were falling from some part of me, and those salty tears made me angry, I cried without wanting to, angry to be crying, like an ocular incontinence, if such a thing exists. I at least would never be a widow, or leave a widower. That night, when I got back to Medellín, I slept hugging Posadita tightly, my strange discovery so late in life, who I hope will be my first and last girlfriend, my final companion. I embraced her, embraced her youth and stopped crying. Before going to sleep I swore to myself that I would never again cry over La Oculta. No more, I was going to banish nostalgia, animism, our silly family traditions, from my life. No more nostalgia, only the present, no future either.

PILAR

What happened was that Toño and Jon had a very important conversation, one night when Jon was unable to sleep and told him he had to confess something very serious, something that he'd never been able to say. Toño told me he'd turned on the lamp on the bedside table and thought that Jon had a lover, something like a double life. But no, what he told him was something else, I don't know whether better or worse, but in any case it changed their life plans radically. He told him that he was very sorry but he was never going to be able to live in Colombia, not even six months a year, not even three, and much less in a town like Jericó, where there was nothing to do. Much less would he live in a city like Medellín or Bogotá, which have neither the charm of the countryside nor the advantages of great cities. That he wasn't prepared to walk down the street in fear, that he wasn't fond of so much rain, so much sun, so much humidity. He also thought the friendliness and kindness of the people of Antioquia was not normal, the excess of courtesy, according to him, was actually hiding a fear of violence. That he had learned to love La Oculta, and to appreciate it, that he was impressed by the exuberance of the tropics, but the way an explorer of inhospitable places is impressed, or someone who goes to a botanical garden to see carnivorous plants with foul-smelling flowers, for a day, a few hours, a little while, but living in that excess was too much for him and even damaging. That he didn't breathe well when it was so humid and among so many plants and that old houses gave him asthma.

He also said that in reality he believed that our family, and in general all of Antioquia, suffered from a type of *finca* madness. He'd been starting to think that for a while. That he definitely did not understand that attachment to land, to the ancestors who'd settled it, to rural property. That it was insane to spend one's life buying and selling farms. That land in the United States was more fertile and cheaper, and besides, it was the campesinos who worked the land and not the people who lived in the cities, who nevertheless always had their minds on *fincas*. That he did not understand this anachronistic, ancestral attachment to an agricultural or small-town family past. That here in the States they were happy to liberate themselves from the unhappy small towns their families were from and to which they never wanted to return, like stubborn homing pigeons, always returning to their first nest. That the Ángel family, furthermore, two or three generations ago, had left the countryside, had made the leap into the liberal professions and the city, had received the blessing of not having to work the land with their hands, crumbling clods of earth with their fingers, but they carried on determined to maintain that root, that attachment to trees, manure, plows, corn, the crowing of roosters and grunting of pigs. That as beautiful as the landscape might be, it was a monotonous landscape, the same every day, and he was not going to be able to bear waking up to the same crags, the same lake, the same blue mountains, the same birds, as incredible as they might be, after a month they started to get repetitive and they were always the same and sang the same cacophony every morning. That to see so many birds he'd rather go to the Natural Science Museum. And he kept talking like that for hours, like someone throwing verbal punches.

Toño told me all this like a Catholic telling the blasphemies of a heretic, a Protestant, or a convinced and aggressive atheist. He told me sadly, and with a lot of anger, that Jon had deceived him for so long and allowed him to get his hopes up that they'd go to Jericó, that they'd donate their modern art collection to the town museum, and that they'd spend a few weeks or months with us each year. But at the same time Toño had always known that Jon didn't understand La Oculta, saying that maybe it was true that the farm was a madness of ours, and in general the fever for farmland a collective madness of Antioquia. Jon had practically given him an ultimatum: he either got those ideas out of his head (the return to that land of his elders, life in a sad little town) or they'd each have to go their own way and just maintain a friendship. Toño had been taken by surprise by this cancellation of their plans, so suddenly, and he started asking more questions, and hearing answers he didn't want to hear: that he should open his eyes, that, frankly, we could not compare Antioquia to the United States. And to look at our crazy way of always being all together; that he had a family too but at most they were obliged to get together once a year, in November, for Thanksgiving, and that was it, because they all spent their Christmases apart. That the Antioquian way of living all together, as if they were puppies for their whole lives, was sort of ridiculous, like an ancient culture, tribal, but without any basis in the contemporary civilized world, in the urban, dispersed, globalized world, in which adults scattered to all corners of the globe and chose their relationships by their own tastes and affinities, and not those relics of blood or land. That a person loved his family, yes, but from afar, because up close families could be a plague, because everyone knows each other too well, and knew how to hurt each other where it hurt most, touched sensitive spots, and clung to shared things and properties, when the best thing to do was sell up and divide the proceeds, and each to his own, follow his own path and make his own life.

Toño understood very well what Jon was saying, but it depressed him anyway. He put on one side of the scales all his nostalgia, all his obsession for La Oculta and the Ángel family, and on the other side his relationship with Jon, his life in New York. He had dreamed of having both, of a life divided between periods here and periods there, but now his partner didn't want to share half his life, or accept that Toño should come here for a few months on his own, nor would he supply the money necessary for him to do it, since it was Jon who had more money of the two and without his help he couldn't afford it. So Toño got depressed, started just going through the motions in his violin classes, lost his enthusiasm for his notes on Jericó and our forefathers; he no longer wanted to tell one by one the life of each couple of Ángels throughout the nineteenth century, to the twentieth century. Now what for, he said. All his plans for a life with Jon in Jericó, near La Oculta, had suddenly gone to hell. To put pressure on him, Jon had asked him to pay his share of the household expenses, something he'd never demanded. And so Toño's earnings started to go toward food, transportation, and half the bills for their Harlem apartment, which Jon used to pay entirely. Now it was hard for Toño to send his share of the farm expenses to Colombia, and they'd come late. He called me, apologized, said to give him a little time until he got paid for some concert. Jon's savings were not going to go to fulfilling his dream of living in the tropics, in Jericó; the collection of work by contemporary artists was not going to go to Dr. Ojalvo's museum in town, either, and Jon was planning to make a local donation instead, to some small museum in the United States.

Toño even considered the possibility of splitting up with Jon and returning to Colombia, but even though he felt full of resentment, he wasn't willing to leave him. He loved him, he still loved him, he was used to his presence and his body, having spent the happiest and fullest years of his life with him. Apart from that, he thought, if he did come back, the only place he'd have to live would be the farm, but living with me and Alberto would also be crazy; exchanging a husband for a sister and brother-in-law was a very strange bargain. "If I went to live with you two," he told me over the phone, "we'd end up fighting; and that's the last thing I want. I don't want to fight with anybody, not with Jon and not with you."

With his crisis, and with our mamá dead for two years now, there was no one to cover the holes for us, for she had always been the one to help us through difficult moments, when any of the three of us had temporary problems covering the costs. My mamá worked miracles, to keep us from fighting and to enable us to keep the farm. But now she wasn't here to help, and without her help we no longer had Christmas or Easter. Until one month, Toño, without even letting me know, didn't send his share for the upkeep, and Alberto and I didn't even have enough to pay Próspero's salary, much less the normal expenses and taxes, which started to mount up again, every trimester. Eva gave the minimum, unwillingly and late. The accounts of La Oculta were always in the red, and we had to pay interest, and the bank manager phoned up more and more often to ask when we thought we might cover our overdraft.

This coincided with the Jehovah's Witnesses giving me notice, and overnight, our main regular source of income, that rent money, dried up as well. We signed the house up with an agency to rent it, but it was no longer a livable house, as the Jehovah's Witnesses had adapted it into a temple and converted it into a sort of shelter with no walls or rooms: a giant open space with a roof. Then we put it up for sale, as a lot, but it wasn't easy to sell either and months went by without being able to rent or sell it. Eva remained fixated on the idea of selling La Oculta, as she always had, and insisted that now more than ever was the favorable moment to do so. These things all happened at once and that's when drastic, sad, mistaken, but almost inevitable decisions get made.

Débora, Lucas's wife, came to the farm one weekend with my grandchildren, and showed me a plan of La Oculta divided into fifteen lots of three *caudras* each. A company belonging to friends of hers were prepared to beautifully develop and parcel out the land, with weekend ranches, a paved road, an enclosed unit with an attended gate where we'd all come in. The planned lots would have security guards, gatekeepers, gardeners, an aqueduct, and ecological paths. It was a luxury development, very tasteful, with tennis courts, a gym, mini-golf shared among all the houses, native trees planted along the ravines, a riding school for all the proprietors, where they would teach them horsemanship. She showed me the landscaping project, designed by a very famous architect, and everything else. "It'll be like living in an exclusive club," said Débora.

Inside I thought it was all horrendous, but I couldn't tell her that, almost couldn't let myself think it. "Very nice, Débora, I see," I said, even though I wanted her to leave the farm that very minute, but how, when she was my eldest son's wife and she was bringing us this proposal for our own benefit, to save us, with the best of intentions. You could tell they'd been thinking about it for months or years, designing it all. They were old friends of Lucas and Débora, who had come here for a change of scene several times over the years, and they'd always loved the farm and the region. And they loved it so much that they came up with the idea of parceling it out and developing it. Alberto looked and didn't say a word, he just huffed and his nose started to sweat, his whole body; his shirt was stuck to his chest, soaked. "This belongs to the Ángel family, it's for you three to decide," was all he said, and he left. He probably went to fertilize the orange trees, or go horseback riding, or have a siesta at the wrong time of day for sleeping. Then Débora whispered in my ear, lowering her voice, an enormous sum of money that each of the siblings would get, if we sold the whole thing. If I insisted on keeping the old house, then I would get a much smaller share. It would be best to sell the old house too, knock it down and build one more in the style of the new subdivision. *If they were offering us such a huge amount of money*, I thought, *what kind of profits were they expecting to make for the company in charge of developing all the lots?* I didn't mention this to Débora, which would have been like accusing her friends of having vested interests, but I did tell her that I wasn't going to sell, that even if I wanted to I couldn't, because I'd sworn I wouldn't to my papá. That I would be staying in the old house with Alberto forever, even if it was without any land, but if Toño and Eva agreed, the way things were, I couldn't object and I would give my signature for the sale of the rest of the land. If they wanted to they could sell my share and my house, when I died. Débora told me that Eva knew about the project and was a hundred per cent in favor, and I would receive part of the money in any case, as compensation. The decision, then, was in Toño's hands. The construction company had foreign accounts, in tax havens, and could pay in dollars, or in euros. I shrugged and thought if everyone who has money takes their capital out of Colombia this country is going to be screwed.

Eva called Toño in New York and convinced him in one minute. Or she didn't even need to convince him: he was in one of the worst moments of his life; he was like a caged beast offered, at the very least, a bigger cage. They could tell he was weak and rushed to send the contract of sale and he went to sign them and have them authenticated at the consulate. He wasn't even able to call me and tell me he was going to do it. I know he spoke to Lucas and Simón and Manuela and that they told him I agreed that my brother and sister should do what they wanted. A short while later Toño and Eva got their money; they deposited dollars in Toño's account in New York, Eva had hers sent in euros to Germany. Alberto and I received a much smaller sum, in pesos, in Medellín. They gave us a fair amount, I won't say otherwise. Alberto and I still have the old house with a small amount of land around it. The lake is still part of the farm, but there are no longer coffee fields, no longer pastures for cattle (we gave them all away, except for two). The three of us settled up with Próspero and Berta and Alberto and I made a new contract with them, just in our names. We were able to sell the house in Medellín to a building contractor and we put all the money into shares that should give us enough to live on until we die. In that same account we put what they gave us for losing our view around La Oculta.

We remain here enclosed, buried, surrounded by noise and people, day and night. People no longer arrive at the farm through the old archway, crossing the cattle guard made out of abandoned railway ties, instead we have to identify ourselves at the attended gate, to some guys in cap and uniform who look out from the sentry box and mistrustfully buzz open the gate, which closes again immediately after we drive through. Our old, dilapidated jeep is the ugliest vehicle in the whole subdivision. The neighbors watch us pass by the way you'd look at a prehistoric pachyderm.

Nothing is the same anymore. Everything began to change a few weeks after we signed the contracts. When they began the construction of the subdivision the whole place filled up with machinery, bulldozers, dredgers, steamrollers, trucks that left with debris and came back with construction materials. They moved the mountain's core to make terraces where the new houses would be built. For two weeks chainsaws were cutting down the teak trees, which toppled almost quietly, resigned to their fate. At the same time they chopped down the coffee bushes, the shade trees in the coffee fields, the groves of old teaks by the entrance, since they had to fix the road, the mango trees from Thailand, the almond trees, the hundred-year-old saman trees, which were like immense, natural umbrellas. I can be very mean, and when they started to cut down all the trees I invited Eva to come, so she could hear how they were chopping down what we'd planted ten or twenty or thirty years ago. So she could feel even a tiny fraction of the pain I was feeling. I think it did hurt her, but she put on a brave face and even went for a swim and had a siesta. She left sour-faced and refused to stay overnight no matter how much we insisted.

On all the new lots you could see all sorts of yellow and red patches of uprooted earth. A hideous green, plastic fabric enclosed the entire perimeter of the old property. Débora told us to relax, that it was normal while they were dividing up the lots, but the peace and lush greenery would return, in a year or two, when they finished digging up and moving the earth and building the houses; that this was a land blessed by rain and sunshine. The former greenness still hasn't come back.

The new owners of the lots began to build their houses: enormous mansions in different styles: California, Bauhaus, colonial, narco-mafioso style. Almost all of them have pools, lawns, stables, open-air Jacuzzis, and manicured gardens. From the back of the house I can no longer see the landscape that my mind remembers, our photos show, and my eyes yearn for: before me are several tiled roofs of immense houses, and blue swimming pools, fake, everything surrounded by tall fences of exotic plants, with thorns, and at night streams of light disturb the dusk and illuminate the bland, geometric gardens. Now the border of La Oculta is the cedar tree where the ashes of my mamá and the bones of my papá are buried, the resting place. At least that was respected in the plans, but behind the cedar, a meter from it, passes the wire and the neighbor's fence. The silence is made up of different music, each one worse, and now there are no trails and animals, but paved roads where motorcycles and quad bikes come racing past at full speed, armor-plated four-by-fours with tinted windows, gigantic, expensive horses, purebreds, Arabian, Spanish, American Quarter Horses, and people who ride them in uniforms, with boots and whips, as if they were cavalry soldiers, Olympic athletes about to jump hurdles, or something like that. Armed guards drive around the perimeter fence on noisy Japanese motorbikes, because many of the buyers are businessmen or dealers from Medellín, nouveaux riches or old money, I don't really know, since we have nothing to do with them, but in any case they're afraid of people coming in and robbing them or kidnapping them or killing them, and they protect themselves.

The following December, to pretend, to feign that everything could be the same again, or at least similar, all my children and grandchildren came to spend Christmas and Eva came with Benjamín. On Christmas Eve Toño arrived from New York.

Jon stayed in Harlem with his new life, finally liberated from his old promise to live in the tropics. Toño looked for a moment toward the lake, and another moment in the other direction, down toward the river. He squeezed his eyes shut and covered his face.

"It's incredible: what the civil wars, guerrillas, and paramilitaries didn't manage to do to us, the businessmen did."

That was all he said. Then he shut himself up in his room for the three days he stayed and only came out to eat or to drink a coffee. He said there was no point in writing what he'd planned to write and that he was going to burn all those fucking papers. That's what he said, swearing. When he came out and saw the disaster all around he couldn't contain his rage and sometimes his tears. "I'm getting used to it now," I told him, to console him, but there was no solace to be had and it wasn't even true that I'd gotten used to it, or would ever get used to it. Eva just swam in the lake; she said it brought her peace, that it was her salvation, her way of meditating. Benjamín accompanied her, rowing the little boat close behind, the way my papá used to when we were girls. Benji said he didn't want to run the risk, that his mamá wasn't that young anymore and he might have to save her, and he always kept a white ring buoy in the boat. It angered Eva that he took care of her like that, following her and treating her like an old lady, and sometimes she'd lift her head out of the water and tell him frankly that she didn't like it, why didn't he leave her alone, read a book or go for a walk, but Benjamín didn't pay any attention to her and carried on smiling and rowing beside her, like a dog, as if he were Gaspar back from the dead, who always swam like that, like him, behind Eva. When she got out of the lake, Eva read books in the hammock, frenetically, to avoid us and pretend everything was normal. Débora said she slept very soundly, knowing no one could come in and attack us in this enclosed, protected unit; that now nobody could come and kidnap Lucas, or threaten Eva's life, like before, when the land was open to the steps of all intruders. Lucas and all my children just played cards, dominoes, and scrabble, and drank beer. For them the parceling off of the lots was nothing strange, but simply the new way young people with money liked to live, enclosed in little protected ghettos, in opulent bubbles. We turned up our own music louder and louder, so we didn't have to hear the music from the other houses. We heard the neighbors' voices and fireworks, the sound of their cars and motorcycles going by.

Two months after that December we spent with the whole family, maybe in March, the owners of the two houses downhill from the lake ordered an inspection by the municipal Secretariat of Public Works because they feared that the lake might burst its banks one day. The relevant authorities came, engineers, health inspectors, and they said the lake was a danger to the houses downhill from it and that it should be drained and dried out. I informed my brother and sister. Eva came for a weekend and swam in the lake for the last time. She brought a very young and very pretty girlfriend, Susanita Posada, who stayed on the dock watching her swim, as if taking care of her, but without following her. She seemed like a daughter. Toño didn't want to or couldn't come; he groaned when I told him over the phone, and hung up rudely. I didn't want to watch, but I saw everything they did, like a masochist. They opened a drainage channel with twelve-inch pipes and the water began to flow out down into the old gulley where the stream once ran. The lake emptied slowly and two weeks later there was a dark, muddy, ugly, foul-smelling bed. It all filled up with insects and a terrible odor. Thousands of rotting fish lay on the bottom; snakes, turtles, and iguanas longed for the water, looking and twisting from the edge, stunned and dried up like me. An almost complete skeleton of a young woman appeared, as white as chalk, which the police took away in a sack, as a Jane Doe. The next day some police came to question us, about this or that, about who it could be, about whether we could go into town and give a declaration to an examining court in Jericó. They looked at us as if we were hiding something. Dozens of vultures circled over the hole where the lake had been, and they ate the dead carp, the rotten tilapias, and the trout flipping about in death throes in the last puddles. Alberto and I went to Medellín for a few weeks, to Florencia's house, until the stench subsided. We'd have to wait for some vegetation to grow up over the old lakebed. We've been left with a pestilential wetland, full of mosquitos that affect all the owners of the houses in the subdivision, who now complain about how many flies and mosquitos there are. They fumigate every three months with a disgusting chemical, which makes us cough, irritates our eyes, and makes us dizzy for two or three days after they spray. The fumigation company, of course, says it's innocuous, that it only affects insects and not humans. On the side of the old lake there is no longer any view, it's just a filthy, unpleasant hollow. On the riverside the house overlooks the roofs and fences of new houses and the wire mesh of the perimeter fence, crowned with rolls of barbed wire, electrified like in a concentration camp. Over the top wires, you can just see the tops of the crags. And the noise is permanent, or that thing that is music to others and noise to us. Not even Alberto, who adores music, likes this mishmash of different rackets, each fighting to drown out the others.

La Oculta is no longer hidden or silent, but exposed to all the indiscreet neighbors' looks, from above and below. In the mornings you hear the buzzing of the lawnmowers cutting the neighbors' grass as short as possible. Their buzzing is almost identical to the chainsaws, although a little less intense.

Everything is worse than before, but now they say our house is worth more because it's inside an enclosed subdivision and our taxes have gone up. We have to pay a fee for the gatekeepers, the motorcycle guards, and the night watchmen. Débora says at least we always have clean water. Yes, and every month they charge us for it, as if they weren't taking it from our own springs. Alberto closed up inside himself and looks after the few orange and mandarin trees we have left around us. Sometimes he goes out riding, but he doesn't like it so much anymore; he says the horses don't trot as well on asphalt as on the old mountain trails, that the noise of their hoofs on the pavement is not natural. The quad bikes startle them. Próspero is getting old and can't find much to do. Sometimes he says it's getting to be time for us to die. Everything is dead, actually, and we are the only things left to die.

Toño never comes down from New York to visit now and much less Eva. She travels a lot, or shuts herself up in her apartment in Medellín, with her books. She travels with that girl, Posadita, as if they were a couple, though they don't live together, I don't think. A little while ago she called to tell me about a trip to France and Germany, to visit Benji, and she said that over there they take good care of the countryside and value it highly, that it's not like here, where they can just build whatever they want all over the countryside, and even to put up a doghouse or a dovecote over there they had to get permission from all the neighbors. That they had laws to protect the land-scape, and nobody can get around them. I couldn't even believe what she was telling me and I just laughed. Toño calls me once or twice a month, but the conversation doesn't flow and is made up of routine questions about me, about Jon, about Alberto and my kids. The sentences are uncomfortable, disconnected like two old rusty hinges on a door that doesn't open very often or ever get oiled. The only new thing he's told me is that his left hand has begun to shake so it's very hard for him to play the violin. We avoid the subjects of Eva and La Oculta and our words come out like strident, out-of-tune screeches. In order not to quarrel we usually hang up quickly and say goodbye with the false promise of seeing each other in the next few months. I hang up and think: yeah, at my funeral.

The months go by and life goes on. I know one day I'll wake up with an urge to get down to work and improve things again. If I can prepare the dead, I can also prepare this house that they've killed for me, compose the view they stole from us. I have plans, but I haven't yet gathered the strength to start putting them into practice. I want to fill in the lakebed with truckloads of rubble and earth, to make a garden. And at the front I'm going to con-struct a fake hill, to shield the view of the neighboring houses, so from the corridors of the house we'll only see the top tips of the crags and no rooftops. I'm going to cover the hills in bougainvillea of all different colors, Cobo's favorite plant, so they'll flower and cheer up my view. That same hill will protect us from the noise and from noticing the other houses; it will hide us away again. One day I'll do it, when I recover from this paralysis I'm in. I have to be able to do it, but for now I can't, I'm like a sleepwalker, quiet and bewildered.

Sometimes I wake up in the early hours and get up and walk around the house. At least during the week, since most of the new houses are weekend getaways, almost all the lights will be off in the surrounding properties and there won't be music, so I can hear the crickets like in the old days, almost the only creatures to have survived the disaster. Because of the fumigations there are no frogs or fireflies anymore, and the bats haven't come back, and there aren't any parrots or macaws nesting in the dry trunks of the royal palms, which were also cut down. The floorboards creak in the same places and I lie down in a hammock, in the outer corridor, to let the morning dew settle on my face. For a moment I have the illusion that everything is the same; that in a few hours day will begin to break over the crags, and I won't have the view of them blocked by neighboring houses or metal fences to keep intruders out of the subdivision. Sometimes I fall asleep in the hammock and dream of the lake, and I walk over the surface of the lake, as in a miracle. Alberto wakes up and approaches in bare feet, with slow, silent steps, but the floorboards creak in the same places and I wake up. He asks me if I'm okay and I say yes. He asks me if I want coffee and I say yes. The aroma of the coffee is still very good and we lie back in the hammock, side by side, our legs entwined, to slowly sip our coffee as the sun comes up. Although I cough and my voice is hoarse, I smoke a cigarette, slowly, in front of him even though he's quit. I like to see the glowing, red tip, and smell the fragrance of tobacco. Until the light arrives, we have the illusion of still living in La Oculta, like we always wanted to. I don't want day to break and it seems sad to prefer nighttime. I tell Alberto: "It used to be that happiness was waiting for the dawn to see the view; daytime was life. Now it's only good at night, when everything's dark."

It begins to get light and a thick, white mist covers the whole landscape. It's drizzling. Little by little the silence starts filling up with birdsong. A veil of compassionate mist has fallen over all the ugliness. It used to be that veil hid beauty and happiness was waiting for it to dissipate. Now we wish that dense veil would stay forever.

"Let's imagine that beneath the mist everything is the same as it used to be," says Alberto.

"I wish I could," I tell him.

He pats my leg and, leaning back in the hammock, we stare into the mist.

ACKNOWLEDGEMENTS

While making this book I've realized, more than ever, that writing a novel is a collective job. That in the end only the one who puts the words on the page should sign it is an imprecision and an injustice. There are some who are completely unaware of the phrases and ideas they contributed. They are the majority: people plundered by my eyes or ear. Others I consulted on specific points and they cleared up my doubts. There are those who gave me peace, time, the wherewithal to live, or company. My Spanish publisher Alfaguara had infinite patience with me, through years of drought and unmet deadlines. *El Espectador* and the Library of the Eafit University also gave me space and free time. I received space, peace, and affection from Beatrice Monti von Rezzori and her idyllic writers' retreat in Tuscany. Time and silence were supplied by the German Academic Exchange (DAAD) and the Freie Universität Berlin, in the form of a Samuel Fischer Fellowship, sponsored by the Holtzbrinck Editorial Group.

I'll mention a few names of people I owe great debts of gratitude, without whom I would have been unable to finish *The Farm*: the historians Roberto Luis Jaramillo and Nelson Restrepo gave me information and shed light on Jericó and the colonization of Southwest Antioquia; any truths, if there are any, in the history of the settlement of Jericó I got from them; the fantasies and errors are mine alone. My friends Ricardo Bada, Eva Zimerman, Ana Vélez, Elena Serrano, Laura García, Ángela Aranzazu, Jaime Abello, Ana Cadavid, Jaime García, Sonia Cárdenas, and Carlos Gaviria kept me from sinking into discouragement and helped me to improve the manuscript. So did my soulmate editor, Pilar Reyes; my publishers in Colombia, Gabriel Iriarte and the succinct and precise Ana Roda, and my German agent, the sweet and efficient Nicole Witt. Próspero, my friend from La Ceja, lent me nothing less than his own name. Elkin Rivera, copyeditor *in extremis*, saved me from, at least, 126 anacolutha. To the writers Mario Vargas Llosa, Javier Cercas, Leila Guerriero, and Rosa Montero I owe something very important: they scolded me for not writing and spurred me on to not give up. Alexandra Pareja, my beloved *pareja*, put up with my absences and even worse, my often absent presence, in addition to revising the manuscript and supplying ideas fundamental to its improvement.

Finally, Amalia and Mario Ceballos (relatives of mine from La Oculta in Southwest Antioquia), my sisters, my mother, and my children know that without them this book would not exist either, because they are its primordial clay and first destination.